Seduction and Snacks

A Chocolate Covered Love Story

Book #1 in the Chocolate Lovers Series

TARA SIVEC

Other books by Tara Sivec

Romantic Comedy

The Chocolate Lovers Series:

Seduction and Snacks (Chocolate Lovers #1)

Futures and Frosting (Chocolate Lovers #2)

Troubles and Treats (Chocolate Lovers #3)

The Chocoholics Series:

Love and Lists (Chocoholics #1)

Passion and Ponies (Chocoholics #2)

Tattoos and TaTas (Chocoholics #2.5)

Baking and Babies (Chocoholics #3)

The Holidays:

The Stocking Was Hung (The Holidays #1)

Cupid Has a Heart-On (The Holidays #2)

Romantic Suspense

The Playing With Fire Series:

A Beautiful Lie (Playing With Fire #1)

Because of You (Playing With Fire #2)

Worn Me Down (Playing With Fire #3)

Closer to the Edge (Playing With Fire #4)

Romantic Suspense/Erotica

The Ignite Trilogy:

Burned (Ignite Trilogy Volume 1)

Branded (Ignite Trilogy Volume 2)

New Adult Drama

Watch Over Me

Contemporary Romance

Fisher's Light

Worth the Trip

Romantic Comedy/Mystery

The Fool Me Once Series:

Shame on You (Fool Me Once #1)

Shame on Me (Fool Me Once #2)

Shame on Him (Fool Me Once #3)

Psychological Thriller

Bury Me

Seduction and Snacks

Print Edition
ISBN: 9781682304334

Disclaimer

This is a work of adult fiction. The author does not endorse or condone any of the behavior enclosed within. The subject matter is not appropriate for minors. Please note this novel contains profanity and explicit sexual situations. All trademarks and copyrighted items mentioned are the property of their respective owners.

For Madelyn and Drew. You are my heart and soul and my reason for living. Thank you for providing me with enough material to fill a million books. I'm so glad I never sold you to gypsies.

Table of Contents

1. Arby's Anyone? 1
2. Beer Pong May Cause Pregnancy 7
3. Have You Seen This Sperm Donor? 16
4. Sex and Chocolate 28
5. Snickers Finger Arm Teeth 40
6. I Got a Big Weiner 49
7. Open Mouth, Insert Vodka 62
8. Cuckoo for Cocoa Puffs 74
9. Claire's Coochie Kills 85
10. Seduction and Snacks…and Snafu's 100
11. Good Vibrations 117
12. P.O.R.N. 130
13. Quivering Loins 141
14. Captain Narcolepsy 154
15. I'm a Dirty Slut 168
16. They're Called Nipples 188
17. Duct Tape for the Win 205
18. Baby Daddy 225
19. This Patient Needs an Enema, STAT 239
20. Have You Seen Mike Hunt? 256
21. Itchy Feet and Fading Smiles 275

1.

Arby's Anyone?

HELLO, MY NAME is Claire Morgan and I never want to have children.

For those of you out there who feel the same way, is it just me or does it seem like you're in the middle of a horrible Alcoholics Anonymous meeting whenever someone finds out you never want children? Should I stand up, greet the room as a whole, and confess what brings me to the seventh circle of hell I constantly find myself in? It's a house of horrors where I'm surrounded by pregnant women asking me to touch their protruding bellies and have in-depth discussions about their vaginas. They don't understand why the words placenta and afterbirth should never be used in a sentence. Ever. Especially over coffee in the middle of the day.

You know what brought me to this decision? The video we saw in health class in sixth grade. The one set back in the seventies that had some woman screaming bloody murder with sweat dripping off of her face while her husband lovingly pat her forehead with a towel and told her she was doing great. Then the camera panned down to the crime scene between her legs: the blood, the goo, the gore, and the humungous porn bush that now had a tiny little head squeezing its way out. While most of the girls around me were saying, "Awwwwwww!" when the baby started to cry, I looked around at them in revulsion muttering, "What the hell is wrong with you people? That is NOT normal." From that moment on, my motto was: I'm never having children.

"So, Claire, what do you want to be when you grow up?"

"I'm never having children."

"Claire, did you choose a major yet?"

"I'm never having children."

"Would you like fries with that?"

"I'm never having children."

Of course there are always those in your life who think they can change your mind. They get married, have a baby, and then invite you over expecting you to be overcome with emotion when you take a look at their new little miracle. In truth, all you can do is look around at the house they haven't had time to clean in six weeks, smell their body they haven't had time to bathe in two weeks, and watch their eyes get a little squirrelly when you ask them the last time they got a good night's sleep. You see them laugh at every burp and smile at every fart. They manage to bring poop into every single conversation, and you have to wonder who the crazy one really is here.

Then you have the people who believe your flippancy is due to some deep, dark, secret issue with your uterus that you're overcompensating for, and they look at you and your vagina with pity. They whisper behind your back and then suddenly it turns into a horrible game of "Telephone," and the whole world thinks you have life-threatening fertility issues where pregnancy will cause your vagina to spontaneously combust and your left tit to fall off. Stop the insanity! All my bits are in working order and as far as I know, I don't have exploding vagina syndrome.

The simple truth is I just never thought pushing a tiny human out of me that turns my vagina into something resembling roast beef that no man would ever want look at, let alone bang, was a stellar idea. End of story.

And let's face it people, no one is ever honest with you about child birth. Not even your mother.

"It's a pain you forget all about once you have that sweet little baby in your arms."

Bullshit. I CALL BULLSHIT. Any friend, cousin, or nosey-ass stranger in the grocery store that tells you it's not that bad is a lying sack of shit. Your vagina is roughly the size of the girth of a penis. It has to stretch and open and turn into a giant bat cave so the life-sucking human you've been growing for nine months can angrily claw its way out. Who in their right mind would do that willingly? You're just walking along one day and think to yourself, "You know, I think it's time I turn my vagina into an Arby's Beef and Cheddar (minus the cheddar) and saddle myself down for a minimum of eighteen years to someone who will suck the soul and the will to live right out of my body so I'm a shell of the person I used to be and can't get laid even if I pay for it."

It just stands to reason that after all the years of preaching I did to everyone around me about how I was never having children, I was the first of my friends to have one—much to their horror, which I was highly offended by. I mean really, any idiot can raise a child. Case in point: my mother. She was absent the day they handed out parenting handbooks and instead turned to the age old, brilliant wisdom of Doctor Phil and fortune cookies to educate me, and I turned out just fine. Okay, maybe that wasn't the best example. I'm not a serial killer, so at least I have that going for me. More on my mother later.

I suppose saying I hate children is a little harsh, considering I'm a mother now, right? And it's not like I hate *my* kid. I just strongly dislike *other people's* dirty faced, snotty nosed, sticky handed, screaming, puking, shitting, no-sleeping, whining, arguing, crying little humans. Give me a cat over a kid any day. You can open up a bag of Meow Mix, plop it down on the floor next to a bucket of water, go on vacation for a week, and come home to an animal that is so busy licking it's own ass that it has no idea you were even gone. You can't do that with a kid. Well, I guess you could, but I'm sure it's frowned upon in most circles. And if my kid could lick his own ass, I'd have saved a shit load of money on diapers, I can tell you that.

To say I was a little worried about becoming a mother given my aversion to childbirth and children in general is an understatement. They say that when you have your own child, the first time you look into his or her eyes you will fall instantly in love and the rest of the world disappears. They say you'll believe your child can do no wrong, and you will love them unconditionally right from the very first moment. Well, whoever "they" are should seriously limit the amount of crack they smoke and stop talking out of their ass while their Arby's vaginas are flopping around in their grandma panties.

The day I had my son I looked down at him and said, "Who the hell are you? You look nothing like me."

Sometimes it isn't love at first sight. "What to Expect When You Weren't Expecting to Get Knocked Up That One Time at a Frat Party" and the rest of the all-knowing baby books like to leave that part out. Sometimes you have to learn to love the little monsters for something other than the tax deductions they provide you. Not all babies are cute when they're born no matter how many new parents try to convince you otherwise. This is yet another lie the half-baked "theys" lead you to believe. Some babies are born looking like old men with wrinkled faces, age spots, and a receding hairline.

When I was born my father George took my hospital picture over to his friend Tim's house while my mom was still recuperating in the hospital. Tim took one look at my picture and said, "Oh sweet Jesus, George. You better hope she's smart." It was no different with my son, Gavin. He was funny looking. I was his mother, so I could say that. He had a huge head, no hair, and his ears stuck out so far I often wondered if they worked like the "Whisper 2000", and he was able to pick up conversations from people a block away. During my four day hospital stay, all I kept doing whenever I looked at his huge head was speak in a Scottish accent and quote Mike Meyers from "So I Married an Ax Murderer".

"He cries himself to sleep at night on his huge pilluh."

"That thing's like Spootnik. It's got its own weather system."

"It's like an orange on a toothpick."

I think he heard me talking about him to the nurses and formulated a plan to get back at me. I firmly believe at night in the nursery he and all the other newborns struck up a conversation and decided it was time for a revolution. Viva la newborns!

I knew I should have kept him in my room the whole time I was there. But come on people, I needed some rest. Those were the last days I would ever get to sleep again, and I took full advantage of it. I should have kept a better eye on which kid they put his bassinet next to at night though. I knew that little brat Zeno would be a bad influence on my kid. He had "anarchy" written all over his face. And who named their kid Zeno anyway? That was just asking for an ass-kicking on the playground.

Gavin was quiet, never fussed, and he slept all the time in the hospital. I laughed in the face of my friends who came to visit and told me he wouldn't be like this once we left. In reality, Gavin did the laughing, waving his tiny little fist of fury in the air for his brothers in the Newborn Nation. I swore I heard, "Infant Pride! Baby Power!" every time he made noises in his sleep.

The moment I got him in the car to go home, the jig was up. He screamed his head off like a wild banshee and didn't stop for four days. I have no idea what a wild banshee was or if they even existed, but if they did, I was sure they were loud as fuck. The only good thing about this whole ordeal was the fact that my kid refused to leave my body via my lady bits. No roast beefy beaver for this woman. All the baby books written by women who had the most perfect birth experience in the world said you should talk to your child in the womb. That was about the only piece of advice I took from those things. Every day I told him if he ruined my vagina I would video tape his birth and show all his future girlfriends what happened to your who-ha when you had sex, ensuring that he will never, ever get laid. Fuck playing Mozart and reading Shakespeare. I went with the scared straight method.

All my threats to him in the womb paid off. He sat there with his arms crossed for twelve hours and refused to move down the shoot. This was perfectly fine by me. C-section, here I come. I would go through having my gut sliced open again in a minute if I could skip the whole baby part and just get the four days at an all-inclusive location that served you breakfast, lunch, and dinner in bed, gave you a twenty-four hour morphine drip, and sent you packing with a thirty-day supply of Vicodin.

Before I get too excited thinking about legal narcotics without the ear-bleeding scream of a newborn, maybe I should go back to the night that got me into this mess. My horoscope that day should have been a warning of things to come: "You'll score a bunch of great computer gadgets and jewelry from your neighbors, who happen to die when you go into their house, shoot them, and take all their things."

I don't know what it should have been a warning of, but come on! Does that not have "bad omen" written all over it? The one and only time in my life I decide to have a one-night stand so I can finally give up the V-card, I get pregnant. I'm telling you, the universe hates me.

I was twenty years old and in my second year of college, well on my way to a degree in Business Administration. Aside from the constant ribbing from my best friend Liz, on the state of my virginity, life was good. Well, college student good. I didn't have VD, none of my friends had been roofied, and at the end of the semester, I had avoided needing to sell my organs to science to pay for food and pot.

Let me just say I do not condone illegal drug use in any way. Unless it's an all natural herb that doesn't make me feel guilty for eating an entire box of Peanut Butter Captain Crunch while watching hours of The Joy of Painting with Bob Ross. "Oh green water, oh that's pretty, and a happy little tree right over there." It also chills Liz out during finals so she isn't screaming and climbing the walls like a rabid howler monkey. Remember that whole "Hugs not Drugs" shit they tried to cram down our throats in high school? We fooled them. You don't have to choose. You can totally have both and not die. But seriously, kids, don't do drugs.

I remember that night fondly. And by fondly, I mean with bitter resentment toward all things alcoholic and with a penis.

2.

Beer Pong May Cause Pregnancy

IT WAS A Friday night and we were spending it the usual way – at a frat party with a bunch of drunken frat boys and sorority freaks of nature. I really don't understand how Liz managed to drag me to these things week after week. These were not our people. Our people were back at the dorms listening to Pink Floyd, "The Dark Side of the Moon" and watching *The Wizard of Oz* while arguing over whether or not the last season of Dawson's Creek jumped the shark. (Pacey and Joey forever!) We did not belong with the crowd of trust fund babies that thought student loans had something to do with a foreign exchange student. As we made our way over to a portable bar on one side of the room, I could hear two completely wasted tools argue back and forth about who paid more for their Coach purse and who slept with the most guys last week. One of them claimed she was ashamed she brought the other to the party since she was wearing a pair of Louboutin's that were "so last year". These were the future leaders of our country, ladies and gentlemen. Christ, I felt like I was watching a live scene from "Heathers" ("I brought you to a Remington party and what's my thanks? It's on a hallway carpet. I got paid in puke."). Thankfully Liz interrupted me before I handed one of them a cup of liquid drainer.

"Oooh what about that one? He's cute. And he has good teeth," she announced excitedly as she tipped her head towards a guy in a sweater vest manning the keg.

"Jesus Liz, he's not a horse," I moaned, rolling my eyes and taking a sip of luke warm beer.

"But you could ride him all night long if you play your cards right," she said with a creepy used car salesman wink and a nudge with her shoulder.

"I'm concerned about you Liz. I really think you spend entirely too much time thinking about my hymen. You're secretly in love with me aren't you?"

"Don't flatter yourself," she replied distractedly as she scoped out more guys. "Come to think of it, I did bat for the other team in high school after one of Tom Corry's Friday night parties. We never got past second base though. Someone knocked on the bathroom we were in and it suddenly occurred to me that I liked penis," she mused.

I stared at her profile like she had two heads. Or her hand in a vagina. Why is it that I'm just now finding out my best friend went through a lesbian phase? Every time I look at her now I'm going to picture vagina-hand. A little hand that looks like a who-ha chasing me around the house and watching me while I sleep. Vagina hand is always watching. Vagina hand sees you.

Liz looked beyond my shoulder and then leaned in closer. "Two tangos staring at us at your six."

I rolled my eyes again and sighed at the attempt Liz was making to be covert.

"Five bucks says free drinks will be ours if we play our cards right," she said conspiratorially.

"Liz, we're surrounded by kegs of beer and we were handed a plastic cup when we walked in. I'm pretty sure that equals free booze," I told her, holding up my red Solo cup in front of her as a reminder.

"Oh shut it. You're ruining the moment. If we were at a bar right now, they'd totally be buying us drinks."

"If we were legal."

"Details," she scoffed with a wave of her ominous vagina hand.

She fluffed up her hair, and then pulled the front of her shirt down lower so she showed enough cleavage to blind a man.

"Liz, if you sneeze there's going to be a nip slip. Put those things away before you poke an eye out."

"They're coming over!" she squealed, batting my hands away as I tried to pull her shirt back up to cover the twins.

"Jesus, is there a homing beacon on those things?" I muttered. I shook my head in amazement at the power that was her boobs. "Your tits are like Bounty. The quicker dick picker upper," I muttered as I finally turned around to get a look at who was coming over. I'm pretty sure to an outsider I looked like Elmer Fudd when he saw Bugs Bunny dressed up like a girl and his eyes popped out of his head and his heart stretched out the front of his shirt. If the music weren't so loud you would be able to hear "ARRROOOOOOGA!"

"Hello there ladies."

Liz not so subtly elbowed me when the one that looked like a line-backer spoke. I briefly raised my eyebrows at the shirt he wore that strained against the muscles of his chest and read "I'm not a gynecol-ogist but I'll take a look." My attention immediately focused on the guy standing next to him with his hands in his pockets. The long-sleeved t-shirt he wore with the sleeves pushed up to his elbows hugged his body nicely and I could see the subtle outline of muscles in his chest and arms. They were nothing compared to Hooked on Steroids standing next to him, but they were perfect to me. I wanted him to turn around so I could see how great his ass looked in the well-worn jeans he had on. Unlike a lot of the college guys around here who were going through some sort of weird Justin Bieber-hair phase, this guy kept his light brown hair cut short, with just enough length on top for some messy spikes. He wasn't too tall, wasn't too short, he was just right. And just... beautiful. I wanted to punch my own face for calling a guy beautiful but it was true. He was so pretty I wanted to frame him and put him on my nightstand in a totally non-creepy, non-Hannibal Lector skin-suit-wearing kind of way. He looked bored and like he'd rather be anywhere but at this party. Before I could introduce myself and tell him he was my soul mate, someone bumped into me roughly from behind and I stumbled forward, smacking gracefully into his chest and spilling my beer all over the floor at our feet.

Holy hell he smelled good. Like boy and cinnamon and a tiny hint of cologne that made me want to rub my nose in his shirt and take a deep breath. Okay, so that might have thrown me back into creepy territory. I didn't want him to start calling me the shirt sniffer. That's a nickname that just doesn't go away. Like vagina hand.

His hands flew out of his pockets and grabbed onto my arms to steady me while I was busy trying not to motorboat his tee shirt and flee the scene in mortification. I heard the sound of cackling laughter behind me and turned to see that one of the Heathers was responsible for my graceful entrance into this guy's life. It turns out slamming into someone is hilarious and her equally offensive twin joined in on the finger pointing and laughing.

What is this, a bad teen movie from the nineties? Did they expect me to cry and go running out of the room while dramatic music played over my exit?

"Jesus, what's your damage Heather?" a masculine voice said irritably.

Their laughter immediately stopped and they looked behind me in confusion. I whipped my head around and stared at the guy in awe, noticing that I still had my hands pressed against his chest and that I could feel the heat from his skin through his thin t-shirt.

"Did you just quote 'Heathers'?" I whispered. "That is my favorite movie ever."

He looked down at me and smiled, the piercing blue of his eyes boring a hole right through me.

"I had a huge crush on Winona Ryder before the whole shoplifting thing," he said with a shrug, his hands still wrapped around my upper arms.

"My name isn't Heather," a whiny voice protested behind me.

"Wow, Winona Ryder," I stated with a nod of my head.

Jesus, I had absolutely no game. Being in close proximity to a guy this hot turned my brain to mush. I just wanted to hear him speak again. His voice made me want to take my pants off.

"I kind of have a thing for quirky, intelligent, dark-haired chicks," he said with a smile.

"Why did he call me Heather? He knows my name is Niki," came the shrill voice from behind me again.

I'm a quirky, intelligent, dark haired chick! Me, me, me, pick me! And who the hell keeps whining and ruining my perfect moment? I will cut a bitch.

"UM, HELLLOOOO!"

The man of my dreams broke eye contact with me to look over my shoulder. "Niki, your voice is making my ears bleed and killing my buzz."

I heard her huff and storm off. At least I think that's what she did. I was still staring at this guy and wondering how soon was too soon to drag him into a spare bedroom. He looked back at me and removed one of his hands from my arms to brush my bangs out of my eyes with his fingers. The simplicity of the action and the ease in which he performed it made it feel as though he'd done it a thousand times before. I wanted to slyly give Liz a big cheesy grin and a thumb's up but she was busy talking to this guy's friend a few feet away.

"You want to go refill your drink, maybe play a game of beer pong or something?"

I want to reach in my pants, pull out my virginity, wrap it up and put a bow on it. Or maybe stick it in a gift bag from Target and give it to him like a present with a nice card that says "Thank you for being you! Just a little virginity to show you my gratitude!"

"Sure," I replied with a shrug, totally playing it cool. It's probably best to play a little hard to get. You don't want to look too eager.

"OH GOD, DON'T stop," I panted as he kissed a trail down my neck and fumbled clumsily with the button of my jeans. After five rounds of beer pong and hours of talking, laughing and standing so close to him that it soon became impossible to refrain from touching him, I forgot the meaning of "hard to get". With a boldness I could only achieve through copious amounts of alcohol, I wrapped a hand behind his neck after losing the last round, pulled him to me, and kissed him with everything I had in me in front of all the people still left at the party that hadn't yet passed out in a pile of their own vomit. I grabbed his hand and dragged him down the hallway and shoved him into the first room we came to. I hoped Liz would have been close by to give me some sort of encouragement or last minute pointers about what I was about to do, but she disappeared after I announced to the room that she would be giving free PAP tests at the end of the night with her lesbian approved hand.

As soon as we got into the dark room we attacked each other. Sloppy, drunken kisses, hands groping all over the place, slamming into random furniture as we stumbled and laughed our way to the bed. I tripped over something on the floor that may or may not have been a person and fell backwards, luckily onto the bed, dragging the guy right along with me. He landed roughly on top of me and it felt like the wind was knocked out of me.

"Shit, sssorry. You'kay?" He slurred as he pushed himself up on his arms, taking some of his weight off of me.

"Yep, good," I wheezed. "Now take your clothes off."

I was so buzzed I almost laughed when he dragged himself off me and took his pants and boxer briefs off. The moonlight shining through the bedroom window provided just enough illumination for me to see what he was doing even though the alcohol coursing through my veins made him look like he was on a tilt-a-whirl. He pushed everything down to his ankles without bending his knees, then stood up and shuffled back to the bed. Thankfully, the miniscule part of my brain that hadn't yet been taken over by beer and tequila shots reminded me it was never a good idea to laugh at a man when he took his pants off. It was just so funny though! I've seen plenty of penises before, just not in living color and two feet from my body. That thing stuck straight out and was pointing right at me. I swear, in my head I could hear the penis talking.

"Aaarrggg, ahoy me matey, thars a great grand vagina over yonder."

Penises talk like pirates when I'm drunk. Probably because Liz calls them one-eyed snakes. And pirates wear patches and only have one eye and…holy shit, Captain Hookpenis was coming closer.

I should probably focus.

He crawled on top of me and kissed me, his scallywag bumping into my leg. This time I did laugh, pulling my mouth away from his and giggling until I snorted. I was drunk as shit, thinking about walking the plank and there was a penis smacking against my thigh in a strange bedroom that may or may not have a dead person on the floor. How can you not chortle like a schoolgirl at that shit? He was oblivious to my convulsions of laughter as he moved his head to the side and kissed my neck. And Jeeeeeeesus if that didn't sober me up long enough to realize how good it felt.

"Ohhhhh yessssssss," I moaned out loud, surprising myself that I'd actually vocalized the words that were sloshing around in my fuzzy, beer-addled brain.

His lips moved up to the spot right behind my ear and when his tongue slid lightly against the skin there, it shot a tingle right between my legs that surprised me. My hands moved up to clutch onto his hair and hold his head in place. I didn't really think anything about this night was going to feel good. It was all about getting this crap out of the way, enjoying myself was a small perk I didn't expect. After a few minutes of fumbling with my jeans, he finally got them unbuttoned and yanked them down my legs, taking my underwear with them. His hands slid up the sides of my body, taking my shirt with them until it was pulled over my head and tossed in the general direction of my jeans. The liquid courage reignited long enough for me to take off my bra and fling it to the side, the sound of the material smacking into the wall making me realize I was now lying on a bed completely naked with a guy kneeling between my legs, staring down at all I had to offer.

Oh my God. This is really happening. I'm naked in front of a guy. Am I really going to do this?

"Jesus, you're so fucking beautiful."

Yes, the answer is yes! If he keeps talking to me like that he can stick it in my ear.

He let his eyes roam over my body and then quickly yanked his shirt off and threw it across the room. My hands automatically reached up to his chest so I could touch him as he sunk back down on top of me. His chest was hard and his skin was smooth. I touched every inch of him I could reach. I wrapped my hands around the back of his neck and pulled him down to me and kissed him. He tasted like tequila and sunshine. Despite our inebriated states, I was enjoying his kisses. Now that we were naked and in bed, they weren't so frantic. They were actually soft and sweet and made me sigh a little into his mouth. He pulled one of my legs up and wrapped it around his hip and I could feel the head of his penis right at my opening.

Oh shit, this is it. This is really happening. And why am I talking to myself when I have my tongue in someone's mouth and he's getting ready to stick his penis in me?

Oh my God …

EVEN THOUGH I was drunk as a skunk at the time, I still remembered what happened after that. Less than two seconds later he was inside me and I was waving good-bye to my virginity. I wanted it to last forever. I saw stars, came three times that night and it was the most beautiful experience of my life.

Yeah right. Are you kidding me? Have you lost your virginity lately? It hurts like a mother effer and it's awkward and messy. Anyone that tells you she had anything even close to resembling an orgasm during the actual event itself is a lying sack of shit. The only stars I saw were the ones behind my eyelids as I squeezed them shut and waited for it to be over.

But let's be honest here, this is exactly how I expected it to be. It's not his fault it wasn't anything to write home about. He was as sweet and gentle as he could possibly be with me considering the amount of alcohol we consumed during the night. We were both drunk as hell and I lost my virginity to a guy whose name I didn't know because I didn't want any distractions and I didn't have time for a relationship. With the state of my virginity out of the way, I could focus more on school and my career and Liz would stop treating every party we went to like a meat market. It went exactly according to my plan. That is, until my period was a week late and I realized I ate an entire loaf of bread and seven sticks of string cheese while I sat at the kitchen table looking at the calendar and wishing I'd paid more attention to math in kindergarten because there was no fucking way I counted right.

3.

Have You Seen This Sperm Donor?

SOMETIMES I BLAME my lack of desire to have children on my mother. She wasn't a bad mother; she just didn't really know what she was doing. She realized early on that living in a small town out in the country wasn't for her and that sitting around day after day watching television with my dad and dealing with a sassy pre-teen wasn't all that she wanted out of life. She wanted to travel, go to art shows, concerts and movies, she wanted to be free to come and go as she pleased and not have to answer to anyone. My mom told me once that she never stopped loving my dad. She just wanted more than he could give her. They divorced and she moved out when I was twelve to get a condo in the city about thirty miles away. I never felt like she abandoned me or anything, I still saw her all the time and talked to her on the phone every day. And it's not like she didn't ask me to go with her when she moved out. She did, but I think it was only because she felt like it was expected. Everyone knew I'd choose to stay with my father. I was and always would be a daddy's girl. As much as I loved my mother, I felt like I had more in common with my dad and it just seemed natural that I should stay with him.

Even though she didn't live with us, my mother still tried to nurture me as best she could. Her parental skills weren't all that great to begin with though, and after she moved out, they pretty much turned into one big train wreck. Regardless of what people might think, she really did love me; she just acted more like a friend most of the time than a mother. Three days after she moved out, she called and told me that according to something she saw on Oprah, we needed to do something life altering so that we could forge a stronger bond between us. She suggested getting matching tattoos. I reminded her that I was twelve and it was illegal. I have enough "Chicken Soup for the Mother/Daughter Blah, Blah, Blah" reference books she's given me over the years to open my own bookstore and have been tagged in one too many photos of her and I on her Facebook page with the caption "Me and my BFF!".

People thought it was strange the way the three of us lived, but it worked for us. My dad didn't have to listen to my mother nagging in his ear all day long about how he never took her anywhere, and my mother was free to do as she pleased while still having a close relationship with us. Some people just aren't meant to live together. My parents got along much better when there was a twenty-five minute car ride separating them.

Aside from the advice she received from bad talk shows, my mother used the "Parenting with Idioms" book to raise me. Every piece of advice ever given to me was in the form of a one-liner she read in a book or heard Paula Dean use on the Food Network. Unfortunately, they never made sense and were never used in the correct context. When you're six-years-old and you tell your mother someone at school made you cry and she replies with, "Don't pee down my back and tell me it's raining," you sort of learn to handle things on your own and stop asking for her advice.

When I found out I was pregnant, I didn't immediately have dreams of being some independent, women's lib, equal rights, "I don't shave my legs because the man won't keep me down" type of person, perfectly content to do things on her own without the help of anyone. I'm not a martyr. As stubborn and self-sufficient as I was, I knew I would need help.

As soon as I took eleventy-billion home pregnancy tests, after drinking a gallon of milk so I would have enough pee for all of them, I realized I needed to hunt this guy down. Of course, this was after I Googled "milk and pregnancy tests" to make sure I didn't just spend thirty-seven minutes of my life staring in horror at positive pregnancy tests littered all over my bathroom that may or may not be correct because pasteurization messed with the hormones in your body and created a false positive.

It doesn't, just in case you were wondering.

I was a twenty-year-old full-time college student, and according to my mother, "You don't have two nickels to pull out of a duck's ass with a penny in its name." My dad, George, worked the same job he had since he was eighteen and made just enough to pay his bills and help me with my room and board. Thank God my dad's best friend Tim was right all those years ago. I was smarter than I looked and received a full ride to the University of Ohio, so I didn't have the burden of student loans or grants. Unfortunately though, that meant I went to school full time and worked my ass off, taking twice the course load as other students, leaving no time for a job and no money saved.

In some ways I took after my mother. I wanted more out of my life than waiting tables at Fosters Bar and Grill where I worked all through high school. I wanted to travel, work hard and one day own my own business. Unfortunately, life doesn't throw curveballs; it throws an eight pound, one ounce infant at your face when you're looking the other way. Life is a vindictive little bitch. I was smart enough to know I couldn't do this by myself and wanted more than anything to keep the inconvenience of my mistake away from my dad for as long as possible. Any other woman would probably call her mother to cry and plead for help as soon as the stick turned pink, but at the time, I wasn't in the mood for my mother to tell me that "Rome was not built with two birds in your bush". That left me with the person who helped put me into this situation. Unfortunately, I had no idea who the guy was I slept with. I was too mortified by my actions that night to ever repeat the performance so I knew without a doubt Mr. Beer Pong was the father. I just had to find him. Who the hell gave a guy her virginity and never even bothered to ask him what his name was?

Oh yeah, that would be me.

The first day I decided to try and find him was spent talking to every single dumb jock that lived at the frat house where the party occurred. No one there had any clue who I was talking about when I tried to describe this guy and the friend he had with him that night. It could have been due to the fact that everyone I talked to smelled like a brewery and stared at my boobs the entire time I was there. Or maybe it was because I wasn't fluent in stupid. Really, either option was viable. On the way back to the apartment I shared with Liz, after my hunting expedition, all I wanted to do was kick my own ass. The morning after when I woke up, I felt silly admitting that the feel of his arm wrapped around my waist made me sigh a little. I should have stayed. I should have waited until he woke up, thanked him for a good time and put his number in my phone. But as much as I itched to run my fingers through his hair or slide my hand down his cheek, I knew I couldn't. At that point, I couldn't afford any distractions in my life and that's exactly what he would have been. If we were together, stone-cold sober, I knew I could have easily lost myself in him and forgot everything I had been working towards all my life. I found it was much easier to brush something off and say you did it because you were drunk than admit you made a mistake. I didn't think sleeping with him was a mistake really, just the way I went about it and my actions the next morning. Instead of sticking around, I slithered out from under his arm and the warmth of his body and thought about how bad it would have been if I woke up next to some ugly troll. At least he was hot as hell in the light of day, and I didn't have to perform a coyote ugly and chew my own arm off to get out from under him. I threw on my clothes as fast as I could and left him naked and sound asleep in bed. No one moved as I stepped over the lifeless bodies spread throughout the house and performed the morning-after walk of shame, out the door and into the bright morning light.

I turned around a total of six times to go back to that house and wait for him to wake up. And each time, I talked myself out of it with the same argument. I used him to finally get rid of my stupid virginity. Did I really want to know why he did it? I was definitely not the best looking girl in that place. People tell me I'm cute and I guess I probably am, but what exactly did he see when he looked at me? Maybe he could just tell I would be a sure thing that night. I'd rather remember him as the sweet, buzzed, hot guy who rid me of my virginity and made me laugh. I didn't want to know if he was some skeezy womanizer that was sleeping his way through the student directory, and I was just lucky enough he finally made it to the M's.

When I got home that day, Liz made me retell the story over and over so she could squeal and tell me how happy she was for me and that it was no big deal she struck out with his buff friend because she found some guy named Jim who was all alone at the party and it was love at first sight.

Her squealing and patting on the back continued until five weeks later when she came home from class and found me sitting on the bathroom floor surrounded by little white plastic sticks that all said "Pregnant" on them, crying hysterically with snot running down my lip as I rambled incoherently about milk and cows taking pregnancy tests.

For two months Liz helped with my crusade to find this guy. She never got his friend's name either because as soon as she made eye contact with Jim "the rest of the world disappeared" or some disgusting shit like that. We contacted the admissions office and we poured through a dozen yearbooks in the hopes that we might recognize him in one of the pictures. We even tried locating that skanky chick Niki that slammed into me, with no luck.

Did these people just appear out of thin air or something? How is there no fucking record of their existence at this school?

Liz even tried talking to the guys at the frat house herself, taking Jim along with her, but she didn't have any better luck than I did. She did however come home completely trashed because every guy she talked to made her and Jim do a shot every time they said the word "goat testicles". Honestly, I have no idea how that word came up in their conversation so many damn times. Do you have any clue how annoying drunk people are when you are forced to be sober? Especially drunk people who are in love, touchy-feely and quoting Walt Witman to each other while you've got red, puffy eyes from crying, haven't showered in four days and just got done throwing up the contents of your stomach because you saw a commercial about goldfish – the crackers, not the real fish. But those damn things looked so much like real fish all I could think about was swallowing a live, slimy goldfish that stared at me with its beady little eyes before I put him on my tongue.

I knew the chances of me finding this guy were slim to none. I couldn't very well move into the frat house and be the boys' token pregnant roommate in the hopes he would one day come back there before the child I was carrying was in college and possibly living there himself.

I also couldn't hold off on telling my dad any longer. I saw the campus nurse that morning and she confirmed with a blood test that I was pregnant, and going by my calculations of the one and only time I had sex, I was thirteen weeks along.

Now, I'm all for a woman's right to choose. I believe it is your body and do with it as you may and blah, blah, blah. With that being said, as much as I dislike tiny little humans, I could never get rid of my own flesh and blood, by abortion or adoption. It just wasn't something I was personally comfortable with. So, with Liz holding my hand, I took the chicken shit way out and told my dad over the phone.

Let me explain something about my dad. He's six-foot-four, two hundred and fifty pounds, has tattoos up and down his forearms of snakes and skulls and other scary shit, and he always looks pissed off at the world. He scared the shit out of several boys in high school when they knocked on the door and my dad would answer. When I came to the door, they'd tell me they thought my dad was going to kill them and I'd reassure them that no, that's just the way his face always looks.

In all honesty, my dad was a nice guy. He got his tattoos when he was young and in the army and he always had a scowl on his face because he was exhausted. He worked twelve-hour days, seven days a week for months at a time before he got a day or two off. He wasn't big on talking about his feelings or being affectionate, but I knew he loved me and would do anything for me. He was a great guy, but he was still a force to be reckoned with and God help the person who ever hurt his little girl. Liz started spewing Chuck Norris quotes in high school and replacing Chuck's name with my dad's. She did it so much that I find myself doing it from time to time. He reacted to the pregnancy news pretty much like I expected him to.

"Well, I'll get your room ready so you can come back home when the semester is done. And if you find this guy in the meantime, let me know so I can rip off his balls and shove them down his throat," he said in his usual deep, monotone voice.

If you spelled George Morgan wrong on Google it didn't say, "Did you mean George Morgan?" It simply replied, "Run while you still have the chance."

After the semester ended, I applied for a leave of absence with the school so they would hold my scholarship. They would only keep it active for one year before I would have to reapply. I never intended to be away from school that long, but I also never intended on a baby completely fucking up my life. Er, I mean, bringing me years of great joy.

For the next six and a half months, I worked as much as my growing stomach and cankles would allow so I could save plenty of money for after he was born. Unfortunately, in the small town of Butler, there's not much to choose from employment-wise that would pay well. Unless of course I wanted to be a stripper at the town's one and only strip club, The Silver Pole. I was approached by the owner at the grocery store when I was seven months. In the middle of the cereal aisle he told me there were plenty of patrons in his club that thought the pregnant body was beautiful. If there weren't children around at the time, I would have told him off. Oh, who was I kidding? If Jesus himself was standing next to me, I would have still told that douche bag that if he ever came anywhere near me again I would rip his dick off and choke him with it. I would have apologized to Jesus before leaving though of course.

On the bright side, the president of the Butler Elementary PTA was standing there with her six-year-old and heard every word. I guess I shouldn't hold my breath waiting for the invitation to join, huh? Shoot. Now where am I going to find the will to live?

With my pregnant stripping career over before it started and my proverbial tail stuck between my legs, I groveled for my old job as a waitress at Fosters Bar and Grill. Luckily, the Foster's still owned it from when I worked there in high school, and they were more than happy to help me out considering my *situation.*

When people in a small town talked about you to your face, they whispered the words that they believed might offend someone if they were to overhear your conversation. In my opinion, they should be whispering words like "fuck", "anal sex" or "Did you hear Billy Chuck got caught with his pants around his ankles down at the Piggly Wiggly with his dog Buffy?" Whispering the word "situation" kind of defeated the purpose. I whispered random words all the time just to mess with them.

"Mrs. Foster, the *bathroom* is out of toilet paper."

"Mr. Foster, I need to leave *early* to go to the doctor."

I talked to Liz every single day after I moved back home, and she kept up her search of the missing sperm donor when she had time. Her family was from Butler as well so she came home to visit me as often as she could but towards the end of my pregnancy, she just didn't have time to make the three and a half hour drive as often. Her professors convinced her to double up on her course load so she could graduate a year early with her degree in Small Business, majoring in Entrepreneurship with minors in Marketing and Accounting. With her full-time studies, part-time internship with an at-home consulting firm and her blossoming relationship with Jim, I knew she had a lot on her plate and didn't begrudge her any of her successes or happiness. I was a big enough person to admit that I was only a tiny bit jealous. Liz and I always talked about owning businesses together. About how we'd rent out buildings right next to one another with a door that led into both and how we'd live in a loft upstairs and throw awesome parties every weekend. We also dreamed about both of us marrying one of the members of N'Sync and living a life of polygamy with our new band N'Love.

Fingers still crossed on that one.

In all of our talk about the future, Liz never really cared what kind of business she ran, she just wanted it to be hers and be in charge. I always knew I wanted to own a candy and cookie shop.

As far back as I can remember I was always in the kitchen covering something in chocolate or baking cookies. My dad always joked that I could never sneak up on him because he could smell the chocolate on me from a mile away. I was pretty sure it leaked out of my pores at this point. I was so happy that my best friend's dream was coming true. I tried not to dwell too much on the fact that my dream was going on the back burner until God knew when.

I missed seeing Liz every day once I moved back home, and I was sad that my future needed to be put on hold, but nothing was as depressing as going into labor on my twenty-first birthday. While all of my friends celebrated their twenty-first birthdays by drinking every alcoholic beverage on the menu, sitting on the floor of a public restroom while singing along to the music piped through the speakers and then hanging out of the passenger-side window of a car on the way home screaming, "I'M DRUNK FUCKERS!", I was stuck in a hospital trying not to punch every twat nurse in the face that kept telling me it wasn't time for my epidural.

I decided then and there that someday, I was going to be a labor and delivery consultant. I was going to stand next to every single woman in labor and every time a nurse or a doctor or hell, even the woman's husband said something stupid like, "Just breathe through the pain," it would be my job to squeeze the living fuck out of their reproductive organs until they were curled up in the fetal position asking for their mommies and I'd say "Just breathe through the pain, asshole!" And anyone that gave the new mother a dirty look after an eight pound, one ounce bloody, gooey, screaming pile of tiny human was cut out of her stomach when she asked her father to grab the bottle of vodka out of her overnight bag because, "morphine and vodka sounds like a stellar way to celebrate the birth of my spawn," would get their McJudgy glare smacked right off their face.

And I guess that brings us up to speed.

The next four years were spent working my ass off trying to make enough money to set aside for my future business, while raising my son and trying not to sell him to gypsies on a daily basis.

After a while, the search for Mr. Cherry Popper fell by the wayside as life got in the way. It didn't mean I never thought about him. Every time I looked at my son, I couldn't help but think about him. Everyone told me that Gavin looks exactly like me. And I guess he does to an extent. He has my nose, my lips, my dimples and my attitude. But his eyes were a whole other story. Every single day when I looked into the crystal blue pools of my son's eyes, I saw his father. I saw the way the corners of his eyes crinkled when he laughed at something I said, I saw the way they sparkled when he animatedly told me a funny story and I saw the sincerity in them each time he brushed the hair out of my eyes that night. I wondered where he was, what he was doing and if "Heathers" was still one of his favorite movies. Every so often I would be struck with a sharp stab of guilt at the fact that this man would never get to meet his son, but it's not like I didn't try. There's only so much I could do. I wasn't about to put out an ad in the paper that says, "Hey, world! So this one time, at a frat party, I was a total slut and let a stranger go where no man has gone before and now I have a son. Won't you please help me find my baby daddy?"

Jim became more of a permanent fixture in my life as well as Liz's. I probably talked to him on the phone as much as I did her. It was a no-brainer that the two of them would be Gavin's godparents. They spoiled him rotten and I liked to put all the blame on Liz for the mouth on that kid. I didn't think anyone screamed louder than I did when I found out Jim asked Liz to marry him and that they were going to move to Butler to be closer to her family and me. As soon as they moved back, Liz began tirelessly working and researching for the next few years to get a solid business plan in place. She told me a few months ago that she finally figured out what she wanted to sell, but she didn't want to tell me until she was certain she could do it. After that phone call, the most I saw of Liz was a blur as she ran from one appointment to the next. She was constantly on the phone with realtors and banks, running back and forth to her lawyer's office to sign paperwork and making daily trips up to the county court house to get all of the small business forms completed. I reluctantly agreed during a night of girl-time, after five too many dirty martinis, that I would help her out on a part-time basis as a consultant. I think my exact words were "I love you Liz. And I love vodka. I shall hug you and squeeze you and call you Lizdka." Liz considered that a yes.

All Liz told me about the job was that it could be considered sales and I would have a blast doing it. Being a bartender, I considered myself pretty damn good at sales.

"What? You say your wife dumped you for a woman in her book club? Here, try a bottle of Patrón."

"Oh no, your best friend's neighbor's ex-wife's dog was hit by a car? Here, Johnnie Walker should do the trick."

Liz liked to make even the most mundane things suspenseful and wanted to keep me in the dark and surprise me about what I would be selling. And since I was drunk at the time, I would have agreed to sell do-it-yourself enema kits and she knew it. I worked a few hours almost every night at the bar after Gavin went to bed and made some money putting together candy and cookie trays for parties around town but I could always use the extra cash, so I was okay with it as long as helping Liz out didn't cut into my time with Gavin too much.

Tonight was my "orientation" so to speak. I was going to tag along with Liz to one of her engagements so I could get a feel for the business. Jim was watching Gavin for the night so I offered to drive, dropping him off when I picked Liz up.

They met us out in the driveway as I pulled in. Liz was lugging the biggest suitcase I had ever seen behind her and shooed Jim's hand away when he tried to help her heft it into my trunk. I should have taken Jim's knowing smirk when we pulled away as a huge red flag. In my defense, I don't get out much. I assumed we would be selling something like candles, Tupperware or beauty products; all things that Liz loved. I should have known better. Or paid closer attention to the words "Bedroom Fun" stitched into the side of the suitcase in pink, elegant script.

4.

Sex and Chocolate

"HE WAS MY favorite uncle. Good old Uncle Willie. I sure am gonna miss him."

I rolled my eyes and drained the last of my beer, listening to my best friend Drew on the barstool next to me try to pick up one of the waitresses.

"Oooooh, you poor baby. You must be so sad," she told him, eating up all of his bullshit and running her hands through his hair.

"I'm devastated. Practically horny with grief."

"What did you say? I couldn't hear you over the music," she shouted.

I snorted and looked over her head to make eye contact with Drew, giving him a look that clearly said "I cannot believe the words that are coming out of your mouth."

With a kiss on his cheek and a smack to her ass, they parted ways and he swiveled around on his bar stool to take a swig of his drink.

"Your Uncle Willie died two years ago. And you hated him," I reminded Drew.

He slammed his beer down on the bar and turned to face me.

"Have you forgotten the awesomeness that was 'Wedding Crashers', Carter? Grief is nature's most powerful aphrodisiac, my friend."

Drew had been my best friend since kindergarten, and yet sometimes, the things that he said still amazed me. The fact that he was a good friend and was here for me in my time of need helped me overlook his obnoxious and man-whorish behavior most of the time.

Drew flagged the bartender over and ordered up two shots of tequila. At this rate I would be going home on a stretcher. My organs were going to start shutting down from liquor running through my veins instead of blood and I'm pretty sure there was a little person in my brain whispering the words to "Ice Ice Baby" and messing with my vision.

Drew and I both worked for the same automotive plant and were recently transferred from the plant in Toledo to the one a few hours away in Butler. We shared an apartment together in Toledo, but after two years of listening to him bang his way through the white pages, the yellow pages, and eight business directories within a ten mile radius, I decided not sharing a small space with him anymore was a necessity. I still had a ton of unpacking to do in the small ranch-style home I was renting and was starting to regret letting Drew convince me to drown my sorrows in the bottom of a bottle. He knew me too well though and knew that if I was at home, I wouldn't be unpacking. I'd be sitting there alone, staring at a picture of my ex wondering why the hell I wasted so many years with her.

The bartender poured the shots, letting them overflow and Drew grabbed them both, handing one over to me and raising his in the air. I reluctantly did the same with mine and tried to focus on holding my hand steady while the room tipped sideways.

Drew's empty hand flew out and grabbed onto my elbow, yanking me upright and spilling some of the shot on my hand.

Oops, guess that was me tipping, not the room.

"Before you face plant off your stool, fucker, I'd like to make a toast. To my best friend, Carter. May he never fall victim to another two-timing, gold-digging whore."

We downed the shots and slapped the glasses on the bar.

"Thanks for not fucking her buddy," I mumbled, trying not to slur.

"Dude, first of all, I'd never fuck any girl you were even remotely interested in, let alone dating for a long period of time. And second, I could never accept a proposition from that skank. I wouldn't do that to my penis. He's done nothing wrong and doesn't deserve the punishment of her vagina."

I sighed, smacked my elbows on top of the bar and rested my head in my hands.

"My poor penis. I should buy him a gift," I muttered to myself.

Finding out my girlfriend of two years was cheating on me two days before we were supposed to move here together and start a new life was a huge pain in my ass. And my penis.

Drew's grief counselor, the waitress, walked back over to console him and interrupted my penis pity party. At the same time, a rush of air surrounded me as someone quickly walked by, their shoes clicking on the hardwood floor. I breathed in right at that moment and the smell of chocolate overwhelmed me and instantly transported me back in time to five years ago.

"Mmmmm you smell so good. Like chocolate chip cookies," I muttered with a raspy, hung-over voice as I pulled her incredibly soft body against my own.

Wow, she doesn't have any bones. Like, at all. Where the fuck are her bones? Am I still drunk? Did I sleep with a blow-up doll? Again? I pealed my eyes open one at a time so the rays of sun shining in the room wouldn't make me go blind. Once my eyes adjusted to the light, I looked down and groaned. Nope, not drunk, just hugging a pillow. I let go of the pillow, rolling over onto my back and flinging my arm out to the side of me to stare up at the ceiling.

She was gone. And I didn't even get her name. What kind of a dick was I? She wasn't too interested in knowing my name either though, so I guess we were even. As drunk as I was last night, I could remember every single second. I closed my eyes and pulled to mind how great her ass looked in those jeans, the smell of her skin, the sound of her laugh and the way her body felt like it was made to fit against mine. I scanned through every memory I had, but for some reason, her face just wouldn't come into focus no matter how hard I tried. God dammit, how was I going to find her if I couldn't remember her face and didn't know her name? I was the king of jackasses. I knew she was beautiful, even if I couldn't remember everything. Her skin was soft and her hair felt like silk and her lips on me could make me whimper like a girl. And best of all, she made me laugh. Not many girls made me laugh. They never got my jokes or were too uptight for my sense of humor. But she got me.

Last night obviously wasn't my best performance. I hope to God I didn't have whiskey dick and was able to at least get it up and keep it up. Shit. She probably ran out of here as fast as she could this morning because I sucked so badly. I never had a one-night-stand before; I didn't know what the protocol was for something like this. Would it be wrong for me to hunt her down? Even if she wanted nothing to do with me ever again, I needed to at least apologize for my God-awful skills last night.

And truth be told, I just wanted to see her again. I wanted to know if she was real or if I just imagined how perfect she was. I grabbed the pillow and brought it up to my face, breathing the smell of chocolate in deep and smiling. I might not have remembered everything, but I remembered her smell. It was like hot chocolate on a cold winter's day, chocolate cake baking in an oven on a rainy afternoon…

Oh my God, I sound like a chick. I need to watch some ESPN and get in a bar fight, pronto.

The sound of the toilet flushing in the connecting bathroom had me bolting upright in bed. Holy shit! Was that her?

I swung my legs around off the bed and started to get up right when the door opened.

"Fucking hell dude, don't ever sleep in a bathtub. That shit is for the birds. My ass is killing me," Drew complained as he shuffled over to the bed, turned around and let his body fall back onto the end, settling after a few bounces. He threw his arm over his eyes and groaned.

"Why the fuck does morning have to come so early?" he whimpered.

I sighed in disappointment, holding the sheet in place so I could lean over and grab my jeans that were crumpled on the floor with my boxer-briefs still shoved inside them.

"I'm never drinking again," he promised.

"You said that last week," I reminded him as I flung the sheet off of me so I could put my pants on.

What. The. Fuck?

"Oh shit. Fucking shit. Mother fucking shit balls."

This can't be good. This really, really cannot be good.

"What are you whining about over there, Nancy?" Drew asked as he removed his arm from across his eyes and sat up.

"My dick is bleeding. Drew – MY DICK IS BLEEDING!"

I was screeching like a girl. I knew it, he knew it, pretty soon the whole house would know it. But my dick was bleeding. Did you hear me? My fucking dick was fucking bleeding. FUCK! It's not supposed to bleed. Ever.

I thought I was having a heart attack. I couldn't breathe. I didn't know much, but I did know the rules about owning a dick. Rule number one: It should never bleed. Rule number two: There was no rule number two. IT SHOULD NEVER FUCKING BLEED.

Did I sleep with a nutcase that decided to carve my dick like a jack-o-lantern while I slept? Or maybe her vagina had teeth. My dad used to always tell me when I was a teenager to stay away from them, because they bite. I thought he was kidding. Oh God, I can't look. What if some of it is missing?

"Calm down. Let's assess the situation," Drew said, crossing one leg over the other and folding his hands on his knee. "Have you noticed any of the following: unidentified discharge, burning sensation when you urinate, lower abdominal pain, testicular pain, pain during sex, fever, headache, sore throat, weight loss, chronic diarrhea or night sweats?"

He sounded like a fucking commercial for syphilis.

"Eeew dude, no. I just have blood on my dick," I answered irritably, pointing to the problem but refusing to look.

He leaned over and looked down at my lap.

"Looks okay to me," he said with a shrug as he stood up. "You probably just bagged a virgin."

I sat there with my bloody, non-chlamydia infested dick flapping in the breeze and my jaw hanging open.

A virgin? That can't be right.

I glanced back down in my lap and took a closer look. Okay so it wasn't the bloody slaughter I originally thought I saw. My dick hadn't been Texas Chainsaw Massacred. There were just a few pink streaks. I wore a condom though. How in the hell does something like this happen? You use those God dammed things as water balloons in middle school and couldn't get them to pop even if you threw them at a bed of nails. The one time you need them to stay in one piece they decide to say "fuck this shit". It was like condom anarchy.

But more importantly – Holy hell! Why would she let me take her virginity? Why in the fuck would she give something like that to me when I was completely shit-faced and couldn't even make it sort of enjoyable for her? What an epic fail. I probably ruined sex for her forever. She's probably thinking right now "Seriously? That's what I waited for? What a joke."

"I have to find out who she is. I need to apologize," I mumbled to myself, standing up and pulling my boxers and jeans on.

"Whoa, dude. You didn't even get her name? Wow, you're kind of a dick," Drew said with a laugh, walking over to the bedroom door and opening it.

I threw my shirt over my head and then followed behind him, hopping on one foot to slide my shoes on.

"Thanks for making me feel a whole lot better Drew. Really. You're a stellar friend," I said sarcastically as we maneuvered our way through a house full of passed out drunks.

"Hey, it's not my fault you banged and bailed bro," he stated as he took a giant step over a naked chick wearing just a sombrero and opened the front door.

"I didn't bang and bail. In case you failed to notice, I woke up alone in bed this morning."

"With a bloody johnson," he added, walking down the steps of the porch.

"With a fucking bloody johnson," I repeated with a groan. "Shit. I have to find this girl. Do you think it's wrong for me to ask your dad to use his private detective resources to find out who she is?"

Drew's dad opened his own PI agency a few years ago when he decided following the rules of the police department didn't fit in with his busy schedule.

"Are you asking me if it's ethically wrong or if I *think it's wrong? Because those are two very different questions my friend," he replied as we crossed the street and got into his car parked by the curb. If only Drew took after his father in some way…*

"I have to find her Drew," I said as he started up the car.

"Then find her we shall my little virginity thief!"

"We never found her, did we big guy?" I muttered to Drew, who I assumed was still sitting next to me.

"Are you speaking to anyone in particular or do your shot glasses usually respond?" replied a very un-Drew-sounding voice.

"NOW, IF YOU'LL direct your attention to the one Claire is holding, that is called the Purple Pussy Eater. It has four speeds: Yes, More, Faster and Holy Shit Balls. It's also got a g-spot stimulator that is sure to tickle your fancy. Could you hold it up a little higher so everyone can see, Claire?"

I shot Liz a look that clearly said "bend over so I can shove this thing up your ass sideways" before I raised the rubber penis above my head with absolutely no enthusiasm.

The living room full of completely trashed women screamed in excitement and bounced up and down in their seats when I raised my arm, like the thing I was holding above my head was the actual penis of Brad Pitt. It's plastic, people. And it's filled with double A's, not sperm.

"Go ahead and pass it around for me, Claire," Liz said sweetly as she reached into her suitcase for yet another rubber rod.

I held my arm out lifelessly in front of me for the drunk-ass sitting closest to grab, but she was too busy complaining about how her husband's spunk always tastes like garlic.

Please God don't let me ever come face-to-face with this man, I beg of you. I will look at his crotch and see cloves of garlic popping out of his dick.

"Yo, Lara," I called, trying to get her attention so she could take this dildo out of my hand.

"Claire, remember to use her Bedroom Fun Party name!" Liz reminded me in a sickeningly sweet voice that was starting to make my ears bleed.

I gritted my teeth and imagined raising my arm back up and chucking the fake phallus right at her forehead so she would have a permanent dick head mark right in the middle of her face that people would point and laugh at. Is that a birthmark? No, it's a dick mark.

"Excuse me, *Luscious Lips Lara*?" I enunciated politely while trying not to vomit in my mouth.

Really, was it necessary for everyone to come up with a stupid ass nickname for themselves? That was the first thing Liz made everyone do when they got here. Come up with a sexual nickname for yourself using the first letter of your first name. And you were only allowed to call each other by those names all night.

Luscious Lips Lara, Juicy Jenny, Raunchy Rachel, Tantalizing Tasha ....

Who thought up this shit? Oh, that's right, Liz – my former best friend. The one who decided to start a sex toy business without telling me so she could con me into working for her.

She should have let me come up with the names. Twat Face Tasha, Jizzbucket Jenny, Loose Labia Lara...those didn't make me want to jam a pencil in my eye.

Liz finished up the rest of her stupid party while I imagined I was doing anything else but this, like getting a Brazilian wax, water boarded by Navy Seals or my big toe shot off at close range for a gang initiation. Any of those would be preferable to talking with complete strangers about lubrication, nipple clamps and anal beads.

I gave her the silent treatment as we drove to the bar an hour later. I was offered an extra shift tonight that I couldn't pass up and Liz was going to keep me company in between customers. I should just open the car door and throw her out of the moving vehicle for what she did to me tonight, but I didn't want to ruin someone else's car if they ran her over.

"You can't ignore me forever, Claire. Quit being a dick," she complained.

"Speaking of dick...really, Liz? Sex toy parties? At what point in our friendship did you think I would EVER want to sell Pocket Pussies for a living? And another thing, Pocket Pussies? What kind of man needs something called a Pocket Pussy? Do men really need to release their seed out into the wild so much that they need to stick a fake vagina in their pocket that they can whip out at a moment's notice?"

Liz rolled her eyes at me and I resisted the urge to reach over the console and punch her in the vagina.

Pussy Punch: when a Twat Tap just isn't enough.

"Claire, quit being such a drama queen. I don't expect you to sell my sex toys forever, just until I can hire a few more consultants. Think about it Claire, this is the perfect opportunity for us. What was the one thing you noticed that was missing from this party tonight?" she asked, turning sideways in her seat to look at me as I got off at the exit for the bar.

"Dignity," I replied flatly.

"Funny. Snacks, Claire. Well, good snacks at least. They had bowls of chips and store bought cookies and enough liquor to choke a horse. These are women with money, Liz. Money they don't mind throwing away on Pocket Pussies for the husbands they don't want to screw anymore or clitoral stimulators for the 'friend' they know whose husband has never given them an orgasm. What goes better with sex than chocolate?"

Sex and chocolate. My chocolate. My chocolate-covered yummy goodness that I couldn't sell as often as I liked because as a single mother working in a bar, it was hard to market yourself. The majority of people I was surrounded by cared more about who was buying the next round than what kind of desserts to have at their next party.

"The building I rented has the potential to be turned into two separate spaces. One of them with a kitchen," Liz continued. "A very large kitchen where you can perform your magic and when women book their parties they can order dessert trays at the same time."

I took my eyes off of the road long enough to look over and Liz, expecting to see a sarcastic smile on her face and waiting for her to say "Just kidding! Wouldn't that be great though?" When none of that happened and she just sat there in her seat staring at me expectantly, I blinked back tears that I hadn't even realized were forming in my eyes.

"What are you talking about?" I whispered shakily in the dark car.

"Okay so I did something big. Something that's probably going to piss you off because you're going to think it's charity or pity, but really, all I did was get the ball rolling. The rest is up to you," she explained. "I've looked everywhere for a building for my business and everyplace I see is too big or too small and way overpriced. My realtor called me a few weeks ago and told me the owners of Andrea's Bakery right on Main Street came into some money and wanted to sell their space as quickly as possible, retire and move to Florida. It was like a sign, Claire. The price was right, the location is perfect and it's exactly what we always dreamed about, minus the whole Justin Timberlake penis time share. With one sheet of drywall, we've got enough room for two connecting businesses: my sex toys and your desserts."

I bit my lip to stop myself from crying. I never cried.

"But I really wanted to share JT's penis with you," I told her with a sad look, trying to take the seriousness out of this situation before I started to ugly cry. No one likes an ugly crier. It's uncomfortable for all parties involved.

After a few minutes of neither one of us saying a word in the dark car, Liz couldn't take it anymore.

"Will you say something already?"

I let out a huge breath and tried to calm my racing heart.

"Liz I don't…I can't believe you…the money…" She put her hand on my arm as we pulled into the parking lot of Fosters.

"Don't turn into a pansy-ass on me just yet. Take some time and think about it. You know the trust fund my grandfather left me has been eating its way through my pocket so we're not even going to discuss money right now. Talk it over with your dad, come and check out the kitchen at the store and then we'll talk. In the meantime, you're going to get your hot little ass in that bar and serve me up some cocktails. I've got some new products to test out on Jim after your dad picks Gavin up later," she said with a wink before getting out of the car.

I sat there for a few minutes after she got out wondering what the hell just happened. My best friend was always a force of nature, but this just defied logic. Did she really just tell me she bought me a business? With every step of my life I felt like I'd made wrong turns. Nothing was going the way I planned. I wanted this more than anything, but part of me was afraid to really get my hopes up. Who knows though? Maybe good things were finally going to start happening in my life.

I glanced at the clock on the dashboard and realized I spent entirely too long sitting in my car and now I was late for my shift. I ran through the parking lot and threw open the side door, tying my little black apron around my waist as I went. Mr. and Mrs. Foster have seen one too many episodes of True Blood and recently decided we should adopt the same uniform as Merlotte's. Tiny black shorts and tiny white t-shirts with the word "Fosters" stamped across our tits in green. It could be worse. At least I don't have to make sure I'm wearing enough "flare" or sing some demented version of happy birthday with the rest of the staff. "Happy birthday to you, with beer goggles on you don't look like you should moo, happy birthday dear random stranger who's dressed like a hooker, happy birthday to you!"

I ran behind Liz already seated on a stool at the bar sipping her usual drink of vanilla vodka and Diet Coke and waved to T.J., the bartender I was taking over for tonight. Thankfully the men didn't have to wear the same uniform. I didn't think I could handle seeing a couple of these guys in tiny shorts with their hairy balls popping out of the leg holes.

On a slow night, I would have just hopped my ass up onto the bar and swung my legs around to get behind it, but the place was packed tonight. I had to do it the right way and go under the hinged, lift-top part of the bar at the opposite end. I jogged past some poor drunk schmuck that held his head in his hands, moaning, and made a mental note to call him a cab if he was here by himself.

Once I was behind the bar and got the skinny from T.J. on the customers here tonight and what they were drinking, he left to go home and I got to work getting refills for the regulars. One of the waitresses brought in an order for ten shots of the cheapest whiskey we had. I rolled my eyes and went to the end of the bar where we kept all of the whiskey. What is wrong with these people? Cheap whiskey equals a bad hangover and having the craps all the next day. I started lining up the shot glasses on my tray when I heard the drunken moaner speak.

"We never found her, did we big guy?"

Oh Jesus. I hate the really tanked ones. I hope this guy isn't a crier. He sounds pitiful. And if he pukes on my bar I'm going to rub his nose in it like a dog that shit on the carpet.

"Are you speaking to anyone in particular or do your shot glasses usually respond?" I asked without looking up as I added a few more shot glasses to the tray and reached under the bar for the bottle of Wild Turkey, trying not to make gagging noises as I unscrewed the top and the disgusting smell wafted up to my nose.

I saw Return of the Living Drunk whip his head up out of the corner of my eye while I filled the glasses.

"You know, the first sign of insanity is when inanimate objects talk to you. Or maybe it's the first sign of alcohol poisoning," I mused to myself.

"Who the hell is ordering that rot gut? They're going to have the shits all day tomorrow."

I laughed that even drunk, he was able to come to the same conclusion as me. Picking up the tray of shots and a bowl of lemon slices, I turned around to tell him so – and stopped dead in my tracks at the sight before me.

What. The. Fuck?

I felt the tray full of glass and booze tipping out of my raised hand but there was nothing I could do to stop its descent to the floor. I stood there like a statue, staring straight ahead as the glasses shattered around my feet and liquid splashed up onto my legs.

5.

Snickers Finger Arm Teeth

IT HAPPENED IN slow motion. Well, for me it happened in slow motion. Probably because the amount of alcohol I've consumed tonight has digested half of my brain cells, and I feel like I'm in the Matrix.

I wonder if I could lean back on my bar stool and do that cool move from the movie where I dodge bullets in slow motion while suspended in mid-air? I need a cool black leather jacket and my hair slicked back. I wonder if they used wires or if that Keanu guy could really bend like that? I bet he does that yoga shit. He looks like the kind of guy that does Downward Facing Dog.

Heh, heh, downward dog. That's funny. I should get a dog.

Wait, what was I doing? Oh, yeah. The bartender turned around and stared at me and before I could even get a good non-drunken haze look at her. I watched the entire tray of shots tip right out of her hand. They crashed to the floor before I had a chance to react, the sound of glass breaking rising above the drone of music and loud voices.

I should have jumped into action and vaulted across the bar to help her. Because you know, right now I had cat-like reflexes—if the cat drank three times its weight in tequila because it just found out its girlfriend of two years never wanted to have kids and decided to turn her vagina into a wiener-warmer for half the population of Toledo.

I should get a cat or two. They're pretty low maintenance. Maybe I can even teach it to piss in the toilet like Jinxy from "Meet the Fockers." Can a guy turn into a crazy cat lady? I suddenly pictured myself as an old man shuffling along the sidewalk covered in cat hair and meowing at everyone who walked by.

On second thought, no cats. I shouldn't be allowed to think when I'm drinking.

The bartender ducked down behind the bar, and I forgot about cats pissing for a minute so I could stand up and lean over as far as I could without the bar stool flying out from under me to see if she needed help.

And by "help" I meant checking to make sure she wasn't bleeding and then sitting back down to before the room tilted too far to the left and I made an ass of myself.

My good deed ended before it began when a tiny little thing with long blonde hair, who looked strangely familiar, got behind the bar and walked over to the spot I was trying to see and looked down.

"Jesus, butterfingers, are you…"

She was cut off by a hand flying up from behind the bar, latching onto her forearm and yanking her down roughly. She disappeared with a yelp and I shook my head at why women were so weird. And such whores.

Fuck you, Tasha. And fuck cats that don't piss in toilets. And fuck you, Keanu Reeves, and your dog.

Drew sat back down next to me and yelled out, "Yo, bartender!"

The girl with the blonde hair popped up suddenly from behind the bar with her mouth wide open, staring right at me.

"Can we get a couple shots of tequila?" Drew asked her. She didn't even look in his direction, just stared at me without even blinking, like we were in some sort of fucking staring contest.

I'll show her. I'm the mother fucking king of staring contests.

Drew leaned over and snapped his fingers in front of her face a few times.

"Hellloooo?"

Dammit! I blinked.

But she never moved from her spot kneeling behind the bar with just her little head peaking over the top of it. What the fuck was wrong with this woman? She was starting to freak me out.

"Um, tequila please?" I asked questioningly, enunciating each word as best as my drunken mouth would allow. So really, it came out as "Ufff, shakira pea?"

A huge psychotic smile broke out on her face and she quickly stood up.

"So what can I get you?" she asked me brightly, resting her hands on top of the bar and leaning into them.

Drew and I slowly turned to face one another. We both shrugged and I turned back to look at her, but not before noticing that Drew was busy tucking his shirt back into his jeans.

"T-e-q-u-i-l-a," I said very slowly, wondering if this bartender was drunker than me.

Her smile got bigger if that's even possible.

"Whiskey, coming right up!"

She quickly spun around and immediately tripped over what I assumed was the other bartender still down there picking up broken glass. Blondie caught herself from falling, huffed and reached down to pull the other girl up. There was some swearing, loud whispering and tugging back and forth before she was finally able to pull the other one up roughly. Her long, wavy brown hair hung in a curtain, obscuring her face as she stood there with her head down. More whispering and erratic hand gesturing continued between the two of them, then they each turned and stomped off in the same direction, both of them taking turns smacking the other in the arm as they walked away. My eyes went immediately to the brunette's ass in the tiny black shorts as she walked away.

"I hate to see you go, but I love watching you leave," I said with a snort.

Drew punched me in the arm and I reluctantly looked away from her great ass and long legs before I started drooling.

"So, did you strike out with the waitress?" I asked him as we waited for whatever it was the chick decided to bring us to drink.

"No, I just fucked her in the bathroom. She tasted like beef jerky and Captain Morgan. Strange, yet oddly satisfying. She threw up when she came though. She's got issues."

"How in the fuck has your dick not fallen off yet?" I asked with disgust.

"Don't be a hater just because you dipped your wick in the same crotch-rot for two years. I like to test the waters, sample the merchandise. Plus, I've got a stamp card for the Quickie Mart by my house. One more box of condoms and I get a free twenty ounce of Pepsi."

The ladies were back with our drinks before I could come up with a clever retort. The short blonde with the staring problem slammed a bottle of Johnnie Walker Blue Label down on the bar, while the other one stood a few feet behind her with her hair still shading her face.

"So boys, what are we drinking to tonight?"

Since she wasn't staring at me like that creepy clown Pennywise from the movie "It" anymore, I figured she wasn't dangerous.

"If you share a drink with us, I might be inclined to tell you," I said with a wink.

At least I thought it was a wink. She was looking at me funny, maybe I just squinted really hard. I tried again.

Fuck, why was it so hard to fucking wink?

"Is something wrong with your face?" she asked.

I had been out of the game for too long. I couldn't even get drunk and flirt anymore. I could however, get drunk and look like a stroke victim. I just shook my head and pointed at the shot glasses, signaling her to pour them.

"You'll have to excuse my friend here," Drew said with a pat to my back. "He's still morning the loss of a shitty girlfriend and he's not happy I made him go out instead of sitting at home watching 'Beaches' and diddling his vagina."

"Shut up, dick-fuck," I muttered as I grabbed one of the shots the blonde poured.

Turning her head, she called to the girl behind her. "Get your sweet ass up here and do a shot with these lovely gentlemen."

"I'm working, Liz. I can't drink," she said, gritting her teeth.

My ears perked up at the sound of her voice like I was a dog and someone just said, "cookie." The shot was halfway to my lips and I held it in place as she took a step forward and shook the hair out of her eyes.

Holy shit, she was beautiful. And not beer goggles beautiful. I was pretty sure that if I was sober she'd still look good. Long, wavy brown hair, smooth skin and the most gorgeous brown eyes I'd ever seen.

"Oh shut your yap. You know the Fosters could care less if you drink while you're on the job. You're like the daughter they never had."

Those eyes. There was something about them that made it impossible for me to look away.

"Liz, the Fosters have a daughter."

"Patty plays softball and can bench press two hundred and fifty pounds. Her dick is probably bigger than this guy's," she said, hooking her thumb towards Drew.

"Heeeeey," Drew said defensively.

I couldn't stop staring. I just wanted her to look at me. Why wouldn't she look at me? Her friend wouldn't shut up and she wouldn't look at me.

"Sorry, big guy. I'm sure you have a very nice dick."

"Well, thank you. How about you and I…"

"Don't even finish that sentence," she said with a roll of her eyes and a shake of her head. "I saw you sneak into the women's bathroom to fuck Jerky Jade not more than twenty minutes ago. Are you seriously flirting with me right now?"

"Jerky Jade? I thought her name was Alison."

"You're such a man whore. Her name is Jade. She always smells like beef jerky so we call her Jerky Jade. And you stuck it to her. You stuck your penis in her meaty vagina."

While Drew and Blondie continued their verbal sparring, I continued to stare at the quiet one. I wanted to touch her hair and see if it was as soft as it looked. I bet I could use her hair as a pillow, a silky, furry hair pillow that I could finger all night to help me get to sleep.

No, that doesn't sound creepy at all. I should really stop drinking. Who keeps putting alcohol in my alcohol?

"Jesus, Liz, keep it down. She's right over there."

My ears perked up like a dog's again when she spoke and pointed in the general direction of the chick that smelled of Slim Jims.

I hope I don't start barking.

"Oh, please, like she doesn't know about the smell of meat products wafting from her lady parts. I think she rubs bologna down there to attract men. Lunch meat is her sex pheromone."

The brunette shook her head in irritation. "If I do a shot, will you please stop talking about Jade's disgusting vagina and never, ever use the word meat product in a sentence?"

"Woof!"

Three sets of eyes all turned to look at me.

"Did I just bark out loud?"

Three heads bobbed up and down in unison.

"I dated a guy once that had wet dreams almost every night. I'd wake up to him humping his pillow and howling in his sleep," Liz said wistfully, taking the heat off of me for a minute.

The beautiful one came right up to the bar then and grabbed the shot glass closest to me but still wouldn't look up. She kept her eyes down in the glass like it held the meaning of life.

"So, what are we drinking to?" she asked the shot glass.

"Do your shot glasses usually respond?" I asked with a laugh, throwing her words from earlier back at her.

Her eyes shot up to mine and I felt like I had been punched in the gut. Her eyes were so bright and shiny they looked like melted chocolate.

Fuck. Why the hell was I obsessing about chocolate again? It had been years since I thought about that night and now all of a sudden I couldn't get away from it. I thought I smelled it earlier and that stupid flashback floated through my mind, and now I was comparing this chick's eyes to it. It was chocolate for fuck's sake. It was everywhere. There was nothing special about chocolate.

Except *she* had smelled like chocolate.

After that night, I'm ashamed to say I went through a phase for a few months of smelling lotion and soap at every single store I was in but they never smelled exactly right. The only thing that came even remotely close was real chocolate. I used to wonder if she rubbed Hershey's behind her ears instead of perfume. And then I'd wonder if she tasted like chocolate, and I'd have to rub one out after kicking myself in the ass for not tasting her that night.

Who was I kidding? It hadn't been years since I thought about her. Every fucking time I was within a mile radius of someone eating chocolate I thought about her. Shit. It was all Tasha's fault that I was here right now obsessing about chocolate. My job relocation was going to give us a brand new start in a new place. The fighting between us those last couple of months were brutal, and we both agreed a change of scenery would do our relationship a world of good. Knowing she was going to make the move to this small town with me made it not seem so shitty. Fucking cock sucker. Literally. Too bad it was never my cock she sucked. She did it once and said she had TMJ or some shit and never did it again.

TMJ my ass.

Women were the devil. They led you along for years, making you think you would have a future together and then one day you came home and found her on her knees with the neighbor's dick in her mouth and porn playing on the television. It was all fun and games until someone else's dick was in your girlfriend's TMJ mouth. And it wasn't even good porn that was playing. It was Looney Toons porn. I shit you not folks. She sucked our neighbor off while Daffy Duck took it up the ass from Bugs Bunny shouting, "P-p-p-p-weathe Bugs, harder." That is some serious shit that could never be unseen.

Does it matter that I'm pretty sure I never loved Tasha? That every day with her felt like I was just biding my time until I found *her* again? I knew it was shitty of me and I probably deserved to walk in on her gargling with the neighbor's spunk, but it still sucked.

Clearing my head of duck-fucking rabbits and depressing thoughts, I raised my glass in the air with an angry growl and waited for the other three to do the same.

"We're drinking to all of the lying bitches in this world that wouldn't know how to tell the truth if it smacked them in the fucking face. Cheers!"

I threw back the shot and slammed my glass down, wondering why the beautiful girl in front of me hadn't drank hers and instead stood there staring at me with a look of horror on her face. I watched her friend elbow her and she quickly sucked that shot down like a champ. And then proceeded to pour herself another. And another. And then, like ten more after that – in a row. She'd obviously overcome her decision that it wasn't a good idea to drink on the job. Drew and I just kind of sat there watching her in awe. I mean, I drank like ten times that much tonight, but not all at once.

Half the bottle was gone by the time Liz reached over and took it out of her hands.

"Okay there, home slice, I think that's enough for now."

I was seriously losing my ability to focus at this point. I wanted to ask her if I could suck on one of her fingers and see if it tasted like a Snickers bar. I wanted to ask her what her name was and tell her I didn't always do stuff like this, but she was already walking away and I couldn't figure out how to lift up my arm to signal her back. I stared down at my arm resting on the bar and it just sat there like a little piece of shit slacker. I stared really hard at it and thought about it moving, but it didn't work.

Fucking arm. It must be in a union and on a break. I can't feel my teeth.

"Drew, I can't feel my teeth." I tapped my finger against them. I had dreams all the time that my teeth were falling out. Fuck, what if this was one of those dreams? But it can't be a dream because I don't remember falling asleep. In my dreams my teeth were always falling in my lap and there was blood everywhere and no one cared that I was spitting them all out. Every tooth I touch just falls right out and no one looked at me funny even though that was some crazy shit, right? I ran my fingers around the hard edges of all my teeth.

Never mind, it's fine. Teeth are still there.

"Yeah, I think it's time to say nighty-night and get you home, little buddy," Drew said as he got up from his stool and threw a wad of bills down on the bar before pulling my dead arm up and swinging it over his shoulders. I looked up at Drew as he helped me walk out of the bar. "I wanna eat her Snickers finger but my arm teeth won't feel."

I don't remember much after that.

6.

I Got a Big Weiner

I WAS HAVING the best dream ever. It was one of those hot dreams where you're having sex and you start having an orgasm and you slowly wake up in the middle of it and you don't know if you really did just have an orgasm or if it was part of the dream, but you know you want it to keep going. I was warm and cozy under the covers, and I slid my hand down between my legs to either do it again or finish it. Right when my fingers started to slip inside my underwear, I opened my eyes and screamed.

"HOLY SHIT!"

My son stood there next to the bed just staring at me. Seriously, two inches from my face just staring at me like those creepy twins in "The Shining." I waited for him to start saying, "Come play with us" in their freaky twin voices while I tried not to have a heart attack.

"Gavin, seriously. You can't just stand here and stare at mommy. It's weird," I grumbled as I put my hand to my aching head and tried to calm my pounding heart.

Sweet Jesus, who kicked me in the head and shit in my mouth last night?

"You said a bad word, Mommy," he informed me as he clambered onto my bed and straddled my waist. My other hand joined the first one on my head and I held on tight, fearing the entire thing was going to explode all over the room.

"Yes, Mommy said bad words. Sometimes mommies say bad words.

Just don't ever repeat them, got it?"

He started bouncing up and down on my stomach like he was riding one of those stupid hopping balls with handles.

"Gavin, come on. Mommy doesn't feel good," I complained.

He stopped bouncing and leaned forward to sprawl his body out on top of me, putting his face right up to mine.

"Do you want me ta' beat up your friends, Mommy?" he whispered conspiratorially.

I removed my hands from my head and opened my eyes to look at him.

"What are you talking about, Gav?"

He brought his hands up and put them on my chest, resting his chin on top.

"Your friends, Mommy. The ones who maded you sick," he said in a voice that clearly screamed, "Duh."

I wrapped my arms around his little body and shook my head at him. "I have no idea what you're talking about, buddy."

He let out an exasperated sigh. Poor kid. He got stuck with a dumb mother.

"Papa says your friends Johnny, Jack and Jose maded you sick. Friends shouldn't do stuff like that, Mommy. If Luke maded me sick, I'd punch him in the nuts!"

"Gavin! Come on, we don't say things like that," I scolded him.

"Fine," he huffed. "I'd tickle him in the nuts."

Jesus Christ on a waffle cone. There's a reason why some animals in the wild eat their young.

"Just don't talk about nuts," I said with a sigh, rolling over so he slipped down onto the bed next to me with a giggle as he went.

"My best friend Luke talks about nuts. He showed me his wiener once. Do girls have wieners? Papa took me to breakfast and I ate fwee pancakes wif syrup and sausages, and Papa let me have Dr. Pepper last night wif dinner, and I told him I'm not allowed to have pop wif dinner but he told me not to tell you, and I said okay but I forgot. Can we go to the park?"

Make it stop. Please God just make it stop.

"SO HOW YOU FEELING THERE CLAIRE?" my dad screamed at the top of his lungs as he lounged against the door frame to my room with a cup of coffee in his hand.

I squinted one eye open and peered at him through it, trying to muster up a dirty look but my face hurt too much to do that.

"Really funny there, old man. Don't make me come over there and punch you. When I don't feel like puking. And my legs start to work again," I muttered as Gavin fidgeted and kicked and scrambled his way over top of me to get off the bed.

He ran across the room to my dad and threw himself at his legs, his head smacking into the family jewels.

"Shit! Gavin, you gotta be careful there, buddy," my dad wheezed as he picked him up.

"Papa, can we go to the shit-park?"

I have to give it to my dad, he never laughed at that shit. Er, stuff. I don't know how the hell he always kept his composure. As long as Gavin didn't do that sh..stuff in public and embarrass the hell out of me, it was hard not to laugh.

"Gavin, remember the talk we had last night about big-people words? Well, *shit* is one of those big-people words. You don't say it," my dad said sternly as he looked into Gavin's eyes.

"Can I says it when I'm a big boy?"

"Yes, you can SAY it when you're a big boy," he replied.

Gavin seemed satisfied with that answer and forgot all about the shit-park. My dad put him down and he ran out the door and down the hall to his room.

"Thanks for watching him last night after Liz got home to Jim," I said as I pushed myself up in bed and leaned against the headboard.

"Yep."

He stood there staring at me silently while he sipped his hot coffee. He knew something was up. I liked to have some drinks every now and then, but getting tanked like I did last night, especially at work, meant something bad happened. Thank God Liz stayed with me at the bar all night and made sure I didn't drop any more glasses or puke in someone's lap.

I don't even know how I'm supposed to process what happened last night. Or more to the point, *who* happened last night. As soon as I saw his face, I knew. Those eyes were a dead give-away. Aside from the fact that I used to dream about those blue eyes and would remember his face no matter how much time had passed, I've had to look into those same eyes every single day for the past four years.

Fuck!

I'm pretty sure the wet dream I was having this morning was about him too.

Double fuck!

His voice was a dead giveaway as well. That deep raspy voice that murmured the words "Jesus, you're so fucking beautiful" in that dark bedroom five years ago floated through my mind all the time. After I tipped the tray full of glasses and dropped down behind the bar, I sent a panicked look to the other end where Liz sat. Without hesitating, she got to my side to see what was wrong. My frantic words of "OH MY GOD, OH MY GOD, OH MY GOD, IT'S HIM, HOLY SHIT LIZ IT'S HIM AND HE'S HERE AND HE SAW ME AND OH MY GOD I CAN'T DO THIS RIGHT NOW!" spurned her into action and she popped her head up to get a better look at him. After just a few seconds she dropped back down to my hiding place and with a squeal and a clap of her hands she confirmed it was him.

My dad stood there in the doorway tapping his foot, waiting for me to proceed. I needed more time to think about what I was going to do, but I never kept anything from my dad. With a huge dramatic sigh, I let it out. "He came into the bar last night."

Dad stared at me questioningly for a few seconds before it clicked and his eyes grew wide and his mouth fell open. He knew exactly who I was referring to. There were only a small handful of men in my life, and we both knew I would call them by name if I was talking about them. The only person we ever referred to as "he" over the last few years was….

Fuck! I still don't know his God damn fucking name!

"Did you get his name this time?" my dad asked sarcastically, practically reading my mind.

I shook my head and let it drop into my hands.

My dad let out a sigh. "Well, if he comes back into the bar and you need me to kill him, let me know. I can make it look like an accident."

If you're George Morgan's enemy and you can see him, it's too late. He already killed you and you just don't realize it yet.

AFTER A SHOWER and two cups of coffee, I almost felt human. I checked my voicemail while Gavin got dressed and there was a message from Liz. She told me to meet her at the old location of Andrea's Bakery as soon as I woke up. She wanted me to look at the place before I had a chance to freak out about the bomb she dropped on me in the car the previous night. Liz knew me entirely too well. She knew as soon as I came to my senses I would tell her there was absolutely no way I would let her buy me a freaking business. She was out of her mind. Forcing me to meet her at the shop was cheating as far as I was concerned. Liz was smart though, I'll give her that. She knew this would take my mind off of my other *situation.*

Butler was a small college town that had a town square right in the heart of it where all of the mom-and-pop-type stores were located. Andrea's Bakery was situated on the busiest corner. I had to clamp down my excitement as I buckled Gavin into his car seat and headed towards downtown. I would not get my hopes up about this yet. There were entirely too many things to work out and consider. How much rent would I have to pay Liz? What would Gavin and I do about healthcare? Would Liz and I be partners with this whole thing or two separate entities just sharing a space? Could our friendship survive something like this? Would Gavin have to skip college and spend his life as a male prostitute just to make end's meet because I stuck every penny into a business that tanked?

Fuck, this was going to throw me into a panic attack.

"Are we going to Auntie Wiz's house?" Gavin asked from the backseat, looking out his window at the cars and houses we passed.

I looked at him in the rearview mirror and reminded myself that whatever I did was all for him. He deserved the best life, and I was determined to give that to him.

"No, bud, we're not going to her house. But we are going to see her," I told him as I pulled up in front of the building a few minutes later.

I sat in the car for a minute staring at our building. It was right on the corner and windows took up the entire front of the store, wrapping around to take up the whole other side as well. It was the perfect corner store where we could each have our own window displays. Andrea's Bakery had recently been repainted bright white and had brand new flower boxes installed beneath the windows overflowing with Gerbera daisies in every color. It looked beautiful.

Our building, *our* window displays. Jesus, I'm already thinking of it as mine. Liz is an evil genius and I haven't even walked inside yet.

Speaking of the she-devil, Liz stepped out of one of the doors, holding it open with her hip.

"Stop gawking and get your ass in here," she yelled out to me, before turning around and walking back inside.

Gavin unfastened his seat belt and tried to open his door but the childproof lock prevented him from doing so.

"Come on, Mommy," he complained. "Auntie Wiz said to get our ass in dare."

"Gavin, language," I said, rolling my eyes at his refusal to listen as I got out and walked around to open his door. I grabbed his hand and helped him jump down out of the car.

"Be good, you got it?" I asked as we walked up onto the sidewalk. "Don't run, don't yell, don't touch anything and stop saying bad words or you're going home to take a nap."

"Naps can suck it."

I will not sell him to gypsies. I will not sell him to gypsies.

A bell dinged above the door as I opened it, and Gavin yanked his hand out of mine to go running into Liz's arms.

"Ooooooh, my handsome man is here!" Liz squealed as she scooped him up and swung him around. "What's new, little man?" she asked as she set him down on top of the counter next to her.

"Mommy don't feel good today and I got a big wiener!"

Liz barked out a laugh.

"Gavin, please. Enough with the wiener talk," I complained.

"But, Mommy, look," he said as he attempted to unbutton his jeans. "My wiener is really big and tall right now and it feels funny."

"Ooookay," I said as I quickly walked over and stopped him from whipping it out. "No one needs to see it and remember what I told you the other night?"

Gavin nodded in understanding and I slid him down off of the counter and told him to go look out the front window to count the cars that go by. When his face and hands were plastered against the window, I turned to face Liz who was silently laughing with her hand over her mouth.

"It's not funny," I hissed at her in a loud whisper. "Why the fuck didn't anyone tell me four-year-olds get woodys? I am not equipped to deal with this shit, Liz."

She wiped tears out of her eyes and looked at me apologetically. "I'm sorry, Claire, but seriously. That is some funny shit right there. Sorry, I know nothing about four-year-old boys. When the hell did it first happen?"

"ONE!" Gavin yelled from in front of the window as a car went by.

"The other night after his bath. He was lying on the floor on his towel and I gave him a book to read while I ran down the hall to get his pajamas out of the dryer," I started.

"TWO!" came another yell from Gavin.

"I walked in the room and he rolled over onto his back and that thing stuck straight up into the air like a lightening rod. It was horrific. He kept smacking at it and saying it felt funny. Jesus Christ, will you stop laughing!"

"FWEE!"

"I'm sorry. I'm sorry!" Liz gasped in between laughs.

"And of all the books he could have been reading when it happened, it had to be Barney. My son gets a hard-on for fucking BARNEY," I screeched and quickly turned around to make sure Gavin didn't hear me.

Liz was hysterical at this point. Her mouth was closed and her shoulders were shaking. Every time she tried to breathe and not laugh she snorted and then choked.

"Did you ask your dad about it?" she asked between giggles and coughs.

I rolled my eyes before responding as I thought back to the conversation I'd attempted to have with my dad the other morning.

"You know my dad. As soon as I said the word *penis* he turned and walked out of the room and told me to call my mother. And she was just as much help as you are right now. When I asked her if it was normal she replied 'Does a one-legged duck swim in circles?' I hung up on her after ten straight minutes of her doing that hyperventilating laugh thing after I told her about the Barney Boner."

Liz finally calmed down and we both turned to check and make sure Gavin was still occupied.

"Now every time it happens he wants to show me and say 'Mom! Look at my big wiener!' So I just told him it was normal and it happens to all little boys and it just wasn't something he should go walking around telling people."

Liz patted me on the back and gave me a look of pity. "Well, that's just proof you need a man in your life, Claire. And speaking of men in your life…."

"Don't. Don't even go there," I threatened, pointing my finger in her face so she knew I was serious. "I am so not ready to have this discussion with you right now. I'm still wondering if last night was a dream and that wasn't really him. Maybe I was just imagining things in the haze of alcohol. I mean, in all the bars, in all the towns, in all the world…"

"Easy there, Humphrey Bogart, it was him. I immediately recognized him and the friend he had with him. That was the guy who tried to make out with me that night right after telling me he usually liked girls with bigger tits but since I was pretty he would make an exception."

I knew I was full of shit trying to convince myself that maybe it wasn't him. But having Liz confirm it made me feel like a dumb ass.

"Fuck. Fuck, fuck, fuck. Did you see his eyes? God, those were Gavin's eyes. They were that same weird blue-grey color with a black outline. What the fuck am I going to do?" I asked in a panic.

"TEN!"

"Gavin, four comes after three," Liz yelled to him while I tried not to throw up on the floor.

"That's boring," he announced.

"Come on, let me give you the tour before he starts showing his penis to all the people walking by and gets an indecent exposure ticket before the ink is dry on this place," Liz said as she grabbed my hand. "You're going to stop worrying about this right now and just enjoy taking a look at your dreams coming true. We'll worry about blue-eyes later."

I WAS STILL in shock and awe mode as I drove us home two hours later. Gavin fell asleep as soon as the car started, so I didn't have any nonsense chatter about wieners and nuts coming from the backseat to break up my thoughts. The kitchen at the store was much nicer than I remembered from the years I spent stopping in there for a cup of coffee and a muffin, and it was stocked with supplies I only dreamed of using, let alone owning. There was an industrial-sized, two-door reach-in freezer with a matching three-door reach-in-fridge, a heavy-duty electric range with six burners, two Cyclone convection ovens, a holding cabinet that could keep sixteen trays of chocolates cool, a refrigerated bakery case that was right below the front counter and two copper kettles to melt chocolate, caramel or pretty much anything I needed. Right in the middle of the room was a four-foot by six-foot island with a cooling marble countertop – perfect for making candy. In all the time I'd patronized Andrea's Bakery, I always loved the open floor-plan. I loved how when you were at the counter paying you could see into the kitchen and watch someone making cakes or pies.

It was too much and I told Liz that as I walked around the kitchen, letting my hand trail over all of the equipment. She tried to tell me that the previous owners recently upgraded everything so all of the stuff in the kitchen came with the space, but I knew she was lying. I'd been in Andrea's Bakery not that long ago and spoke with the manager. I knew for a fact they didn't upgrade. Plus, Liz could never look me in the eyes when she lied and she swore twice as much.

"Liz, this is too much. I can't let you do this."

"Oh for fuck's sake, Claire. This fucking shit came with the fucking place and the previous fucking owners just want to fucking get rid of it."

Liar liar, fucking pants on fucking fire.

Liz's side of the store was just as nice, only without the amazeballs kitchen that my side had. She showed me where she wanted the wall to go that would separate the two spaces right down the middle, but not extend all the way to the front. She wanted enough room up by the windows for customers to walk back and forth between the two stores. It would provide just enough privacy in case my customers weren't too keen on looking at the dildos, lingerie and lube on Liz's side and she said we could put a door back by my kitchen where the two of us could easily go back and forth without going to the main parts of the stores. The front of both of our sides had a counter where a cash register would go. Liz's side had display tables littered throughout the front so she could display the items she would have for sale. Mine was left empty right now, so I could possibly add some tables for people to sit down in the future. I realized she made changes to the place long before she clued me in, knowing full well I wouldn't be able to turn it down once I saw the hard work she put in to it. Where my side was wide open so when you were standing in front, you could see the entire kitchen in the back, Liz's side had a wall right behind the front counter since the only thing in the back of her store would be inventory. She'd thought of everything and I was completely amazed at all she'd done in such a short amount of time.

While Gavin ran amok, we sat down on the floor with all of the paperwork strewn around us. We were knee deep in zoning permits, sales tax licenses, business plans, insurance policies and a hundred other different forms that made my head spin. This dream was so close I could touch it, but the fear of not being able to afford it had me biting my fingernails down to stubs. I could take up extra shifts at Fosters to save some more money and of course there was the additional income I would get from suffering through a bunch of Liz's sex toy parties, but it still wouldn't be enough to swing the rent and I refused to let Liz invest any more of her money for me. Liz called my father before I could protest and he met us up at the shop to take a look around.

"So, what do you think?" I asked him as he opened up the fuse box and took a look inside.

"Wiring is good. The kitchen is on a separate circuit from the security system," he replied.

"That's not what I mean."

I wanted him to knock some sense in to me like he was famous for. Tell me I was insane for thinking I could do something like this; call me an asshole for having my head in the clouds.

My dad closed the fuse box and turned around to stare up at the ceiling.

"You know how when you were in college I was paying your room and board every month?" he asked as he checked out all of the light fixtures. "Well, for the past five years, I've been putting that money into a savings account every month just in case you needed it one day. With the interest it's earned, it's a little over fifty thousand right now."

My mouth dropped open in shock and Liz, who was standing close by and not even trying to pretend that she wasn't eavesdropping, started squealing loud enough to break the sound barrier. She jumped up and down and flung her arms around my dad while I stood there trying to process what he'd just told me.

"Mr. Morgan, if you weren't my best friend's father I would totally hump your leg right now," Liz told him excitedly.

"There's a...I have...my dog's at the vet," my dad stuttered awkwardly as he pulled himself away from Liz and walked out of the store.

"You're dad doesn't have a dog," Liz stated as the bell over the door jingled with his departure.

"Nope. Your dry humping threats have finally made him go insane."

It took another hour for Liz to convince me that it wasn't selfish to take the money my dad offered. It was money he put away for me to do with as I wished, so why shouldn't I use it to start up the business I've always dreamed of? With money worries out of the way for the time being, Liz asked me to make up a tray of items to take to the party she booked me to do tomorrow afternoon. Jenny, a friend of her cousin, was having it and she was a computer designer. She offered to help Liz with brochures and flyers and things like that. Liz let her know I would be doing her party and that I would need help creating something to advertise my store as well. She agreed to help us out as long as she got to test out some free samples. I'd let her sample my vagina if she did this for me.

After the party, I was going to head over to Liz and Jim's house for dinner and some wine so we could talk more and come up with names for our business.

Our business. I repeated those words over and over to myself as I drove home from the store, trying to make it sink in. It was all happening so fast. Just two days ago the idea of owning my own business was a pipe dream that I figured was years and years away from ever happening.

I pulled into my driveway and quietly unbuckled a sleeping Gavin so I could take him in the house and lay him down. As I lifted him out of his car seat and held his head to my shoulder, he wrapped his arms around my neck and squeezed.

"You hafta mow the lawn wiffa snake marshmallow," he mumbled sleepily. "I slipped on a penny."

I let out a chuckle at my son's sleep-talking habits as I walked into the house and got him situated in his bed.

I wonder if *he* talks in his sleep too.

Liz sufficiently took my mind off of Gavin's father all morning, but now that I was alone with my thoughts, his reappearance in my life screamed through my head and it was all I could think about. For all I knew, he could have been passing through town and I'll never see or hear from him again. He was too drunk to remember me the first time we met, and obviously history was repeating itself. He had no clue who I was last night.

I refused to admit it stung a little that I hadn't made any kind of impact on him almost five years ago, when I had to live with a reminder of him every single day.

7.

Open Mouth, Insert Vodka

SHE RESTED HER *elbows against the bar and leaned closer to me. I was mesmerized by her eyes. They looked like pools of Hershey's chocolate syrup. It was her. All these years and I could finally see her face. She was just as stunning as I remembered.*

"I've been looking everywhere for you," I said.

She laughed and goose bumps rose on my arms. I remember that laugh; it was like music to my ears. She reached across the top of the bar and ran her hand down my arm and rested it on top of my own.

"Do your shot glasses usually talk to you?" she asked with a smile.

"Wait, you're the girl from the bar," I said in confusion.

"Am I?" she asked with a smirk.

She leaned completely across the top of the bar and pressed her cheek to mine, her lips close to my ear.

"Ask me what my favorite movie is," she whispered.

I turned my head and slid my nose against her cheek. She still smelled like chocolate. But that didn't make sense. Someone started knocking on the door to the bar and she pulled away and whipped her head around in that direction. She started backing up as the banging continued.

"Wait! Don't go. Just tell me your name," I pleaded.

She kept backing away and I stared at her face, memorizing every single detail: brown eyes, thick chestnut hair, full-heart-shaped lips, and a dimple on each cheek.

That's what the girl from the bar looked like. But this one had the same eyes and the same voice as MY girl. What the hell is going on?

"Please, tell me your name!" I yelled after her.

I jerked awake to the sound of banging and my heart pounding like I just ran a marathon. I slid my hand through my hair and flopped back down, trying to remember what I had just been dreaming about. It was right there at the edge of my consciousness but I just couldn't grasp onto it. There was something I needed to remember about that dream. I closed my eyes and tried to bring it back. The silence lasted for two seconds before the pounding against my front door started again and interrupted my thoughts.

"SHUT THE FUCK UP!" I screamed at the incessant banging, irritated that I couldn't make myself remember.

Oh, sweet Jesus, I am never drinking again.

I have the weirdest dreams every fucking time I drink. Why the hell can't I remember this one? I picked up a pillow from next to me and hugged it against my ears, trying to muffle the sound of my door being kicked in.

"Open the door, goat-fucker!" Drew's muffled yell shouted as he continued to pound his fist against my front door. I know if I don't get up, he'll keep making noise and then I'd have to kill him.

The banging continued as I sat up, threw the covers off angrily and stumbled through the rental house with my eyes closed. I still had boxes of shit all over the place that I had yet to unpack and I kicked them angrily out of the way as I went. I made it to the front door without breaking any limbs and flung it open with an angry growl.

"Holy shit, dude, you don't look so hot," Drew said as he shouldered his way past me and into my house, wearing one of his signature t-shirts. I swear this guy owned at least two-hundred-and-fifty of these things. Today's shirt said "I pooped today".

"Sure, come on in Drew," I muttered to myself as I slammed the door shut and followed him to the living room. "You totally interrupted a good dream I was having. At least I think it was a good dream, I can't remember."

"Were you dreaming about the hot bartender you couldn't stop drooling over last night?" he asked with a laugh.

"Funny," I deadpanned as I leaned against the doorway and crossed my arms in front of me.

"If only I were kidding, dude. Her friend with the blonde hair asked me if you rode the short bus to the bar after you picked up your beer and poured it down the front of your shirt instead of your mouth—which was wide open staring at the bartender's ass.

Wow, definitely not one of my better nights.

"Maybe I should go up there and apologize to…."

Shit, I was drawing a blank.

"Yet another girl whose name you didn't get." Drew finished. "At least this time we know where she works. This place is a fucking mess," he said as he shoved boxes away with his foot so he could make his way over to the couch.

"Did you just come over here to insult me, or is there a reason for this early morning visit?"

"Early? It's twelve-thirty, dumb ass. We've got orientation at one," he said as he slid a box of books over and flopped down on the couch.

"SHIT! Are you kidding me?" I yelled as I ran into the kitchen, tripping over boxes along the way. Sure enough, the clock on the microwave read twelve-thirty-four. Fucking hell. I do not need to be late for orientation at the new plant. I pulled the front of my t-shirt up over my nose, took a whiff and cringed. I smelled like a distillery.

I ran to the bathroom and took the fastest shower known to man and threw on a clean long-sleeved t-shirt and pair of jeans. Drew broke every speed limit, and we managed to get to the Butler Automotive Plant with five minutes to spare.

The plant was closed for production on Sundays, so our small group of transfers were the only people that would be here today. There were about twenty of us that transferred from different plants around the United States and would start working tomorrow. All of the plants ran basically the same way, so we wouldn't need to learn how to do our jobs or anything. We would just get all of our paperwork to fill out for Human Resources and watch a few videos about the history of the company and about how you shouldn't sexually harass your co-workers. The latter was always our favorite. It was the same video they've been showing for over thirty years that they recorded back in the seventies and it was set to porno music. Getting a group of rowdy, blue-collar workers together in one room and putting in a tape that shows a guy in a leisure suit putting his hand on his secretary's ass and you've got complete and total anarchy, ladies and gentlemen.

We walked through the employee entrance to the plant and went into a conference room right by the door. Drew and I signed our names in to the attendance log hanging on the door and took a seat at one of the tables towards the back of the room. We looked around at all of the other people that would be starting with us, seeing if we recognized anyone.

"So, what kind of a douche bag do you think our foreman will be?" Drew said in a low voice. A guy sitting on the other side of Drew leaned forward and spoke before I could answer.

"He's actually an okay guy. He's been here for about twenty years and as long as you don't fuck up, he leaves you alone to do your work. I'm Jim Gilmore," the guy said, holding his hand out for us to shake while Drew provided the introductions.

"Hey, man, I'm Drew Parritt and this is Carter Ellis."

We each shook his hand while Drew kept talking.

"So how long have you worked here?"

"Only a few months. My fiancé and I just moved here from Toledo," he said.

"Seriously? That's where we just moved from. We worked at the Toledo Automotive Plant and got relocated here," I explained.

Jim laughed. "Small world I guess. My fiancé is originally from Butler and we met in college at The University of Ohio. She wanted to move back here as soon as we graduated, so here we are."

"Hey, we went to a party one weekend there. Gee, Carter, you probably don't remember that party, do you?" Drew asked sarcastically, knowing full well just how much I remembered about that party.

"Shut up, asshole," I grumbled. "So Jim, how come you had to come to orientation today?"

"They suckered me into coming to give you guys a tour of the plant when it's over and introduce you to your foreman."

"As long as he leaves me alone and doesn't ride my ass, we'll get along just fine," Drew said.

"I thought you liked it when big, burly men rode your ass," I joked.

"You must have me confused with you and that new vagina you grew. Remind me again when the last time it was you got laid? Because I'm pretty sure I got my dick wet last night while you barked like a dog and passed out in the parking lot."

"I don't think I'd be bragging about tapping some girl's ass that has a meat-product nickname for her vagina," I reminded him.

"Yeah, that wasn't really my finest hour. I'm so disappointed in myself I can practically taste it."

"Does it taste like semen?" I asked.

"Fuck you. She wasn't a dude," Drew replied, leaning back in his chair and crossing his arms in front of him.

"Jim, please tell me you know some hot girls," Drew begged.

He let out a chuckle. "You might be in luck boys; my fiancé has a few single friends."

"Don't worry about the pussy here to the right of me," Drew said while Jim took a drink of his bottled water. "He's been hung up on a one-night-stand he had five years ago with a girl that smelled like Cocoa Puffs."

Jim spit out some of his water and started choking on the rest. Drew had to reach over and pat him on the back. After he recovered, he sat there staring at me funny.

What the fuck is up with people staring at me lately? Last night at the bar and now today. There was something wrong with the people in this town.

Just then, one of the supervisors walked in and shoved the sexual harassment video into the machine. Everyone started clapping and cheering as soon as the music started.

"Why don't you guys come over tonight for dinner and some drinks," Jim said over the rowdy employees as he started to turn back around to face the front of the room. "My fiancé can see if you guys are worthy enough for her friends," he said with smirk.

"HEY, CLAIRE, DOES this lube really taste like strawberry cheesecake?"

"Um, sure," I replied.

"Does the Jack Rabbit hit your g-spot or do I need to get something else for that?"

"Are you sure this massage oil candle burns cool? The last time my boyfriend and I tried hot oil his penis got second degree burns."

Kill me. Just kill me right now.

"Where exactly do you put the cock ring on a guy? We must not have put it in the right spot because after a few minutes it got lost in my vagina. That was an awkward emergency room trip, let me tell you."

I'm going to lose my shit if someone asks me one more fucking question that I can't answer. That's all anyone has been doing for the last half hour. FUCK! These people need to just buy something already and quit talking to me.

"Do you let a guy use a vibrator on you? I've heard that's really hot."

"Okay look," I shouted, holding my hands up so they'd shut their yaps. "I have zero experience with any of this shit. I'm only doing this as a favor to my friend so I can make some extra money for my new business. I have had exactly one and a half sexual partners in my life and they were both pretty shitty experiences. The first one was in college and we were both completely trashed, I never got his name and he knocked me up. The next one was a friend of mine, and I decided to try it again and see if got any better. His dad had a key to his house and walked in on us two thrusts in, which completely killed any mood that might have been started. I've decided that my vagina is cursed. My orgasms have all been self-induced and have never been with anything that required batteries, a special cleaner, instructions or a weapon of mass destruction warning. If you want to place an order, I'll be in the kitchen. Try the chocolate-covered potato chips."

I turned and stalked out of the room and straight into the kitchen. Where was a giant, gaping hole in the floor to swallow you up when you needed one? Every woman in there was probably talking about what a loser I was and how they were going to tell everyone they knew to never do business with us. Shit, Liz was going to fire me. I was going to have to tell people I got fired from selling dildos. I can't even sell fake cocks to a room full of horny women. How do you come back from that shit? And on top of it all, I just spilled my deepest, darkest secrets to a room full of strangers.

"Oh, honey, you poor thing," Jenny said as she hurriedly walked into the kitchen and threw her arms around me. One thing new people learned about me real quick – don't invade my personal space or you will get punched in the neck.

I stood there stiff as a board with my arms out to the side. I don't understand huggers. I really don't. A nice, solid pat on the back worked just fine.

"I'm buying you a Jack Rabbit," Jenny proclaimed.

"Whoa, no, really that's okay," I tried to argue as I pulled out of the hug. That thing scared the shit out of me. Four speeds, ears and beads that spun around. You should have to get a permit from the city to even power that thing up.

After several minutes of cajoling, Jenny managed to pull me back into the living room, and after she announced that she was going to buy me a toy, the whole room erupted in agreement. Much to my mortification, all of them began commenting to one another about what they were going to buy me. I had to draw the line when they started talking about throwing me a Vibrator Virgin party. I heard the words penis-shaped ice cubes and penis pasta salad, and I started getting a headache from hell. Any moment now they were all going to join hands and sing Kumbaya to my vagina—my poor, unloved vagina that never knew the pulsating touch of a rubber penis. I'm sorry vagina, I should have taken better care of you, I guess.

At the end of the show, I sold twice as much as normal because everyone bought two of everything, one for them and one for me. If my vagina wasn't covered in cotton and jeans, it might have taken offense to their looks of pity. I swore as they all placed their orders they looked down between my legs. Now, I know how chicks with huge boobs feel when a guy won't look you in the eyes.

When the last girl left with a hug for me and Jenny and a goodie bag of fun in her hand, we both collapsed on the couch in the living room.

"Thanks for doing the party tonight, Claire," she said with a smile. "And thanks for the awesome tray of desserts. Seriously, you have a gift. Those chocolate-covered pretzels drizzled with caramel almost gave me an orgasm. And that's saying a lot considering I was surrounded by fibrillators all night."

My eyes popped open and I raised my head from it's spot resting on the back of the couch to stare next to me at Jenny's profile while she absentmindedly check out her manicured nails. She was a nice person and we got along really well, but some of the things that came out of her mouth tonight boggled the mind.

"Um, Jenny do you mean *de*fibrillators?"

Why she was even using that word in a sentence about a sex toy party was beyond my scope of imagination, unless she assumed something in my bag of tricks would stop someone's heart. Come to think of it, I almost had a heart attack when I saw the size of the Grape Gargantuan. Where exactly is a woman supposed to stick that thing, in the Hoover Damn to plug it up?

"Wait, what did I say? I meant vibrator. Oh my gosh that's so weird!"

I just shook my head and got up off of the couch to pack up all of the stuff into the extra suitcase Liz gave me for the supplies. Just my luck, I get to keep all of this shit in my house. If anything ever happened to me and the police or some other authority figure had to go through my house, I was going to be completely humiliated from beyond the grave if they find this suitcase.

Oh, Jesus, what if my dad found this thing? He was going to think I was a freak. What woman needed a suitcase with thirty-seven vibrators and nineteen bottles of lube? Shit, I needed to store this stuff at Liz's house. I didn't tell my dad yet about Liz's part of the business. No girl should ever be forced to have a conversation about dildos with her father. That was just wrong on so many levels. He could find out the first time he walked into the store just like everyone else.

"So, I'll get started on your flyer this week as soon as you send me photos of the items you want featured on it. I'm going to do one for you, one for Liz and then one that combines both of your stores. You said you guys were going to get together tonight and decide on a name?" Jenny asked.

"Yeah, I'm headed over to her and Jim's house tonight," I explained as I zipped the suitcase closed. "Hey, why don't you come with me? You can help us brainstorm."

"Oh, I don't know. I don't want to impose."

I pulled the plastic handle out of the top of the case and glanced over at her.

"You will definitely not be imposing. You already know Liz and she always makes enough food to feed an army. Really, she won't mind at all."

"Well, if you think it will be okay, I guess I'll stop by. I really need to get out and have some fun. Maybe she can find me a single man. I'm so desperate that I might settle for ugly and unemployed as long as he has decent hygiene and knows how to go down on me."

I stared blankly at her, wishing I could erase that that entire sentence from my memory.

"I'm going to finish cleaning up here, and I might try to fit an orgasm in too. I'll just meet you there."

I'm pretty sure my head just exploded.

"Um, Jenny? Did you just say you were going to try and fit an orgasm in?"

Please God, let me have heard her wrong.

"Well, duh! I have to make sure what I bought works properly don't I? If it doesn't get me off fast enough, I'm returning it. I have a two point five minute rule."

Oh Jesus. Please don't let her give me a used vibrator with her vagina funk all over it. What the fuck am I supposed to do with that? Do I need a hazmat suit to handle a returned vibrator? This was not a topic included in my new employee packet.

"Okay, well, I'll just see you at Liz's house then," I said as I ran from her house, pulling my suitcase on wheels behind me as fast as the wobbly legs on that thing would allow.

FIFTEEN MINUTES LATER I was walking up to Liz and Jim's house and letting myself in. Liz flew around the corner into the foyer with a panicked look on her face.

"Elizabeth Marie Gates, you owe me big time. That was the single most horrific experience of my life," I yelled at her while I unbuttoned my coat.

"Claire, I have to tell you…"

"When I invited Jenny over for dinner, she decided to tell me she was going to pencil in some alone time with her vibrator before coming here," I said in horror, interrupting her. "I'm not going to be able to look her in the eye at all tonight."

"Claire, there's something…"

"You could have warned me that these women would be asking me a thousand questions about lube and g-spots that I wouldn't have a fucking clue how to answer. 'Oh, all you need to do is stand there and take everyone's orders,'" I complained in my best Liz voice as I yanked my jacket off.

"You need to…"

"I lost my shit after the question on cock rings getting stuck in vaginas and told them all about my stellar sexual history. Jesus H. Christ, Liz, a woman who has had one point five lays and didn't even come close to getting off during them should NOT be selling sex toys!" I screeched, throwing my coat on the hook next to the door and turning back to face her.

"Claire, you might want to keep it…"

"I told them about Max, Liz. MAX! The thing we swore to never speak of again. I told them all about him getting two thrusts in before his dad walked in on us," I said as I started walking backwards out of the foyer. "I can tell by that horrified look on your face that you realize how awesome this evening was for me."

"Don't say any…"

"Why in the hell did you ever think I would be good at this?" I asked as I came to a stop in the living room. "By the end of the night, every woman in that room was giving my vagina sad looks. My vagina is going to get a complex Liz. It's already judging me because it's only gotten off with my hand. And I don't count dry humping your leg that one time we were really drunk after finals freshman year," I argued as Jim came up next to me with a bottle of Grape Three Olive vodka in his hand.

I glanced at him and then back to Liz.

"Why the hell are you staring at me like that?" I asked her. Her mouth was open and she kept looking behind me over my shoulder.

Oh fuck.

I looked at Jim and he gave me a reassuring smile and held the bottle of vodka out to me.

Oh fucking fuck.

"There's someone behind me, isn't there?" I whispered.

Liz just nodded her head. I swallowed thickly and blindly reached to my side to grab the bottle out of Jim's hand. He already took the cap off for me so I brought it up to my lips and took and huge swig of it, my eyes watering as the burn of the alcohol slid down my throat and warmed my stomach. I slowly turned to face the music and die of humiliation. When I finally made it all the way around, the bottle of vodka slipped out of my grasp. Thank God for Jim's quick reflexes. His hand shot out and grabbed the bottle before it crashed to the floor.

"So, who wants another drink?" Liz asked cheerily from behind me.

8.

Cuckoo for Cocoa Puffs

ORIENTATION TOOK A few hours. When we were done, Jim, Drew and I decided to stop for a drink before heading over to Jim's house. We were sitting by the window at a tall table in a sports bar in the next town over. I really liked Jim. He was down-to-earth and friendly. He gave us a bunch of tips on places to go and things to do in this area. The conversation flowed easily and it felt like we had known this guy for years.

"I think I need to hear some more about Miss Cocoa Puffs," Jim said after he took a drink of his beer. I closed my eyes, wishing he forgot all about that comment Drew made back at the plant.

"I thought you'd never ask," Drew said with a smile as he leaned back in his chair and put his hands behind his head.

"Oh, you are so not telling this story, asshole," I said.

"Carter, I am the best possible person TO tell this story. I have an outside perspective on the situation and can give a better recollection of the events that took place that night. Plus, I've had to deal with your whiny ass for the past five years and your constant need to stop in chick stores and smell girly lotions. Maybe Jim can talk some sense into that brain of yours."

I could feel my face turning red and it wasn't because it was stuffy in here. I could not believe Drew was saying this shit. I would really need to evaluate his best friend status when this night was over. His membership card to the Carter Ellis Friendship Club was getting revoked. And yes, I realized I sounded like a complete douche just by thinking that.

"So, it goes like this," Drew began, completely ignoring the pissed-off looks I was throwing in his direction. "Five years ago, we crashed a frat party at your alma matter."

"Wait, so neither one of you went to school there?" Jim interrupted excitedly.

Try to contain your excitement at my humiliation, dick.

"Nope," Drew said, popping the 'p'. "Heard about it from a friend of a friend…you know how it goes. Anywho, we get to this party and little Carter here sees this girl across the room right when we get there. I swear to fuck you could almost hear 'Dream Weaver' start playing and see stars circling his head. He stares at her for like a half hour before I finally tell him to quit being a pussy and to go talk with her. She's got a hot friend so I'm all over that shit."

I rolled my eyes at his retelling of the story. As I recall, Drew made me take him to see a voodoo priestess he found in the yellow pages that week because he said the friend put a hex on his penis. For two weeks he slept with a two-pound package of boneless, skinless chicken breasts on his junk since he refused to sacrifice a live chicken.

"So, he starts talking to her. They're doing some stupid movie-quoting shit that bored the fuck out of me, and I turned my charms onto her friend to pass the time. We totally hit it off and left those two losers to their geekiness. This girl was smokin' hot and had an ass that wouldn't quit. We found the closest empty bedroom and fucked like rabbits all night."

Drew had a faraway look in his eyes like he was remembering every detail.

"That's funny, because you couldn't remember shit about her the next day except for the fact that she put a curse on your twigs and berries so they would shrivel up and fall off. All of a sudden you have perfect clarity? You woke up in the bathtub alone, dip shit," I said with a laugh.

"Hey, we're talking about you, not me. And I thought we agreed to never ever speak of *the curse* again. Her highness, Zelda Crimson-Grass stressed how important that was," he stated seriously.

"So, anyway, where was I?" Drew asked, after looking over each of his shoulders in case the great and powerful Zelda, who charged thirty-five dollars a minute and accepted Visa, Mastercard and traveler's checks, was standing behind him holding a voodoo doll with pins stuck between its legs. "Carter wakes up the next morning freaking the fuck out because he thinks his dick is falling off."

Jim laughed and clunked his bottle of beer down on the table to wipe off the drops that dribbled down his chin. "Okay, why the hell would you think your dick was falling off?"

I huffed. "Because…"

"Because Carter here banged a virgin whose name he never got and had a bloody one-eyed snake," he said, interrupting me with a laugh.

I thought I heard Jim growl a little under his breath and I looked his way to see what his deal was, but he brought his beer back up to his mouth right then and wasn't looking at me. I must have just imagined it. I turned to face Drew to find him still laughing.

"Okay, seriously, you are making this whole thing sound really awful. You need to work on your storytelling skills, idiot," I complained.

"There is nothing about what I've said that isn't true. You're just pissed off after all these years of searching you have never been able to smell her again."

No, that didn't sound weird at all.

After getting a strange, almost angry vibe from Jim the last several minutes, he finally seemed to relax.

"Wow, so you actually looked for this girl and never found out who she was?" Jim asked.

Drew started to answer him, but I punched him in the arm.

"You shut your mouth. It's my turn," I said to him.

I sighed. I hated thinking about this part. For some reason it made my chest hurt.

"Yes, I looked for her. I would have given anything just to talk to her again and I don't care how much of a pussy that makes me sound. I asked everyone on that fucking campus and no one could tell me anything. I even went to admissions and tried to bribe the secretary into letting me look through yearbooks," I explained.

"Ha ha, she called the cops on you, remember?" Drew laughed.

"Um, yeah I remember. She called the cops because *you* told her we needed to look at pictures of all the female student body, pun intended, and see which one gave me a hard-on. She thought I was a pervert."

"So, why did you want to find her so badly? I mean, everyone has one-night-stands at some point. Most guys would consider themselves lucky they didn't have to deal with the whole morning-after bullshit," Jim stated.

I should feel embarrassed about this shit, but in all honesty, I didn't. Even though we just met him, I felt like Jim was the type of guy I could confide in and he wouldn't judge me, as opposed to my ex-best friend who was miming the act of playing a violin to go along with my sad tune.

"There was something about her," I said with a shrug. "Something that drew me in and made me want to just be near her. We talked for hours while we played beer pong. She got my sense of humor and we had the same taste in music and movies. Everything I can remember about her just makes me want to find her and see if she really existed. And it had nothing to do with the sex. Although, I would like to apologize to her for ruining her first time since I was completely trashed. It's more than that though. No woman has ever been on my mind as much as her. And it drives me fucking crazy that I can't remember her face," I said irritably as I flicked my beer bottle cap across the table.

Understanding seemed to wash over Jim's face and he nodded his head. The anger I swore I saw flash in and out of his features during this entire exchange suddenly vanished.

"Okay, now that you got all the touchy-feely shit out of the way, tell him about the creepy stalker shit you do," Drew said pointedly.

"Fuck you. It's not stalker shit."

"Right, because dragging my ass into every single fucking girly store and making me stand there while you smell everything that's made with chocolate, made near chocolate or made by something that shits chocolate isn't weird at all. And don't think I haven't forgotten about that last time a few months ago when the clerk asked us how long we'd been dating and you put your arm around me and said, "Well, sugar plum, this big, strong, sexy beast and I have been together for ages now," he said, mimicking the high-pitched voice I used at the time.

Jim threw his head back and laughed and even I had to snicker at the memory. When Drew turned to run out of the store I smacked him on the ass. It really was priceless.

"Alright, so after five years I can't get the smell of her out of my head. Big fucking deal. And it's not like I Google every store that sells lotion and just go down the list every weekend. If I happen to be in a store that sells lotions or soap, I go and smell a few to see if by some off chance I'll find the one that smells like she did. I just can't pass up the chance to find that smell again. It drives me God damn crazy."

Both men sat there staring at me. Fuck, I really was growing a vagina.

"You, my friend need to bang this chick out of your system once and for all. We really need to find you a nice girl that won't fuck you over and will make you forget about the Count Chocula Cooter," Drew said with a sad shake of his head.

"I may have just the girl for you," Jim said with a smirk.

"Perfect!" Drew proclaimed with a hard smack to my back. "You see, little buddy? There just might be hope for you yet. Hey, maybe we can even convince her to slather some Three Musketeers on her vagina. We'll just tell her you have a Willy Wonka fetish," Drew said with a laugh, finishing off his beer.

I kicked the leg of his chair while he leaned back on two of them. While I watched him windmill his arms to get his balance and not fall backwards onto the hardwood floor, I thought I heard Jim whisper something that sounded like, "That won't be necessary."

WHEN WE GOT to Jim' house, his fiancé came out of the kitchen to greet us and Drew and I both stopped dead in our tracks.

"Hey, aren't you the girl from the bar last night?" I asked. It was the woman with blonde hair that hadn't been afraid to call Drew out on his lame attempt at trying to get in her pants. "Liz, right?"

As soon as she saw us her eyes got wide and her mouth flew open. But she gained her composure quickly and smiled.

"Wow, I'm surprised you remembered. When you left the bar you were crying and singing at the top of your lungs 'I got ninety-nine problems and the bitch is all of them'."

I grimaced at the memory that frankly, I didn't remember at all.

"Really, don't worry about it," she laughed when she saw my discomfort. "It was quite fun pointing and laughing at you all night," she teased.

"Remind me never to get drunk around you again. I might wake up with my head shaved," I said with a laugh. Liz motioned for us to follow her the rest of the way into the living room.

"Don't worry, I'd never do something like that," she promised with a smile as we all found a place to sit and she relaxed next to Jim on the couch.

"Don't lie, sweetie," Jim laughed as he swung his arm around Liz and rested it on the back of the couch. "The night I met you, I had to pry a black Sharpie marker out of your hand because you were going to write 'insert penis here' on some guy's cheek with an arrow pointing to his mouth. Wasn't he passed out in some room in a ba-"

Liz jumped up from the couch suddenly and grabbed Jim's hand.

"Hon, can I talk to you for a second in the kitchen?" she asked, pulling him up before he could answer.

"Sorry, we'll be right back," Jim said over his shoulder as he was quickly ushered out of the room.

Drew leaned forward, placed his elbows on his knees and whispered across the coffee table to me.

"Fuck, that chick still looks so damn familiar. I hope I didn't sleep with her. That would be kind of awkward, right? I mean, we just met this guy. He's nice. I don't want to have to tell him I've seen his girlfriend's vagina. He might not let us eat dinner and I'm fucking starving."

"Drew, I'm pretty sure she would have said something by now if that happened," I assured him.

"I don't know man. She looked surprised to see us just now. I bet you they're in there right now arguing about my penis. What do you think she's saying? Do you think she's telling him it was the best sex she's ever had? I haven't gotten in a fight in a while. Maybe I should stretch."

"Jesus, how do you fit your ego through doorways?" I asked as the sound of the front door opening and closing stopped Drew's musings.

Faster than I've ever seen anyone move, Liz flew out of the kitchen and bolted to the front door. They had a foyer around the corner from the living room so we couldn't see who had just got here, but we could definitely hear her.

"Elizabeth Marie Gates, you owe me big time. That was the single most horrific experience of my life."

Holy fuck, I know that voice. And why am I suddenly thinking about barking dogs?

Muted voices filled the room as Jim sauntered in from the kitchen with a giant bottle of grape vodka in one hand and two bottles of beer in the other. He cocked his head and stared at Drew with a funny look on his face and for a minute, I wondered if maybe Drew was right about sleeping with Liz. After a few seconds though, he smirked like he just remembered the punch line to an inside joke, placed the beers on the coffee table in front of Drew and me and turned to face the direction of the foyer but didn't move from where he was standing.

The voice from the foyer suddenly got really loud.

"I lost my shit after the question on cock rings getting stuck in vaginas and told them all about my stellar sexual history. Jesus H. Christ, Liz, a woman who has had one point five lays and didn't even come close to getting off during them should not be selling sex toys!"

Ouch. We should probably not be listening to this. She's going to be pissed.

Jim unscrewed the lid to the vodka and tossed it down on the coffee table where it clattered a few times before coming to a stop. I thought he was going to take a drink straight from the bottle or something, but he just stood there holding on to it, as if waiting for something. At least Liz was trying to get her to talk a little quieter. We heard a few of her attempts but they went completely unnoticed.

Shit, one of us should say something. Alert her to our presence by walking around the corner or coughing or something. But like the assholes we are, we just sat there waiting to hear more.

The name Max was yelled and something about him getting two thrusts in before his dad walked in on them. Okay, now I wanted to hear more. Drew must have had the same idea because both of us leaned our bodies closer to the door so we could hear better. Fortunately, there was no need for that. Suddenly, everything was loud and clear as she walked with her back to us into the living room while Liz followed her, shaking her head frantically.

"Why in the hell did you ever think I would be good at this?" she said as she came to a stop and put her hands on her hips.

It was the girl from the bar last night. Halleluiah! And don't judge me just because I knew it was her as soon as I saw her ass. That was a really, really nice ass right there. I wanted to get down on my knees and praise God and the makers of the jeans she was wearing. I wanted to fuck that ass.

Wait, that didn't come out right. I mean, yeah what guy wouldn't? But she might not be into that sort of thing. That's something you have to discuss with a woman. You don't just go poking around or you'll get punch in the face and the words, "EXIT ONLY!" screamed at you.

The word 'vagina' being yelled right at that moment was the only thing that pulled my mind and my dream dick out of this chick's ass.

"By the end of the night, every woman in that room was giving my vagina sad looks. My vagina is going to get a complex, Liz."

Jim was the only one of us with any brains at this point. He walked over to the two women and stood quietly next to the one with the great ass, vodka bottle still in hand.

"It's already judging me because it's only gotten off with my hand. And I don't count dry humping your leg that one time we were really drunk after finals freshman year."

I have now lost all motor function. Someone check and see if I just came.

"Oh my God, I think I just wet myself," Drew whispered excitedly.

"Why the hell are you staring at me like that?" the woman asked irritably as she looked back and forth between Liz and Jim. She whispered something and Liz just nodded her head and looked in our direction. By the speed with which her hand flew out and grabbed the vodka bottle and chugged it, I'm guessing she just realized there were other people in the room listening to her talk about blah, blah, blah, masturbation, blah, blah, girl-on-girl-action. She slowly turned her body around and her eyes flew right to mine. I felt like the wind had been knocked out of me and watched the bottle of vodka slip from her hands. Jim calmly stuck his arm out and caught the bottle before it hit the floor, while I just sat there staring at the most beautiful woman I had ever seen.

Okay, I knew I saw her last night, but I was drunk and objects in drunk eyes may appear hotter than they actually are. My recollection of her face in my mind might not have been as accurate as I thought it was. Thankfully, she was just as beautiful as I remembered. And now I felt really bad that she looked so horrified by everything she blurted out to Liz when she thought no one else was here.

"So, who wants another drink?" Liz asked cheerfully as she moved around the brown-haired beauty.

Drew and I wordlessly lifted our beer bottles to show Liz we were all set. She grabbed onto the poor girl's arm and dragged her into the living room. I watched her bring the vodka bottle back up to her lips and take another swig as she walked. Liz snatched the bottle away from her and slammed it down on the coffee table.

"Carter, this is *Claire*. Claire, this is *Carter*," Liz said, emphasizing our names for some reason. I feared for Liz's life a little right now. I was afraid Claire might claw her eyes out.

"We sort of met last night," I said with a smile, trying to move the attention to me and save Liz from disfigurement.

Claire let out a hysterical laugh.

Liz sat down on the couch, pulling Claire down next to her.

"Well, we have a few minutes before dinner will be ready. Jim tells me you guys just moved here from Toledo, is that right?" Liz asked as Jim walked in front of the women to take a seat on the other side of Claire.

I nodded my head. "Yeah, we were transferred here from the Toledo Automotive plant."

I turned my gaze back to Claire. Her knee was bouncing up and down at a frantic pace. Liz reached over and put her hand on it to stop the movement.

"So, Claire, how long have you been a bartender?" I asked. I wanted to know everything there was about her. And I wasn't going to lie, I was dying to hear her voice again and learn more about her vagina and how often she found herself humping girlfriends. Shit, please don't let me get a hard-on right now.

"Almost five years," she said as another awkward laugh bubbled out of her and Jim reached up to pat her on the back a few times.

How much of the vodka did she chug from that bottle?

"Liz, I can't take it anymore," Drew interrupted. "You look so fucking familiar."

Claire jumped to her feet, her knee slamming into the coffee table and knocking over the two beer bottles. Thankfully they were already empty.

"I think I heard the timer go off on the oven. Liz, did you hear the timer go off?" she asked.

Liz shook her head casually. "Nope. Definitely didn't hear the timer," she said with a smile.

I watched as Claire turned her back to us and faced Liz.

"The timer definitely went off. You just didn't hear it because you weren't paying attention. We need to go check on the food. Because the timer. It went off."

"Hey, Liz," Drew said. "I think she's trying to tell you the timer went off!"

He laughed at his own joke and I reached over and smacked his arm.

Watching her go from horrified to embarrassed to nervous was fascinating. She was like a beautiful train wreck and I couldn't stop watching.

Liz sighed and finally stood up, smiling at Drew and me while she excused herself and followed Claire into the kitchen.

Drew leaned over and whispered in my ear, "Did you see the way Liz looked at me? I think I definitely banged her."

9.

Claire's Coochie Kills

OH, JESUS CHRIST. Oh, fuck. Can a person die from humiliation? Shitfuck-damn.

"I think I'm having a heart attack. Or maybe a stroke. Which is the one that makes your left arm numb?"

I've lost all brain function. This is it. I'm dying. Tell my folks I love them.

"A stroke," Liz said in a deadpan voice as she followed me into the kitchen.

"Shit. I'm having a stroke. Feel my pulse. Does it feel weird to you?" I asked, thrusting my arm out to her.

Liz smacked my hand away. "For fuck's sake, Claire, get a grip."

"Carter. His name is Carter. And he has no idea who I am," I whined.

Fuck, I hate whiney girls. I'm turning into an insecure, whiny girl. I'm going to have to kick my own ass. Liz bent down in front of the oven and took a peek at the lasagna cooking inside. She stood back up and crossed her arms in front of her chest, leaning her hip against the front of the oven.

"You think you have it bad? That fucktard Drew thinks he slept with me. I can see it in his eyes. He's trying to remember if he knows what I look like naked. Like I would ever let my lady bits near someone who wears an 'I pooped today' shirt. He doesn't even remember hitting on me that night or how close he was to having cock and balls permanently drawn on his face. I wonder if he remembers the hex I put on his dumb stick? He really believed I was a witch that night. What an idiot."

"Really Liz? You're comparing the fact that a guy doesn't remember telling you he'd make out with you because you had nice tits to my sperm-donor'ing one-night-stand sitting twenty feet away and not know who the fuck I am? Really? Is that what you're doing right now because I just want to make sure I understand this correctly and didn't accidentally hit a bong full of bad crack on the way over that I don't know about," I ranted.

Liz rolled her eyes at me. "Jesus, Cranky VonHyperAss, simmer down."

I put my hands on my hips and gave her my best "I'm gonna fuck you up look".

"Okay, so this isn't the most ideal situation for meeting back up with your baby daddy, I'll give you that. But it's done. He's here and there's nothing we can do about it now. After all these years of wondering, you finally know who he is so you can tell him about Gavin. So pull up your big-girl thongs and get your ass out there."

We stared at each other blankly for a moment.

"I know what you were going for with that but it didn't work so well," I told her.

"Yeah, I realized that as soon as I said it. Next time I'll just stick with big-girl panties."

I started pacing back and forth across the kitchen.

"What are the fucking odds, Liz? First, he shows up in the bar out of the clear blue and now he's here. In your house. And he's talking to me like I'm some new chick he just met that he wants to get to know."

"Well, technically, you *are* some new chick he just met," she said with a shrug, like it was no big deal. "I know we wondered last night if he just didn't recognize you because he was drunker than Mel Gibson when he called his wife a pig in heat, but I think it's safe to say, he really doesn't remember who you are. It's time to face facts, Claire. Your vagina just isn't that memorable."

"Fuck you," I mumbled.

"Not tonight dear, I've got a headache."

It wasn't her fault she could be so nonchalant about this whole thing. I never really told her just how much I actually thought about him over the years. She had no idea how much that man sitting out in her living room had occupied my thoughts and dreams. In all the scenarios I made up in my head about someday finding him, they always began the same way. He remembered me and everything about that night immediately and apologized for never trying to find me. We would kiss in the rain, jump hand-in-hand together into a pool and ride horses together along the beach.

Or maybe I've seen one too many tampon commercials.

Seeing him again, knowing that he had no clue about the night we spent together, sucked big time. Especially since I was raising a reminder of that night and had to think about it every time I looked at my son.

"How am I supposed to even begin telling him about Gavin when he has no idea who I am? He is never going to believe me. He's going to think I'm some nut job who's looking for child support," I stopped my pacing and moved to stand next to Liz by the oven.

"Not necessarily. Jim didn't realize who Drew was until just before you got here when I dragged him into the kitchen, but he knew immediately who Carter was. Said he talked all about you this afternoon when they were at the bar. He knew right away when the poor guy mentioned something about you smelling like chocolate."

I stopped my manic pacing and stared at her. My heart started beating furiously again.

"What?!"

"I guess he told Jim about a girl, and I quote," she paused and brought her hands up to make air quotes. "That he met at a frat party and how he's thought about her for five years. Jim didn't get a chance to elaborate on what all was said because you chose that moment to walk into the house telling everyone about your neglected vagina and two-pump-chump Max."

"Fucking hell," I whispered.

"That's why Jim invited them over. I didn't have a chance to tell him that we saw Carter last night at the bar so he had no idea until our kitchen pow-wow."

He DID remember me! Well, not me-me, but the 'me' from that night. The 'me' he met at the party. The 'me' whose virginity he took.

I need to stop saying 'me'.

"A little advanced notice would have been nice. You know there's this nifty little gadget called a cell phone right?" I complained.

"Oh, shut the fuck up. I was just as surprised as you were. They got here right before you did and Jim had all of thirty seconds to blurt out what was going on while we hung up their coats," she argued as she pulled plates down out of the cupboard.

"There is no way you were even remotely as surprised as me. If I woke up tomorrow with my tits sewn to the curtains, I wouldn't be this much in shock," I replied petulantly.

"Hey, I tried to shut you up. Several times. It's not my fault everyone now knows you have an irritable vagina. Heh, irritable vagina!" she laughed at her own joke. "Maybe it's like irritable bowel and you can get some medication for it."

Jim chose that moment to stick his head in the kitchen.

"If you two yentas are finished discussing Claire's rabid who-ha, me and the boys would like to eat sometime this century."

"You and 'the boys?' You just met them today. Does the Ya Ya Brotherhood already have a secret handshake and a password?" Liz joked.

Jim made a production of grabbing his crotch. "Secret handshake – check. And the password is 'Claire's Coochie Kills'."

I threw an oven-mitt at him, hitting him square in the face. Just then the buzzer to the oven went off and the doorbell rang.

"That's probably Jenny," Liz said as she opened the oven door and pulled out the pan of lasagna. Being the good friend that I am, I had the foresight to send her a text with the news about Jenny joining us for dinner.

"Perfect timing. We'll all sit down and eat, she will inevitably say a bunch of stupid shit and everyone will forget about your pikachu. That should give you enough time to figure out a way to tell Carter his boys can swim."

FIFTEEN MINUTES LATER we were all seated around the dining room table, filling up our plates. Thankfully, my earlier embarrassment was pushed to the side while I watched Drew fall all over Jenny. Unfortunately, I couldn't ignore the Carter situation since he was sitting right across from me and I couldn't stop staring at him.

Fuck he's hot. I mean, really, really hot. He filled out a lot in five years. I bet he works out. He's probably a runner. He's got that lean look to him. I wonder who cuts his hair? It looks like he pays a small fortune to make it look like he doesn't care what it looks like. Totally works for him.

Shit! Focus. Who cares what kind of hair products he uses? How are you going to tell this man he's a father?

Hey Carter, how about this crazy weather we've been having? Speaking of crazy, your spunk has a crazy backstroke.

The hum of conversation around the table shook me from my thoughts.

"So, I was in the left-hand lane and some idiot tried to come over to where I was. I had to slam on my breaks so I didn't hit the medium."

Everyone stopped what they were doing and waited for Jenny to correct her mistake. Unless she really meant that she almost ran her car into someone who could communicate with the dead.

"Um, Jenny, do you mean *median*?" Jim asked when the silence around the table lasted for far too long.

She paused with her fork halfway to her mouth and looked at him funny. "Isn't that cement thingy in the middle of the highway called a medium?"

Carter tried to cover up a laugh by coughing, and I saw Drew punch him in the side.

"It's alright, Jenny. You can call it whatever you want to," Drew said, patting her hand in reassurance.

"Oh, Claire, I forgot to tell you. The purchase I made tonight worked awesome!"

I should never have taken a drink of my water at that moment. As soon as the words left Jenny's mouth, I took a deep breath in shock and the water went down the wrong pipe. I started hacking and coughing, tears running down my face as Liz put her fork down and started smacking me on the back.

"What did you buy?" Drew asked as over a mouthful of noodles and sauce, completely ignoring the fact that I was dying across the table from him.

Carter at least gave me a concerned look and did that half-sitting, half-standing thing like he was getting ready to vault over the table to make sure I was okay. His concern for me was hot.

Hey Carter, speaking of hot – your hot beef injection had a play date with my eggs.

"The best vibrator I've ever owned," Jenny announced proudly, answering Drew's question.

It was his turn to choke. Some of the lasagna flew out of his mouth as he pounded his fist against his chest and Carter reached over to slap his palm against his back.

It was starting to look like a Heimlich convention in here.

"Seriously, Liz, you have some great products for sale. I can't wait to try out the rest of the stuff I bought. What about you, Claire? Did you get some alone time yet with all the toys everyone bought you tonight?" she said with a wink and a wag of her eyebrows.

"Wait, the girls at the party bought *you* vibrators?" Liz questioned, suddenly forgetting about the fact that everyone was supposed to be thinking of something other than my down-there-place.

"Nope, this isn't at all uncomfortable. Thanks for asking," I said under my breath, with a roll of my eyes.

"Can we go back to what Jenny was saying? I'd like some more details about her alone time: location, mood lighting, standing up or sitting down and if she's in need of a spotter next time. I have excellent upper body strength," Drew said with a wink as he recovered from having noodles lodged in his windpipe.

"Eeew," I muttered.

"So you really sell sex toys?" Carter said to me with a dreamy look in his eyes as he leaned in my direction with his elbows resting on the table.

I could feel my face heating up. This was not a conversation I wanted to have with him of all people. I was trying to figure out a way to tell him his love mayonnaise had mad skills and no one at this table could stop talking about vibrators.

"Technically, she doesn't sell them. She's just doing it as a favor to me," Liz chimed in, saving me from trying to explain. "We're starting up a business together. I'm selling sex toys and she'll sell cookies and candies."

"I like sex and....caaaaandy yeeaaahhh," Drew sang, completely fucking up the words to the song.

"Oh, so in answer to your question Liz—yes!" Jenny said over top of Drew's poor rendition of the sex and candy song. "Everyone tonight bought Claire a vibrator! How many did you end up with? Eleven?" Jenny asked. "I still can't believe you have never used one on yourself. That's just insanity right there. No orgasm comes close to the ones you can have with one of those puppies."

This was not happening right now. This was a dream wasn't it? Like one of those where you're in front of your entire high school naked and everyone is pointing at you and laughing. Except this time, I'm lying on the dining room table naked and everyone is pointing dildos at me.

"Oh my gosh, I know right?" Liz agreed, leaning forward so she could see around me. "I can have multiple orgasms in seconds with the Jack Rabbit."

Liz was a traitor. Benedict Liz. That's what I was calling her from now on. Fucking Benedict Liz.

"No offense baby," she said sheepishly to Jim.

"None take, love. As long as you get off, I'm happy," he said with a smile as he leaned over and kissed her shoulder.

"Claire, you absolutely have to go home tonight and use the Jack Rabbit. And then call me immediately after and give me a report," Jenny said excitedly.

"No, she shouldn't go with JR her first time out of the gate, that will scar her for life. She needs to ease herself into using toys. Did anyone buy you a bullet?" Liz asked casually with a glance in my direction. "A bullet is the best bet for your first time. It's small, doesn't make a lot of noise but it's powerful as shit," Liz explained. "It will take you thirty seconds, *tops*."

Are these people seriously discussing how I should give myself an orgasm at the dinner table like they were discussing the directions for putting together a book shelf? Insert slot A into your vagina and twist. What the fuck is happening right now?!

"Sorry," I said to Carter. "My vagina usually isn't dinner topic conversation."

He was the only one that heard me since everyone else at the table was…fuck! Still talking about my God damned vagina.

"Maybe she should use the blue dolphin. It's so cute with its bottle nose and adorable little eyes and fin! She could make up a whole story about it swimming up her channel!" Jenny proclaimed.

Carter laughed and gave me a reassuring smile and for some strange reason I wanted to climb over the table and lick his mouth.

"Alright, now I'm curious. Bullets, rabbits, dolphins…are we still talking about vibrators or are you freaky people into bestiality? I want to see these things and what they can do. Claire, go out to your car and bring them in," Drew said as he pulled his cell phone out of his pocket. "This thing has a video camera on it somewhere…" he trailed off, pushing a bunch of buttons.

"Um, no. I am not bringing in vibrators that I have neither confirmed nor denied to receiving. So shut up and eat your dinner, all of you."

"Too bad that Max guy didn't have a bullet on him. You could have at least gotten off before his dad came home," Jenny laughed.

"Ooooh, is this the guy you were talking about when you walked in the door? What happened?" Drew asked, momentarily forgetting about filming amateur porn on his cell phone.

"No. Absolutely not," I protested.

"Come on, Claire, it's no big deal, just answer it," Jenny begged with a laugh.

"Come on, Claire," Drew argued while I sat there with my arms folded glaring at him.

"Answer the question, Claire!" Drew and Jenny said sternly at the same time while trying to reign in their laughter.

"Yeah, because I've never heard the Breakfast Club reference before," I muttered.

"Awww, don't feel bad, Claire. Everyone's got an embarrassing sex experience. Hell, Carter here had sex with a virgin when he was drunk one time in college and never found out her name."

Somewhere in heaven, baby Jesus is weeping. Or maybe that's just me and the sound of my dignity dying. I'm sure Jim, Liz and I looked like we just witnessed a horrific car accident. And technically, we kind of did. I felt like blocking off the table with crime scene tape. "Keep it movin' folks, there's nothing to see here – just my self-respect being flushed down the crapper."

I'm pretty sure I stopped breathing and Liz smacked Jim in the chest so he'd close his mouth which was currently stuck in the "holy shit, did that just happen?!" wide open position. I wondered for a minute if this whole thing was one big elaborate plan to trip me up and get me to confess and that everyone at the table was in on it. My eyes glanced over to Carter to see his reaction and he looked embarrassed, not like he wanted to wring my neck for keeping a secret from him that he knew and he knew that I knew that he knew.

Aaaaack!

I started tapping my foot nervously, my leg bouncing up and down. Liz reached over under the table and put her hand on my knee.

"Drew, Jesus, man," Carter muttered, shaking his head.

"Claire…"

I interrupted Liz. She was giving me a look that clearly said now was a perfect opportunity to come clean, but I wasn't ready for that yet. This was not something you blurted across the table in front of people. Instead, I let the word vomit flow.

"So, I used to work with this guy Max at the bar. We were pretty good friends and seemed to have a lot in common."

I conveniently skipped over the part that our primary mutual interest was that we were both single parents at the time.

"We tried to tack on a friend with benefits thing a few years ago. His recently widowed father had just retired and moved in to the apartment above his garage. It was the middle of summer and we were all in the house watching a movie. His dad decides to get up and go fishing for a few hours. So, he leaves and we start going at it on the couch."

Everyone at the table stopped eating and stared at me as the story flew from my mouth in one long, continuous run-on sentence.

I can't believe I'm doing this. I'm covering up one humiliation with another.

"So, we're naked from the waist down and he dives right in. Exactly two seconds later, the front door opens and in walks his dad. He's too busy trying to get through the door with a fishing rod and a tackle box that he doesn't notice us scrambling around on the couch trying to throw a blanket over the bottom half of us."

Drew's shoulders were shaking in silent laughter, Carter looked sorry for me and everyone else just nodded their heads up and down since they had heard this story before.

"So, his dad walks right into the living room, sits down in the middle of the floor with his back to us and starts organizing his tackle box and rambling to us about how the lake was closed for fishing. Meanwhile, we're under a heavy, wool blanket on the couch behind him in the middle of July."

"Totally not suspicious at all," Carter joked.

I finally looked at him and when I realized he wasn't outright laughing *at* me, I took a deep breath to go on.

"Yeah, not at all considering Max didn't have air conditioning and it was about ninety-eight degrees out that day."

Drew shook his head in amusement. "So what the hell did you do?"

"Well, I sat there horrified and Max started digging in the couch cushions for his boxers. The more he dug, the more the blanket was threatening to get pulled right off of my naked lap. I was holding on to that thing for dear life while his dad continued to mumble about lures and bait three feet in front of us. Max finally finds his boxers and shorts and starts shimmying into them under the blanket. Meanwhile, I'm still trying to hang onto the blanket and dig for my underwear at the same time, but can't find them anywhere. I found my shorts though so I yank those on and almost scream in victory when Max flings the blanket off of our lap because I was sweating my ass off under that thing."

Everyone was thoroughly amused by my story, and I didn't mind too much at this point since they weren't talking about me getting myself off or Carter's cherry popping blunder.

"You're forgetting the best part, Claire," Jim reminded me.

"Oh yeah. So when Max yanked the blanket off of us, my underwear must have been stuck somewhere in there. It went flying through the air and hit his dad in the back of the head."

"So what did you do?" Carter asked.

"I did what any self-respecting, grown woman would do when faced with a situation like that. I stood up, ran like hell out of that house and pretended like it never happened."

THE REST OF the night went pretty well, aside from the wide-eyed looks and head nods in Carter's direction Liz kept shooting me every couple of minutes when there was a lull in the conversation. She seriously expected me to just blurt this shit out in between courses in front of everyone. "Why yes, this apple pie is delicious. Did you know apple comes from the Latin word *alum*, which means *you knocked me up*?"

We finished dinner and Liz made the men do the dishes so she, Jenny and I could start brainstorming some names for the business. We had it narrowed down to three that we loved and couldn't decide between. And then the guys joined us and the suggestions immediately went in the gutter. It's amazing, really, how quickly they can go from zero to filthy.

Plastic Penises and Pastries.

Cocks and Cookies.

Sex and Candy (I'll give you one guess who suggested that one.)

Lubes and Lady Fingers.

Cock Rings and Confectioneries.

I sat on the couch the entire time pretending to pay attention but all I could do was stare at Carter. Every time he smiled I felt like someone punched me in the stomach which was just stupid. I didn't even know him. He was a one-night-stand.

A one-night-stand I felt comfortable enough with to give him one of the most important gifts a girl has to give and the little time I spent with him was enough to create a lasting memory of how alike the two of us were. It was also enough time to create another lasting memory that I've had to love, nurture and mold all by myself into something that I hope resembles a well-behaved child and will not need years of therapy due to my parenting skills.

None of the similarities in our personalities or how attracted I was to him then and now has any bearing on this moment, though. As soon as I tell him he's a father and has a four-and-a-half year old son, he was probably going to hate me. At least I had nine months to get used to the idea. What single, gorgeous man in his twenties wanted to be told he was now saddled with the giant responsibility of a kid for the rest of his life?

He was going to head for the hills when I told him. He was going to scream, turn and run. Like one of those cartoon characters that go charging through a door and all you see is a giant hole in the wood shaped like them running. I needed to just prepare myself for that. And it wasn't like I could blame him. It was a completely insane situation that no one in their right mind would ever believe. Gavin and I did quite well on our own so far anyways. You couldn't miss something you never had. If he chose to never speak to us again, so be it.

So why did the thought of that suddenly make me sad?

I glanced at my watch and realized it was almost ten o'clock. I needed to get home and relieve my dad of babysitting duty.

"Hey, where are you off to? It's not even ten yet," Drew said as I stood up from the couch and started moving to the foyer to grab my coat.

"Sorry, I need to get home to Ga…et some laundry finished," I said, stumbling over my words.

Dammit, I almost said Gavin. I am a chicken-shit. I should have just said it and gotten it over with. Liz winced at my almost-slip and Jim coughed.

"I'll call you tomorrow and we can *go over a few more things*," Liz said with a raise of her eyebrows.

I know by "go over a few more things" she meant that she was going to beat the shit out of me for not saying something to Carter tonight.

Super, looking forward to it.

I waved good-bye to everyone and quickly walked out into the foyer. I had just gotten my coat on when Carter came rushing around the corner.

"Hey, I'll walk you out to your car," he said as he opened the front door for me with a smile.

I stood there like an idiot, just staring at him. I should tell him. Right now, while we're out here alone.

Hey, you don't remember me, but I'm the one whose virginity you took five years ago and well, guess what? It's a boy!

I couldn't do it. I broke my stare and walked out the door, rushing down the steps to my car and putting as much distance between us as I could. Didn't Liz say that Carter mentioned to Jim something about his "mystery girl" smelling like chocolate? I didn't need him putting the connection together. Not now. I needed more time. I needed to figure out what to say and find out what kind of guy he really was. Did he even want children? Did he plan on staying in town for long or was he going to put in for another transfer? Maybe he already had six other children spread around the world that he didn't support. Oh God, what if he decides he wants to be a father to Gavin and sticks around, then something happens to all the mothers of his illegitimate children and suddenly he gets custody of them and we have not one but seven children? And they all hate us because we were never there for them and Gavin turns to life on the streets and turning tricks for crack because a homeless guy named Fromunda Cheese told him crack ISN'T whack. I needed more time. I needed to formulate a plan that kept Gavin out of the hood. I also needed to calm down. It's not like Carter was begging for my attention or asking to see me again. He was being nice and walking me to my car. End of story.

Carter followed right behind me and stopped by the hood as I opened the door and turned to face him.

"I'd like to see you again, Claire," he said softly.

"Well fuck me gently with a chainsaw," I muttered as I stood there with the car door open.

His mouth dropped open and for a second I thought I saw recognition flash across his face.

Shit, I just quoted Heathers. I didn't even realize what I was saying. The non-bat-shit crazy part of me willed him to remember, to put two and two together and realize that *I* was the girl from the frat party. Jesus, we'd practically acted out the entire movie while we played beer pong. We traded quotes back and forth until our sides ached from laughing. But his silence proved that whatever memories he may have had about me were still locked up tight in the far recesses of his mind.

"Call me. Liz can give you my number," I blurted before I could change my mind. I scrambled into the car, started it up and pulled quickly out of the driveway, glancing into the rearview mirror to see Carter, still standing in the driveway, get smaller and smaller as I drove away.

10.

Seduction and Snacks...and Snafu's

I COULDN'T STOP staring at Claire all through dinner. I felt bad that everyone seemed to be picking on her, but she was so adorable when she got embarrassed. Her cheeks flushed pink and she looked down at her lap and tugged on her left ear lobe.

Jesus, I just used the word adorable like I was talking about a fucking puppy. Wait, that didn't sound right. Although if she *was* a puppy, she'd probably be fucking something because she's so hot. So in reality, she *would* be a fucking puppy. I mean come on, what dog wouldn't want to tap that ass? I need to stop watching Animal Planet. Claire is not a puppy – one that fucks or one that doesn't. Period.

I had a hard time finishing my dinner. The lasagna was amazing, but all I could think about was Claire pleasuring herself with a vibrator.

Or her hand.

Or a vibrator and her hand.

Or a vibrator and her hand and my hand.

Well, hello there, Mr. Hard-on.

I clearly had issues when it came to this woman I just met. Part of me wanted to rip that guy Max's head off just because he got to touch her, kiss her and be inside her. But when she was finished with the story, I just wanted to find him so I could point and laugh at him. What kind of a douche tried to have sex with a woman on his couch with his daddy living there, coming and going as he pleases? Real smooth there, buddy.

I stopped being jealous of the guy at that point. Now, all I wanted to do was show her how a real man should act. I had an irrational need to show her everything she'd been missing.

Right, because I am the king of all things sexual. My penis can make grown women weep in the streets.

Things got silly as the men drank more beer and the women tried thinking up business names for Liz and Claire's place. I didn't know why they shot down "Candy-Coated Cunnilingus." That was brilliant. And it made me think of sucking on a Jolly Rancher, brushing the wet piece of candy between Claire's legs and then sliding my tongue along candy trail.

Then I remembered the one time in middle school when I put a half-eaten Jolly Rancher on my dresser and somehow it fell into one of the drawers. Three socks, a pencil and a G.I. Joe guy were stuck to it when I found it a month later.

Probably wasn't a good idea to put something like that anywhere near a vagina, especially Claire's vagina. No harm should ever come to Claire's vagina.

I was probably imagining things, but I swear every time I glanced over at her she looked away quickly. It made me smile to myself thinking that she might be staring at me too. I knew Drew was right. I needed to stop fantasizing about a girl I was never going to see again. It was five years ago for God's sakes. I was acting like a pussy, holding on to the tiny bit of information I had on her. For all I know she looks like Sloth from The Goonies now and smells like Drew's sweaty balls. I tried to forget about her by getting into a relationship with Tasha a couple of months after that frat party. Almost five years later and I was still stuck in the same rut of fantasizing about someone I'd never see again. To be fair though, I should have known from the start that Tasha and I weren't the best idea. We spent the majority of our time together in some sort of argument or another. She had a jealous streak that bordered on psycho and hated that I didn't behave the same way if another man glanced in her direction. What I should have done was hold out for someone like Claire. Someone sweet, and funny and smart;

someone who didn't have a whole other side to her like Tasha. Right in front of me was a beautiful woman that made me think dirty thoughts just by watching her breathe. I needed to cut this shit out and take a chance.

Aside from the jealousy and fighting, I knew one of the main reasons Tasha and I didn't last was because I just wasn't able to give the relationship one-hundred percent because I couldn't stop wondering if *she* might still be out there somewhere.

That and the fact that Tasha's vagina had the same slogan as McDonalds: Over ten billion served.

I digress.

I needed to put a stop to this stupid fixation on some faceless mystery girl who could very well be a figment of my imagination. I needed take a chance on someone who was sitting right here in front of me or I was going to be alone forever. I was too busy contemplating my pathetic life to notice that Claire was no longer across from me and had gotten up to leave. She was already rounding the corner into the foyer when I snapped out of it.

I sat there staring at her back (fine, her ass) long enough for Drew to punch me in the arm. He not so subtly nodded his head in the direction she went and suddenly I realized all eyes were on me. They were looking at me like, "what the fuck are you waiting for?" Liz narrowed her eyes at me and I'm not gonna lie, I was a little scared of her. I jumped up from the couch and ran out of the room, catching her right as she finished putting her coat on. Circling behind her back, I opened the door and stood next to it.

She was surprised by my presence and jumped a little at the sound of my voice and the door opening. I couldn't tear my eyes away from her. I need to kiss her. I need to kiss her like I need to breathe. What the fuck is this woman doing to me? Before I made a complete ass of myself by drooling or pushing her up against the wall so I could attack her lips, she turned and walked through the door without saying a word to me after I told her I'd walk her to her car. I had an irrational need to spend more time with her. I wanted to learn what made her blush (aside from talk about her vagina), what song was on repeat on her iPod and what her favorite book was. I wanted to hear her say my name.

Fuck, I wanted to hear her sigh, shout and scream my name.

So, I told her just that. Well, not all of it. I didn't want her to get a restraining order. I watched the corners of her mouth twitch when I said her name, almost like it made her happy to hear it. For a second, I thought she would just get in the car and peel out of the driveway without answering me. Then she muttered something that I almost didn't hear over the sound of a car starting next door. The words she spoke force my mouth to drop open and pushed the memory of a dream I had recently to the forefront of my mind.

"Ask me what my favorite movie is."

She interrupted my thoughts by telling me to call her. By the time I remembered where I knew that quote from, her car had pulled out of the driveway and was speeding down the street.

FOR THE NEXT two weeks Claire and I talked every night on the phone. Unfortunately, the plant put me on night shift and overtime for the first few weeks so our schedules never meshed so we could see each other. The only spare time we both had to talk was during my first fifteen minute break around midnight every night. I always apologized to her for calling at such a shitty time but she swore it was absolutely perfect. For the first time in as long as I can remember, I actually looked forward to going to work because I knew I'd get to hear Claire's voice. Drew, who worked directly across from me on the assembly line, got entirely too much pleasure out of watching me rush to a quiet corner of the plant to make the call. The first time, he asked me where I was going and when I didn't answer, he followed me the entire way, shouting to every single person that I was calling my parents to tell them I was coming out of the closet. A well-placed punch to the nuts curbed his desire to do that ever again, but people were still coming up to me and patting me on the back in congratulations.

For fifteen minutes every single night, Claire and I talked about nothing and everything all at the same time. I told her about growing up with two older brothers who confirmed my belief in the boogey man and had their friends call me and tell me they were Santa Clause and that I would never get another toy again if I didn't clean their rooms while wearing a pair of their underwear on my head.

Claire told me about her parent's divorce and her decision to live with her father, who I hadn't even met and already feared. He went to a birthday party the previous weekend and when trying to break up a fight, some guy said to him "What are you going to do about it grand-pa?" Claire's dad knocked him out with one punch and said "THAT'S what I'm going to do about it, asshole." Claire tried to convince me that her dad was a giant teddy bear, but where I come from, you're not afraid to meet a teddy bear in a dark alley at night for fear that he'll scalp you and tattoo his name on your ass.

I regrettably told her about Tasha and the reason for the breakup. I even spilled my guts to her about how I didn't know if I ever even really loved Tasha and was just biding my time until the right person came along. I didn't tell her more about the one-night-stand from college that Drew brought up at dinner that night and she never asked about it, thankfully. Even though it was easy to talk to Claire about Tasha, it seemed wrong to talk to her about the woman I'd dreamed about for five years. Claire was sweet and smart and funny and I didn't want to taint any of that with a stupid dream. The more I talked to Claire and got to know her, the more it became clear that she could be the one I was waiting for. I felt like the majority of the time we talked more about me than we did her and when I pointed that out, she just laughed and said there wasn't much to tell because her life was so boring. Still, with each phone call I learned something new about her and I was willing to spend as long as it took to know everything there was to know about her.

Finally, after fifteen days of hovering in corners at work away from the loud machines to listen to Claire's softy, husky voice as she lay curled up in bed under the covers talking to me, I was going to see her again. The plant finally gave me a Saturday off of work and I was more than happy to spend it checking out Claire and Liz's shop (fine, Claire's ass). Claire had sent me a few pictures on my cell phone in the last week and from what I could tell, they were making enormous progress on the place. In reality, I didn't care if I was meeting Claire in a garbage dump; as long as I could be close to her I would be happy.

At ten that Saturday morning, I pulled up in front of the address Claire gave me for the shop. I sat in the car for a minute, tapping my fingers against the steering wheel. I probably got around three hours of sleep last night. All I did was toss and turn, thinking about seeing Claire again and being close enough to touch her. I'm not gonna lie though, the thing that gave me the sleepless night was the quote she used absentmindedly on the phone the previous night. It was the second time she'd used it around me and no matter how much I tried to push it from my mind, that stupid nagging though about *her* popped back up. A lot of people have seen the movie Heathers. And really, "fuck me gently with a chainsaw" could be a very popular way to say "holy shit" nowadays.

Uh-huh, yeah right.

Her use of that saying could be the biggest fucking coincidence in the history of the world, or I just boarded the crazy train headed straight for cuckoo city. I pulled my cell phone out of the cup holder and checked the time, smiling when I saw the picture of Claire that I was using as my screen background. I caught a lot of shit from Drew when he saw it, but I didn't care. I covertly asked Liz to send a picture of Claire to me and she was more than happy to oblige. The picture she sent was a black and white close up of Claire, laughing unabashedly at something, with one hand held up to her face and her fingers spread in such a way that you could still see her beautiful smile, the mirth in her eyes and the dimples in her cheeks. It was stunning, and I only hoped I would be able to put that look on Claire's face myself one of these days and be there to witness it.

Looking at the picture of Claire on my phone erased the confusion and questions from my mind and made me just want to concentrate on her, not ghosts from the past. I shut the engine off and got out, finally taking a good look at the building I parked in front of. I was impressed. It was bigger than I thought it would be and it looked great from the outside. I could see Liz through the front window on what must have been her side of the store, so I rounded the front of the car and stepped up on the sidewalk. I started walking towards the front door and had to stop short when a little boy went flying in front of me, arms and legs flailing all over the place.

"Gavin, get your ass back here!"

On instinct, my arm flew out and I grabbed onto the back of the kid's shirt, halting his progress of running away. A guy, probably close to fifty, jogged over to where I was.

"Hey, thanks for stopping him," he said, looking down at the boy with a stern face that would have made me cringe if I was on the receiving end of it. I let go of his shirt, confident that the little runaway wasn't going anywhere now that he'd been caught.

"Gavin, how many times have I told you that you can't just take off when you get out of the car? You have to hold my hand."

The kid shrugged. "I don't know. I was just hurryin' my ass to the ice cream store 'fore it all meltses."

I covered my mouth with my hand to hide my laugh. This kid had balls! The poor guy just rolled his eyes at the boy and let out a sigh.

"If you enjoy your sanity at all, don't have kids," the guy said to me before grabbing the kid's hand and walking away.

"Thanks for the advice!" I yelled to him as the two of them walked into the ice cream shop next door.

Liz noticed me on the sidewalk through the window just then and opened the door for me.

"Good morning!" she said brightly as I walked inside.

Everywhere I looked I saw bras, underwear and all sorts of frilly shit on hangers and displayed on tables. I could almost feel my dick shriveling up and retreating back inside my body. I didn't mind taking this stuff off of a woman, but standing in the middle of a room surrounded by this crap made me feel entirely too in touch with my feminine side.

Jesus fuck, what is THAT?

"That's a ball gag mask, Carter. I take it you aren't into bondage?" Liz asked seriously, noticing the direction of my gaze.

"Uh, I….umm…"

Is it hot in here all of a sudden?

"Have you ever tied up a partner? Used whips? Experimented in anal play? Had a threesome? Would you say you're more of a dominant or a submissive? When was the last time you were checked for STD's?"

"What? I mean, I…."

"How many sexual partners have you had in the last five years? Have you ever been convicted of a sex crime against another human, animal or plant?"

"ELIZABETH!"

Oh thank God. I don't think I've ever been happier to hear the sound of Claire's voice.

"I've got my eye on you," Liz whispered, looking me up and down and doing the whole two-finger point from her eyes to mine.

"Duly noted," I muttered as I walked past her and over to the doorway behind the counter where Claire was currently standing with her hands on her hips. Since she was busy staring over my shoulder shooting dirty looks at Liz, I had the opportunity to take her in unnoticed. It was unbelievable how she seemed to have gotten even more beautiful than the last time I saw her. Maybe it was because I knew her so much better than before. Her hair was up in a messy ponytail with stray pieces falling down around her face. I noticed a smudge of flour or maybe powdered sugar on her cheek and I wanted to lick it off. My dick got hard just thinking about tasting her skin.

"I'll deal with you later, Liz," Claire threatened.

"Shut your mouth and get your scraggly ass back in the kitchen where you belong, whore!"

Claire rolled her eyes and jerked her head behind her.

"Come on, I'll show you my part of the store."

She reached for my hand like it was the most natural thing in the world. When our skin touched I had a hard time forcing my feet to move. I just wanted to stand there and stare at her. Claire smiled at me and turned, pulling me gently along behind her. We walked through the storage room of Liz's store and it took everything in me not to reach out and grab her ass. Fuck, she was wearing jeans again. This woman in a pair of jeans should be illegal. My brain didn't work when she wore jeans.

"And here is my half of Seduction and Snacks," Claire stated proudly as we left Liz's storage room and entered her kitchen. With her hand still in mine, she led me through the kitchen to the front of the store, pointing things out to me. Where Liz's store was all dark colors and rich fabrics, Claire's side was light and airy and full of bright colors. In the front of the store, she had three light yellow walls and one light pink wall. Behind the counter there was just enough wall hanging down from the ceiling to hold three large chalkboards, filled with all the store had to offer along with prices. Below the chalkboards, the wall ended and you could see straight into the kitchen. All around the room were framed pictures of cupcakes, candies and different sayings that had to do with her business. A pink and brown wooden sign on one wall stated "Money can't buy happiness but it can buy chocolate, which is kind of the same thing." and a yellow and brown one by the door read "A balanced diet is a cookie in each hand." Aside from the warm, inviting atmosphere, the smell alone would put you in a good mood. For once, the smell of chocolate didn't bother me like it usually did. Maybe, because Claire was standing right next to me, and all I could think about was tasting her instead of the memories that scent usually brought me. I moved a step towards her and took the fact that she didn't move away or let go of my hand as a good sign.

"Seduction and Snacks is a great name. It's probably more appropriate than Blow Jobs and Baked Goods."

She laughed nervously, but still didn't move away from my close proximity. This near to her, I could see that her eyes weren't just liquid brown. They also had tiny specs of gold in them that made it look like someone had sprinkled a handful of glitter in them.

"The place looks great," I told her, taking another step in her direction, wanting to be as close to her as possible. I reached down by her side and slid my free hand into hers, the fingers of both of our hands intertwining. She swallowed and licked her lips nervously but didn't move.

"Thanks," she mumbled, her eyes staring straight at my lips.

Fuck, did she want me to kiss her? Should I do it? Just lean in and press my lips to hers? Why do I feel like a twelve year old that has no experience? Why can't I stop asking myself these annoying questions?

I took one last step, closing the distance between us. I let go of her hands so I could slide mine behind her and rest them on her lower back, pulling her flush against me in the process. Her hands flew up to my chest but she didn't push me away. She rested them there and finally looked up into my eyes.

"It smells good in here. What did you make?" I asked quietly, leaning my head down closer to her lips, thankful that she was finally in my arms and amazed at how right she felt there.

"N-nothing," she stammered. "I was just making a list of all the supplies I need to order and stocking the flour on the shelves."

I stopped with my lips hovering directly over hers. I could feel her breath on me, and I had to count to ten to stop myself from pushing her back against the door and pushing myself between her legs.

"It smells like chocolate in here," I whispered, ghosting my lips back and forth across hers.

I had absolutely no self-control being this close to her. Two weeks of only hearing her voice was like the most torturous foreplay in the world. I kissed the corner of her mouth, her cheek and right below her ear, taking in a deep breath of her skin. All of the blood rushed to my head and my arms tightened around her small waist.

Whoa, what the fuck?

I could feel her heart thumping in her chest which was pressed against my own, but that wasn't what made the room suddenly seem tipsy.

This can't be right. Why in the hell is my subconscious playing tricks on me right now? I kissed the spot below her ear again just to make sure I wasn't losing my mind and felt her shudder in my arms. I took another deep breath of her skin, nuzzling my nose into the soft pieces of hair that rested against the side of her neck.

Jesus Christ, I have officially gone off the deep end. How is it possible that she smells like this? I stood there and just breathed her in. Five years of searching for this and it was right here in my arms. And now I was going to look like a total assy pervert because it was killing me. I need to know what that smell is. It had to be some kind of lotion or some shit and in some crazy, twisted act of fate, Claire used the same product. Once that mystery is solved, I can finally, once and for all, let go of this nonsense.

"It's probably just me. I always smell like chocolate," she whispered, her arms sliding up to my shoulders and around my neck, her fingers gently sliding through the hair at the nape. Something about the feel of her fingers sliding against the back of my head felt so familiar that it was my turn to shiver.

Did you just quote 'Heathers'? That is my favorite movie ever.

I kind of have a thing for quirky, crazy, intelligent, dark-haired chicks.

I forgot how to breathe for a minute as bits and pieces of the past tried to make their way to the forefront of my mind. She felt so good in my arms; like she belonged there or maybe she'd been there before....

No, don't be a dick. Claire is sweet and beautiful and a nice girl. Don't confuse her with a memory, especially not now.

"Well, fuck me gently with a chainsaw."

"Ask me what my favorite movie is."

The past, present and stupid dreams were all flying around in my brain trying to fight for first place. Suddenly I had a memory of falling down on top of her on a strange bed. Her body was soft in all the right places and her skin was smooth and I couldn't get enough of touching her. She made the most amazing noises when I licked the skin of her neck right below her ear. I remembered pushing into her and squeezing my eyes shut because she was so fucking tight and hot, and I didn't want it to end before we even got started. I remembered moving slowly in and out of her and hoping to God it felt good for her because I wanted to do this forever with only her. I remembered waking up the next morning, breathing in the smell of chocolate that still lingered on the pillow and the sheets and praying that I'd be able to find out who she was.

I pulled away from Claire enough so I could see her face. I stared into her eyes, willing every single one of my memories to come back to me so I wouldn't feel so confused. Her fingers continued to play with my hair on the back of my head, bringing everything into focus.

"What's your favorite movie?" I whispered.

I held my breath, desperate for the answer. I watched her face go from content to puzzled to nervous. Why was she nervous? It was a simple question. Unless…

She looked back and forth between my eyes and I watched her blink back tears. Seeing her eyes like this, so bright and nervous jarred a memory loose and I choked on a breath. With perfect clarity I saw myself above her, pulling her leg up and wrapping it around my hip while I stared down into her eyes. I remembered looking into her eyes as I pushed inside of her and forcing myself to stop when I saw her quickly blink back tears.

I remembered hearing her gasp like she was in pain and I asked her if she was okay. She never answered me; she just stared up at me with those beautiful, bright brown eyes, pulled my face down to hers and kissed me. Claire's face, Claire's eyes, Claire's body…

"Heathers," she whispered.

My mind flew back to the present at the sound of her whispered admission. All I could do was stare at her in disbelief. The feel of her in my arms, her breath on my face, the sound of her laughter and the way she blushed when she was embarrassed, I remembered it all. Bumping our shoulders together conspiratorially as we played beer pong, the way her lips felt the first time I kissed her…it was her. *It was Claire.*

"My favorite movie. It's Heathers," she repeated, mistaking my stunned silence for a hearing impairment. She stared at me like she was willing me to remember. Hoping that I would finally get a clue as to why she and Liz acted so weird when they met me. Why she was so nervous around me that night we showed up at Jim and Liz's and tried to avoid looking me in the eyes at all cost. Why everyone at the table looked like they'd seen a ghost when Drew brought up the virgin comment. Why she was reticent to share too much with me during our many conversations over the last few weeks – I already knew everything about her. She'd shared it all with me that night so many years ago.

"It's you," I whispered, bringing my hand up to cup her cheek. "Holy shit."

She let out a watery laugh and closed her eyes, leaning her forehead against my chin.

"Oh thank God," she muttered to herself, but loud enough for me to hear.

I reached under her chin and pushed her face back up so I could see her.

"Why didn't you say anything? You probably thought I was a complete asshole."

She smirked at me. "I did. At first. Liz wanted to kick your ass."

"I think she still does," I deadpanned.

She smiled and it made my knees weak.

"Honestly, I didn't know what to think when I first saw you and you didn't say anything. I figured you were just a typical asshole that had countless one-night-stands in college. But after some of the stuff Jim told us you said, Liz figured out pretty quickly that you must have just been too drunk that night to remember everything about me. I'm still going with the idea that I just wasn't very memorable to begin with."

She laughed at her own words but I could tell that idea bothered her.

"Don't even joke about that. Do you have any idea how long I've looked for you? How bat shit crazy Drew thinks I am because I keep trying to find lotion that smells like chocolate and nothing ever comes close to the way I remembered you? I was beginning to think I imagined you."

I pulled her body back against mine and rested my forehead against hers, afraid to let go of her for fear she would disappear again. How could this be real? Drew is never going to believe this. Fuck, I still didn't believe it. Now that she was this close, I could smell her skin without even trying and it made me smile.

"You either didn't have as much to drink that night as I did or you just have a damn good memory. How in the hell did *you* recognize *me*?" I asked.

Claire opened her mouth to speak, but right then, the door to the store burst open and she pulled back out of my arms suddenly as we both turned in that direction. The little boy with the mouth flew through the door and I let out a laugh, figuring he had gotten away from his dad again.

"Mommy! I gots ice cream!" he yelled as he ran towards us.

I stood there with my mouth open as Claire bent down and caught the little guy as he threw himself into her arms. She looked up at me in complete and utter horror.

Holy shit. She has a kid. I've been looking for her for five years and she went off and had a kid. Well doesn't this sunk donkey dick.

"Sweetie, that kid is about two steps away from getting one of those kid leash things they sell at the store. Or a shock collar. I wonder if you need a concealed carry permit to get a taser."

In walked the dad I saw earlier, and I tried not to cringe as he walked over to where Claire was crouched down still hugging the boy and looking a little bit like she might puke.

Claire has an old man fetish. This guy has to be pushing fifty. I'd puke too if I was her. That's kind of gross. She's touched those old, wrinkly balls. When he comes I bet it's just a puff of smoke poofing out of his elderly penis. The guy finally glanced over at me, looking me up and down.

"Who are you?" he asked, obviously forgetting our encounter just moments ago due to the Alzheimer's.

"You have old balls," I mumbled angrily.

"George! I thought I saw your car pull up a little bit ago!" Liz exclaimed as she walked over from her side of the store and right up to Claire, helping her off the floor. I stared at the back of the guy's head as Liz walked over and he turned to give her a hug. He's got thinning hair for fuck's sake. Can his balls even grow hair anymore? I want to punch his hairless old balls.

Claire looked nervously back and forth between Old Man Winter and me. I wonder what he would think about the fact that Claire and I had a past. And that she almost made out with me right before he got here and interrupted us.

"I slept with your wife," I stated, crossing my arms in front of me and staring him down.

All three of them gaped at me with equal looks of confusion on their faces.

"You swept wif my Nana? Did she read you a bedtime story? Papa says she snores."

George took a step towards me and I actually gulped. Regardless of how old his balls were, I was sure he could kick my ass. Or kill me and make it look like an accident.

"Dad," Claire said in warning.

Dad? Oh, fuck. I really *am* an asshole. I have Tourette's of the mouth. Claire never once mentioned his name when she talked about him. This was the man who punched someone in the face for calling him grandpa. And now I just told him he had old balls. He was going to straight up murder me.

"Shit. I didn't sleep with your wife. Total mistake."

He stopped walking towards me and if I had a brain I would have kept my mouth shut from that point on. Obviously I was drunk the day they were handing those things out.

"I got confused. I meant to say I slept with your daughter."

I heard Liz groan and saw Claire's mouth fall open.

"But it's not what you think," I continued quickly. "I mean, we were both really, really drunk and I didn't even know who she was until a minute ago."

Oh my God, stop. STOP!

One of his eyebrows cocked and I swear I heard him crack his knuckles.

"She smells like chocolate and I don't like to be spanked," I blurted in a panic.

"Jesus Christ…" George muttered, shaking his head.

I saw Claire smack Liz from behind George. Liz was snorting with laughter. Of course she found this funny.

"I don't like to be spanked either. How's come I don't have hair on my balls? Mommy, you aren't going to spank him are you?"

"Yes, Mommy, tell us. Are you going to spank Carter for being a bad boy?" Liz said in her best Marilyn Monroe voice. In the chaos of the shit storm that was happening, I never really got a good look at the kid Claire was holding. His back had been facing me up until a few seconds ago and I hadn't been paying much attention when I caught him from running away outside. Claire had to shift him to her other arm so she could smack Liz. He was staring right at me now. He was a really good-looking kid. But that wasn't surprising since he looked just like her. But there was something about him…

I cocked my head to the side and he did the same. I realized no one was speaking but I couldn't take my eyes off of him. The edges of my vision started to turn black and I felt like I was going to pass out. He had my eyes. He had my fucking eyes! I quickly tried to do the math but my brain was a jumbled mess and I couldn't remember what number comes after potato!

What the fuck is happening right now? This couldn't be real. My sperm betrayed me. I suddenly had a vision of my sperm swimming around and talking in Bruce Willis's voice like in Look Who's Talking. "Come on! Swim faster! This little shit has no idea we escaped from the condom! Yippee-ki-yay, motherfucker!"

My Bruce Willis sperm is bad ass and thinks he's John McClane from "Die Hard." That is the only explanation for this fuckery.

"Who are you?" I asked the kid with my eyes when I finally found my voice.

"I'm Gavin Morgan, who the hell are you?"

11.

Good Vibrations

OH FUCK.

My dad was going to kill Carter before I even got a chance to tell him that he was a father. Although, I was pretty sure that ship has sailed. He's either mentally challenged or in shock. Or I completely missed the fact that he liked to shout about hairy balls and being spanked.

Gavin *did* like to talk about his balls all the time. Could be hereditary…

"Who are you?" Carter whispered, staring straight at Gavin like he was trying to figure out the square root of pi in his head.

"I'm Gavin Morgan, who the hell are you?"

"GAVIN!" we all scolded, except for Carter. He still looked like he might throw up.

Shit, this was so not how I saw this happening. I knew after all of our conversations and how much I'd gotten to know Carter that I was going to have to come clean soon. And I had planned on telling him today, easing him into it.

After I plied him with enough alcohol to choke a horse.

"This is one of mommy's friends, buddy," I told Gavin. "Friend" seemed better than "the father you never knew you had" or "the guy who knocked mommy up" at the moment. I could wait until he was a teenager to scar him with that information.

Gavin started to get bored with the lack of excitement in the room since everyone pretty much just stood there and waited for Carter's brain to explode. Gavin had the attention span of a two-year-old with ADD on crack. He started to squirm in my arms so I put him down. I held my breath as he stalked right over and stood in front of Carter with his hands on his hips.

"You're Mommy's fwiend?" he questioned.

Carter just nodded with his mouth open and no sound coming out. I'm pretty sure he didn't even hear Gavin. Someone could have asked him if he liked to watch gay porn while painting pictures of kittens and he would have nodded his head.

Before anyone could react, Gavin pulled back one of his little fists of fury and slammed it right into Carters manhood. He immediately bent over at the waist, clutching his hands between his legs and gasping for breath.

"Oh my God! Gavin!" I yelled, as I scrambled over to him, bent down and turned him around to face me while my dad and Liz laughed like hyenas behind me.

"What is wrong with you? We don't hit people. EVER," I scolded.

While Carter tried to breathe again, my dad managed to stop laughing long enough to apologize.

"Sorry, Claire, that's probably my fault. I let Gavin watch 'Fight Club' with me last night."

I am Claire's complete mortification.

"Your fwiends got you sick the other night. You said he was your fwiend," Gavin explained, like it made all the sense in the world.

This just made my dad laugh even louder.

"Not helping, Dad," I growled through clenched teeth.

"You don't make my mommy sick, dicky-punk!" Gavin yelled at Carter, putting his two little fingers up by his eyes, and then pointing them right at Carter just like Liz had done to him earlier.

"Jesus Christ," Carter wheezed. "Did he just threaten me?"

"Jesus Cwist!" Gavin repeated back.

Liz scurried over then and scooped Gavin up into her arms.

"Okay, little man, how about me, you and Papa go for a walk and talk about big-people words?" she asked him as she walked over to my dad and grabbed him around the elbow.

I stood up and shot her a look of thanks. She just smiled and dragged my dad out the door with Gavin talking her ear off about something he saw on Spongebob.

When Carter and I were finally alone, I chanced a look at him. He didn't look pissed. He didn't look sad. He just looked like he had no idea where he was or what day it was. We stood there looking at each other for several minutes until the silence finally got to me.

"Would you please say something?" I begged.

Just moments ago I was blissfully happy that he finally figured out who I was. He held me close and he was going to kiss me. Now everything was ruined and it was my fault for not telling him sooner.

Carter shook his head as if trying to clear it.

"That was a kid," he stated. "I don't like kids."

I bit my tongue. He was still in shock. I couldn't just go off on him because he said something like that. Hell, I don't even like kids and I live with one. I love my kid, but that doesn't mean I like him all the time.

"I used a condom. I know I used a condom," he said in an accusatory tone, shooting me a panicked look.

Okay, that was it for the tongue biting. The pleasure I'd felt earlier when he'd had his body pressed up against mine and his lips on my neck flew right out the window.

"Really? You can actually remember that? Because I'm pretty sure up until about twenty minutes ago you had no fucking idea who I even was. You're right though, you did use a condom. You put it on three thrusts *after* you took my virginity. But let me clear something up for you there Einstein, they aren't one-hundred percent effective, especially when they aren't used properly," I fumed.

"I dry heave whenever anyone pukes. And I don't know how to change a diaper," he said in horror.

"Carter, he's four. He doesn't wear diapers. And he's not Linda Blair from the Exorcist. He's doesn't walk around spewing vomit all day," I said with a roll of my eyes.

"My wiener hurts. I need a drink," he muttered before turning and walking out the door.

BY THE TIME Liz and my dad came back to the store with Gavin, I was in no mood to talk to either one of them. I put Gavin in the car and went home without saying a word. I was probably acting like a big baby, but I didn't care. I was mad at them for thinking this whole thing was funny, I was mad at myself for not telling Carter as soon as I saw him, and I was mad that I was mad about all this.

Who cares that he freaked out and would probably never talk to us again? It wasn't like we were missing out on anything. Gavin had no idea who he was. How could you miss something you never had?

But I *did* have him. Literally. And even thought I was fucked up at the time, I know what I'm missing. For two weeks he opened up to me and I knew so much more about him than I did before. I know he loves his family and wants more than anything to have one of his own some day. I know he's a hard worker and would do anything for those he loved. For just a moment, it was nice to have him here. To be in the same room with him, to see him smile and hear him laugh, to feel his arms around me and know I wasn't alone in this crazy parenthood thing.

Shit. I was good and fucked. I *did* care. I wanted him in my life; in Gavin's life. I wanted Gavin to know his father and I wanted Carter to know what kind of an awesome little person he helped to create. I want to spend more time with him and I want him to know me. Not the partial version I gave him on the phone for fear of slipping up about Gavin or the chocolate-scented fantasy version he held onto all these years, the *real* me. The one who put her dreams on hold to raise his son, the one who would do it all over again in a minute if it meant she got to have Gavin in her life, the not so perfect crazy me who jumps to conclusions and freaks out about the most mundane things and who would give anything to go back to that morning five years ago and stay curled up in that boy's arms who smelled like sweet cinnamon and whose kisses were hotter than an inferno.

I spent the rest of the day cleaning the house from top to bottom. This was a sure sign I was agitated. I hate cleaning.

I was on my hands and knees pulling shit out from under the couch. A pop-tart wrapper, a sucker stick and a sippy cup with something chunky in it that was probably milk at one time.

Jesus, Gavin hasn't used sippy cups in over a year.

"Mommy, are we havin' people over for a party?"

"No, we're not having a party, why?" I asked him as I picked up two pennies, a nickel and four empty fruit snack wrappers.

"Cuz you're cleanin'. You only clean when people are comin' over."

I pulled my head out from under the couch and sat back on my feet.

"I do not only clean when people are coming over," I argued.

"Do too."

"No I don't."

"Uh-huh."

"Do not."

"Do too."

Gaaaaah! I'm arguing with a four-year old.

"Gavin, enough!" I yelled. "Go clean your room."

"Freakin' hell," he mumbled.

"What did you just say?" I asked him with a stern voice.

"I love you mommy," he said with a smile before he threw his arms around me and squeezed.

God dammit. I am way too easy.

I ignored three calls from Liz throughout the day and one from my dad. Liz's voicemails weren't surprising.

"Stop being a dick. Call me."

"Did you pull the stick out of your ass yet?"

"…..OH YES! Harder Jim! Oh fuck yes…"

That bitch actually butt-dialed me while she had sex with Jim.

My dad's voicemail showed just how concerned he was for my well-being.

"Did I leave my Budweiser hat at your house last week?"

As the day wore on, I started to feel sorry for Carter. I mean really, he did kind of get blindsided. One minute he was leaning in to kiss me and the next he found out he was the father of a four-year-old.

Good God, he almost kissed me.

My hand paused in the process of putting our plates from dinner into the dishwasher, and I stared off into space as I remembered what happened between us before everything went to shit. I should be trying to think of what I was going to say to Carter when we spoke again, but the memory of this morning was too fresh in my mind and it had been too long since I let a man get that close to me. My body was starved for affection. And even *I* couldn't deny that some small part of me had always dreamed about being with Carter again. Completely sober this time so I could remember every single detail. I was embarrassed to admit that he had always been the star in my spank bank reel. Except it was always made-up things since not much about our first encounter could be used as masturbation material aside from the kisses and how hot he looked. I had real life facts to use now. His lips had been soft and warm on the sensitive skin of my neck. I felt the tip of his tongue sneak out and taste me and I wanted more. His breath against my cheek made my heart speed up and warmth explode between my legs. When his firm hands and strong arms wrapped around me and pulled me up against him, I felt every inch of his body, including how much he wanted me. I had been on a small handful of dates over the years that never went much beyond kissing. None of those men ever made me feel even a tiny bit of what Carter did. I never craved more with any of them; I never daydreamed about what it would be like to feel their lips and tongues moving over every inch of my naked body. What would it be like to be with him without the haze of alcohol? Would he take his time? Would his hands be strong and demanding on my body, or soft and gentle? The beep of a new text message on my phone startled me from my fantasies, and I almost dropped the plate I was holding. I shoved it into the dishwasher and shut the door before walking over to the table and snatching up my cell.

If you're not going 2 call me, @ least do something 2 ease your tension. Take bullet u got @ Jenny's party out for a test drive. Report back 2 me 2morrow.

~ Liz, The Bullet Bitch

I rolled my eyes and deleted her text without responding. Why am I not surprised that Liz just sent me a text ordering me to masturbate? I turned the light off in the kitchen and made my way down the hall to peak in on Gavin. He was sound asleep so I quietly shut his bedroom door and walked across the hall to my own room. After throwing on a tank top to wear to sleep and brushing my teeth, I was curled up in bed staring at the ceiling, thinking about Carter.

And his hands.

And fingers.

And lips.

Fuck!

Shouldn't I be thinking about how I was going to deal with this situation? My one-night-stand shows up after almost five years and he was just as gorgeous as ever and he was making me feel things I had no business feeling. I should be making plans. Driving over to his house so I could apologize for the way this huge bomb was dropped on him. I had nine months to prepare myself for this. He had no time and no one there he trusted or really knew to help him get a grip.

My heart threatened to melt as my brain quickly switched gears and I thought about the look on his face when he finally recognized me. Had he really been looking for me all this time? It just seemed so impossible and far-fetched. But Jesus, the look in his eyes when he realized it was me…it was almost too much. He looked like a dying man that had just been given the reprieve of life. His face lit up and his smile made me weak in the knees.

No, that was his tongue and the hard-on you felt poking you in the hip.

God he smelled amazing. He still smelled like cinnamon and boy. Well, that would be man now wouldn't it? And my-oh-my, what a man. I rubbed my thighs together when I felt that familiar tingle between my legs. Shit, I was never going to fall asleep at this rate. Or make any important decisions. I felt like a live wire about ready to burst into flames. I ran my fingertips over my bottom lip as I remembered the feel of his lips gently brushing back and forth over them. God I wanted him to kiss me so badly right then. I wanted to feel his tongue against mine, and I wanted to see if he still tasted the same as he did all those years ago. I was agitated and now, horny as hell. I knew I needed to take care of this or I'd never get to sleep. I *wanted* to take care of this with thoughts of Carter fresh on my mind, but suddenly, the thought of my own hand bringing me the release I needed didn't sound very thrilling. I wanted it to be his hands touching me, his fingers sliding through me and pushing me over the edge. My hand just wasn't going to do it for me at this point. I reluctantly glanced over at the black suitcase leaning against my wall and gave it a dirty look.

"God dammit, Liz," I muttered to myself as I angrily flung the covers off of me and stormed over to the suitcase. I pulled open the zipper, reached in and closed my hand around one of the clear plastic, factory sealed bags containing what I needed. As soon as it was in hand, I paused and looked around the room to make sure no one had seen me. You know, just in case I suddenly lived with ten people who might be standing in my room watching me without my knowledge. I huffed in frustration, crawled back into bed and leaned against the headboard. I was an independent, twenty-four-year-old grown-ass woman. Why the hell was I so freaked out about using a vibrator? This was the twenty-first century for Christ sakes. My grandma probably owned one of these things.

*Uuuughhh, *gag*. I just threw up in my mouth a little. Note to self: thinking about masturbating grandmas is not, I repeat NOT on the list of approved spank bank material.*

Determined to do this thing before I had any more disgusting thoughts about relatives that may or may not own a battery operated boyfriend, I tore open the plastic with my teeth and dumped the contents of the package onto my lap. I picked up the blue, oval, plastic remote, letting the twelve inches or so of thin cord that was attached to the remote unfold until a small, silver cylinder was dangling from the end in front of my eyes like a pendulum, slowly swaying back and forth.

You're getting very horny. I'm going to count backwards and when I get to one, you will be a satisfied woman.

I rolled my eyes and scooted my body down until I was lying flat on my back. Setting the remote down by my hip, I stared at the little silver peanut of pleasure. I had a moment of panic trying to figure out if I really believed in ghosts and if I did, were they watching me right now? Was Mr. Phillips, the dirty old man who lived across the street when I was little and died of a heart-attack when I was twelve, standing in the corner waiting for me to diddle myself? Was my great-grandma Rebecca standing there waiting to yell at me and tell me I was going in time out if I couldn't keep it down?

Son of a bitch!

"You better be worth all this self-doubt, my little friend," I threatened the battery operated toy.

I shook my head at my stupidity for talking out loud to a vibrator, closed my eyes and flicked the damn thing on with my free hand that was still resting on the remote before I lost my nerve.

That thing may be little, but it had a kick. It jerked alive in my hand and if there weren't any ghosts in my room before, the whirring sound of this thing was sure to wake those fuckers up from the dead and bring them right to the source of the noise to see what the ruckus was.

I flew under the covers, dragging the bullet with me and hugging it tight against my stomach in an effort to muffle the noise. When you were little and you were afraid of the boogey man, getting under the covers meant he couldn't see you or grab your foot while you were sleeping. True story. I figured the same rules applied with dead people watching you masturbate. Under the covers means it wasn't really happening. You can't see me! My sheets are magic and they make my vagina disappear!

Oddly, the vibrations of this thing against my stomach felt good. Sort of like a massage that lulled some calm into me. Calm is good. I need calm. I took a deep breath, relaxed into the mattress and closed my eyes once again, conjuring up images of Carter from this morning—Carter's eyes, Carter's mouth, Carter's wet, warm tongue dipping between my breasts.

Okay, that didn't happen. But this was a diddling daydream and I could make daydream-Carter lick me if I wanted to. And I wanted to. I wanted him to lick and suck on my neck. I wanted him to lick and suck on my nipples. I wanted him to lick and suck a trail down my stomach and sink his mouth between my legs. My hand holding the bullet followed the same path Carter's mouth did in my mind, until the tiny vibrating tube rested right outside of my underwear.

Whoa. Okay, this is good.

I pushed the bullet a little harder against myself and my hips jerked forward as tiny pin-pricks of pleasure shot through me.

"Jesus, God…." I mumbled, along with a few other incoherent words of shock and awe.

My hips rocked against the vibrator and I let out a small, whimpered moan at how good this felt. This was insane. I was not going to last more than a minute with this thing. I could feel the wetness in my underwear and the throbbing all through my sex and suddenly I wanted more than anything to feel the cold, smooth metallic toy directly against my bare skin. Faster than I've ever moved, I slid the bullet away and up to my stomach and pushed it and my hand beneath my underwear, quickly shoving it back where it belonged. As soon as the vibrations and the smooth metal came in direct contact with the bareness between my legs, a loud moan escaped from my lips, my head flew back and my eyes squeezed shut. With this thing pulsating between my legs, I didn't really need images of Carter, but I still wanted them. I pictured his smooth fingers pushing into me, his lips pulling my nipple into his mouth and his thumb rubbing circles around the very sensitive area the bullet currently touched. The sensations were almost too much and I cried out in surprise, arching my back as the first wave of an orgasm rocked through my core while I rubbed the bullet quickly against me.

"Holy hell," I moaned as I rode wave after wave of pleasure that made my toes curl. I was panting from my release and the energy slowly drained out of me but my hands still slid the bullet through my wetness and rubbed it quickly against my overly sensitive clit out of their own accord. Before I could even form a coherent thought, another orgasm, slightly less intense than the first, pulsed through me and put a stop to all of my movements. My mouth was open but no sound came out as I held my breath and felt the intense throb of my release pound through me. Several minutes passed before my brain started to function again. I yanked the bullet out of my underwear before I had a chance to and turn into one of those crazy nut jobs on the show "My Strange Addiction" who locked herself in her room and did nothing but masturbate and watch the Food Network all day. I quickly shut the vibrator off, the sudden lack of a buzzing sound making the room seem eerily quiet all of a sudden.

I laid there like a slug in the bed, unable to lift any of my limbs for several minutes while my eyelids drooped with fatigue. When I finally recovered the use of my arms, I reached over to the nightstand without sitting up, grabbed my cell phone and started a new text.

Bullet Bitch: Homework assignment completed. My vagina will never be the same. ~ Claire

A knock on the door shook me from my thoughts. Okay, maybe not thoughts, catatonic state might have been more accurate. I'd done nothing but go to work and stare at the empty walls in my house for two days since Claire dropped the bomb on me. I shuffled morosely over to the door and threw it open. Drew stood there wearing a black shirt that said "Alice in Chains" with a picture of Alice from the Brady Bunch wearing a ball gag, handcuffs and chains. He smiled and held up a six-pack of beer.

"Sober man enters, drunk man leaves."

I shut the door in his face and walked back over to my spot on the couch.

He reopened the door himself and walked in.

"Alright, Mary, there's no need to act like a baby," he said as he set the beer on the coffee table and flopped down on the couch next to me. My nose curled up in disgust at the smell coming from him.

"Jesus, Drew, what the fuck is that smell?" I moaned as I covered my nose with my hand.

"Don't be a hater. I picked it up today. It's Tim McGraw's cologne."

"You mean it's Tim McGraw's balls. That smells like pure cat piss dude."

"Fuck you," Drew grumbled.

"No thanks. The smell of piss does nothing for me."

Drew huffed and crossed his arms over his chest and stared me down.

"Alright, out with it. Before I run to the store and buy you Midol and tampons."

My head fell to the back of the couch. I knew I was being a little bitch but I couldn't help it. My world just blew up in my face.

"She has a kid. I'm somebody's dad," I muttered.

"Yeah, I got that already from the voicemail you left me last night. Although, I have to say, trying to decipher 'Bruce Willis got her pregnant with my chocolate hairy balls at the frat party' took some time to figure out. Luckily, I was able to get a hold of Jim and Liz since you wouldn't answer my calls."

"What the hell am I going to do?" I asked him as I lifted my head up to look at him.

"First of all, you're going to talk to her and get the whole story. I know you're in shock but sitting around here all day fingering your vagina isn't going to make anything better. So man-up. Go talk to her.

You spent all these years trying to find her and here she is, right in front of you. So she's got a little baggage. Who doesn't?"

"A little baggage? Drew, she has a son. That's more than a little baggage," I complained.

"Wake up and look in the mirror baby-daddy. He's your son too. And you spent the last few years trying to fuck her out of your system with some chick you could barely stand. That's not just baggage, that's luggage, bags, suitcases, carry-ons, back-packs and Clinique make-up bags."

I gave him a questioning look.

"What? I like to moisturize. Healthy skin is the sign of a healthy life. I need a make-up bag for my exfoliators, pore cleansers and firming skin lotion."

Drew stood up and turned to face me.

"In the words of the great Maury Povich, You ARE the father."

I thanked him for the beers and the pep talk and watched him leave for his date with Jenny. Not a surprise there, considering the way he almost humped her leg at dinner the night they met. According to Drew, they'd spent every waking moment together since then. People were going out, falling in love, living their lives and I was stuck here with my head up my ass Googling litigations against condom companies and realizing that I CAN'T HANDLE THE TRUTH.

Could I do this? Could I really be someone's dad?

I guess there was only one way to find out.

12.

P.O.R.N.

THE NEXT WEEK flew by pretty quickly when I wasn't thinking about Carter, which was practically every second of every day.

Okay, so I guess it didn't really fly so much as go so fucking slowly I wanted to shove a rusty fork in my eye. I wanted to talk to him and see if he was okay but every time I decided to pick up the phone and get his number, I put it right back down. Regardless of how shitty the way he found out was, now he knew. If he wanted to know the whole story, if he had questions or concerns or just wanted to bite my head off, the ball was in his court. He knew where I worked, and he knew how to find me if he wanted to talk. Maybe I was being stubborn, but oh well. I was a girl and it was my right to stomp my foot and hold my breath.

I handled two parties for Liz this week and got three orders for cookie trays from the women there so things were looking up in that regard. Aside from the parties, I was keeping fairly busy. During the day, I baked and finished getting things ready at the shop and in the evenings, I bartended and tried not to stare at the door every time someone walked in, hoping it was Carter.

By Thursday I had tested out every single product from Liz's magic suitcase and decided to hell with men. I was going to marry the Jack Rabbit. We were going to run away together and would be very happy making little tiny Jack Rabbit babies together. That thing was going to have to grow some arms and legs though. After a few years of being married to JR, I was not going to be able to walk anymore. JR would have to carry me to Pleasure Town.

I spent all day Thursday in the kitchen at the shop making white chocolate covered potato chips and baking Snickers Surprise cookies for the party I was doing Saturday night. It would be the last party I would do since the shop was opening next week. Now that I knew what all the fuss was about with these sex toys, I was a little sad to see the parties go. Liz told me I could keep my suitcase of fun though.

I made her sign a waiver that stated that in the event of an emergency or the death of Claire Donna Morgan, she was required to remove the suitcase from the premises within fifteen minutes of said emergency and/or death. It was always a good idea to have a plan like this in place. God forbid your dad or your grandmother got to the scene first and found your stash. You just couldn't allow that to happen. It's also probably a good idea to have them delete your internet history. No one really needs to wonder why you Googled "turtle having orgasm" or were closely watching an EBay auction of a Jesus candle with a penis.

Don't judge me. Google is my enemy after a few glasses of wine.

I was under similar contractual obligations to get to Liz and Jim's house and erase the web history on their computer within fifteen minutes and dispose of any and all pornographic movies in their nightstand, under their bed, on the top shelf of their closet, saved on their DVR, packed in the third box from the left in the garage and in the cupboard in the kitchen where the cutting boards are.

I'm not kidding. She made me a list.

As I dipped a potato chip into the big silver bowl of melted white chocolate, I looked out to the front of the store and smiled. Gavin was lying on his stomach by the windows coloring a picture. When I walked out there a little while ago, he covered it up and told me I wasn't allowed to see it. I held the chip above the bowl to let the excess chocolate drip off and then set it down on the sheet of wax paper next to me just as I heard the door connecting mine and Liz's store open.

"You can just turn right back around and go back to your side. For the last time, I am not going to tell you on a scale of one to 'holy shit' how good my orgasm was last night with the butterfly vibrator."

"Well that sucks. Can I at least watch next time?"

My head jerked up and my mouth hung open at the sound of Carters baritone voice.

Why the fuck am I always talking out of my ass around him? And why the hell is he standing there looking so God dammed hot that I want to mount his face.

"Um, you're dripping," he said.

"I know," I muttered, staring at his lips.

He laughed and I blinked myself back to reality as he pointed at the bowl.

"I meant the bowl is tipped. The chocolate is dripping out."

My head flew down and I muttered profanities as I righted the bowl and used my fingers to wipe the drips off of the lip of the bowl and the counter.

Carter walked over to stand next to me and just like our last few encounters, his close proximity forced my pulse into overdrive.

"I'm sorry I snuck up on you like that. Liz caught me as I was getting out of my car and dragged me into her side so she could hand me my ass," he explained as I concentrated on wiping up the chocolate and tried to ignore the heat from his body. "I hope you don't mind me dropping by like this. I feel like such a dick that it's taken me this long to talk to you"

I stood there like an idiot, trying not to touch anything since my fingers were full of chocolate. I turned my head to the side and found his face inches from my own. I saw the sincerity in his eyes, and I knew I could never be mad at him about this.

"It's okay, believe me. I've had a lot of time to get used to the idea. I'm sorry that it was sprung on you like that out of the blue. I swear that I fully intended to tell you. I don't want you to think I intentionally kept this from you. I planned on telling you from the start. I was just trying to figure out how. And then it all blew up before I could do anything about it," I explained.

I realized right then that I didn't want him to be mad at me. I wanted more than anything for him to be able to handle this and to stick around. Spending the last week going to bed without hearing his voice was sad and depressing. Having him here right now made me realize just how much I missed him.

"We have a lot of things to talk about I guess. You have no idea how many questions are swirling around in my head right now," he said.

I nodded my head and before I could say anything, he changed the subject.

"But for right now, I am in a kitchen with a beautiful woman who has melted chocolate all over her fingers," he said with a smirk.

Before I could grab a towel, he reached over and wrapped his hand around one of my wrists and pulled my hand towards him. I held my breath as he opened his mouth and slid my chocolate coated index finger into his mouth. The pad of my finger slid along the roughness of his tongue as he sucked all of the chocolate off while he slowly pulled my finger back out through his warm, wet lips.

Check please!

"Mommy, I finished coloring my picture!"

The excited yell and pounding footsteps of Gavin as he barreled into the kitchen doused a bucket of cold water all over my vagina. For once, I was glad I had a built-in cock-blocker in the form of a four-year-old. I was one more finger suck away from dropping Carter down on the floor and showing him that I was quite bendy.

Quickly wiping my hands on the apron I wore, I turned away from Carter and bent down to my son's level.

"Can I see your picture now?"

Gavin held it tight to his chest and shook his head no.

"Sorry, Mommy. I maded this picture for the little maggot," he said earnestly.

I heard Carter laugh behind me.

"Um, did you say 'little maggot'?" I asked.

"Yup," he said, popping the 'p'.

"Do I even want to know who you're talking about?"

Gavin pointed behind me to Carter.

"Him. Papa called him dat the day we met him."

I groaned in embarrassment. One of these days my father was going to have to realize that Gavin is a parrot.

"I don't like your name. It's weird. And you don't look so little to me," Gavin said to Carter. "But I still drewed you a picture."

He reached around me and handed the paper to Carter. I took a quick glance at it and realized it was a picture of a big stick figure being punched in the junk by a little stick figure.

"Well, at least now I have a photo to commemorate our first meeting," Carter deadpanned quietly.

"Gavin, how about you just call him Carter," I said, looking to Carter with my eyebrows raised in question to make sure he was okay with that.

He nodded his head at me and smiled, then squatted down so we were both eye-level with Gavin.

"Thank you very much for my picture," he said with a smile.

Gavin wasn't big on strangers, mostly because I put the fear of God into him when we had the discussion about stranger-danger. In hind sight, telling him all strangers wanted to eat him wasn't my finest hour. Having to explain to a bunch of crying children in line to see Santa why my kid was screaming "DON'T GO NEAR HIM! HE'LL EAT YOUR FINGERS!" was no picnic. Liz had to talk me out of taking him to the vet and getting a GPS chip put in his neck. Something told me though that anyone who took my kid would bring him back within the hour. They wouldn't be able to take the kicks to the nuts and the cursing.

Gavin didn't usually talk to strangers unless I prompted him to do so. The ease with which he talked to Carter surprised me.

"You're welcome, Carter. My papa is coming to get me so Mommy can give beer to people. Papa lets me watch movies that Mommy don't let me watch and I get to have pop and I wanna get a dog but my friend Luke has a jeep that he rides in the yard and I hurted my knee and it got cut and Mommy put a band-aid on it and told me to 'shake it off' so I wouldn't cry and did you know vampires suck?"

"Gavin!" my dad bellowed before I got a chance to.

He had walked into the store during Gavin's run-on-sentence and was almost to the kitchen when he heard him drop that bomb. I quickly stood up and faced him with my hands on my hips.

"Dad, I told you he wasn't allowed to watch that movie."

"Hey, Carter, I'm team Jacob, bitch!" Gavin yelled.

"Gavin Allen! Do you want me to put soap in your mouth?" I asked him sternly.

Gavin shrugged. "Soap tastes like Fruity Pebbles."

My dad came around the counter and picked up Gavin before I could punt him like a football.

"Sorry, Claire, 'Vampires Suck' was on cable the other night and there was nothing else on. You'll be happy to know that he covered his eyes during the s-e-x stuff," he explained.

"Super," I muttered.

"I saw boobs!" Gavin yelled happily.

"Okay, he may have peeked a few times," my dad admitted after Gavin's announcement.

Of all the times for Gavin to act completely like...well, Gavin, of course it had to be when Carter showed up. No wonder he hadn't said a peep in the last few minutes. He was probably stunned stupid.

I glanced behind me and saw Carter standing completely still, staring over my shoulder at my dad. I turned back around in time to catch my dad doing the whole two-finger eye-point to Carter that Gavin and Liz did the other day.

Oh for fuck's sake. It's like we suddenly have a family salute.

"Dad, quit it. Carter, you haven't been formally introduced. This is my dad, George."

Carter stuck his hand out towards him, "It's a pleasure to..."

"Cut the s-h-i-t," my dad cut him off."

Somehow he didn't sound as threatening when he had to spell everything. This could work as long as Gavin was here as a buffer.

"I've got my eye on you. I was in Nam and still have shrapnel in my skin from the b-o-m-b-s. You like the smell of napalm in the morning son?"

"DAD! Enough!" I scolded.

I leaned over and gave Gavin a kiss on the cheek.

"I'll see you later, baby. You be good for Papa okay?"

He slyly reached over and tried to pull the front of my shirt down.

"Lemme see your boobs."

I grabbed his hand before he could give everyone a peep show and shot a dirty look to my dad who was just standing there laughing.

"Hey, I did *not* teach him that. He must be a boob man."

Carter laughed but quickly stopped when my dad looked over at him.

"Are you a boob man Carter?" he asked menacingly.

"I…well…um…I…don't."

I rolled my eyes at my dad and rescued Carter from him.

"Say goodbye to Carter," I told Gavin.

"Bye, Carter!" Gavin said with a smile and a wave as my dad turned and headed out of the kitchen.

"Papa, what's Nam? Is it a park? Can we go there?" I heard Gavin ask as they walked out the front door. With a big sigh I turned to face Carter.

"Sorry about that," I said sheepishly. "I will completely understand if you turn around right now and run far, far away. Really, I won't hold it against you."

"Claire?"

I stopped fidgeting with my apron and finally looked up at him.

"Shut up," he said with a smile.

AFTER MY DAD and Gavin left, Carter helped me clean up the kitchen and put everything away. We talked more in depth than we had on the phone now that I wasn't so worried about slipping up. I finally found out that Carter was crashing the frat party that night and didn't even go to The University of Ohio. He felt awful about all the time I spent with Liz and Jim trying to find him, and I felt guilty all over again about leaving him that morning. Especially right now, when he was being so nice and amazingly understanding about everything.

For the time being, Carter was sticking around. I wasn't going to hold my breath though. He said he wanted to spend time with us and do this the right way, but he also hasn't spent time alone with Gavin yet.

As Gavin so nicely put it, I had to give beer to people tonight, so after we finished cleaning Carter walked me down the street to the bar so we could continue talking. I remembered how easy it was to talk to him five years ago and how he seemed to get me and my humor when no one else did. He made me feel comfortable and he made me laugh. All of those things happened when we talked on the phone but sometimes it was harder to duplicate that level of comfort when you were face to face. In all honesty, it almost seemed easier to be with him like this, to be able to gauge his face for reactions to things I said and to see his expressions when I told him something about Gavin. It made me wish I'd done so many things differently. I was sad that he had missed out on the beginning of Gavin's life. He saw him now as a walking, talking, mouthy little boy, but he didn't get to experience the best parts, the parts that made his attitude and temper tantrums and bad habits all worth while-the first smile, the first words, the first steps, the first bear hug, and the first, "I love you."

Those were all the things that kept me from selling my child at a garage sale on a daily basis, and Carter didn't have those things. It worried me that his expectations might be too high. What if he just couldn't form a connection with Gavin? I felt connected to Carter in a way I never had with anyone else. He made me feel things I'd only dreamed about. But I didn't have just myself to consider anymore. I had to think about my son and how all of this was going to affect him.

For now, I suppose I needed to just let Carter into our lives and see where it took us.

When we got to the bar, I changed quickly into my black shorts and Fosters Bar and Grill t-shirt and was surprised to see Carter making himself comfortable at the bar when I came out of the bathroom.

I got behind the counter and walked over to stand in front of him.

"I thought you were going home," I said as I leaned onto my elbows.

He shrugged at me and smiled. "I figured, why go home to an empty house when I can sit here and stare at a hot chick all night."

I felt myself blushing and tried to suppress the giddy smile I felt coming on.

"Well, you're outta luck. It's just me here tonight."

No, I am absolutely not fishing for compliments.

"Then I guess it's a good thing that you are the hottest, sexiest woman I have ever seen."

Here, fishy, fishy, fishy.

I leaned over the bar a little to bring myself closer to him and he did the same. I didn't care if I was at work, I wanted to kiss him. And there were hardly any people here right now anyway. It was still early.

I licked my lips as I stared at his mouth and I heard him groan quietly. One more inch and I could run my tongue across his top lip.

"OUCH!"

I jerked away from Carter and yelled when something smacked against the back of my head.

Rubbing my hand against the spot, I turned around to see T.J. with both his arms in the air doing a victory dance.

"Direct hit, Morgan! That's another point for me!" he yelled as he ran over to the chalkboard behind the bar at the opposite end from me and put a tally mark under his name.

"Son of a bitch," I muttered as I turned back around to Carter.

"Um, what the hell was that about?" he asked with a laugh.

Before I could tell him it was just T.J. being a dick, the man in question ran up and stood next to me behind the bar. He slapped a ping pong ball down on the top right in front of Carter.

"That, my man, is a little something we like to call P.O.R.N."

"Wow, your idea of porn and mine are slightly different," Carter said as he picked up the ping pong ball and rolled it around in his hands.

"No, no, no. Not porn. P.O.R.N.," T.J. spelled out.

Carter looked completely lost.

"It's just this little game we play when it's slow in here," I said.

T.J. rested one hand on the bar and the other on his hip.

"Claire, don't underestimate the awesomeness that is P.O.R.N. You are completely devaluing the one thing that makes me not want to kill myself every time I come to work. A little more respect for P.O.R.N. please."

T.J. turned his attention to Carter. "Claire made up the rules," T.J. said excitedly as he pulled a piece of paper out from under the bar.

"Rules?" Carter questioned. "Don't you just throw the ball at someone?"

T.J. pushed the paper across the top of the bar and Carter picked it up to read through it.

"Au contraire my friend. There always need to be rules in P.O.R.N. Otherwise, he'll throw a ball, she'll throw a ball, they'll all throw a ball…it'll be anarchy."

"Alright there, Breakfast Club, walk away before I break the ten-foot distance rule and chuck one at your face," I told him.

T.J. walked away and Carter laughed as he read the rules out loud.

"Rule number one: P.O.R.N. is more fun with friends, invite them. Otherwise, you just look pitiful engaging in P.O.R.N. alone. Rule number two: Sharp objects should never be used in P.O.R.N. Poking someone's eye out will ruin the moment. Rule number three: Sneak attacks or 'back door action' must come with advanced warnings or have prior approval. Rule number four: Only two balls allowed in play at all times to avoid ball-confusion, unless approved by the judges. Rule number five: P.O.R.N. is over when the other player(s) say it's over. Otherwise, someone is left holding useless balls."

Yes, sometimes I act like a twelve-year-old boy. Don't judge me.

"So what exactly does P.O.R.N. stand for and how do I get in on this action?" Carter asked with wag of his eyebrows.

"Well, the official title is Pong Organization Rules and Notices. But sometimes we shorten it to 'throwing shit at each other.' Frankly, I'm not sure you can handle P.O.R.N., Carter. It's an intense game of skill, determination and craftiness," I explained with a grin as I took the ball from his hand, turned quickly and whipped it across the bar to hit T.J. square in the ass as he was wiping down one of the tables.

"MOTHER FUCK!" T.J. yelled.

"It's all about being talented with your hands really," I said as I turned back around to face Carter.

I have absolutely no idea where this boldness shit was coming from. I felt like I was channeling Liz.

"Don't worry, Claire, I'm pretty good with my hands. I have a feeling I'd be *excellent* at P.O.R.N. It's all about how you angle your fingers and the stroke you use…when throwing the ball. Sometimes you have to do it slow and gentle, and other times you have to do it hard and fast."

Sweet baby innuendos, Batman.

"What time do you get off?"

In about ten seconds.

"Not until one. I have to close by myself tonight," I told him while I squeezed my thighs together and thought about his fingers stroking and pushing and hard and fast and gentle and…fuck!

"Can I just wait here while you work? I can help you close up and we can talk…or whatever," he said as he stared at my lips.

YES! Holy shitballs mother of YES! Yes, yes, fuck yes!

"Yeah, whatever," I said with a shrug as I walked away to stock the beer cooler and stick my vagina in there to cool it down.

13.

Quivering Loins

FOR THE NEXT couple of hours I stared at Claire's ass – er, I mean watched her work and chatted with her when she had a few seconds.

I also became a proud member of Team P.O.R.N. when I managed to throw a ping pong ball that ricocheted off of T.J.'s head and hit Claire in the tits. There was talk of making me the team captain after that one. Claire told me I really knew how to handle my balls, and I started to wonder if I was turning more than a little pervy by the fact that it turned me on whenever she said "balls."

I wonder what it would take to get her to say "cock?"

T.J. walked by just then, untying his apron and stowing it under the bar. I probably should have felt a little jealous at the fact that he was a good looking guy and he got to be in close proximity to Claire all the time, but watching them interact just made me laugh. They were like brother and sister with the way the shoved each other, threw insults back and forth and tattled to anyone who would listen. As a result, I decided I liked T.J. and I didn't have to kill him.

"Hey, T.J., do me a favor. Get Claire to say 'cock' and I'll give you twenty bucks."

"Deal," he said automatically before turning away from me.

All of the patrons were gone and Claire had just switched on the "closed" sign and was in the process of walking back from the front door.

"Hey, Claire, remember that one guy who came in here a few months ago, smacked your ass and called you Cutie Claire? What was it you called him?"

"A cocksucker," she replied distractedly as she got back behind the bar and began organizing bottles.

With a dreamy smile on my face, I slid a twenty across the bar to T.J. and he walked away. This was going to be a beautiful friendship. If he could get her to say, "Fuck me hard Carter," I might buy him a pony.

T.J. said good-bye and walked out the door while Claire finished straightening up. After a few minutes, she came around the corner of the bar and sat down next to me on a stool.

"You look exhausted," I told her as she rested her chin in her hand and let out a sigh.

"Is that a nice way of telling me I look like shit?" she teased.

"Absolutely not. If you looked like shit, I'd tell you. I would also tell you if the jeans you're wearing make your ass look big, if something you cooked tasted like it came from the bottom of my shoe or if a joke you told was not funny at all."

"Wow, that's very kind of you," she said with a laugh.

"It's what I do."

We sat there for several minutes just looking at each other. None of this seemed real yet. I couldn't believe she was sitting here in front of me. I couldn't believe she was still so remarkable and funny and beautiful and I couldn't believe she had a child, *my* child.

"You kind of amaze me, you know that?" I said, breaking the silence.

I watched the blush brighten up her cheeks and she looked away, her gaze locked on a drink napkin that she started to shred.

"I'm not that great, believe me."

I shook my head in disbelief at how she clearly didn't see herself very well.

"Are you kidding me? You hooked up with a total loser one night at a frat party, got pregnant, had to give up your dreams and quit school, worked your ass off and raised an awesome little boy and now you're opening your own business. If that's not amazing, I don't know what is."

She continued to rip up the napkin at an even faster pace while I continued.

"You're strong and confident and beautiful and you make everything look so damn easy. I am so grateful to have met you again. I will be forever in your debt for taking care of…of our son. You've done such an amazing job with him and you're so selfless that I am just in awe."

Whew, I said it. *My son.* Gavin is my son. Oddly, it didn't make me want to hurl myself on a rusty nail.

She still wasn't looking at me, though, and it was starting to make me nervous. And I felt really bad for the drink napkin that now resembled a small pile of snow. I reached over and placed my hand on top of hers to make her stop fidgeting with the mess.

"Hey, what's wrong?" I asked.

She finally turned her face towards mine and I'm not gonna lie, it really freaked me out to see tears in her eyes. I didn't do crying. At all. If she asked me to set myself on fire right now I would do it just so I wouldn't have to see her cry.

"Gavin is wonderful. He is smart and perfect, he's funny and he's the best little boy in the world. He has his moments but he's very well-behaved and just perfect. Perfect! Every single person who meets him adores him and I love every second of being his mom….," she trailed off.

I knew she was sugar-coating things. If she said the word "perfect" one more time I was going to start crying myself. I didn't want the watered-down version. I wanted to know it all, everything I missed. The good, the bad and the ugly. Her foot was tapping nervously on the rung of the bar stool, and she looked like she was about to explode. I knew with everything going on right now she had to be under a lot of stress. She was a single mom with a lot on her plate and I knew for a fact

Gavin wasn't flawless. What kid was? But she definitely wanted me to think so. Was she really afraid I would change my mind if I knew the horrors of being a parent? I'd always wanted to have kids someday. It was one of the biggest issues between me and Tasha. I knew it wasn't all rainbows and kittens. I knew it could suck the life out of you and make you second-guess your sanity.

"It's okay if you want to complain. I can only imagine how tough it is for you."

"I love Gavin," she repeated with conviction.

I chuckled a little at how panicked she looked.

"No one is questioning that. But you don't have to act like you have everything under control a hundred percent of the time. I'm not going to think less of you *or* Gavin if you need to vent, believe me. I want to know everything. I wasn't lying when I said that to you earlier."

She was softening a little. The napkin was finally free from her abuse and her foot wasn't tapping manically anymore. She still looked at me warily, though. I knew one way I could get her to calm down and open up. I stood up and leaned over the top of the bar, reaching my arms as far as I could, and wrapped my hand around what I needed.

I sat back down, grabbed a clean shot glass that rested upside down on the bar and filled it with Three Olive Grape Vodka, which I now knew to be her favorite. I set the bottle back down on the bar and slid it out of the way.

"Be honest," I said as I pushed the shot glass in front of her.

She bit her lip, looked down at the shot glass and then back at me. She was like an open book and I could see all of the conflicting emotions as they ran across her face until she finally let go.

"IloveGavintodeathbuthedrivesmefuckingcrazy!" she said as fast as she could and snapped her mouth shut immediately.

"Take a shot," I told her, nodding at the shot glass in encouragement.

Without hesitating, she picked up the glass and tipped it back, slamming it down onto the bar when she was done.

"Keep going," I told her as I leaned closer to her and poured more vodka into the shot glass.

"The first time he said, 'Mommy,' my heart completely melted. But that kid never shuts up. Ever. He even talks in his sleep. One time when we were driving he was going on and on about sheep and french fries and his wiener and the lawn mower, I stopped the car in the middle of the street and got out. After I walked around the car and then got back in, he was still talking, asking me if lawn mowers have wieners. He never. Stops. Talking."

"Take a shot," I said again with a smile.

She downed it, slamming the glass in front of me this time so I could refill it. I did, pushing it back towards her.

"I gained fifty-six pounds when I was pregnant with him. Do you have any idea what it's like to look down and not be able to see your vagina?"

"Uh, no," I muttered.

"My ass had its own zip code."

"If it makes you feel better, it is an awesome ass," I told her honestly.

"Thank you."

I poured her another and didn't even need to prompt her to drink it.

"His hugs are a magical cure for everything. But do you have any idea how much a baby shits and pukes and cries? He projectile vomited every bottle he drank. Drink, burp, spew. Lather, rinse, repeat."

Down went the shot.

"He didn't sleep through the night until he was three and a half years old. I got so fed up I told him Shasta the Sleep Monster lived under his bed and would bite his feet if he got out of it in the middle of the night for anything other than the house being on fire."

She tipped her head back and finished another shot.

"I can't believe you don't hate me right now," she said.

"Why would I ever hate you?"

"Because I basically used you for sex and then never spoke to you again," she explained.

"Honey, where I come from, that's like Christmas to a guy," I said with a laugh, trying to lighten her mood. "I should be the one apologizing to you." I reached out with my hand and turned her face towards me.

God she was so beautiful. And I was a complete dick for wanting to take advantage of her being a little tipsy. But fuck, I needed to kiss her. I waited five years to taste her again. She tilted her head so that she could rub her cheek against the palm of my hand, and I almost forgot what I had been trying to say to her.

"Granted, we were both pretty out of it that night, but if I would have ever known that you had never…that you…that I was your first, I would have done things a hell of a lot differently," I admitted.

Like stare at your naked body and memorize every inch of it, swirl my tongue around your nipples and suck them into my mouth until you moaned my name. I'd taste your skin and burry my face between your legs and make you come so hard you'd forget your name.

"Holy fuck," she whispered with a glazed look in her eyes.

I just said all of that out loud didn't I?

She sat there staring at me with her mouth open, and I worried that I royally fucked up. It was too soon for me to talk about her vagina and how much I wanted to become BFF's with it. Sure, I spent the past five years glorifying every single thing I could remember about her, and I worried over the past week that maybe my memories were better than reality, but that was just stupid. She was just as amazing sitting here in front of me as she was in my dreams, and I needed her to know that. I opened my mouth but before I could get the words out, she jumped down off of the stool, mumbling something about stocking beer in the cooler in the back. She brushed past me and I was left sitting on my stool with a bottle of vodka and the smell of chocolate lingering in the air.

OH MY GOD. Oh holy fucking shit.

I was such a fucking coward. I ran away from him as fast as I could and now I was in the storage room pretending to stock beer.

I'd taste your skin and burry my face between your legs and make you come so hard you'd forget your name.

Jesus Christ on a cracker. I had no experience with this shit. I wanted to hump his leg as soon as those words left his mouth. He clearly didn't mean to say them out loud going by the shocked expression on his face.

"Shit!" I muttered loudly, punching an empty case of beer.

Except it wasn't empty and my fist connected with full cans of beer.

"Son of a bitchfuck!" I cursed while I shook my bruised hand, kicking my foot out and connecting with a bottle of tequila that went rolling across the floor.

"I hope this alcohol abuse isn't because of something I said."

I turned around to find Carter lounging against the door frame. Why does he always have to witness my mortifying stupidity?

"I mean really, what has that bottle of tequila ever done to you?" he asked as he started to walk towards me.

"You mean aside from impairing my judgment so that I lost my virginity to some really hot guy I met at a frat party, got knocked-up and never got the guy's name because I am a complete and total bitch and now that he's here I feel like I am so out of my league whenever he's around because I have zero experience with this shit?" I rambled.

Carter stopped right in front of me and gave me a crooked grin.

"You think I'm hot?"

I rolled my eyes at his attempt to lighten the mood and completely gloss over my nervous admission.

"You know, you're absolutely right. That tequila is a real asshole. Go ahead and kick the shit out of it. You might as well finish off the beer, too. I saw him looking at you funny."

I laughed at the ridiculousness of this conversation. I wasn't drunk but I was pleasantly buzzed enough from our earlier game of Truth or Truth to be able to see the humor in this situation. When I stopped laughing, he reached out and brushed a piece of hair off of my cheek that had escaped my pony tail and it reminded me so much of the night we met that I let out a small sigh.

"Let's get something straight here. You are not a bitch. I don't blame you for anything that you did. I'm not going to lie and say that it didn't totally suck ass to wake up the next morning and not have you there with me and then spend five years wondering if I had imagined you. But I would never think you were a bitch for doing what you did," he said as he inched closer. "I wasn't lying before when I said I would have done things very different with you that night," he said softly as he moved so close to me that our chest and thighs were touching. I swallowed roughly as he brought his hand up and rested it on my hip.

"I would have kissed you more," he said, leaning in and placing a soft kiss on the corner of my mouth.

"I would have held your body up against mine longer so I could feel every inch of you," he whispered against my cheek as he wrapped his other arm around my waist and pulled me up tighter against him.

His hand that rested on my hip slid up the side of my body. It grazed up my ribs and brushed against the side of my breast until his palm was flat over my heart.

"I would have touched you everywhere and took the time to feel your heart beat against my hand."

I licked my lips and tried to control my breathing. God, I loved the way he smelled, the way he spoke and his hands on me. How had I lived so long without these things?

"Most of all, I would never have taken even one sip of alcohol that night so that every single moment with you would have been etched into my brain and the memory of how your skin felt against my hands would be clear as a bell."

I was certain he could hear the pounding of my heart echoing through the room. I knew he could feel how fast it was beating with each word he spoke.

"Fuck, Claire," he muttered. "Just being close to you drives me crazy."

He bent his knees slightly and then pushed up against me so I could feel exactly what he was talking about. Both my hands flew to his shoulders in an effort to hold on and pull him closer. My one leg automatically lifted to wrap around his waist and bring him closer to me. His lips ghosted over my neck, and I was pretty sure I moaned. When he was back by my ear he whispered, "If this is too much, too soon, just tell me to stop and I will."

Was it too soon? Was I acting like a complete slut right now rubbing myself all over him? I was a mother for fuck's sake.

A mother that had never been laid properly and was horny as fuck.

"If you stop, I will straight up murder your ass," I whispered as his lips found their way to mine and connected.

No sooner had our mouths collided when I felt his tongue gently push its way past my lips. I slid my tongue against his, and he moaned into my mouth, pushing his hips into me harder. I was tingling all over like in some cheesy romance novel. My breasts were heaving and my loins were quivering.

I HAD QUIVERING LOINS!

I felt like I was going to explode if he didn't touch me. I wanted him to touch me so much it almost hurt. I am so not good at dirty talk. Just the thought of saying "touch my *ack* pussy" made me want to cringe. I could try "let your fingers do the walking". Or maybe "put your digits in my divot."

Focus Claire!

Oh my God his tongue was like magic. Where the hell did he learn to kiss? I bet his dad taught him.

Wait no. That sounded gross.

Jesus, I was turning into a puddle of goo and so was my underwear.

TOUCH MY VAGINA!

If I screamed it in my head maybe he'd figure it out. His tongue circled mine and his hand went down to my ass to slide me up and down against his hardness.

PUT YOUR HAND ON MY VAG!

My leg slid down his hip and the feel of the rough denim of his jeans against my bare thigh made me whimper. He walked us backwards and pushed me up against the wall of the storage room, deepening the kiss and slowing it down at the same time. My hands were clutching the hair at the back of his neck so hard I think I pulled some out by the roots.

His hand that was palming my ass moved away and I almost yelled in frustration until I felt him slide it around to the front of my thigh and slowly inch it up towards the hem of my shorts.

OH MY GOD HE'S GOING TO TOUCH MY VAGINA!

Did I remember to put on sexy underwear and not period panties? You know what I'm talking about. The ginormous granny panties that you only wore when the crimson tide is flowing. The ones you'd never allow man nor beast to see.

He broke the kiss as his fingers snuck under the leg of my shorts and – Oh thank you sweet baby Jesus and the wise guys, I just remembered I put a Victoria's Secret thong on when I got dressed earlier.

"I know this doesn't make up for the shittiness of that night, but I want to make you feel good, Claire. Can I touch you?" he asked softly against my lips while he looked into my eyes.

Could he not feel my quivering loins and the brain screams?

I need your fingers inside me!

Yep, you guessed it.

"Fuck. That was the hottest thing I have ever heard."

I didn't have time to be mortified that I'd spoken out loud. He was doing what I asked and his hand was sliding all the way under the edge of my shorts until I felt his fingers slide up the front of my underwear.

"Holy fuck," I muttered and jerked my hips into his hand.

No one had ever touched me like this. I thought touch was all the same and brought on the same feelings whether it was a guy or myself fumbling around down there.

Clearly I was mistaken.

Carter's fingers moving up and down ever so slowly against the thin scrap of satin made me want to scream my head off in pleasure.

"I can feel how wet you are," he whispered as his fingers moved to the side and toyed with the edge of my underwear.

Hearing dirty talk from other people always made me blush and feel embarrassed for them and the weird stuff that came out of their mouths. I mean really, can they hear themselves? It's corny and all "fuck me harder big boy" and "oh you're so tight baby". Who says that crap? Obviously I had been missing out on Carter's dirty talk. It was hot. And I didn't want him to stop. He could talk about how tight, wet and fan-fucking-tastic I was all night long. He placed several small kisses to my lips as he took his sweet time working his fingers under the thin scrap of material and used the heal of his hand to push the leg of my shorts open wider to give him better access. I held my breath and tried not to think about the fact that I'd never had a guy touch me like this. That was just sad, really. And even more depressing was the fact that I was feeling sorry for myself when his fingers were getting ready to go for a swim at the Y.

I broke up the pity party when I felt two of his fingers come in contact with my bare, wet skin.

"Oh my God," I mumbled, letting my head fall back against the wall with a thud.

Yep, much better than my own fingers. My own fingers were now going to feel like Sinbad's hands in the movie Houseguest when he gets Novocain all over them and they flop around like dead fish, knocking shit off of the table. His fingers were smooth and soft and holy fuck they were touching me, feeling just how much I wanted this and that Liz forced me get waxed regularly.

Note to self: apologize to Liz for calling her a Sadistic Vagina-Nazi Bitch every time she made a Brazilian wax appointment for me. Because of her dedication to my who-ha, Carter doesn't have to discover a wildebeest in my pants right now and stop what he's doing to go in search of a weed whacker.

He swooped in and placed an open-mouthed kiss on my neck and slowly pushed a finger inside of me, letting his thumb rest against my clit while he gave me time to adjust to what he was doing.

He held his finger perfectly still inside me, and I clutched harder onto the back of his head and pushed my hips forward, making his finger go in deeper and his thumb slide against me.

This was too much and not enough and I felt like this was going to be over long before I wanted it to because the way he moved his fingers was pure genius. And that was just shocking in and of itself. I always needed a full reel of clips from porn movies flipping through my mind in order to finish. I couldn't think about anything but what he was doing to me right now. Naughty Neighbors, MILF Madness – none of those were necessary.

He started pushing and pulling his finger in and out of me slowly and did some glorious maneuver where he curled his finger before he started pulling it out that made me want to pant like a dog and lick the side of his face. His lips and tongue found every inch of my neck and his thumb circled faster until I was rocking my hips into his hand almost forcefully.

I was whimpering and moaning and I didn't have time to be embarrassed that I sounded kind of like a dirty slut or that there was a real live guy who was really touching my vagina because I was really one second away from exploding.

Really.

He pulled his finger out of me and used the pad of two fingers to circle my clit until I completely fell apart against his hand.

"Ohhh, oh, God! Fuck. Carter!"

His fingers didn't stop and he swallowed my cries with his mouth while I pushed against his hand, never wanting this feeling to stop. I made all kinds of noises into his mouth while he continued to kiss me and pull every ounce of my orgasm out of me until my legs were trembling and I could barely stand. When I stopped moving my hips and the last of my release faded away, he pulled his hand out from my shorts and wrapped his arm around me, kissing me slowly, letting his tongue lazily slide against my own. I didn't know how long we stood there in the storage room wrapped in each other's arms kissing. I could have spent hours kissing him and never come up for air.

We finally pulled our mouths apart and stood there staring at each other.

"That was the hottest thing I've ever seen. I should have done that five years ago," Carter said with a smile.

"Baby, if you would have done that five years ago, I would have handcuffed my vagina to your arm and made you do that to me every single day."

Carter laughed and then his face immediately got serious.

"Claire, I need to ask you something. And it's really important."

Oh my God, he was going to ask me to have a threesome. Or tell me he was really from Canada and needed a green card and that's the only reason he was here. Oh shit, what if he didn't like my vagina? Did it feel funny? I should have felt around down there more often. My gyno never complained. In fact, he told me I had a very nice uterus. Why the hell didn't Carter like my vagina? Shit, what if he was into dendrophilia and liked to have sex with trees?

"I'd like to spend some time with Gavin."

I knew he was going to say that.

"It's okay if you don't feel comfortable with me being alone with him just yet since he really doesn't know me. But I'd like to come over and see him."

I couldn't stop the smile that took over my face. Not only did his fingers deserve a major award, like a leg lamp or a national monument erected in his name, (heh, heh, erected!) he actually took the initiative and asked to spend time with Gavin – even after getting punched in the nuts and threatened with the two finger eye-watching signal.

Gavin would finally get to hang around a man other than my father and Jim.

And I'd get to have Carter tiptoe through the twolips again soon.

14.

Captain Narcolepsy

"SO WHAT YOU'RE telling me is, our little Claire's got hardwood floors, terracotta pie, a leather sausage wallet, a who-ha with no hair-ha," Drew yelled over the noise of the assembly line.

"Wow, I am really regretting that I told you anything about last night," I yelled back.

I reached above me for the hydraulic drill attached to the rig in the ceiling and pulled it down to fasten the car door to the body of the vehicle. I had three minutes before the next car came down the line and having to deal with Drew being an ass was going to make me screw everything up and force the line to shut down.

That and the fact that I really couldn't stop thinking about what had happened between Claire and I last night in the back room of the bar. Sweet Jesus she was beautiful when she came. And the little sounds she made…fuck, just thinking about them was making Carter Junior stand up and start begging for her. I hope she didn't think things were going too fast because I really wanted a repeat performance. And I didn't even care about not getting off. Watching her and feeling her come apart in my hands was enough satisfaction for me.

"Dude, you know your secret is safe with me. I will never tell a soul that you got to third base with your baby-mama last night and that Chewbacca does not live in her underwear. At least now I don't have to worry about you."

I turned off the drill and looked across the car at Drew who was attaching the front door handle.

"Why were you worried about me?"

"Aww, bro, come on. You were one step away from lathering chocolate ganache on your dick and trying to give yourself a blow job," he said.

"Did you just say ganache?"

Drew shrugged. "Yeah. Jenny makes me watch the Food Network all the time now. Ever since she started designing the flyers for Claire, she's decided she wants to learn how to cook. She spent twenty minutes the other day looking up a recipe online for frosting made with *confederate* sugar."

Laughter bubbled out of me and I got back to work on the car.

"Did you tell her to try looking in the Deep South for that sugar? You might also want to warn her about the Rebel sugar," I laughed.

"Come on, man. Don't be a dick. I didn't have the heart to tell her it was called convection sugar."

Nope, not going to touch that one.

"So, are you and Jenny going to Claire's tonight?" I asked, changing the subject.

Claire was definitely on board with letting me see Gavin. She figured starting off in a group setting would be the best thing so she invited everyone over to her place tonight for dinner.

"Wouldn't miss it for the world. I even got a new shirt just for the occasion," Drew said with a smile.

AT SIX O'CLOCK I knocked on Claire's door. I heard footsteps pounding against the floor and suddenly the door was flung open.

I looked down at the little man that stood there staring at me and I couldn't help but smile. Jesus he looked so much like Claire. But his eyes...wow they were exactly the same as mine.

"Hi there Gavin," I said as I pulled a wrapped present out from behind my back and handed it to him. "I got this for you."

Gavin snatched it out of my hand, turned and ran away from the door screaming for Claire.

"MOOOOOOOM! That guy bought me sumfin!"

I laughed and stepped into the house, closing the door behind me.

Claire lived in a small, Cape Cod bungalow and the first thing I noticed when I walked into the living room was how homey it was. There were candles lit on the coffee table and the mantle of the fireplace and the smell of dinner coming from the kitchen was mouth watering. I walked around the room looking at all of the pictures she had on practically every surface: pictures of her when she was little, pictures of her with her dad, pictures of her friends and pictures of Gavin. My heart clenched when I saw a picture of Claire, her belly round with our son. She looked so young. I lifted the picture off of the mantle to get a better look. This was how she looked when I met her, minus the pregnant belly. Looking at this picture made me sad and angry – not with her. I could never be angry with her for anything. We were both young and stupid and neither one of us used any brains that night. I was just upset that I had missed this. I had missed watching her stomach grow, I missed being able to put my hand on her and feel him kick.

"OWWWW!" I yelped as I felt a foot connect with my shin.

I looked down to see Gavin standing there staring at me.

So much for missing out on feeling him kick. I think my shin will remember that forever.

"Hey, I forgotted your name. Can I just call you dog poop?"

Before I could formulate any type of response to that request, I heard Claire's voice from behind me.

"Gavin!"

"I didn't do it!" he swore, with a panicked look on his face.

"Yeah, right," she deadpanned. "This nice man's name is Carter, remember? Stop trying to call everything dog poop."

I turned to find her leaning against the doorframe leading into the kitchen given Carter the evil eye.

"Don't take offense," she said, turning her gaze to me. "Last week, every time you asked him a question he replied 'stupid fat cows are stupid' no matter what the question was."

I laughed, grateful that the whole dog poop thing wasn't just because he already decided he hated me. Claire made her way across the room to where I was and glanced down at the picture still in my hand.

"Oh my God, please don't look at that picture. I look like I have a giant tumor growing out of me. A tumor that kicked the shit out of my vagina and made me pee myself when I sneezed," she said with a groan. "I just told you I peed my pants didn't I?" she asked.

"Yeah, you kind of did. It's okay, I'll only send a text to four of my contacts about it instead of my whole phone book."

I suddenly realized we were toe-to-toe and I was close enough to kiss her. I leaned forward to do just that, completely forgetting that we weren't alone in the room.

"Mo-om, can I open my pwesent now?"

We stopped inches from each other's mouths and looked down next to us.

Claire sighed and leaned back away from me.

"Yes, you can open your present now," she replied.

He plopped down on the floor right where he was and started tearing into the paper, pieces of it flying in every direction.

"You didn't have to get him anything," she said softly to me.

I shrugged. "It's no big deal, just something little."

"Mommy, look! It's crayons and markers and paint and wow I can color stuffs and make pictures!" Gavin said excitedly, holding everything up for Claire to see.

"That's awesome, baby. Can you go put them in Mommy's room on my bed and we'll play with them later?"

"But I wanna paint now," Gavin complained, dropping the box of crayons on his foot. "Shit!"

"Gavin Allen!" Claire yelled.

I knew I shouldn't laugh, so I looked away and thought of dead puppies and that scene from "Field of Dreams" where Kevin Costner's character got to play catch with his dad. God dammed scene got me every time.

"The next bad word that comes out of your mouth is going to get you a spanking, do you understand me? Tell Carter thank you for the present and go in your room until it's time for dinner."

"Thanks, Carter," Gavin mumbled as he trudged down the hall.

When he was out of earshot I started laughing, and Claire smacked me in the arm.

"Sorry, but he is funny as hell."

She rolled her eyes at me and walked back to the kitchen with me following behind her.

"Yes, he's a riot. Come back to me after you've been out in public with him. Like, say in church. And when it gets to a really quiet part and all you can hear is the fountain in the back of the church and then Gavin's voice say really loudly 'Mom! I hear Jesus taking a piss!' It's not so funny then."

I glanced at the counter behind her and my jaw dropped. Covered over every available surface were chocolate, cookies and candy – every kind imaginable.

"Am I in Willy Wonka's workshop?"

She laughed and opened up the lid of a huge pot on the stove and stirred the contents.

"Well, I decided to make you guys my guinea pigs tonight. And Jenny is going to take a few pictures of some of the items for my advertisements since I don't have anything better than my cell phone camera."

I stared dreamily at everything. I may have a slight weakness to sweets.

"Holy hell, what are those things?" I asked pointing to a row of white chocolate clumps the size of my fist with caramel on top.

"Oh, those are something new I'm experimenting with. I melted a bowl of white chocolate, added crushed up pretzels and potato chips to it and then once the dropped spoonfuls solidified, I drizzled caramel on top. I may have gone a little overboard on the size of them. Right now they're called Globs."

Sweet Mary in heaven. I wanted to ask this woman to have my babies.

Oh, wait...

A knock sounded on the front door and Claire asked me to answer it for her while she set the table and finished up.

Jenny and Drew were the next to arrive. I held the door open for them and shook my head at Drew while Jenny walked in and made her way into the kitchen to talk to Claire.

"Really, Drew?" I asked, looking at his shirt.

There was a picture of a little kid on it shooting a gun above his head. The shirt read "Don't hit kids. No, seriously. They have guns now."

"What? Kids nowadays are the devil. This shirt is a PSA for you, dude. You'll thank me one day. So, where is the little guy? Does he need his diaper changed or anything? Maybe I can show him my car or give him some candy," he said as he looked around me and rubbed his hands together.

"He's four Drew. He doesn't wear diapers. And you might want to dial down the creepy kidnapper vibe just a notch."

"Whatever. Take me to your demon seed," Drew said.

We walked past the kitchen and I stuck my head in and asked Claire if it was okay to head back to Gavin's room. She told me where it was and we went down the hall and found him sitting on the floor in the middle of his room, squirting a tube of toothpaste right onto the carpet.

"Whoa there, big guy. What are you doing?" I asked as I quickly made my way over to him and took the now empty bottle out of his hand.

He just shrugged his shoulders. "I don't know."

Shit. What do I do? Should I go get Claire? I don't want the kid to think I'm a traitor though. He would get mad at me for tattling on him. Wait, I was the adult. I couldn't let him walk all over me. I needed to let him know who the boss was. And right now, it wasn't Tony Danza.

"I'm pretty sure you're not supposed to be putting toothpaste on your floor, are you?" I asked.

"That's a dumb question, Carter. Of course he's not supposed to put toothpaste on the floor," Drew said seriously.

I looked back over my shoulder and gave him a dirty look.

"I know that. I'm trying to get him to admit what he did was wrong," I said through clenched teeth.

"Okay there, Dr. Phil. I'm pretty sure he knows it's wrong otherwise he wouldn't have done it. Kids are dumb. They do things they aren't supposed to all the time because they can. Being an adult sucks. I could never get away with putting toothpaste on my floor now."

It was like dealing with two children.

"Why would you…you know what? Never mind," I said, turning back around to face Gavin.

"Your mom wouldn't be too happy about you making this mess. How about you show me where the towels are and we'll clean it up before she sees it."

There. He won't hate me for telling on him and I still let him know it was bad. I am an awesome parent.

Obviously Gavin was very excited to clean if it meant we didn't tell Claire what he did. I briefly wondered if she was going to find out and possibly cut my penis off or smother me in my sleep. And then I wondered if I told her, would Gavin punch me in the nuts again, or maybe go for the throat this time? I don't know whether to fear my kid or his mother.

Twenty minutes later, the carpet was good as new and Drew and I were sitting Indian-style in the middle of Gavin's room, praying to every higher power we knew that the girls wouldn't walk in the room right this minute.

Gavin had decided we should play dress up. We tried getting him to play something manly like cops and robbers, running with scissors or lighting shit on fire – anything but this. Unfortunately, you couldn't win an argument with a four-year old no matter how much you tried. Drew and I were both currently dressed as babies, complete with pacifiers in our mouths and holding on to stuffed animals. He stuck us each in these giant sun hats of Claire's that flopped down over our faces. Drew's was pink and mine was white. I drew the line at putting on one of his old, unused diapers that he found in a drawer in his closet from before he was potty trained.

"Hey, Uncle Drew, I have a secret to tell you," Gavin said.

Drew pulled the pacifier out of his mouth.

"Give it to me."

Gavin leaned in by his ear and whispered just loud enough for me to be able to hear him.

"You smell like beef and cheese."

Gavin pulled back from Drew's ear and Drew rolled his eyes at him.

"Dude, your secret sucks," he said.

"YOU SUCK!" Gavin yelled.

"Guys, dinner is ready so you should..."

Claire's words were cut off when she rounded the corner of the room and caught us. The abrupt halt to her feet caused Jenny, who had been following close behind, to smack into the back of her. Claire put her hand over her mouth to hide her giggles. Jenny couldn't have cared less about shielding her enjoyment of the situation. She bent over at the waist laughing her ass off out loud and pointing.

"Oh my God, someone tell me they have a camera," Jenny said in between laughs.

"Do you want me to spit up? Because I'm not afraid to go there," Drew threatened.

Both of us ripped off our baby crap while the girls laughed and gave Gavin high-fives. Drew and I stood up while Jenny lifted Gavin into her arms and told him how awesome he was and cooed all over him. He ate up every word and I swear that kid smirked at us as he put his head down on Jenny's chest – which was currently on full display with her low-cut top and push-up bra.

"Oh my God, I am so jealous of that kid right now. I wish I was cradled to her tits. Cradled like a baby," Drew whispered.

"Do you hear yourself right now?" I asked as we all walked out of Gavin's room and into the dining room where we were greeted by Liz and Jim who were already seated.

AFTER AN EXTREMELY delicious dinner where there was only minimal fighting between the two children, and by children I mean Drew and Gavin, Claire started bringing out tray after tray of all her sweet goodies.

Now all I could think of were Claire's sweet goodies on a tray; her delicious num-nums on a silver platter. I would love to eat her off of a tray. I want to lick her Globs.

"Carter, do you want some?"

"Fuck yes."

"Awwwww, Carter said the t-u-l word mom!" Gavin tattled.

Oops.

"Who taught you how to spell?" Drew asked with a sneer.

"Dude, I'm four," Gavin replied.

I excused myself to go to the bathroom before I did something even more embarrassing. I stood there peeing and trying not to think about Claire being naked on a tray when the bathroom door suddenly opened and Gavin walked in.

"Oh, hey there, Gavin," I said nervously as I tried to turn my body away from him without interrupting the flow. "Uh, I'm kind of going to the bathroom here buddy. Can you shut the door?"

He did as I asked, however, he didn't leave the room before he shut the door. Now he was locked in a small, enclosed space with me while I tried to take a piss. And now he was staring at my junk. Okay, this wasn't awkward at all.

"Um, Gavin can you look somewhere else? Oh hey, look at that duck in the tub. That's pretty cool."

Still staring. Was this something I should be concerned with?

"Wow, Carter. You've got a HUGE wiener."

Suddenly, Gavin being in the bathroom with me didn't seem so bad.

If only he could have been in the bathroom with me in eighth grade and passed that little tidbit around for Penny Frankles to hear, I might not have gone to the eight grade graduation dance solo.

I finished pissing, zipped up my pants and flushed the toilet, all while trying not to pat myself on the back. Yeah, I had a huge wiener. You bet your sweet ass I did. I almost needed a wheelbarrow to carry it around. And because a toddler said it, it must have been true.

We got back to the table and I couldn't keep the shit-eating grin off of my face.

"What are you smiling about? Do you have gas?" Drew joked.

"Hey, Mommy, Carter has a HUGE wiener," Gavin said around a mouthful of cookie, holding his hands up in the air about three feet apart, like you do when you're telling someone how big the fish is you just caught.

Claire quickly reached over and pushed Gavin's arms down while everyone else at the table laughed. I just sat back and smiled and tried to keep my anaconda penis tucked under the table so it wouldn't scare anyone.

"Hey, Uncle Drew, you wanna hear a dirty joke?" Gavin asked excitedly.

"I don't know, will it get you punched?" Drew replied seriously. It was almost touching how concerned Drew was with getting Gavin in trouble.

"The pig fell in the mud and walked across the street to the dirt and then climbed the roof!" Gavin shouted, falling immediately into a fit of giggles at his "dirty joke".

Everyone chuckled at Gavin's attempt at humor – except Drew.

"Dude, that wasn't funny at all," Drew said with a straight face.

"You wanna piece of me?" Gavin shouted, holding his little fist up in the air at him.

"Alright, that's enough. Gavin, go put your pajamas on, and I'll be in shortly to read you a story," Claire told him.

Gavin scampered down off the chair, giving one last threatening look to Drew before running to his room. Five pairs of eyes all turned their attention to Drew.

"What?" he asked. "It wasn't funny and I totally didn't get it."

"Okay Claire," Liz said, turning her face away from Drew, probably so she wouldn't feel the need to choke him. "Time for the real show. Tell us what you've got here," she said, pointing to all the trays on the table.

Claire went around the table pointing out what each item was. Snicker Surprise cookies, homemade turtles, Pretzel Turtles, White Chocolate Buckeyes, white and milk chocolate covered potato chips, pretzels, cashews, peanuts, raisins, rice krispies, bacon and a cookie called a Cranberry Hootycreek – which Drew kept calling a Hooterpeep.

Everything was amazing and I think we were all in a sugar coma by the time we sampled everything. Jenny circled the table and snapped a few pictures of everything for the advertisements before we inhaled the stuff and Claire blushed a bright shade of red at all the compliments we threw at her.

"I definitely got some good pictures, Claire. I think for the front cover of the brochure we should pacifically focus on the chocolate-covered stuff," she explained.

"You mean specifically?" Jim asked.

"That's what I said," she replied. "Pacifically."

"Hey, Claire, can I come with you to put Gavin to bed?" I asked, hoping to divert the attention from Jenny's weird use of the English language.

Her face lit up with my question which instantly made me grateful I had the foresight to ask.

We left everyone to clean up the dining room table and walked back to Gavin's room to find him asleep on top of his toy box. I laughed as soon as I saw him.

"Don't laugh," she whispered with a smile on her face. "That's not the funniest place I've seen him fall asleep. I've got an entire photo album dedicated to his sleeping habits. On the back of the couch like a cat, sitting up at the dinner table, face down at the dinner table, under the Christmas tree in a pile of toys, in his closet, on the toilet…you name it he's fallen asleep on it. He's like a horse. He can practically fall asleep standing up. Jim gave him the Indian name of Chief Sleep-sanywhere and Liz recently changed it to Captain Narcolepsy."

She moved quietly into the room and scooped his little body up easily, placing a kiss to his head as she walked over to his bed. I leaned against the door jam, trying not to get too sentimental and girly at just how sweet it was to see her taking care of him. She covered him up with a blanket, smoothed back the hair off of his head and kissed him again before turning around and walking to me.

"So, Mr. Ellis, how freaked out are you right now by all of this domesticated parenting crap?" she asked.

There was a smile on her face as she stood right in front of me but I could tell it was just there for show. She really was nervous about how I was handling all of this. I glanced over her shoulder at the little boy that was fast asleep in his bed and my heart started beating faster. I had an undeniable urge to grab onto him and never let him go, to protect him from anything bad that might come his way and to shelter him from scary things like the boogey man and clowns.

Shut up, clowns are scary as fuck.

I looked back down at the incredible woman standing in front of me and knew I felt the same way about her.

"I don't want the boogey man to get you and I hate clowns," I blurted out.

She laughed and patted my cheek in sympathy. I sucked at this. I didn't do well under pressure. I cared about her and Gavin and I just wanted her to know I wasn't going anywhere. How fucking hard was that to say?

"That's not what I mean. I mean, yes, I hate clowns. They are dumb and creepy and grown men should never wear anything with polka dots or giant shoes."

God dammit, stop the word vomit!

Before I could open my mouth and stick a giant clown shoe in any further, Claire covered my mouth with her hand.

"It's okay if you're freaked out. I wouldn't blame you, believe me. This is a lot to take in," she said softly. "All of a sudden you go from single and free to having a built-in family."

I took a deep breath and tried it again, reaching up and pulling her hand away from my mouth and resting it flat against my chest.

"Let me just start off by saying I really, really suck ass at doing the whole 'touchy-feely, talk about my feelings' shit. Although if you ask Drew, he would surely disagree since he spent five years listening to me whine like a baby about how much I wanted to find you. After all that time and spending years driving everyone around me crazy just trying to find your smell again, I am not about to fuck this up and run screaming into the night."

Her thumb moved back and forth over my chest and she brought her other hand up to my cheek before leaning forward and placing a soft kiss on my lips. When she pulled her face back, I wrapped my arms around her small waist and rested my forehead against hers.

"I know after I found out I fled the scene like a hit-and-run driver, but I promise you Claire, I will never get spooked again."

She pulled back and looked me in the eye, the corners of her mouth turning up in a smile.

"Did you really just quote Cocktail to me right now?"

"Yes, yes I did. If you'd like me to go all crazy Tom Cruise and jump up and down on a couch for you, I'll totally do it."

"ARE YOU KIDDING ME?! I WOULD RATHER TAKE IT UP THE ASS!"

Drew's booming voice from the living room pulled our attentions away from each other. We took one last look at Gavin before closing his door, and then walked hand in hand down the hall to find everyone sitting around the living room playing a twisted game of "would you rather".

Claire and I sat down next to each other on the couch. I put my arm around her shoulders and she snuggled into my side. Nothing had felt this perfect in a long time.

"Alright, my turn," Drew said. "Jim, would you rather have your porn name be Hugh G. Rection or Mike Unstinks?"

15.

I'm a Dirty Slut

"CHAINS AND WHIPS excite me…c-c-c-come on, come on…S-S-S-S-M-M-M…"

"Gavin Allen Morgan, if you don't stop singing that song I am going to put you on the curb for the garbage men to pick up," I yelled for the tenth time today as I finished cleaning up the kitchen from lunch.

"That's boring," Gavin muttered before stomping off to his room.

"Speaking of garbage, when is that Christy guy going to be here?" my dad asked from his seat at the kitchen table.

Why is everyone determined to get on my nerves today?

"It's CARTER, Dad. Stop being an ass. He'll be here when he wakes up."

My dad made a production of looking down at his wrist where there wasn't even a watch.

"It's 12:48. What kind of a slacker is this guy?"

I threw the dish towel on the counter and turned to give my dad a dirty look.

"He works the nightshift, dad. We've been over this already. One more comment out of you and I'm changing your Facebook status to 'I love penis.'"

I walked over to the fridge to add a few things to my shopping list that hung off of the freezer and tried not to glance at the clock. I was definitely anxious to see Carter.

I was up to my eyeballs in stuff for the grand opening and Carter was working a lot of overtime so we hadn't seen each other since the night of dinner a week earlier. But we talked on the phone and he also called a few times just to talk to Gavin, which totally made my heart melt.

Thoughts of our time in the storage room earned me extra credit in Liz Homework by making my way through my suitcase of "who needs a man" products for a second time. Liz got all choked up on the phone when I told her. It was a beautiful moment for the two of us.

I was working at the bar tonight so Carter was going to give me a ride up there. I called Liz and told her she and Jim should come so Carter wouldn't be bored.

"I think maybe I'll hide behind the couch and jump out when he gets here. Put the fear of George into him," my dad said with a nod of his head.

"Not funny. And don't you mean 'fear of God'?"

He shrugged. "Same thing."

God said "Let there be light" and George Morgan flipped the switch.

This was the most my dad had spoken about Carter since they met. Granted, it wasn't very flattering but hey, it was progress. At least he was acknowledging his existence and not thinking up new ways to kill him. Dad had been going down the alphabet for a week now and finally stopped at the letter S.

Death by shopping cart suffocation, in case you were wondering.

The doorbell rang and I hurried to answer it. I wiped my hands on the front of my jeans, smoothed my hair and bent forward to reach my hand down the front of my shirt and tug each of the girls up so their prime real estate was on full display. I stood back up, took a deep breath and flung the door open. My heart actually skipped a beat when I saw Carter standing there.

"You know there are windows on either side of your door right? And that your curtains are see-through?" Carter said with a smirk.

Why? WHY, for the love of God!

"I would give you my entire paycheck for a month if you bent over in front of me and fluffed your boobs again," he said as he stepped through the door, and I closed it behind him.

I closed my eyes, fully prepared to be mortified and not make eye contact, but before I could wish for a giant hole in the floor to swallow me up, Carter's lips were on mine. He slid his arm around my waist and pulled me up against him, cupping my cheek with his hand as he slid his tongue past my lips and slowly stroked it through my mouth. I could kiss this man for days and never get enough. His lips moved against mine, soft and sensually, while his hand slid from my cheek, down my neck, and stopped on the bare skin right above my heart. I wanted to reach up and push his hand down into my bra. My fists clutched onto the front of his shirt and a whimper escaped from me as his hand inched just a tiny bit lower. If my mouth wasn't fused to his right now, I might wonder if I said that last part out loud. Or maybe he could read my mind.

Touch my boobs. Do it. The power of my mind commands you.

His hand stopped its downward descent and I wanted to scream. His tongue continued to slide against mine ever so slowly and I really wished I had one of those green flags from the NASCAR races. I would've waved that thing all around. Wave it in the air like I just don't care.

Carter, start your engine! You have been given the green flag. All systems go. Hit the gas and let your hand grab the boob.

"If you touch my daughter's boobs while I'm standing right here, I'm gonna have to put taffy in your trachea until you terminate."

Carter and I broke apart so fast you would have thought we were teenagers that just got caught having sex instead of grown adults that had a child together.

"Did your dad just tell me he was going to choke me to death with taffy?" Carter whispered.

"Yeah. He's on the letter T. Behave or an umbrella up your Uranus will be in your future," I whispered back.

My father walked over to us and looked Carter up and down.

"You got any tattoos, son?"

Carter looked at me in confusion and I just shrugged my shoulders. You never knew what was going to come out of my dad's mouth.

"Uh, no. No, sir, I do not," Carter replied.

"You own a bike?"

"Well, I have a pretty nice mountain bike that's still in storage because I just haven't had time to take it out for a…"

"Motorcycle, Cathy," my father interrupted with a sigh of annoyance. "Do you own a motorcycle?"

Carter shook his head, "No, and my name is Cart-"

"You ever been arrested or get in a bar fight?" my dad interrupted.

"No, I've never been arrested or gotten into any kind of fight, Mr. Morgan," Carter said with a confident smile.

My dad leaned over towards me.

"Claire, are you sure this kid isn't gay?" he whispered to me.

"Jesus, Dad! No, he's not gay," I yelled back.

"Hey…" Carter said, insulted by my dad's question.

My dad turned to face Carter and sighed.

"Fine, you can date my daughter and get to know your son. But if you knock her up again…"

"DAD!"

My dad looked over at me with my hands on my hips and smoke practically coming out of my ears and then continued with his warning like I wasn't there.

"…I will comb the face of the earth, hunt you down like a dog, and drop her cranky ass off on your doorstep. I'm not dealing with another nine months of Miss Pissy Pants over there."

Oh for the love of God.

I looked back and forth between them as they stared each other down.

Carter nodded his head and stuck out his hand for my dad to shake.

"Deal," Carter said as they shook on it.

Wonderful. One big happy cray-cray family.

Just then, Gavin flew through the living room holding something above his head.

"Carter! Look at the new sword I gots!"

Christ almighty!

My son was running into the room with my Jack Rabbit above his head like he was a gladiator going into battle. A gladiator with a purple "sword" that had five speeds.

"Oooh, what does this button do?" Gavin asked as he stopped and pressed the button that made the beads swirl around.

I flew over to him and tried to snatch it out of his hand, but he wouldn't let go. I frantically pressed all of the buttons to get it to stop while I played tug-of-war with Gavin and suddenly I hit one that switched it to warp speed and made the whole top part start rotating and vibrating so hard Gavin's arms shook.

"M-m-m-m-m-o-o-o-o-m-m-m-m-m th-th-th-th-i-i-i-i-s-s-s-s t-t-t-i-i-ck-l-e-s-s-s."

Fucking hell. When did this kid get so strong?

"Gavin, cut it out. This is not a toy," I said through gritted teeth.

I was playing tug-of-war with a rubber penis and my son. This is not okay people!

"It is too a toy. Why do you get all the good toys?" Gavin huffed as he put all of his weight into pulling the thing out of my hand and I actually stumbled forward.

"No, really guys don't worry. I've got this," I said sarcastically at my dad and Carter. They were standing shoulder-to-shoulder, a few feet away watching the show. They looked at each other and burst out laughing.

Of course. NOW they bonded – when I was trying to wrestle a sex toy out of my kid's hand.

"Gavin, let go NOW!" I yelled.

"You better do as your mom says, Gavin. She gets grumpy when she can't play with her toy," my dad laughed.

Carter laughed right along with him until I shot him a look that clearly said "If you don't shut the fuck up and help me, I will never let you in my pants again."

His mouth quickly shut and he finally moved.

"Hey, Gavin, I got something for you I left on the front porch. And it's a much better toy than your mom's. Why don't you run out and grab it," Carter suggested.

Gavin released his death grip on the vibrator without another word and ran out the front door.

"You are so lucky you helped me when you did or there would have been serious repercussions," I told Carter angrily.

Obviously he didn't get the severity of the situation since he was actually giggling right now. And my dad was wiping tears out of his eyes. Then I looked down and realized I had been enunciating my point by shaking the vibrator in Carters face.

I quickly put my arm down, opened one of the end table drawers and shoved the damn thing inside just as Gavin ran back into the house with a toy gun, cowboy hat and sheriff's badge stuck to his shirt.

"Bad boys, bad boys, whatcha gonna do, whatcha gonna do when they cut your wiener," Gavin sang as he pointed his gun at random objects.

"Wow, cops have gotten pretty hardcore lately," Carter muttered.

I FORGAVE CARTER on our ride to the bar because come on, look at him. I couldn't hold a grudge and fantasize about his penis. It was a major conflict of interest.

Business was just starting to pick up at the bar as the after-work crowd started filing in around seven. Liz and Jim ate dinner with Carter at one of the booths and the three of them moved over to the bar after they were done. On one of my many trips walking past them, Carter reached out and grabbed my arm. He swiveled his seat to the side so he could pull me between his legs. I set my empty tray on top of the bar next to him and he rested his hands on my hips.

"Remember when I told you that I would always tell you if your ass looked fat?" he asked.

Oh man, I knew I shouldn't have licked the bowl of milk chocolate clean last night after I finished making turtles. I could feel my thighs getting bigger while I stood here. Were they rubbing together tonight when I walked? I bet he was worried my rubbing thighs were going to start a spark.

Only you can prevent thigh fires. That Smokey the bear jerk only cared about the forest. Fuck the forest. My vagina could catch on fire because Carter thought I was fat.

"Shut your brain off. I wasn't going to tell you that you looked fat," he scolded.

I knew that.

"I was just going to say, I forgot to also mention that I will always tell you when your ass looks so fucking amazing that I want to wrap my hands around it every time you walk by."

I bit my bottom lip and smiled.

"Anything else?"

Yeah, I was fishing for compliments again. I just had a meltdown about a thigh inferno. I earned this.

"Yes," Carter answered after kissing me softly. "I will also always tell you when your legs look so long and sexy that all I can think about is having them wrapped around my waist."

He kissed my lips again.

"And I will always tell you when you are so beautiful that somebody better call God, because he's missing an angel."

"Awww did you just use a cheesy pick-up line on me?" I asked.

"I've been waiting to use that since I was fifteen," Carter said with a smile.

"Are you guys done yet? I just threw up in my mouth a little listening to this shit," Liz muttered from her seat on the other side of Carter.

"Well aren't you two just the cutest couple?"

I turned away from Carter when I heard the female voice behind me dripping with sarcasm.

"Tasha, what the fuck are you doing here?" Carter demanded as he stood up behind me.

Whoa, fucking whoa! Tasha? The ex? This was who Carter dated before he came here? Isn't this just a pickle on the crap sandwich that is my life. Of course she had to look like a porn star. Miles of long blonde hair, bright blue eyes and a perfect complexion. Not to mention the tiniest waist known to man and the nicest set of boobs I've ever seen. They had to be fake. Real boobs weren't that perfectly round. If I didn't hate her on sight, I might have asked her if I could touch them. She looked familiar. She flipped her hair behind one shoulder and it suddenly came to me where I knew her from.

"Hey, you were at Jenny's sex toy party a few weeks ago."

I felt Liz walk up next to me.

"Oh yeah, I remember her. Twat Face Tasha," Liz said with a smile as she crossed her arms in front of her.

Twatty huffed in irritation. "It was Tantalizing Tasha."

"Nope, I'm pretty sure it was Twat Face," Liz said, looking to me for confirmation.

I nodded in agreement.

"Oh it definitely was. She probably doesn't remember because we talked about it behind her back," I said with a shrug.

Before I knew it, Cunty was up in my face.

"Listen slut, just because you're Carter's new flavor of the week doesn't make you anything special."

All hell broke loose then. Carter started yelling at Tasha, Tasha yelled at all of us and Liz pushed her away from me. I just stood there in the middle of the commotion in shock.

"That's enough Tasha," Carter said angrily. "Tell me what you want, or leave. You will not just show up here out of the blue and insult Claire."

She gave me another snide look before turning her gaze back on Carter.

"Wow, it sure didn't take you long to find some little whore to dip your wick into did it?" Tasha asked Carter sarcastically.

Oh hell no! She did *not* just call me a whore.

I took a step towards her, my hands shaking with the urge to punch that smug look off of her face.

"That's pretty rich considering I heard you fucked your way through the phone book when you were with Carter. Your vagina is a giant gaping hole like the one the iceberg left on the titanic. It's a crime scene in your pants with hundreds of people screaming in horror and trying to jump the fuck off."

I didn't even know what I was saying at this point. I was just spouting nonsense because I was pissed. And it looked like I hit the nail on the head – or the vagina. Tasha charged me like a bull. Everyone moved at once. I moved out of the way, Carter, Liz and Jim all got in front of me and grabbed onto Tasha while she screamed about killing me. It turns out, porn star-slut-ex-girlfriends aren't so pretty when they have tomato-red faces, spit flying out of their mouths and their limbs are flailing all over the place.

Carter finally managed to grab Tasha's elbow and started pulling her with him over to the front door while she continued to yell insults and death threats at me. Carter made eye contact with me and mouthed *'I'm sorry'* before he disappeared out the front door with the nut job.

I'm not gonna lie, I was a little freaked out. It felt like everyone in the place was looking at me. It was so loud in here, no one had any clue what had just happened, but it still unnerved me. I hated being the center of attention. And I hated how insecure I felt because right now, Carter was outside, alone, with his ex-girlfriend. Granted, she was obviously one window lick away from riding the short bus, but that knowledge did nothing to ease my mind.

I let one of the other waitresses know when she walked by that I was going to take a break for a few minutes. Liz pushed me down onto her barstool and Jim stood behind me rubbing my shoulders to try and ease the tension. Neither of them said much. I think they were waiting for me to have a mental breakdown or curl up in the fetal position and suck my thumb. I had never been in any kind of a fight before. I talked a good game but the first time someone came at me I ran the other way. One time in high school, Liz and I were walking through the mall and some crazy emo chick walked by us and slammed her shoulder into mine. Without thinking, I turned and shouted "Stop writing poetry and crying and watch where you're going!"

She stopped dead in her tracks and turned around, along with the rest of her depressed, too-much black eye make-up posse. I quickly stuck the straw of my cherry slush in my mouth and pointed my thumb at Liz.

"What did we miss, kids?" Drew asked, coming up behind us a few minutes later with his arm around Jenny as the rest of us just stood there staring at the door where Carter had disappeared.

I turned around to face him and his shirt that said, "I shaved my balls for this?"

"Somebody just tried to kill me," I told him in a horrified voice.

"What? Who?" Drew asked.

"Tasha." Liz said with disgust.

Jenny immediately looked guilty.

"Oh shit! She was here already? Claire, I'm so sorry. Tasha is all my fault."

"What the hell are you talking about? You know that crazy bitch?" Liz asked.

"We went to college together and she called me a few weeks ago and said she'd be in town and wanted to get together. That's why she was at the sex toy party. She was only supposed to stay for that weekend but she decided to stick around longer. I had no idea she knew Carter until a little bit ago. She asked me if I knew Carter and said she was an old friend and wanted to say hi. It wasn't until after I told her where you guys were going to be tonight that I remembered she used to date a guy named Carter. That's why we came up here. I really thought we'd get here before her so I could fix this."

Drew removed his arm from around Jenny and turned to face me, jumping into action.

"Okay, Claire, here's what we need to do first. Do you know how to throw a punch?" Drew asked as he grabbed my arms and stared seriously into my eyes.

"What? No. What are you talking about? I'm not going to fight her," I said with a roll of my eyes.

"You don't understand. I've known this freak for years. Did she threaten you?" Drew asked.

"Yeah, that cum dumpster said she'd kick Claire's ass," Liz told him.

"Oh it's on now! It's on like Frogger!" Drew shouted in excitement.

"Don't you mean Donkey Kong?" Jim asked as he stood behind Liz and slid his arms around her waist.

"I never really liked Donkey Kong. So it was never *on*. Frogger just works better for me."

"Drew, nothing is going to be *on*. I have never been in a fight and I'm not going to start now. Carter took her outside and is hopefully telling her to go to hell. Problem solved," I said.

Drew looked at me in horror. "Claire, I don't think you understand the seriousness of this situation. Now, as much as I hate Tasha like a fire burning rash on my dick, she's still hot. And Claire, you're a total MILF."

I looked at him in confusion. "Drew, what the hell does this have to do with anything?"

"It's like you don't even know me Claire," Drew said sadly with a shake of his head.

He let go of my arms and stepped back, wiping an imaginary tear from under his eye.

"Jim, help me out here man. I'm too upset to continue."

Jim untangled his arms from Liz and took a step forward to pat Drew on the back.

"As Drew has pointed out Claire, you're hot. And while we all agree that Cray-Cray needs to be put in her place, unfortunately, she's hot too.

And you're both chicks with long hair. And we're in a restaurant that has approximately four different flavors of Jell-O in the back room," Jim explained seriously.

"Oh my God are you fucking kidding me?" Liz asked. "This is about wanting to see two chicks fight in a pool of Jell-O?"

"Liz. It's ALWAYS about wanting to see two chicks fight in a pool of Jell-O. Never, ever forget that," Drew said without any trace of humor in his voice. "Jell-O is *delicious*."

Liz looked over at me. "You know, even though these two morons are speaking with their dicks right now, you should probably learn how to hit something. You know, just in case Carter can't talk any sense into her. If she comes back in here, obviously we'll all take her out, but what if she sneaks up on you when you're unloading groceries from your car? Or jumps up from your backseat while you're driving down the highway?" she asked.

"Oh my God, what is wrong with you?! This is not helping me AT ALL!" I screeched.

"Alright, that was probably an exaggeration. Besides, her tits are too big to squeeze down in the backseat of a car. You'd totally see her first," Liz replied with a shrug. "And now, you can learn how to pop one of those implants without breaking a nail."

This was really not happening was it? I didn't want to learn how to fight. I should have kept my mouth shut with the twat face giant vagina comments.

Drew turned to face me and put both of his hands up in the air with his palms facing out.

"Alright, strap on your brass balls and hit me," Drew said, widening his stance.

I stood there with my hands on my hips looking around at everyone. They all stood there waiting for me to punch Drew's hands.

"This is the dumbest idea ever," I complained.

"Come on Claire, let 'er rip. Then you can go outside and tear her shit up like a Cyclops," Jenny said.

"Cyclops?" Jim asked.

"You know, that other name for like, a hurricane or tornado. Cyclops."

We all cocked our heads at her in confusion.

Drew sighed. "It's cyclone, baby."

I took that moment to wind back and punch Drew's hand so I could take him by surprise. Drew looked at me in confusion while I bounced back and forth on my toes like a boxer. That felt good. That felt *really* good. I hit the shit out of his hand. Bring it on bitch!

"Claire, what the fuck was that?" Drew asked.

"Scared you didn't I? That was my fist of fury, BITCH!" I yelled.

Drew put his hands on his hips and stared at me.

"You have the punching power of a drunken baby. I hope you throw down your vagina harder than that. Otherwise, I feel bad for Carter's penis."

"Why are we feeling bad for my penis?"

Carter came up behind me before I could tell Drew that my vagina and Carter's penis were none of his business.

"So what's up, man? What the hell did Slut Bag McFuck Stick want?" Drew asked.

Carter sighed. "Oh just to tell me what a big mistake she made turning her vagina into a twenty-four hour seven-eleven. And how 'you don't know what you got till it's gone.'"

"Wow, she quoted a Cinderella song. She's not afraid to bring out the big guns is she?" Liz asked.

Everyone was laughing and making a big joke about this, but it wasn't funny. It wasn't funny at all. That bitch wanted to kill me. Or at least punch me in the face. Did everyone forget about that fact already? She wanted to punch me. In the face. With her FIST.

"I hate to break up the fun, but Crazy Train wants to beat up my face."

Liz gave me a reassuring look.

"Calm down Long Duk Dong. You may punch like a grandma after drinking a forty-ounce, but remember Claire – you know how to *take* a punch. That's what's most important here right now," Liz said with a pat to my back.

I looked at her in confusion for a few seconds before I remembered what she was talking about – drunken Fight Club night last year.

"I'm sorry, but why does Claire know how to take a punch? I'm not sure I like where this is going," Carter said nervously.

"Well, last year Jim made us watch Fight Club for like, the ten-thousandth time. And while I'm all for a little shirtless Brad Pitt action, Claire and I decided to take a shot every time Edward Norton talked in third person. By about twenty minutes in, we were trashed. I don't know whose idea it was, but Claire and I started our own fight club in the living room," Liz explained.

"It was your idea, Liz. You stood up in front of me, lifted your shirt and said 'Punch me in the stomach as hard as you can, fucker.'"

Jim started laughing as he remembered back to that night. It wasn't my finest hour. I punched even worse when I was drunk, barely even grazing Liz's skin. She, however, could punch like a WWF wrestler on steroids.

"Oh yeah, that's right! That was one of the best ideas I've ever had while drunk. We punched each other back and forth until you started wheezing and yelled, 'I am Claire's internal bleeding and you need to cut this shit out!'"

Carter looked back and forth between us just shaking his head in disbelief.

"Don't worry about our girl, Carter. She went a good ten rounds before she tapped out," Jim said with a laugh. "And you'll be happy to know I got it all on video."

"Was there Jell-O? Tell me there was Jell-O?" Drew asked excitedly.

MY SHIFT ENDED a few hours after that and I desperately needed a drink after tonight's events. I threw my apron behind the bar and everyone moved back to a large table so we could all sit together. After we sat down at the table, Carter told us what happened outside. Tasha claimed that she made a huge mistake and she wanted Carter back. He laughed in her face and told her to take her crab-infested vagina back to Toledo. He also informed her that he had always wanted me, even when he was with her and now that he found me, he was never letting me go.

Cue the applause.

I lost track of how many drinks I consumed the rest of the night. Every time I set my empty glass down it was magically refilled. I think Carter knew I was stressed about the Tasha situation and wanted me to just relax and have a good evening.

Or he wanted to get me drunk and take advantage of me.

My lady bits started jumping up and down, clapping her hands and screaming, "Yes please!"

I kept looking towards the door expecting Tasha to come charging back in. After a while though, I didn't know which door she would come through since there were at least thirty of them when I looked in that direction.

I glanced down into my glass, trying to count the ice cubes and lost track after one.

Wow, what did they put in this vodka?

Carter kept looking over at me and smiling and it took everything in me not to straddle his lap. I really wanted to make some sort of move, but I didn't know the first thing about that crap. My hand was on his thigh and I slowly moved it upwards. I stopped just a few inches below the bulge I couldn't stop staring at. I want to rub my vagina all over that shit.

Yes, I was aware that I was sitting here at a table full of people, just staring down in Carter's lap like it was a desert oasis and I hadn't sipped water in months.

I thought about things I could whisper in his ear that might turn him on.

"We should have the sex."

Carter laughed and kissed my cheek.

"I thought that out loud didn't I?"

"Yes, you definitely thought that out loud," he said with a smile.

I turned away from him and grabbed Liz's arm, pulling her up with me.

"Be right back," I mumbled to the table in general.

I pulled Liz over to the bar, about ten feet away from the table.

"I don't know how to sex," I complained.

"Um, what?" Liz asked.

"I mean, sexy. I don't know how to sexy."

Liz laughed.

"You mean you don't know how to *be* sexy?"

I just nodded. Liz got me. My best friend was the best ever. She was so pretty and nice and pretty.

"Hon, you're doing just fine. In case you hadn't noticed, Carter hasn't been able to keep his hands off of you all night. And you couldn't see it, but when you put your hand on his leg, he kept swallowing and staring off into space like he was trying not to jizz in his pants."

I was starting to panic. Which was probably the booze talking but so what? I didn't know the first thing about seducing a guy. I was going to make a total fool of myself.

"You're seriously freaked out about this?" Liz asked, all traces of humor gone from her face when she saw how worried I was.

"I feel like I'm going to puke I'm so nervous."

Liz sighed. "Claire, you're a hot bitch. You could stand there and do nothing and he'd still want to hump your leg. You just need some confidence. Repeat after me, 'I am a dirty, dirty slut.'"

Liz stood there with her hands on her hips waiting for me to comply. I looked back nervously at Carter but he was deep in conversation with Drew.

"This is ridiculous," I complained.

"What's ridiculous is that you don't think you can be slutty. Do you honestly think I would be friends with you if I thought there wasn't a dirty whore lurking in there somewhere? Give me a little credit please.

You are the quintessential lady in the streets, freak in the sheets."

"You need to stop quoting Urban Dictionary," I told her.

Carter had probably been with lots of women. Women who could suck a golf ball through a garden hose and dance on a pole. Liz meant well, but I just didn't know if I could pull this off.

"You're starting to piss me off. Just say it. I am a dirty, dirty slut."

I rolled my eyes. I might as well do what she says or she'll never let it go.

"I'm a dirty, dirty slut," I mumbled quietly.

Well, that *did* feel a little good saying it out loud. Maybe Liz was on to something.

"Come on dirty girl, you can do better than that. Do it again, and put your vagina into it," Liz encouraged.

I took a deep breath and said it a little louder. Thank God there was music playing and people talking.

"Wow, did you see that?" Liz asked. "Carter's disco stick just shriveled up and died. You suck at this, and not in a good way. Again!"

I clenched my fists at my sides and my breathing sped up. I could be a dirty slut; I could be dirtier than a hooker at a gang-bang.

Okay, maybe not that dirty.

I took in a big gulp of air and let out all of my nerves, all of my anxiety and all of my irrational fears with one sentence.

"I AM A DIRTY, DIRTY SLUT!"

Unfortunately, the jukebox decided to move to a new song right then, so the decibel level of the bar had dropped considerably. I was too busy empowering the slut within to notice. Too bad for me no one else had been preoccupied with anything other than my screaming confirmation.

Everyone within shouting distance immediately started clapping and cheering. There were a few cat calls and wolf whistles and one overzealous person who yelled, "Save a drum, bang a dirty slut!"

Drew got smacked in the arm by Jenny for that one.

Everyone felt so sorry for me that free drinks were sent to me for the next hour. And I couldn't be rude. I had to drink them. Which was why Carter was now helping me walk into my house because my feet just did not want to cooperate and – oh look, pizza!

I stumbled away from Carter and flipped open the cardboard box my dad left on the counter, shoveling an entire piece into my mouth.

"Mfmmff soooo fucking good," I mumbled around bites.

Carter stood behind me holding onto my hips to steady me while I inhaled two more pieces and guzzled two glasses of water.

"Fuck, this pizza is like…good and shit," I told him, wiping my greasy hands on a towel next to the box.

Alright, enough stalling. Time to do this shit.

I turned in Carter's arms and gave him my best sultry look, chanting my mantra over and over.

I'm a dirty slut. I'm a dirty slut.

"Are you okay Claire? Do you have something in your eye?"

Carter cupped my cheeks and tilted my head back so he could look in my eye that did NOT have anything in it but sex appeal.

I am a drunk, dirty slut. I am a drunk, dirty slut.

I pulled my face away from his hands and decided to stick with a smile. It was safer.

I could do this; I could so totally do this.

I lifted the hem of my shirt up over my stomach, my black lace bra, and my head.

Except, my shirt got caught in the bobby pins on the top of my head. I was standing here in front of Carter with my shirt stuck around my head and chin and my arms stuck out in front of my face.

I am the great Cornholio. I am the great Cornholio. I need TP for my bunghole.

I started snorting and Carter bent his knees so he could peak into the opening of my shirt.

"Baby, what are you doing?" he asked with a laugh.

"I might need some help getting nuded," I said through snorts of laughter.

"Did you say neutered?"

Carter's question just made me laugh even harder, which naturally made me cry – deep, heaving sobs with snot running down my nose.

Ladies and gentlemen, we have now entered the drunk crying portion of our evening. Please put your seatbacks in the upright position and try not to stare at the train wreck to your left.

Carter helped me get my shirt back on and put his hands back on my face, wiping away the tears with his thumbs.

"Hey, why the tears? What's wrong?" he asked softly.

That just made me cry harder. He was so nice and pretty and…nice. I sniffled loudly.

"I just wanted to be a slut so you'd like me and I don't want your penis to be disappointed and Twat Face is going to beat me up because I called her vagina a clown car."

Carter chuckled at my ramblings, bent down and scooped me up into his arms bridal-style. He walked down the hall towards my room, and I laid my head on his chest.

"First of all, I will never let Tasha beat you up, so don't even give that another thought," he reassured me as he gently set me down on my bed. He grabbed a couple of tissues from my nightstand and handed them to me as he knelt down next to my bed.

"Second," he said softly as I blew my nose and he held up the covers so I could crawl under. "You don't need to do anything to be dirty or sexy. You are already all of those things and more just by breathing. I am in a constant state of horniness whenever I'm near you or thinking about you. I don't want you to be nervous or worried about anything involving you and me and sex. You are everything I have ever wanted Claire. Never doubt that."

I really wish I wasn't drunk. I would so put his penis in my mouth right now.

Carter groaned and I was too drunk to care that I had just said that out loud. I snuggled into the covers.

"If you keep saying things like that, I am going break the rule I made to myself when I found you again," Carter said with a shake of his head as he pulled the covers up around my shoulders and smoothed my hair off of my cheek.

"What rule?" I whispered, unable to keep my eyes open any longer.

Carter leaned forward and put his lips by my ear.

"The rule that the next time I'm inside you, you will remember and enjoy every single second."

I wanted to tell him he was awfully cocky but that just made me think of cock and wonder why male roosters were called cocks.

I passed out singing Alice in Chains "They come to snuff the rooster" lyrics.

16.

They're Called Nipples

CLAIRE'S BODY SLID down the front of mine and she got to her knees, flicking the button of my jeans open as she went. The sound of my zipper sliding down filled the quiet room. I looked down at her on her knees and had to force myself not to grab onto her hair roughly and push her where I wanted her. Her soft, smooth hands reached into my pants and pulled my erection out, holding it right by her full lips. She glanced up at me through hooded eyes and smiled before she plunged her warm, wet mouth down on me. She swallowed the entire length and swirled her tongue around and around. She hallowed out her cheeks, sucking as hard as she could while she moved her mouth up and down. The tip touched the back of her throat with each suck in and caused me to moan loudly. Her hand pumped quickly up and down my length right below her mouth and I could feel my balls tighten with the force of my release. She ran her tongue from base to tip, swirling it around the head several times before pulling back and saying, "What's wrong with your wiener?"

I moaned again and tried to push her head forward so she could take me back in her mouth.

"HEY, WHAT'S WRONG with your wiener?"

I jerked awake and turned my head, screaming at the top of my lungs when I saw Gavin standing a foot away from me on the couch, staring down between my legs. I followed his line of sight and groaned when I saw the huge morning wood I sported poking up under the blanket.

I sat up quickly and bunched the blanket around my lap as best I could as Claire came running into the living room, a look of panic on her face from my scream moments ago.

"What happened?" she asked in alarm as she ran over and knelt down next to Gavin.

Stop thinking about Claire on her knees. Stop thinking about Claire on her knees. Think about that old lady from Titanic naked.

Gavin pointed to me. "Carter's got a big wiener, Mom. Sumfin's wrong with him. He was making the same noises I do when my tummy hurts."

Claire smothered a laugh and finally looked me in the eyes.

"I guess I don't need to ask if you slept well!" she said brightly.

I shook my head at how chipper she was this early in the morning after last night.

"How are you even able to function this morning?" I asked, looking her over. Aside from looking a little sleepy, she still looked amazing. Her hair was wild, she had a little bit of make-up smudged underneath one eye and she wore an old tank top and shorts that had seen better days, yet she was the most beautiful woman I had ever seen.

She laughed and pointed to Gavin.

"You learn real quickly that as a parent, you don't have time for a hangover. Extra Strength-Rapid Release Tylenol and I have become very close over the years."

The phone rang and she hurried out of the living room to answer it, leaving Gavin to stand there and stare at me.

"So, how was your sleepover at Grandpas last night?" I asked as I flung the blanket off of me now that my morning glory was under control.

He shrugged.

"Do I have a vagina?"

I stared blankly at him, not quite sure I heard him correctly.

"Uh, what?" I asked, swinging my legs around and placing my feet on the floor.

He let out a huff of irritation with me.

"I said, do I have a vagina?"

I turned towards the kitchen to see Claire on the phone, pacing back and forth. Shit, I was on my own with this one. How the hell does he even know the word vagina? Wait, maybe he doesn't. He's four for fuck's sake. He probably thinks vagina means Cleveland.

"Well, Gavin, um…do you know what that words means?"

Please say Cleveland. Please say Cleveland.

"Papa watched a movie last night and the guy said he felt like he was driving around in a vagina. Can I drive a vagina? Does a vagina have windows and a horn?"

Oh holy mother of shit.

"Shit. Son of a bitch!" Claire cursed as she walked back into the living room.

Gavin opened his mouth but Claire was quick to cut him off.

"Don't you even think about repeating what I said. Go to your room and find some clothes to wear. You have to go to work with Mommy today."

Gavin scampered off and his vagina comment was momentarily forgotten when I saw the look of worry on Claire's face.

"What's going on? What happened?"

She flopped down next to me on the couch, rested her head on the back of it and closed her eyes.

"My dad was supposed to watch Gavin today so I could finish up some things at the shop but he got called in to work," she said with a sigh.

Light bulb.

"I can watch him for you," I said immediately.

She lifted up her head and stared at me with her mouth open.

"Seriously, Claire, let me do this for you. I would be happy to take him today and get to spend some time with him."

After forty minutes of Claire listing all of the small objects he could fit into his mouth, making me repeat the number for Poison Control back to her eight times and drawing me a diagram with stick figures on a paper towel of how to do CPR, Gavin and I kissed Claire good-bye, got into my car and headed to the library for story time.

It was a public place, full of kids and parents who knew how to take care of kids in case I had a problem or questions. What could possibly go wrong?

"...AND THE SEX? Oh you can just kiss that shit good-bye right now. Before we had our son my wife was a dirty little whore. She'd give me blow jobs while I drove down the freeway, she'd dress up in a naughty nurse uniform and greet me at the door when I got home from work and whenever we went out, we always pulled the car over on the way home and fucked in the front seat."

The man sitting next to me let out a great big sigh. He was another father I met when Gavin and I arrived at the library. He was there with his three-year old son and eight-year-old daughter. His daughter was from a previous relationship and he had his son with his current wife. We started talking when I sat down next to him on one of the couches while the boys sat in a circle with a bunch of other kids a few feet away listening to the librarian read them a book. After telling him the condensed version of my relationship with Claire and Gavin, I asked him for some parenting tips since he'd been around the block a lot longer than me. Little did I know it would turn into a "how much kids fucked up my life" speech.

"But after our son was born, my penis got put on the 'do not call' list. Sometimes, if I listen really closely, I can often hear the sound of 'Taps' being played from my lonely balls," he whispered to me as he waved his hand and smiled at his son.

Jesus. Claire and I hadn't even got to the sex part yet. Was this really how it would be? Before I demanded that this guy tell me something good so I wouldn't have nightmares tonight, his daughter Finley ran over to him with a book in her hands.

"Daddy, can you read me this book about horses?" she asked sweetly as she climbed up onto his lap.

"Sure, baby girl," he replied, wrapping an arm around his daughter and taking the book from her hand.

See? Look at how sweet kids could be. They might be little hellions sometimes but they definitely had hearts of gold. And there was nothing sweeter than watching a father with his daughter.

"Oh Jesus, Mary and Joseph…where did you get this book?" the man asked as a few parents looked in his direction and shot him dirty looks.

I glanced over to see what the problem was and noticed the book in his hand read "The Big Book of Lesbian Horse Stories." My mouth fell open in horror and I looked around to see if anyone had noticed that there was porn in the children's section of the library.

"Honey, go pick out another book," he told her calmly as he hid the book behind his back.

"But I want that one, it's got horses in it," she argued.

"Well, you can't read that one. That's a big person book. It's not for kids."

Finley rolled her eyes and huffed, handing him the other book she brought over with her, "Poop Eaters".

This time, her father was the one to roll his eyes. "Poop Eaters"? Again? Really, Finley. You need to find another hobby."

"She's got this thing about poop," he told me as he took the book from her. "When she was little, she used to finger-paint her room with the poop in her diaper."

He chuckled at the memory and I covered my mouth with my hand to keep the vomit inside. I stared at the little girl's hands expecting to see it covered in shit.

"A few times when we were at the park she would run up to me and say she had a present for me. She'd hold out her hand and it would be filled with cat poop she found in the sand box. Ahhhh, good times," he said with a bob of his head.

A few times? This happened more than once? Poop finger-painting?

Poop presents? Shouldn't kids be born with the knowledge that you never touch poop? Is Gavin aware that this is a rule no one should ever break?

I looked over at him rummaging through a box of books someone placed next to the reading circle and wondered if he would find poop in there and bring it to me. What if he tried to finger-paint *me* with it? I'd scream. And you can't scream in the library. What do I do? WHAT DO I DO???

"So yeah, good luck with the whole father thing, dude," the man said to me as he stood up to leave.

I sat there on the couch trying to stop the panic attack I was pretty sure I was having. I need a paper bag to breathe into. Why the fuck didn't I bring a paper bag? Oh Jesus. Poop hands. POOP HANDS!

"Carter! Hey, Carter!" Gavin shouted as he ran towards me and several other adults shushed him.

I stared at his hands, praying to God there wasn't shit on them. How would I explain to Claire that I made our son walk home from the library because I didn't want shitty hand prints inside my car? I winced as he raced towards me, bracing myself for a shit pie to the face or a shit ball to the arm. He was running so fast he couldn't stop himself in time and he slammed into my legs with an "Oomph."

Oh fuck, please let there not be shit on my legs right now.

As soon as he hit my legs, he scrambled up onto my lap, careful not to drop whatever was clutched in his hand. One can never be too careful with a handful of shit, obviously.

He put his knees on my thighs and I felt him crawl up onto my lap. My eyes were squeezed so tightly closed that I was giving myself a headache.

Oh sweet Jesus. Here it comes. A shit sandwich. He's going to make me pretend to eat it like kids do when they make you a Play-Doh cookie. The term "shiteating grin" will finally have meaning in my life.

"I got you sumfin' Carter. Guess which hand?" he said excitedly.

Oh, God, please don't make me choose. It will always be the hand without shit in it.

Gavin quickly grew impatient with my silence. "Come on, Carter, open your eyes. Don't be a wuss."

I swallowed nervously, trying to think of all the ways to disinfect shit from your skin.

Does bleach burn? Probably after I took a layer of skin off with sandpaper, it would. I slowly opened one eye at a time until I could see that Gavin had his arms behind his back.

"Come on, pick one of my arms and see what I gots," he said excitedly.

"Gee, I guess I'll pick that hand," I said unenthusiastically as I tapped his right arm.

Good-bye clean, shitless skin. I'll remember you fondly.

Gavin bounced up and down on my thighs and swung his right arm around in front of him.

"You picked the right one! Here ya go!" he said excitedly.

I looked down nervously and breathed a deep sigh of relief when I saw what was in his hand.

A book. A beautiful, crisp, brand new library book. Not a book covered in shit, or a book made out of shit. Just a book. The title read "Come on Get Happy!"

I took it from his little hand and held it up in the air to look at the picture of puppies frolicking in a field on the front cover.

"This is a pretty awesome book. How come you picked this one?" I asked him as he put the hand that used to hold the book up on my shoulder and looked me in the eye.

"Because I like you. And Mommy says it's nice to do things that make people happy. I want you to be happy."

All I could do was sit there and stare at him. I got it now. I got why Claire hadn't crumbled when she found out she was pregnant, why she dropped out of college and gave up everything for this little boy. I suddenly realized that my heart was sitting there on my lap and even though I wasn't here for the first four years of his life, I loved him unconditionally simply because he was mine. He was a part of me. I knew without a doubt, I would give my life to make sure he was safe. I wrapped my arms around his little body, hoping he didn't still think of me as a stranger and would let me hug him.

He leaned into me without hesitation and I rested my forehead against his.

"Buddy, I am already the happiest guy in the world," I told him softly.

Gavin stared at me for a few minutes and then pulled his other arm out from behind his back. "Good, then after you read that one, you can read this one.

I pulled away from him and glanced down in his hand at a book titled "The Vagina Monologues".

AFTER WE LEFT the library, I took Gavin to get ice cream and then we headed back to Claire's house. True to form, Gavin talked the whole way home and I started to wonder if he was like a record player that was skipping and maybe I needed to smack the side of him to get him to stop.

I resisted the urge. Barely.

When we got back to the house, I sat down on the couch and Gavin grabbed a photo album from one of the end table drawers and curled up on my lap with it. He flipped through all of the pages, explaining each picture to me. I saw every single birthday, Christmas, Halloween and everything in between that I missed, and with Gavin's commentary about each event, it almost felt like I had been there.

I also learned quite a few things about Claire. Like the fact she has cousin she can't stand.

"That's Heather. She's mommy's cousin. Mommy says she's a whore," Gavin said, pointing at the group photo that looked like it was taken at some sort of family reunion.

I also learned that Gavin seemed to have a penchant for squirting things all over the house, showcased by at least five pages in the photo album. I guess I should have taken a picture of the toothpaste incident a few weeks ago.

"Gavin, how come there are so many pictures of you making messes?" I asked as I flipped to the next page that showed a picture of him sitting on the kitchen floor in a pile of coffee grounds, cereal, oatmeal and what looked like syrup. "I hope you cleaned up all this stuff for mommy."

"Cleaning is ridiculous," he replied.

Considering the current state of my own home, I couldn't really argue that fact.

We continued to look at the rest of the pictures in that album and four others before I noticed that Gavin was unusually quiet on my lap. I glanced down and saw that he had fallen asleep sitting up. I awkwardly scooped my hands under his legs and carried him to his room exactly how he fell asleep – with his back against my chest and his legs dangling down off of my hands. I knew there was some sort of rule about "never wake a sleeping baby" and I figured that had to apply to toddlers as well since they could get into much more trouble than a baby.

After getting him tucked into bed, I came back out into the living room and relaxed on the couch. I turned on the TV, flipping through the channels until I found something to watch. An hour later, right when I started to doze off, my phone buzzed for probably the tenth time since I left the house earlier with Gavin. I smiled as I pulled my phone out of my pocket, knowing it would be Claire again.

How's it going? Is everything ok? ~ Claire

I couldn't even be offended that she was so worried. It was understandable. Surprisingly, being alone with Gavin wasn't bad at all. He was really well behaved, better than any child I had ever been around.

Perfect. Gavin just got his first lap dance. He's hopped up on Red Bull and crack right now and I found out he doesn't like whiskey. ~ Carter

I laughed to myself and hit send. My phone buzzed immediately with her reply, like I knew it would.

I hope you at least sprang for the hot chick and not some butter face with VD. And your son prefers vodka, like his mother. ~ Claire

My laugh at her reply was so loud I glanced down the hall to make sure it didn't wake Gavin. I quickly typed a reply back. Even though she made a joke, I knew without a doubt she was masking a tiny bit of fear.

Everything is fine, Mom. Same as it was five minutes ago when you asked ;) ~ Carter

My phone buzzed not five seconds later.

Oh shut up! It's not him I'm worried about. I was afraid you were duct taped to a chair or had your head shaved by now. ~ Claire

The doorbell rang and as I got up to find out who it was, I quickly sent off another text letting her know that our son was not able to overpower me.

Yet.

I opened the door to find Drew standing there with a box in his hands.

"What are you doing here?" I asked.

Drew pushed past me into the house.

"Nice to see you too, pig fucker. I've got all of Claire's flyers, brochures and whatever other shit Jenny was doing for her. She asked me to drop them off here for her. What are *you* doing here? And why are you still wearing the same clothes from last night? Did you finally bump uglies with your MILF?"

I took the box out of his hand and rolled my eyes at him.

"Will you shut up already, dick? Gavin is sleeping."

Drew looked past me towards Gavin's room.

"Good, I've got a present for the little spawn," he said with a smile as he pulled a shirt out of his back pocket. He held it up in front of me and all I could do was shake my head.

"You didn't. Oh my God, Claire is going to kill you," I told him.

I looked down at my watch, realizing that Gavin had been out for quite a while.

"Hey, how long do kids sleep?" I asked.

"You're asking me? How the fuck should I know? When was the last time you checked on him?"

I looked at him blankly.

Shit, I was supposed to check on him? He was asleep. What the hell could happen while he was asleep?

I turned and ran down the hall to Gavin's room with Drew right on my heels.

"Shit! Oh fucking shit."

Gavin's bed was empty, the covers thrown back like he woke up and flung them off.

I charged into the room, looking behind the door, under the bed and in the closet.

"Oh, Jesus. I lost him. I already fucking lost him!" I yelled in panic as I rummaged through his closet and pulled out a stuffed clown from the bottom of the pile.

Didn't that kid from Poltergeist get sucked into his closet by an evil clown? Shit!

"You didn't lose him. It's not like he could have gotten far. There's only one way out of this house and he would have had to walk right past you to get to it."

Drew walked out of the bedroom while I stood there trying not to cry as I choked the fuck out of the stupid clown that took my kid.

Claire was going to hate me. Our son was sucked into the pits of hell while I was watching General Hospital. God damn you, Brenda and Sonny for making me lose focus.

What if he crawled into the ventilation and passed out somewhere in the walls? Oh my God, he could have gotten into the fridge and suffocated. Didn't they tell you to put rope around your fridge? Or wait, that was just when you put it out to the curb, wasn't it?

Fuck! I didn't know anything!

"Carter! I found him!" Drew yelled from down the hall.

I raced out of Gavin's room and down the hall, finding Drew standing in the doorway of the bathroom laughing his ass off.

"What the hell are you laughing about?" I asked angrily as I pushed passed him.

And then I saw it.

Gavin, sitting on the edge of the sink with white shit all over his face.

"Gavin, what did you get all over your face? Is that Mommy's make-up?"

He shook his head.

"Nope, it's this," he said, handing me the empty tube.

I took it from him and looked down. Diaper rash cream. My son put diaper rash cream all over his face. And when I say all over his face, I mean it. Practically every surface was covered, including his lips.

Drew came up behind me and looked over my shoulder.

"Dude, he put ass cream on his face. You do know I'm going to have to start calling your son Ass Face now, right?" Drew laughed.

"Shut up, dicky," Gavin told him.

"You shut up. You're the one with the ass face," Drew retorted.

I got a washcloth out of the linen closet and ran it under the sink.

"Both of you shut it and quit arguing," I told them as I started to scrub the white shit off of Gavin's face. What the fuck do they make this stuff out of, cement? It's like it's been spackled on. And why does this towel smell like mint?

The white goo was starting to come off, but in its place was now blue goo. What the…?

I held up the towel and noticed it was full of whatever this blue stuff was. I brought it up to my nose and smelled it.

"There's toothpaste on this towel," I muttered.

Drew reached into the linen closet to grab me another one.

"Eeeew, what the fuck?" he said, dropping the towel on the ground.

I looked at his hands and they were covered with toothpaste. I walked back to the closet and picked up a few of the towels. Each one was smeared with toothpaste. And stuck way in the back corner of one of the shelves was the empty tube.

I turned back around to face Gavin.

"Why did you put toothpaste all over everything?"

He shrugged. "I don't know."

I managed to find a clean towel at the bottom of the pile on one of the shelves and got Gavin cleaned up. Drew took him to play in his room while I cleaned up the toothpaste and diaper rash cream mess and put all of the minty-fresh towels into the wash. I was walking past the front door after I started the washing machine when Claire walked in.

"Honey, you're home," I said with a smile.

She laughed and came up to me, snaking her arms around my waist.

"Would I sound really girly if I told you how awesome it is to walk in the door and see you here?" she asked.

I kissed the tip of her nose.

"Yeah, you'd totally sound like a needy chick. Just don't start getting clingy otherwise it's going to get really awkward."

She smacked my chest and rolled her eyes at me.

"I'm pretty sure you might like my kind of clingy," she said with a smirk as she brought her hips up against mine. I put my hands on her waist and rubbed her against the hard-on I had since she walked in the door.

"I think you might be right, Miss Morgan," I said, as I leaned forward to kiss her.

"Get your hands off my woman!"

I pulled my lips away from Claire's and we both laughed at the sound of Gavin's angry rant.

"Gavin, what are you wearing?" Claire asked as she stepped out of my arms and walked over to him.

Drew walked up behind him and smiled.

"Hey there, hot stuff! Like the shirt I got him?"

Gavin stood there proudly, pulling the hem of his shirt down so Claire could read it.

"Hung like a five-year-old?" she read, giving Drew the evil eye.

"I could have got him one like mine. They had it in his size," Drew said.

I think we can all say the shirt Gavin was wearing was a lot better than having one on that said, "Stare at me in disgust if you want to blow me".

Claire kicked Drew out, after thanking him for dropping off her stuff from Jenny, and decided to let Gavin keep the shirt on because, let's be honest, it was just too funny to take off of him. I was nowhere near ready to leave Claire and Gavin yet, but I needed a shower and some clean clothes. Since Claire worked all day, I invited her and Gavin over to my place for dinner. And I told her to pack a bag for both of them.

I WAS FRANTICALLY racing around my bedroom trying to find something to wear that said, "I want to bang your brains out after our kid goes to sleep but I don't want to look too slutty or desperate". I washed and conditioned my hair three times, shaved my legs twice and put on enough lotion that Carter might be able to just borrow my legs the next time he wanted to jerk off. I stood by my dresser, holding up a pair of white lace thongs and tried to keep my towel wrapped around me by squeezing my arms against the sides of my boobs. I threw the white underwear back in the drawer. White was for virgins. I didn't want to be a virgin. I wanted to be a freak, a freaky hot chick that wore slutty red underwear. But not too slutty.

My cell phone rang and I struggled with the towel as I pawed through my dresser and reached for the phone. I answered it and held it against my ear with my shoulder.

"Wear the low-rise, red, lace boy shorts with the matching push-up bra."

"Liz, what the fuck? How do you…I didn't…" I stammered into the phone.

She let out a dramatic sigh.

"Well, crotch rot, since you weren't going to tell me you'd be riding the Carter Express tonight, I had to find out elsewhere."

"Liz, I just found out thirty minutes ago. I was going to call you, I swear. How the fuck do you know anyway?"

"Oh, Jim ran into Carter buying condoms at the grocery store – extra small. I didn't realize they made them in children's sizes."

"Ha ha, very funny, thunder cunt," I replied sarcastically. "Speaking of giant vaginas, I haven't gotten any butt dials from you lately. Has Jim taken a break from spelunking in your bottomless pit lately?"

Gavin walked into my room then with his Toy Story backpack on. He was very excited at the idea of having a sleepover at Carter's house. He argued with me that he could pack his own bag. I'd have to sneak a look into it when he was busy. The last time he went to my dad's, he packed one dirty sock, eight stuffed animals and a plastic fork.

"Liz, I have to go. Your godson just walked in and I need to finish getting ready," I explained as Gavin scrambled up onto my bed and started jumping up and down on it.

I snapped my fingers and pointed to the bed. He immediately kicked his legs out in front of his body and landed on his butt.

"Make sure you pack Children's Benadryl and duct tape. You don't need anyone yelling, 'Mommy,' when there's a penis in you. And no matter how much Carter tries to tell you otherwise, it is never hot if he says it. Never. Trust me."

I really didn't need the mental image of Jim screaming, "Mommy," while he railed Liz. I quickly ended the call and grabbed the red bra & underwear set from my second drawer. Liz bought it for me two years prior to wear on a blind date she'd set me up on. The guy showed up an hour early asking if we could just hit it so he could go. Apparently his mom needed her car back and wanted him to clean his room before she got home. Needless to say, the tags never got removed from the red lace underwear.

I shimmied into the bra while Gavin sat there staring at me through the mirror. I learned early on that it was impossible to do anything by yourself when you had a toddler. Covering myself up and running to hide behind a door if he walked in when I was getting dressed just made him even more curious and inquisitive. And by inquisitive, I mean annoying. It was best to just go about my business and if questions arose, I could handle them in a proficient and mature manner. In theory.

"Are you puttin' your boobs on mom?" Gavin asked.

I laughed and shook my head at his question.

"Well, this bra is mostly padding so I guess I *am* putting my boobs on."

I turned around to face him as I finished pulling the straps up and reached for my jeans I left laying across the foot of the bed.

"Hey, Mom, what are those red thingys?" he asked.

"What red things?" I replied distractedly as I pulled on my jeans and stood there staring at the four different shirts I laid out.

"The red thingies on your boobs."

I closed my eyes and bowed my head.

Okay, this was my chance to be an adult. He asked a reasonable question, so I should give him a reasonable answer. Right? But he's only four. What is the appropriate age to learn the word "nipples"? Should I be honest with him or make something up? He was going to preschool in a few months. What if they were talking about baby bottles or saw a kitten drinking milk from its mother? If I made something up, my kid was going to be all, "Nuh-uh teacher. My mommy said those are called noo-noo-cows and they're just there for decoration."

My son would grow up scarred for life when everyone made fun of him for putting a noo-noo-cow on a baby bottle. I could hear Robert Dinero's voice in my head.

"I have noo-noo-cows, Greg, can you milk me?"

"They're called nipples, Gavin."

Honesty is the best policy. Let's go with that.

He sat there for a few minutes not saying anything. I was mentally patting myself on the back for being a good parent and being able to be truthful with my son.

"Nipples," he said softly.

I nodded my head, proud that he had no problem using the big-people word and not something silly. I still had nightmares about the fact that my father called a vagina a choo-choo-laney when I was growing up.

"Nipples, nipples, nipples. That's fun to say!"

Shit. I may have spoken too soon.

He jumped down off of the bed and ran out of my room, singing "Twinkle, Twinkle Little Star" but replaced each and every word with "nipple."

17.

Duct Tape for the Win

TROJAN, DUREX, LIFESTYLES, Trojan Magnum (oh yeah, my three foot cock definitely needed those), Contempo, Vivid and Rough Rider.

Seriously? There was a condom brand called Rough Rider? Why not just go with Fuck Her Hard and be done with it?

I stood in the "Family Planning" aisle of the grocery store, trying to decide which condom brand was more effective. Family Planning…give me a break. How many people came to this aisle because they were planning a family? They came to this aisle to AVOID planning a family.

I couldn't buy Trojan. Every time I opened the box I heard that god damn jingle from the commercial, "Trojan Man!" and then I thought of a guy on a horse. Durex made me think of Playtex which made me think of tampons, which made me think of periods, which made me want to dry heave. Lifestyles made me think of Robin Leach and caviar. Fish eggs were not sexy and neither was Robin Leach.

I wasn't going to make myself look like a major asshole and buy Trojan Magnum. If I bought those things, I'd have to talk like Dirty Hairy in the bedroom. "Do you feel lucky today, seeing my giant penis, punk?"

Claire probably wouldn't take too kindly to me calling her a punk before I had sex with her.

Contempo just sounded boring, like contemporary music, John Tesh or some shit like that. Snooze fest. If people fell asleep while you were having sex with them, you needed to get your shit together.

Rough Rider was already out so that left me with Vivid. Vivid video was a porn making company. And the things I wanted to do to Claire could definitely be in porn. I think dressing up like a FedEx guy so I could deliver my big package to the horny housewife while she bent over the kitchen sink may have to wait at least a few weeks though.

I grabbed the forty-eight count bulk box that came with a free bottle of KY Warming Liquid and a vibrating cock ring and threw them in the cart. The cock ring scared me just a little. The idea of something vibrating by my balls made me nervous. What if it short-circuited? Great Balls of Fire didn't need to occur in the bedroom. And the smell of burning nut hair was sure to kill the mood.

"Stop worrying. I'm sure Claire isn't going to even notice that you have a tiny tallywhacker."

I turned around to see Jim standing in the aisle with a smirk and a box of tampons in his hand.

"Very funny, asshole. Looks like you're on the rag this week. Make sure to get yourself some Midol and a copy of Terms of Endearment so you can have yourself a good cry," I quipped.

"Hey, Terms of Endearment is a very touching, beautiful story about the dynamics in a mother/daughter relationship. Show some respect for Shirley McClain and Debra Winger for fuck's sake. That movie won five Oscars for…"

"Jesus, calm down, Nancy. Does Liz know you're using her vagina today?" I asked in mock horror.

Jim smiled, "I'm going to pretend you didn't say that because if I told Liz, she would cut your nut sack off, dude."

He was right about that. Liz was a bulldog with rabies and mad cow disease. She would fuck me up if I crossed her.

"Since I just caught you buying condoms, and Claire is like a sister to me, I feel I must say a few words at this time," he explained, shoving aside some bottles of lube on a shelf next to him so he could put his box of tampons down and cross his arms in front of him.

I nodded. "By all means."

"I like you, Carter, but I met Claire first and I'm engaged to her best friend, so that means, by chick laws, I have to like her more. I feel it's necessary that I use the words of some of the greats in history to establish the sincerity of the situation we find ourselves in."

He paused and I waited for him to continue by resting my elbow on the handle of my cart.

"You mess with the bull, you get the horns."

"If you want to throw down fisticuffs, I've got Jack Johnson and Tom O'Leary waiting for ya, right here."

"I'll get you my pretty and your little dog too."

"I will gouge out your eyeballs and skull-fuck you."

I nodded my head, impressed. "Full Metal Jacket?" I asked.

"Yep."

"Nice touch," I replied.

Jim turned around and grabbed his tampons off of the shelf.

"Well, alrighty then. My work here is done. I've got a few more items to pick up so I'll talk to you later."

AN HOUR AND a half later, I managed to clean up the house, change the sheets on my bed, make up the extra bed in the spare room for Gavin and set up a couple of the things I bought for him over the past week. Maybe it was a little bit much, but oh well. I'd missed out on four years of birthdays, Christmases, Valentine's Days, Arbor Days, Sundays and every other day I could have bought him something. I had a lot of time to make up for.

My son was going to spend the night at my house.

I kind of wanted to jump up and down and clap my hands like a girl. I was excited to curl up with him on the couch in his pajamas and watch the new movie I picked up earlier. I couldn't wait to tuck him into bed and wake up with him tomorrow morning and get him breakfast. I wanted to experience all of the things that made up his day. I wanted to hear him laugh, listen to him talk and watch him interact with Claire.

Claire.

Beautiful, smart, funny, sexy Claire who was going to be spending the night at my house as well. I couldn't wait to wake up with her next to me in the morning. I missed out on that five years ago, and I wasn't about to go without this time. I wanted her face to be the first thing I saw when the sun came up and her body curled up next to mine to be the first thing I felt. But most of all, I wanted to be coherent for every single second. I didn't want the haze of alcohol to take anything away from this night for either one of us.

I hope she didn't think it was too forward of me to buy condoms. If she didn't want to do anything, there was no way I would pressure her. But if she asked my throbbing python of love to come out and play, I wasn't going to complain.

I just poured a box of noodles into a pot of boiling water when the doorbell rang. I set the timer on the stove and quickly walked through the living room and answered the door. As soon as it opened, Gavin barged past me and into the living room.

"Hi Carter! Mommy has nipples! Do you have nipples?" he asked as he took off his backpack and dumped the contents in the middle of the floor.

"Oh my God, Gavin, filter!" Claire scolded as she walked through the doorway, rolling her eyes at me. I laughed as I shut the door behind her and tried not to grab her ass or sniff her hair.

Jesus, she really did have a great ass.

"What's the deal with the nipples question?" I asked as we both stood in the entry to the living room, watching Gavin sort through the stuff he brought.

"He was in my room when I got dressed earlier and he asked me what they were. I thought I should be honest with him and now I realize it was a big mistake. He spent the whole way here singing 'All I want for Christmas are my two front nipples.' I almost opened the door and shoved him out into oncoming traffic," Claire said with a laugh.

"Mommy stopped the car and unlocked the doors and told me to get out and walk," Gavin informed me.

"Okay, *almost* isn't exactly accurate," she told me with a shrug. "In my defense, I did tell him if he said the word 'nipples' one more time I was going to stop the car and make him walk. According to his pediatrician, it's important to always follow through with your threats."

I helped Claire take her coat off and scooped up Gavin's that he'd thrown on the floor and hung both of them up in the closet.

"Maybe now isn't the best time to tell you that he asked me if I he had a vagina this morning and then asked me to read him 'The Vagina Monologues' at the library."

Claire groaned and shook her head.

"What the hell am I going to do when he starts preschool in a few months? He's going to be like that kid in the movie, Kindergarten Cop, except he's going to announce 'Boys have a penis and girls have a vagina and my mommy has nipples!' I wrapped my arm around her waist and pulled her against my side, noting again how good her body felt next to mine.

"You mean what the hell are *we* going to do?" I corrected her. I needed to make sure she understood that I wasn't going to change my mind about all of this.

"Don't forget, he's also going to tell everyone just how huge my wiener is. At least I hope he is. Maybe I should remind him about the awesomeness that is my wiener."

Claire raised her eyebrows at me and I realized that didn't come out right at all.

"That sounded a lot skeazier than I meant it too."

Claire turned her body into mine so that we were chest-to-chest and my back was to Gavin. She rested her arms on my shoulders, letting her fingers play with the hair on the back of my neck. I got goose bumps on my arms and Mr. Happy just woke up from his evening nap and started drooling.

"Can we please ban the word wiener?" she asked with a laugh.

I glanced over my shoulder at Gavin. He had his back to us and was busy talking to his Batman figurine, asking it if it had nipples. I looked back at Claire and let my hands slide down her hips and around to her ass to pull her up against me.

"Only if you use the word 'cock' from now on," I told her with a smirk.

She pushed her hips into me and I let out a groan when she came in contact with my raging erection.

"T.J. told me you paid him twenty dollars the other night to get me to say that."

Shit. T.J. was going down the next time we played P.O.R.N. He was going to get a ball right to his throat. I placed my lips to the corner of her mouth and then kissed a path across her cheek. When I got to the soft skin right behind her ear, I let my tongue snake out so I could taste her.

She let out a little moan and pushed her hips back into me. She turned her face so her lips hovered by my ear.

"Cock, cock, c-o-c-k," she whispered, drawing out the syllables in the last one.

"Holy fucking hell..." I mumbled, wrapping my arms around her waist and hugging her tightly so her hips stopped moving against me.

The timer in the kitchen went off and all thoughts of Claire's lips and "cock" were put aside. I unwound myself from her and we all made our way into the kitchen so I could finish the spaghetti.

Dinner went very well even though Claire had to remind Gavin every ten seconds to stop talking and eat. I've never heard a kid talk so much in my life about anything and everything and I enjoyed every second of it. After dinner was over, I sent Claire and Gavin to the spare bedroom while I cleaned up the dishes.

A few seconds later I heard Gavin's yell.

I GRABBED GAVIN'S hand and we took off towards the back of the house where Carter said the spare room was. I thought it was really sweet that Carter had made up a room for Gavin.

We got to the door and I pushed it open. Gavin took a step inside and let out a yell.

"WHAT THE FRIGGIN' HELL?"

He immediately ran into the room and I stood there with my mouth open, unable to muster up the ability to tell him to watch his mouth.

Carter had Toys R Us in his spare room. There was a fucking tree house in the corner! A tree house! How did he even get that in here?

I slowly took in every inch of the room and then did it again just to make sure I wasn't seeing things. Nope, there was definitely a pile of at least one hundred stuffed animals in the corner, a bunk bed with race car blankets, three Hotwheels tracks that intersected all over the room, a pile of puzzles, a drawing table filled with coloring books and crayons, and a shelf filled with multicolor bins that held cars, monster trucks, army men, leggos and God knows what else. Gavin zipped all around the room, touching everything.

"Holy shit," I muttered.

Gavin stopped his climb up into the tree house and looked at me.

"Mom, you can't say shit," he scolded.

I laughed hysterically.

"Oh yes I can. I can say shit. I'm an adult for shit's sake. You're the one that can't say shit. Shit! Shitballsack!"

I could feel the burn in the back of my throat and a sting in my eyes that indicated I was going to cry. Shit! That did it. Now I was in love with the jerk. He bought my…our son a fucking toy store. He wouldn't have done this if he wasn't serious. I know he told me he was – several times. I wanted so much to believe him, but I didn't just have myself to think about. I couldn't really move forward and turn this into something real until I was one hundred percent certain he would never leave Gavin. He could leave me, he could change his mind about us and I knew I'd survive. But I would never, ever let my son be hurt like that. Looking around this room, thinking about how easily he let us take over his life and change whatever plans he had for his future, I knew without a doubt

I wanted him to be Gavin's dad. He wasn't just a sperm donor anymore. He was a father. And I knew he would be a damn good one.

I let the tears slip out of my eyes and run down my cheeks as I smiled at our son, happily checking out all of his new toys. I heard a throat clear behind me and I whipped around to see Carter standing there sheepishly with his hands in his pockets.

"So, um, how much trouble am I in? I didn't plan on getting this much but once I got to the store, I couldn't help myself. They make Hotwheels that change color in the water, Claire! And a garbage truck named Stinky that moves on its own and picks up toys and then burps. Did you know there was something called Moon Sand? Oh, oh and Aqua Sand that strangely looks like siding insulation when you put it in the water but when you pull it out…"

I launched myself into his arms and cut off his words with my lips. He was obviously surprised but caught me easily in his arms and returned my kiss. I poured everything I had into that kiss, all of my happiness, all of my trust and all of my love. I let him know with my lips just how thankful I was to have been blessed with a man like him in my life. I could have kissed him for days and never come up for air. The only thing that made me stop was the sound of absolute silence in the room behind us.

I broke from the kiss and Carter let out a groan of complaint which made my girly parts tingle knowing that he didn't want to stop. Keeping my arms around him, I turned my head around.

"Where's Gavin?"

"Ooooh this is warm. And it makes my hands tingle," we heard Gavin say from another room.

I sighed. "Shit, what did he get into now?" I muttered as I reluctantly pulled out of Carter's arms.

Carter started to smile but immediately got a horrified look on his face. He turned and raced out of the room before I could ask him what was wrong. I followed after him and was right on his heels when he rounded the corner to his bedroom. It was like something out of a movie. Carter jumped up and dove through the air, arms stretched out in front of him like Superman. He sailed across the room and landed on his stomach on the bed right next to Gavin, but not before smacking something out of his hand. I just stood there with my mouth open, trying to understand what the hell was going on.

"Heeeeey," Gavin complained with a frown.

Carter was face down on the bed, his shoulders shaking so hard that Gavin's body was bouncing. Was he crying? Oh my God, was he having a nervous breakdown?

"Carter, what the hell?" I asked.

"What the hell, Carter?" Gavin repeated.

"Gavin!" I scolded while Carter continued to have a seizure or whatever the hell he was doing.

"But Mooooom, he took my lotion," Gavin pouted.

I walked up to the bed to see what Gavin was pointing at. A small tube of something was by Carter's hand on the bed. As soon as I got close enough to see it, Carter grabbed it and flipped over on his back. And now I could see that he wasn't dying from an epileptic seizure, he was laughing his ass off.

"It's not funny, Carter. You took my lotion," Gavin complained.

This only made Carter laugh harder until he was gasping for breath. I looked at him in confusion. He just lifted his arm and handed me the tube of…

KY Warming Liquid?

Oh Jesus fucking hell. Lube? He put lube on his hands. It only took seconds for me to notice that Gavin was surrounded by condoms. A couple of them open and out of their wrappers.

"Your balloons suck, Carter," Gavin complained.

I collapsed on the bed next to Carter and laughed right along with him.

TWENTY MINUTES INTO Toy Story 2, Gavin fell fast asleep with his head on Carter's lap. I got up to go to the bathroom and grabbed my cell phone off of the kitchen table so I could sneak a picture. It was just too cute not to document.

I tapped Carter on the shoulder once I stowed my phone away and pointed to Gavin and then motioned back to his room. He awkwardly tried to finagle his arms around Gavin and you could tell he was freaked out about waking him up.

"It's okay," I whispered to him. "He won't wake up."

Carter shook his head and muttered something that sounded like "Yeah right, until suddenly he disappears and you realize he's been eaten by a clown."

He moved quickly, scooping Gavin into his arms like he'd done it a thousand times before and Gavin never batted an eyelash at the disruption. I followed behind Carter down the hall and smiled at the sight of Gavin with his head nestled into the crook of Carter's neck and his arms hanging limply at his sides. We walked into the bedroom, stepping over all of the toys so we wouldn't trip, and I stood back while Carter gently put Gavin down on the bottom bunk and covered him up. It took everything in me not to sob when he brushed Gavin's hair off of his forehead like I usually did every night.

"My lunch box makes cow nipples," Gavin mumbled in his sleep before rolling over to face the wall.

Carter looked back at me.

"What the hell was that?" he whispered with a laugh.

I stepped around him, bent over and kissed Gavin's head.

"Your son talks in his sleep," I informed Carter as I took his hand and pulled him off the bed. "I was kind of hoping it was hereditary. I don't talk in my sleep and if you don't either, then maybe it has to do with what he eats before bed."

Carter held onto my hand as we walked across the room. "Sorry to say, I don't talk in my sleep. What does he eat before bed?"

"LSD, shrooms, the usual bedtime snack for toddlers."

Before we got to the door, Carter let go of my hand, walked over to the wall and plugged in a nightlight that was shaped like a race car. He joined me at the doorway and took my hand again.

"See? This is what's wrong with the youth of America," he whispered. "Too many chocolate chip cookies and not enough acid."

I just stood there looking at him. A room full of toys *and* a night-light? This man had thought of everything.

"What?" he asked, when I didn't move.

"You just amaze me, that's all," I told him with a smile as I pulled him out into the hall, shutting the door to Gavin's room behind me.

We walked silently down the hall to Carter's bedroom, both of us knowing without a doubt that this was the next step. I wanted to sleep with him again the first moment I saw him in the bar. It felt like this was a long time coming, but here, in this moment, it finally felt right.

Carter shut the door to his room and I reached around him to lock it just in case. Gavin slept like the dead, but he was in a strange place so I didn't know how well he'd do. Maybe that was selfish of me, but after five long years and no alone time, I think I deserved this. Plus, I'd much rather get a knock on the door warning us he was awake instead of him just barging in and asking why we were wrestling naked.

The only light in the room came from a small lamp on the bedside table that cast a soft glow around the room. We stood there by the door just staring at each other. The weird thing was it wasn't awkward at all. I wanted to take it all in. I wanted to remember every single second of this moment. I didn't want to just have bits and pieces of a drunken night flowing in and out of my mind. I wanted to remember every touch, every look and every feeling. I would never regret the first time we had sex because it brought me Gavin. But this time would mean more, because this time, I loved this man with all of my heart.

In just a few minutes I was going to be totally naked in front of him.

Oh my God, in just a few minutes I was going to be naked. In front of Carter.

Shit, I have stretch marks on my ass. Okay, just keep his eyes off of my naked ass.

He reached down and took my hand, pulling me to his chest. He didn't let go of my hand as he wrapped both of our arms behind my back, clasping our fingers together. His other hand came up to rest on my cheek while he looked into my eyes.

"Before we do this, you need to know something," he whispered.

He's going to tell me he's gay.

"I am one hundred percent, absolutely in love with you and Gavin."

My lip quivered and my heart soared. I closed my eyes and tried to keep the tears inside as I rested my forehead against his. Once I got my emotions under control, I pulled back so I could see his face.

"I love you too, Carter," I whispered back.

A smile lit up his face and I brought my hand up and let my fingers trace the shape of his lips. He kissed me fingertips and started walking me backwards towards the bed. I loved the way he looked at me, like I was his whole world. I didn't think we even made eye contact our first time together.

When the back of my knees hit the edge, he leaned me backwards, holding me tight and lowering me slowly, until I felt the softness of the bed against my back and the hard heat of Carter against my front. His arm held me tight around my waist and he lifted me just enough so he could move us both further onto the bed. I brought my legs up and wrapped them around his hips. I placed both of my hands against his cheeks and craned my neck up so I could kiss him. The kiss started out gentle and sweet but quickly changed. I could feel his hardness right in the apex of my thighs and a burst of heat surged through me and dampened my underwear. Carter shifted his hips slightly and I whimpered into his open mouth. That sound must have gave him the "all systems go" signal because he pushed his tongue deep into my mouth and moved the hardness in his jeans right against me. I moved my hands down to hem of his shirt and slid them underneath. The heat of his smooth skin instantly warmed my chilled hands as I moved them up the front of his stomach and chest. I pushed my forearms higher to raise his shirt up the front of his body. He broke the kiss to reach back behind him and grasp a handful of his shirt, yanking it up over his head and tossing it to the side.

He raised himself above me on one arm, repeating the motions I just performed on him. He flattened his hand on the lower part of my stomach, his fingers slipping under the hem of my shirt. He watched his hand as it slowly moved up my stomach and between my breasts. I grabbed the bottom of my shirt and pulled it up, arching my back so I could get it off of me and toss it in the same direction that his shirt went. His flattened palm that rested on my chest slid to the side, running over the top of my breast that spilled out of the top of my red, lace push-up bra. I sighed, closing my eyes and tilting my head back as his hand engulfed my breast over the top of my bra.

"You are so beautiful," he whispered as he kneaded the soft mound, making me moan. Before I could think any coherent thoughts, his fingers slipped the edge of my bra away and his head dipped down so his warm, wet lips could capture my nipple and pull it into his mouth.

I was done for at that point. My hands slapped down onto his shoulders and my nails dug into his skin as he swirled his tongue around and around. How did I never know that there was a nerve that connected from my nipple right to my vagina? Holy hell! Every time he sucked I felt a tingle down there and it was driving me insane.

"You have too many clothes on," I muttered as I reached between us to unbutton and unzip his jeans. He pulled away from me and stood up next to the bed to pull his pants and boxer briefs down while I unfastened my own jeans.

Holy shit, there's his penis – his mighty, mighty penis that was going to be inside of me any second now. Does it look bigger? Maybe it's the lighting. This lighting better not be like dressing room lighting and make my ass look bigger.

"You're making me self-conscious staring at my penis so hard. It doesn't do any tricks, so I hope you're not waiting for it to juggle or anything," Carter said with a smile as he leaned down and hooked his fingers into the waistband of my jeans and underwear and slowly started to pull them down my legs.

Don't think about the c-section scar or the stretch marks around it. If you don't think about them, they aren't real.

Shit, he's going to see me naked. Maybe if he glanced away or closed his eyes, I would look better. It could be like that Old Spice commercial.

Look down, back up, now look at me. I'm a Maxim model.

"I'm just wondering if you have a permit for that thing and if it's going to fit in me," I joked, slyly resting my hands over top of the scar nestled at the top of the little triangle of pubic hair I had. Okay, I wasn't really joking. How the fuck did that thing get in there last time and why didn't I walk funny the next morning?

Carter saw through my actions and immediately pulled my hands away and held them down at my sides.

If I suck in my stomach any harder I'm going to pull a muscle.

"Don't cover yourself up, please. I love every inch of your body," he said sincerely as he rested one knee on the bed next to my thigh and placed a soft kiss right on top of the c-section scar. He loved every inch of my body *before* Gavin stretched it out like a rubber band on a sling shot. Granted, his memory of my body that night wasn't very clear, but I'm pretty sure he'd remember that my ass didn't have a map of stretch marks on it back then and I could very well teach a geography class with it if getting naked in front of students wasn't frowned upon.

He let go of one of my hands and used his arm to hold himself up as he leaned over me and looked at my body. The tips of his fingers followed the line of my scar back and forth several times. He had a sad look in his eyes for a moment, and I absolutely would not allow that when we were seconds away from having sexy time. I took his fingers and moved them up, placing them over top of my breast.

Alright, I'm getting better at this. That wasn't awkward at all. I wanted his hand on my boob, so I put his hand on my boob. Done.

He looked up and smiled at me then knelt down on the floor next to the bed. I gave him a questioning look as he slid both of his hands down my hips, across my thighs and skimmed them back behind my knees. I started to tell him to get back up here when all of a sudden he pulled me towards him until my knees were bent at the edge of the bed and my legs hung down on either side of him. Before I could utter a protest, he leaned down and kissed the inside of my thigh.

Oh, Jesus. Oh holy fuck, he's going to put his mouth on me.

The tip of his tongue made a trail from the inside of my thigh to my hip bone where he placed his lips and sucked gently. I squeezed my eyes shut and fisted the sheets as he kissed his way from my hip to my pubic bone.

Oh fuck, he was right there. I was wet as hell and he could probably smell me now. I should have eaten strawberries or melon or a dozen roses or an entire mint plant. Did that work for women? I read an article that it worked for men. Their spunk tasted like what they ate. Did my vagina taste like spaghetti right now? God dammit! I shouldn't have eaten dinner.

His hands glided back up my legs to the tops of my thighs until his thumbs slid through the lips of my sex. He stopped kissing the area all around my triangle of curls, pulled his head up a little and watched what he was doing with his fingers. I had one eye open at this point so I could see what his next move was. Even though I was freaking out about the fact that my vagina might taste like Chef Boyardee, it was kind of hot to watch Carter stare at me as his hands rested on my thighs and he slid his thumbs up and down through my wetness.

His thumbs slid up one last time, spreading me open as he went. He groaned, and before I could apologize for not letting my lady parts gargle with mouthwash, he dipped his head and wrapped his lips and tongue around me.

A strangled cry flew from my mouth as I arched my back and smacked my hand down on the bed.

All embarrassment was forgotten when his mouth made contact with me. Every thought flew out of my mind and all I could do was feel what he was doing to me. He licked and sucked me into his mouth, letting his lips and tongue slide down to my opening and back up. He flattened his tongue and lapped over top of my clit, up and down, over and over again. The roughness of his tongue and his warm breath hitting my wet skin made me gasp and start moving my hips with the rhythm of his tongue. He moved his lips away, using just the firm tip of his tongue to flick back and forth against the most sensitive spot at a feverish pace.

I could already feel the tingles of my orgasm lurking just beyond my reach. I could hear the sounds of his lips and tongue on me and I didn't even give a shit right now how much those sounds echoed around the quiet room. Carter was going to make me have an orgasm with his mouth and just thinking that in my head made every inch of me throb and my hips thrust faster against him. His tongue slid down my slit and pushed its way inside me. My legs started to shake with the need for release and I could hear myself panting with need. He pushed his tongue in and out of me slowly, over and over, before sucking his way back up. He kissed my clit like he kissed my mouth all those times before – soft lips, swirling tongue, sucking skin. One of his hands moved away from my thigh and I felt the tip of his finger swirling against my opening. Around and around his finger teased while his mouth continued to devour me.

In the haze of pleasure I heard myself chanting "yes, yes" over and over, encouraging him to push his finger inside. His lips and his tongue never stopped their ministrations against me while he complied with my wishes. His long finger slowly glided into me until he was so deep I could feel his knuckles pressed against my skin. With boldness I never knew I possessed, I grabbed onto the back of his head and held him against me, my hips thrusting erratically while his finger began moving in and out of me. He moved his head from side to side so that his mouth glided back and forth over me while he continued pushing and pulling his finger out of me. Before I knew it, my orgasm was rushing through me. I clutched his hair with my fists and held him in place while I bucked my hips and shouted in pleasure.

"Oh God! Ohhhhhh YES!"

Carter continued to lick every drop while I panted and whimpered through my release and slowly came down from the high. If I didn't pull him away, he would probably never stop. But I needed him now. I let go of my death grip on his hair, yanked on his arms and tugged him up my body. He crawled up the length of me, hovered over top of my body and smiled.

"You taste so fucking good. I could do that all night."

Once again, Carter's dirty talk surprisingly turned me on. I'm pretty sure I let out a growl as I slid my hand down between our bodies and wrapped it around his hardness that rested against my inner thigh. I channeled my dirty slut and pumped my hand up and down his smooth, hard length. I rubbed my thumb back and forth over the wetness that leaked out of the tip, spreading it all around.

"Fuck, shit I need to be inside you," Carter mumbled incoherently. He quickly slid his hands all around the top of the bed next to us and blindly reached for one of the condoms. When his hand finally made purchase, he stood up on his knees between my legs and I watched him take the condom out of the wrapper, place it on the tip of his penis and slide it down. I never really thought something like that would be hot, but son of a bitch! Watching him touch himself, even if it was just to put on a condom was fuck-awesome. As soon as he was sheathed, I reached back down between us and wrapped my hand around his length, needing to touch him. He leaned down over top of my body, wrapping his arm around my waist so he could pull me against him and slide us up to the middle of the bed. I slung my free arm around his shoulders and pulled him closer so I could position him right at my opening. I bent my knees so that his body was cradled in between my legs. He pushed his hips forward just enough that the swollen head slipped inside.

So different from our first time and yet, the same. His body still fit against mine like it was made to be there. His skin against mine still made my entire body tingle with anticipation. I moved my hand off of him and wrapped it around his back, clutching on to him tightly.

He looked into my eyes and I blurted out, "I love you."

He let out a shuddering breath, "So much," he whispered in reply. "I will never, ever regret our first time, but I would give anything if it would have gone a little more like this."

I pulled him even closer to me until he bent his elbows and rested his forearms on either side of my head, angling his wrists so his hands could smooth the hair off of my forehead.

"The only thing that matters to me now is that I'm here with you," I replied softly.

He looked into my eyes while he placed a soft kiss on my lips and slowly pushed himself the rest of the way inside me.

Jeeeeeeesus.

All the air left my lungs and I thanked the wet vagina Gods that there was enough lubrication down there and he didn't have to force his way in. He didn't move and I could tell he was holding his breath. I should be the one holding my breath. He pretty much just stuck a giant red whiffle ball bat into a straw. I felt full and I was completely shocked how I could stretch to fit him. And even more shocked about how good it felt to have him inside me this time. He started breathing again as he slowly pulled back out and just as gently pushed back in.

"Fuck, you feel so good," he groaned as he continued to leisurely move in and out of me. I could tell he was trying to hold back in fear of hurting me. I knew it killed him to think about how he hurt me our first time together, but I was a virgin then, the pain was inevitable. I didn't need him to control himself so rigidly. Not now. I wanted to feel his passion and the force of his need for me. I boldly slid my hands down his back, clutching onto his ass and pushed him deeper inside me.

"More," I moaned against his lips.

He immediately pulled almost all the way out and then pushed back in hard, slapping his pelvis against me. Holding himself perfectly still, he let out a shuddering breath and rested his forehead against mine.

"Shit, I'm sorry. I don't want to hurt you. I just want you so badly," he whispered.

"I'm not going to break, Carter. Please, don't hold back. I need you."

He pulled his head away from mine so he could look into my eyes and I tried to convey to him as best I could that I was okay. He must have seen the truth. His arm moved from next to my head as he let his hand skim down the side of my body until it got to my thigh. He wrapped his hand around my leg and lifted it up high so my knee rested against the side of his body. He placed another sweet kiss to my lips, pulled his hips back and slid his length out of me. I tightened my leg against his side in anticipation, and then he pushed back all the way inside of me in one swift motion. He went much deeper this time and I pushed my hips forward to meet his thrust. He moaned against my lips and I swallowed the sound with my mouth, kissing him with everything I had in me. My hands still clutched his ass and I pushed harder against him so he would continue. He didn't hesitate, beginning a rhythm with his movements in and out of me. He kept up a steady pace, slamming into me as deep as he could go until we were both covered in a thin sheen of sweat, gasping and moaning around kisses.

"Fuck, baby, I'm not going to be able to last if I keep this up," he groaned as he tried to slow down his movements.

"Don't stop. I want to feel you," I whispered against his lips.

I couldn't believe those words came out of my mouth but they were true. I wanted to feel him lose control and get pleasure from my body. I needed to know I could do that to him.

He growled and attacked my mouth with a deep, mind blowing kiss as his hips slammed into me at an even faster pace. The bed creaked with each thrust. I dug my nails into his back and wrapped both of my legs around his waist to hold on for the ride. His tongue pushed through my mouth just like his hard length pushed into me and it was so hot I might have had another orgasm if I didn't just think I heard a tiny knock at the bedroom door.

Carter was oblivious so I closed my eyes and hoped our son wasn't outside the door listening and being scarred for life.

Carter pulled his mouth away from my lips and started thrusting erratically. I knew he was close. I really didn't want to stop but I definitely didn't imagine the knock at the door this time.

Shit! Shit! Shit! For the love of God, Gavin, please don't say anything. I want this to be good for Carter and not ruined by a tiny voice saying he had to pee.

I am a horrible mother.

"Oh fuck Claire, oh fuck," Carter groaned.

Oh God, should I shush him? Subtly put my hand over his mouth?

He thrust hard one last time and I felt him pulse inside me with his release.

Oh thank God. I mean, oh darn, is it over already?

"Mommy, I'm thirsty."

Carter laughed in the middle of his release, sliding in and out of me a few more times before he collapsed on top of me. We laid there for a few seconds trying to catch our breaths.

He is never going to want to have sex with me again. Forget about scarring our kid, I just scarred his penis. I just had the best sex ever and I will never get a repeat performance because Carter's penis just died.

Rest in peace, my friend, rest in peace. Here lies Carter's penis. Beloved member, hard worker and all around good guy.

"Mommy!" Gavin yelled from out in the hall.

"Just a minute!" I yelled back right next to Carter's ear.

Carter pushed up and looked at me with a smile.

Here it comes, the penis kiss-off.

"Give me thirty minutes and we're doing this again. Next time though, we're duct taping him to his bed."

18.

Baby Daddy

I'M NOT GONNA lie. Mid-thrust, I swore I heard someone knock on my bedroom door. I couldn't, for the life of me, think of who would be knocking on my bedroom door. Especially at one o'clock in the morning, while my dick was buried in the girl of my dreams. What if it was a serial killer? Frankly, even if one did kick the door down right then, I wasn't stopping. Unless he had a gun. We could quite possibly outrun someone with a knife. A gun, though, we weren't going to get away from that. I might as well die happy and inside of Claire.

Then I wondered briefly if Jim broke in and was going to stand outside the door harassing me by yelling things like, "I hope you know what you're doing with that thing," or "Claire's like a sister to me. If you don't make her orgasm six times, I will gut you like a fish."

Thinking about Jim during a time like this was all sorts of wrong and almost made my dick go soft.

Almost.

Claire did some super power maneuver with her vagina that made it feel like that thing had a fist and squeezed my penis like a stress ball. Holy mother of vaginas!

My head was back in the game at that point—a little too back in the game. She felt so good I never wanted to stop, but her little vagina hand kept squeezing me and I wanted to weep it felt so good. She was warm and tight and fit me so perfectly. I wanted to be a total douche and tell her that her vagina felt like warm apple pie, just like in the movies. But not just any apple pie, McDonald's apple pie. The kind that are so warm and delicious they had to put them on the dollar menu so you could afford to eat eleven of them. I would eat eleventy-billion Claire vaginas. The little sounds she made as I drove into her forced my orgasm up through me faster than I wanted it to. Hearing her tell me she didn't want me to stop and that she wanted to feel me almost made my head explode…both of them.

I kissed Claire in an effort to try and slow down my impending orgasm but that just made it worse. Her mouth was the most delicious thing I ever tasted and her tongue sliding against mine made my dick pulse inside of her. Pushing into her welcoming heat as deeply as I could go, my orgasm burst out of me and I almost had a moment of panic that I was going to come so hard it would burst through the condom.

We all knew I had super powerful sperm. It could happen. Again. Those little fucker's heads were banging against the end of the condom screaming in anarchy, "The man is trying to keep us down! Damn the man!"

After the first throb of my orgasm, a little voice came through the closed bedroom door.

"Mommy, I'm thirsty."

I burst out laughing in the middle of shooting thousands of furious, fist-shaking little sperm into my condom. Claire's legs and arms were wrapped tightly around me and I collapsed right on top of her, careful not to put all of my weight on her. I would like her to still be alive so we could do this again. I'm not much into necrophilia.

We lay there breathing heavily for a few minutes and I started to chuckle again. How could I have forgotten there was a kid in the house? I actually thought an axe murderer might have broken in and was courteously knocking on my door before barging in. For some reason, that seemed more logical than remembering I had a child and he was in the house.

"Mommy!"

"Just a minute!" Claire screamed right by my ear.

I pushed myself up so I could see Claire's face and asked her if we could duct tape him to the bed the next time we did this. I really didn't expect her face to light up as brightly as it did. I was joking about the duct tape. Sort of.

"We'll have to come up with some kind of lie to tell him about what we're doing," she said.

"Do you – fuck, shit-fuck, unnngf! I sputtered while making the 'o' face.

There it was again. That vagina squeeze. What the fuck was that?

"Okay, what the fuck did you just do with your vagina? I think I just came again."

She laughed and the motion pushed my shrinking dick right out of her vagina. I wanted to pout at the loss, but then I realized Gavin was still outside our bedroom door.

Wow, we suck. I hope he isn't bleeding from the head or anything.

Sorry, son, mommy and dad were busy playing hide the salami. How's the head wound?

I shifted off of Claire and grabbed some Kleenex from the nightstand to dispose of the condom. I almost smirked at the jizz inside and gave them all the finger. Ha ha little fuckers. Not this time!

"Kegels," Claire said as she quickly grabbed her shirt and threw it over her head and then shimmied into her skirt. It didn't escape my notice that she didn't put her underwear back on.

"Wait, what? Did you say kegels? Why are we talking about cereal?"

At this point Gavin was rattling the door handle so hard I wouldn't be surprised if the thing came off in his hand. I swung my legs off the side of the bed and threw on my boxer briefs, walking over to the door with Claire.

"Not Kellogs, Jenny, kegels," Claire laughed. "And they are the explanation for my awesome vagina."

I wanted to swat her cute little ass for the Jenny comment but didn't have time. She swung open the door to find Gavin standing there with his head against the door jam looking bored.

Claire knelt down and took him in her arms.

"Hey, bud, are you okay? Did you get scared or something?" I asked, ruffling the hair on top of his head.

"What were you guys doing in here?"

Geeze, nothing like getting right to the point.

Claire pulled back from him and looked up at me.

"Uh…ummmm," she stammered.

"Were you guys playing a game?" he asked.

I snickered at that, wondering if Claire would punch me if I told him about the rules of hide the salami. *The first rule of hide the salami is never knock on a locked door during the game unless you are bleeding from the eyes or something is on fire. Like your hair. Anything else can wait until the game is over.*

"Well, we were making a phone call. A very important phone call," Claire explained.

Gavin looked at her like he didn't believe her.

"It was a long-distance phone call," I explained. "And it was really big and important. We couldn't wait one more minute to make the phone call and once we made the call, we couldn't stop or it would have been…painful. So that's why we didn't answer the door when you knocked. Yep, really big phone call. Your mom screamed when she saw how big it was."

Claire reached up and pinched my thigh for that one, but I couldn't help it.

"Your father is over exaggerating how big this phone call really was," she said dryly.

My mouth popped open and Gavin looked at me funny. Claire just knelt there giving me an annoyed look, not even realizing what she just let slip.

A swarm of butterflies started flapping around in my stomach, and I wanted to reach down and scoop both of them up and jump around the room. We hadn't talked yet about telling Gavin who I was. I wanted more than anything for him to call me "Dad," but I didn't want to rush things with Claire. She had done this all on her own for so long, I didn't want to step on her toes. I wanted her to come to this decision on her own, knowing that she trusted me with Gavin.

I could see when the realization hit. Her face got horribly pale and I was a little worried she might barf on my bare feet for a second. She looked back and forth between Gavin and me several times before her eyes landed on mine and she quickly stood up.

"Oh my God. I'm sorry. I have no idea why I just blurted that out," she whispered, glancing back down at Gavin to see if he could hear her. He just stood there looking at both of us like we were idiots.

"Shit. I'm sorry! I'll just tell him I was kidding. I'll tell him I was talking about the phone call or something. Oh my God! I am such a dumbass," she mumbled.

I rubbed my hands up and down her arms to calm her.

"Hey, listen to me. It's fine. Actually, it's more than fine. I wanted to ask you about telling him but I was afraid you would think it was too soon," I explained.

She let out a sigh of relief.

"Are you sure? I don't want you to do something you're not ready for."

"Baby, I was ready for this as soon as I pulled the stupid out of my ass and came to talk to you after that first week."

She leaned up and gave me a quick kiss before turning around to pick Gavin up.

"So, Gavin. Do you know what a daddy is?" she asked him.

He stared at me and thought about it for a few minutes. I started to get worried. What if he didn't want me as his dad? What if he thought I was too strict or too stupid? Shit, I shouldn't have made him clean up the toothpaste on his floor. Cool dads didn't make their kids do shit like that. Cool dads took their kids to strip clubs and let them throw big parties at their houses and smoked pot with them on Sunday afternoons while they picked their fantasy football teams.

"Is Papa your daddy?" he asked.

Claire nodded. "You are very smart, little man! Yes, Papa is my daddy. And Carter is your daddy."

We both stood there in silence while Gavin looked back and forth between us.

He is totally sizing me up right now.

"I'll take you to get a lap dance and smoke pot with you during fantasy draft week," I blurted.

Claire looked at me like I lost my mind.

"Can I call you punk-daddy?" Gavin finally asked nonchalantly, ignoring my outburst.

Gavin asked for a father and saw that he was good.

Yes, I quoted the bible and compared my son to God. Shut up.

Claire laughed at Gavin's request.

"How about you just call him 'Daddy'?" she asked.

"How about I call him 'Daddy-face'," Gavin countered.

This kid was bartering on what version of daddy he could call me. He was a genius. And I was concerned for no reason at all. I reached over and took Gavin from Claire's arms.

"How about we let Mommy go to sleep and you and I discuss my new name while I put you back to bed?" I asked.

Claire reached up on her toes to kiss Gavin's cheek and then leaned over to do the same to mine. Gavin put his head on my shoulder and wrapped his arms around my neck.

"Okay, baby-daddy."

Claire and I both burst out laughing at that one. As I walked out into the hall, I turned my head and mouthed the words, "thank you" to her before walking Gavin back to his room.

I REALLY DIDN'T know why I was so worried about Carter freaking out when I called him Gavin's father. It proved to me yet again just how wonderful he was.

While Carter was putting Gavin back to bed, I reached into my overnight bag and pulled out the tank top and boy shorts I brought for pajamas and changed into them. I brushed my teeth and then got back into bed to curl under the covers and wait for Carter to come back. I just started to doze off when I felt the bed dip and his arms circle around my waist. I smiled and snuggled back into his warm body.

"Everything go okay?" I murmured sleepily.

"Yep, he decided he wasn't thirsty anymore but he made me read him a story. And we compromised on 'Daddy-o' for now," he said with a chuckle.

"You're getting off easy. Two weeks ago he kept referring to me as 'Old Lady'."

I lay there wrapped in Carter's arms and it was the most comfortable I had ever been.

For about five minutes.

This just proved that everything they did in the movies was a load of bullshit. His arm was under my neck on the pillow which tilted my head at an awkward angle. I could already feel the beginnings of a kink. I was starting to sweat like a whore in church with his other arm heavily draped over my waist and his legs tangled with mine. With my sweaty ass and his itchy leg hair, it felt like I had a hundred mosquito bites on my legs.

It would be wrong to kick him now, right?

I shifted my body just the tiniest bit. I didn't want him to think I didn't want to cuddle, but I was going insane trying to lie perfectly still. Maybe if I waited long enough, he'd fall asleep and I could shove him off me. The Cunninghams had it right when they slept in separate beds on "Happy Days." That's why all those people back then looked so well-rested and blissful. Marion didn't have Howard's hairy legs rubbing all over her.

"Out with it, Claire," Carter mumbled close to my ear.

Shit. Now it was going to get awkward. We *just now* had sex for the first time in years and I was going to tell him to get away from me so I could sleep. I am the most unromantic person in the world.

"Out with what?"

"You've been fidgeting and sighing for the past ten minutes," he replied.

I have tourettes, restless leg syndrome or a baboon heart that gives me the shakes and makes me sigh every time the furry thing beats.

Crap, wasn't I always teaching Gavin about honesty? And here I was trying to figure out a way to tell Carter I had monkey organs instead of just telling him the truth.

"Soooooo, I've never spent the night with anyone before. Well, except for Liz but we've always been drunk."

Carter made some sort of choking, cough sound behind me.

"Can you say that again? Slowly, and with more details," he mumbled.

I laughed and smacked his arm at my waist.

"I'm being serious."

"So am I. You were naked when you did this correct? Tell me you were naked," he replied.

Baboon heart, truth. Baboon heart, truth…

"My neck is killing me and I'm so hot right now my skin could start a blanket fire," I rambled.

Carter was quiet. Too quiet.

Shit, I hurt his feelings.

"Oh, thank fucking God," he said as he pulled both of his arms out from around me. "My arm fell asleep and my legs were getting a cramp."

"THE BUGS GOT lotion when the dog tickled. Ha ha farmer!"

I had been lying in bed for a few minutes, watching the first light of dawn creep through the curtains. I had to slap my hand over my mouth when Carter started talking in his sleep.

Jesus, talk about "like father, like son." Obviously no one ever clued Carter in on his sleeping habits. Just the thought of some other woman sleeping in the same bed as him made me feel stabby so I pushed those thoughts away for the time being.

He was on his back with one arm flung above his head on the pillow and the other resting on top of his stomach. If I was in a porno, he would be naked under the sheet with his olympic-size penis sticking up, and I would be all slutty and pull the sheet down to blow him.

Bow-chica-wow-wow.

I wasn't slutty, and this wasn't a porno. But I had seen enough of them to sort of know what to do. I glanced at the clock on the night stand and figured I had at least an hour before Gavin would be up. I looked back at Carter's peaceful face and remembered how it felt to have his mouth between my legs last night.

Okay, I could do this. He gave me two mind-blowing orgasms since I met him. Right now, I'm in the lead. Time to even things up a bit so I didn't feel so selfish.

I slowly reached over and tugged the sheet down his body until it pooled around his shins. Leaning up on my elbow, I used the tips of my fingers to gently pull the waistband of his boxer briefs away from his skin so I could peek inside.

Well, hello there, big guy.

Wow, I felt all sorts of slutty now. I wanted to lick his dick.

Heh, heh. That rhymed.

Focus!

I scooted my body closer to his and then eased my way down lower so my face was even with his waist. My elbow slipped a little on the sheet, making my fingers jerk away from his underwear so I could brace myself and not fall right on top of his sleeping form. The elastic snapped back against his skin and I stopped all movement and held my breath, staring at his face for any sign of waking up.

"Muffins in the basement," Carter mumbled in his sleep.

I glanced back between his legs and noticed that Sir Cums-a-lot was waking up. Huh, go figure. Dreaming about muffins turned him on. I should make muffins for breakfast. I wonder if Carter had any blueberries. You really couldn't beat fresh blueberry muffins but I guess if I...

Dammit! Why was it so hard for me to focus on the penis? Especially a really nice one like Carter's.

Heh, hard penis!

I closed my eyes and channeled Jenna Jameson but without the nasty lip injections and black eye from Tito. As slowly as I could, I got up on all fours and straddled Carter's legs. Without giving myself anymore time to think about muffins or porn stars, I dipped my head and nuzzled my nose against his length on the outside of his boxers.

Wow, he just got harder when I did that. Neat! I wanna see it grow.

Cha-cha-cha-chia!

Shit, no Chia Pet theme songs right before licking a dick.

I rested my elbows on the bed on either side of Carter's hips, my ass sticking up in the air so I wouldn't touch his legs and disturb him. Ever so carefully, I pulled the elastic away from his skin and peeled it down over his erection.

I glanced quickly up at his face, satisfied that he was still asleep. Letting out the breath I had been holding, it skimmed over his penis since my mouth was about an inch away at this point. I watched him get incredibly harder and longer.

Seriously? My breath on him did that? Or is he still dreaming about muffins?

I shrugged to myself. I was not going to question the penis. It was great and powerful, like the Wizard of Oz. And right now, the Wizard wanted me to lick his yellow brick dick. I jutted my chin forward and placed my tongue against the base of him, right above the edge of his underwear that I still held onto. I slid my tongue up the length of him, completely amazed at how smooth and soft the skin was there. My tongue dipped into the little valley right below the head of his penis and I added some pressure with the tip of my tongue like I saw in "Beat the Heat."

Carter let out a little moan in his sleep and I smiled to myself.

I inched my body up a little further, letting my tongue glide up and over the head of his penis. I swirled it around the tip a few times then brought my lips down around the head and sucked it into my mouth.

Carter whimpered this time and I glanced up to see he still had his eyes closed.

Okay, this wasn't too bad. I could do this. I was a dirty cock sucker! Liz would be so proud.

That reminded me I needed to call Liz later and see if she wanted to help me make three-hundred chocolate penises for one of her parties this weekend.

I dipped my head a little lower and took more of Carter into my mouth, letting my tongue continue to swirl around the head. I tasted a bit wetness that leaked out of him and it was magically delicious, like Lucky Charms. But saltier. And without the leprechaun.

Green clovers, yellow horseshoes, pink penises!

I giggled a little when I thought that. I was giggling with Carter's penis in my mouth. Thank God he was still sleeping. I don't think laughing at a man's penis would make him feel good.

I sucked harder on him and took him as far into my mouth as I could without gagging. Throwing up on his penis wouldn't be a good introduction into the world of blow jobs.

He was big and full in my mouth and I seriously couldn't believe this was happening right now and no one was witnessing it. I, Claire Morgan, had a penis in my mouth. There should be applause or pats on the back. Maybe I should have waited until Carter was awake for this. I bet he'd give me one of those slow golf claps like in the movies. Or at least say "way to go".

I slowly moved up and down his length, letting my wet lips glide over his smooth skin.

Carter's hips jerked forward a little and he moaned again, making me completely giddy with power. Until I made one more pass up his length with my Hoover Mouth (Yes, I was changing its name to that of a vacuum cleaner. Don't judge me.) and I glanced up to see his eyes jerk open and his body completely freeze.

My lips were fastened around the head of his penis when he let out a yell.

"THERE IS NOTHING WRONG WITH MY WIENER! IT HAPPENS TO EVERY GUY!"

His legs jerked out from under me, sending me sprawling backwards to the foot of the bed while I watched him scramble up to the headboard, covering the part of his penis sticking out of his underwear with both of his hands.

"Where's Gavin?" he asked, his eyes frantically searching around the room. "He doesn't have a vagina."

I lay there on my back at the end of the bed, propped up on my elbows, wondering what the fuck just happened.

"Um, I'm assuming he's still sleeping. And I'm guessing you are too," I replied.

"Where's the farmer with the muffins?"

I extended one of my legs and shoved his thigh with my foot.

"CARTER!" I yelled. "Wake up!"

He finally looked at me then, his face scrunched up in confusion. He blinked rapidly and shook his head quickly like he was trying to jar things into place.

"I had another dream that you were giving me a blow job, just like the other morning when Gavin was in the living room watching me sleep. Damn, this one seemed so fucking real," he muttered.

I had no idea what he was talking about right now.

His eyes still glanced worriedly around the room like he expected Gavin to jump out from under the bed or something and shout, "Surprise! I saw Mommy blowing you!"

He looked back at me again. "Why are you laying at the bottom of the bed?"

I sighed and then pushed myself up so I could move back to the top of the bed next to him. When I got up there, I leaned my back against the headboard and glanced down at his lap – where his hands were still crisscrossed over his penis that stuck out of the top of his underwear. He followed my line of sight, moved his hands quickly and yanked his underwear up to cover himself.

What a shame.

"Well, Carter, this time you weren't dreaming. My mouth was on your penis when you decided to start flailing about, yelling about your wiener and our son with a vagina."

The look on his face would have been hilarious if my mouth wasn't depressed from the loss of his penis in there. His penis should be allowed to have the Twizzler slogan, "Makes mouth happy."

"Oh my God. Tell me I didn't interrupt a blow job wake-up call. Say it isn't so and we can pretend I didn't just kick you off of my dick. I don't think my ego will recover from something like that."

I reached up and patted his cheek.

"Sorry, sweets, my mouth and lips were in fact all over your penis while you slept," I whispered.

He groaned.

"I have to say though, I'm a little surprised I never knew blow jobs included donkey kicks to the sternum."

He groaned again but this time in irritation.

"Shit! It's not my fault. Whenever I'm around you, even if I'm unconscious, my dick gets hard and I have dirty dreams about you. I thought I was having a repeat of the other morning and I freaked out."

He looked at me and pouted his lips.

"Pretty please, do it again?" he begged.

I laughed at how much he sounded like a child right now.

The door to the bedroom suddenly burst open and Gavin flew in the room, scrambled up onto the bed and in between the two of us.

"Morning, Mommy," Gavin said as he snuggled into my side.

Carter sighed, knowing there was no use in begging any more. He smiled though and watched me wrap Gavin in my arms and slide down the headboard to get under the covers.

Once we were situated, Gavin looked over his shoulder at Carter.

"Morning, crabby-daddy," he said, before turning back to face me and play with my hair.

I laughed at that one. Carter did look a little crabby.

He just shook his head and laughed right along with me.

Gavin's hand cupped my cheek and he looked seriously into my eyes.

"Hey, Mom," he said.

I squeezed him tighter and smiled.

"Yeah, baby."

"Lemme see your boobs," he said.

19.

This Patient Needs an Enema, STAT

HER MOUTH WAS *on my penis.*

We were sitting on the couch after lunch and all I could do was stare at Claire's mouth over top of Gavin's head.

This is wrong on so many levels.

But Jesus fuck, those red, plump lips were wrapped around my penis and I kicked her away. Sure, it was unconsciously but still… I punted her like a football off of my dick. That was like rule number one in sex. Never kick a girl away from your dick if she's got her mouth there. If her teeth were clamped down on it and she's whipping it around like a chew toy, that's another story.

I let out a big sigh and turned my attention back to the movie.

"What is this one called again?" I asked.

Gavin was curled up into my side with his feet on Claire's lap.

"Finding Nemo," Gavin mumbled.

We watched the movie in silence for a few minutes and I felt like a kid again as I enjoyed the happenings on the screen. It had been a long while since I watched a cartoon.

"Holy shit, did they just kill off that fish's wife?" I blurted in shock.

"Yep," Gavin replied. "That big, mean fish ated her."

He said it so calmly – like it was no big deal that a sweet, loving cartoon fish just got murdered. What the fuck was wrong with this movie? This couldn't be appropriate for kids. I didn't think it was appropriate for me.

"Are you sure this is a kid's movie?" I asked Claire.

She laughed and just shook her head at me.

An hour later Gavin was asleep with his head on my lap and Claire was leaning in the opposite direction from me, her elbow on the arm of the couch and her head in her hand.

If I had to listen to Nemo calling for "Daddy" one more time, I was going to blubber like a baby. I snatched up the remote and turned the movie off.

Claire lifted her head off of her hand and gave me a questioning look.

"We need to put another movie in. This is too depressing. They killed off the poor fish's wife in the first five minutes and then we have to spend the rest of the movie watching that same, poor sap search for his son who ran away. What kind of sick fucks made this into a kid's movie?" I whispered angrily, trying not to wake Gavin up.

"Welcome to the Disney/Pixar School of Hard Knocks," she said dryly.

I laughed at her comparison.

"Oh come on. There's no way they're all like this. I do not remember being horrified by a children's movie when I was little."

"That's because you were a child. You didn't understand what was happening at the time, just like Gavin doesn't really understand. I think they make these kids movies more for adults anyway," she explained.

I shook my head in disbelief.

"Sorry, but I remember all of the great Disney classics and there is no way you can find anything nightmare-inducing in any of them."

She raised her eyebrow at me in a challenge.

"Okay fine. Bambi," I said.

She just laughed.

"Oh please! That's the easiest one. Bambi's dad headed for the hills as soon as the stick turned pink. His mom was a single deer, living in low-rent housing in the crack-whore part of the forest where there are gangs of bunnies. His mom gets killed in a drive-by shooting, leaving Bambi alone and forced to grow up much too soon."

Damn. I forgot about that. It had been a while since I watched Bambi.

"Okay, fine. How about the Little Mermaid? Beautiful sea creature falls in love with the handsome prince."

Shut up. I had little cousins. And Ariel was hot. Men could spend hours looking at a hot mermaid and wonder just how in the hell he could stick it in her.

But seriously, how do mermaids bang?

Claire nodded her head, "Oh yes. Sweet Ariel who has to give up everything, including her identity, for a man. God forbid Prince Eric grows some gills. Nope, Ariel has to give up her friends, her family, her home and her entire life for him. Eric just takes and takes and never gives."

I racked my brain trying to think of another classic kid's movie and continued to contemplate the process of fucking a mermaid. Maybe you could just bend a mermaid over a chair and your dick magically finds the hold in the one-legged fin thing.

"Fine, then how about Beauty and the Beast? The most beautiful girl in all the land falls for the beast's personality instead of his looks. You can't find anything wrong with that. Plus, it teaches a great lesson."

I gave her a smug grin.

Maybe there was a magic button that made a mermaid's legs separate long enough to bang her. Ooooooh, like a magic nipple! Push the nipple and watch her spread.

"Wrong," she replied. "A pretty girl with no money falls for a rich, abusive monster. But she loves him so much that she makes excuses for the abuse. 'Oh that bruise? I tripped down a flight of stairs.'"

She angled her body to face me.

"I could go on all day with these, believe me," she said. "You also can't forget the awesomeness that is the penis drawn on the original Little Mermaid VHS box cover and the whisper of, 'Kids, take off your clothes,' in Aladdin."

I looked at her in horror.

And I'm not gonna lie, I glanced down to her boobs and wondered what it would be like if she had a magic nipple. That would be some Nobel Peace Prize shit right there.

"From now on, Gavin only watches wholesome movies like 'Anchorman' and 'The Seed of Chucky,'" I told her. "And you're dressing up as Ariel for Halloween this year."

Claire just rolled her eyes at me, reached over to scoop Gavin off of my lap and then disappeared down the hall. A few minutes later, she was back and I watched her walk across the room to me. She straddled my lap and my hands went right to her hips to hold her in place while she slid her hands around my neck and tangled them in my hair.

"He should be out for a little while. Wanna mess around?" she asked with a giggle.

"Can I touch your boobs?" I asked hopefully.

It wasn't like I'd tell her no if she wouldn't let me play with the twins, but it was always good to set the ground rules ahead of time so there weren't any awkward foul plays.

She laughed and kissed the corner of my mouth.

"Yes, there will most definitely be boob touching," she said against my lips. "I'm not wearing a bra."

Easier access to the magic nipple.

"Sweet!" I cheered.

I swallowed her laugh with a kiss, taking my time while I explored every inch of her mouth. I had been in a state of semi-hardness since she walked in the room. Listening to her soft moans while I kissed her was enough to send me right into boner territory. My hands rubbed her ass and pulled her down so she nestled right onto my hard length that strained through my jeans. She slid her hips back and forth over me and I ran my hands up under the back of her shirt so I could feel here bare skin. My finger tips skimmed her spine all the way up and then back down, slowly, until I felt goose bumps break out over her skin.

Our tongues swirled together while I wrapped both of my arms around her body, underneath her shirt, so I could pull her right up against my chest. Her hips continued to move against me, and I felt like a teenager again, dry-humping on my parent's couch in the basement.

Except this time, Abby Miller's braces wouldn't get stuck in my hair when she tried unsuccessfully to lick my ear lobe. And by lick, I meant drooled a gallon of spit in there until it sounded like I was swimming under water.

I slid my hands around to Claire's sides and up the front of her body. My palms moved in circles around her breasts, and I felt her nipples harden beneath my hands. She pushed herself down harder on my dick and it made us both let out a gasp. Fuck, I wanted to be inside of her but it wasn't something we could do out here on the couch with a four-year-old down the hall.

Her hands retracted from the hair on the back of my head and she pushed them up under her shirt until they rested on top of my own. She squeezed my hands and helped me put more pressure on the soft flesh that I would give my left nut to put my mouth on right now.

Okay, maybe not my left nut.

Or the right one for that matter.

Shit, forget the nuts. I just really, really wanted to lick her boobs.

The kiss deepened as we worked together, cupping and stroking her breasts. Her thighs squeezed my hips tightly and she whimpered into my mouth as she ground herself harder against me. Making Claire have an orgasm every single day was my new mission in life. The sounds she made and the way she moved against me were heaven, but I needed to touch her. I needed to feel how much she wanted this.

Just as I had that thought, she pushed my hand off of one breast and down the front of her body until both of our hands slid under the waistband of her yoga pants.

"Fuck, you're not wearing any underwear either," I muttered as she pushed my hand through her soft curls and my fingers easily slid through her wetness. She couldn't do much more than moan softly as I coated my fingers with her. Claire's hand stayed on top of mine and showed me when to increase the pressure or slow down the speed. It was the hottest fucking thing ever to have my fingers sliding through her heat while her small, soft hand guided my way.

With her other arm wrapped tightly around my neck, she flung her head back so her neck was exposed. I easily slid two fingers inside of her and kissed my way down her neck while my thumb moved in quick circles around her most sensitive spot. Her hips bucked against my hand while I started moving my two fingers quickly in and out of her. I held my thumb in place so that the motions of her hips made her slide back and forth over the pad of my thumb and she could set the pace for her release.

I grabbed the back of her head and pulled her down for a searing kiss. As soon as our lips and tongues collided she exploded. Her moans and whimpers were muffled by my mouth which was a pretty good thing. I had a feeling she would be screaming if our mouths weren't fused together.

She rode my fingers while I kept them inside of her tight heat until every last drop of her orgasm surged through her. She pulled away from my mouth and collapsed against my chest with her face nestled in the crook of my neck.

My fingers stayed deep inside her while she caught her breath, and I felt every single pulse of her. Claire lifted her head and spoke with a dreamy look on her face.

"Give me two seconds to recover and I will suck you like…"

"Ga ga ah-ah-ahhhh, rama llama llama, want your bad bromance."

The sound of Gavin singing at the end of the hall froze us in place. He was headed this way and we both turned to stone.

Claire stared at me with wide eyes and I couldn't move my fingers from her vagina.

Why the fuck couldn't I move my fingers from her vagina?!

I wanted them there twenty-four hours a day under normal circumstances, but I started to see the error of my ways. There are some situations that do not condone having your fingers in a vagina. Like when you're getting an oil change, having your teeth cleaned, or when your four-year-old is in the room.

"Whatcha doin'?"

The only saving grace was the fact that the couch faced away from the hallway. Right now all he could see was the back of my head and Claire's mortified face.

"Um, Daddy needed a hug," Claire replied.

"Ooooh I wanna give Daddy a hug!"

"NO!" we both screamed.

Claire looked down at her lap and then back up to my face with a look of panic.

I just shrugged. I refused to move my fingers now. What if Gavin wanted to shake my hand? I know that's not a very four-year-old thing to do but Jesus H. Christ! He would need therapy for years after that.

I tipped my head back as far as it would go, so I could see an upside-down Gavin standing there absently kicking his toe into the carpet.

"Hey, buddy, can you do me a favor? In my room on my dresser is a whole bunch of money. Can you carry it into your room and put it into your new piggy bank?" I suggested.

His eyes got big and he started bouncing on his feet.

"Yes! I LOVE money!"

With that, he turned and ran down the hall. We could hear the jingle of change as he scooped it off my dresser and took it to his room.

We finally relaxed when we realized it would keep him busy long enough for us to get our act together, or at least for me to get my fingers out of Claire's vagina.

She slid off my lap and collapsed next to me on the couch while we listened to the clunk of coins being dropped into the ceramic pig and another verse of "Bad Bromance".

"I really need to teach him some better music. Like Zeppelin or The Beatles," I said as I shifted the problem in my pants to a more comfortable position.

"Actually, I was thinking about recording our own Kidz Bop album. Except I'd called it Kidz Bop – The Forbidden Songs," she said with a smile.

"That's a stellar idea. That kid has been loafing off of you long enough. It's time he gets a job."

She nodded with a serious face.

"This is true. He's already got 'S&M' down pat. Maybe we could throw in a little 'Golddigger' from Kanye."

"I think he might sell more if he did some rap," I said. "'Bitches Ain't Shit' or 'Ninety-Nine Problems.' We just need to teach him a little more attitude."

While we laughed, Gavin ran back to the living room.

"You got eleventy-seven nickels, Daddy-O. Go buy me some beef turkey for lunch, dicky."

I guess we could skip the attitude lessons.

AS THE NEXT couple of days went by, all I could do was thank God for Carter. He helped me with everything he could and took Gavin off my hands every single night when he got home from work. Well, almost every night. He took a night off when Liz offered to keep Gavin overnight so we could finally have some alone time without the fear of another dick kick. I swore Liz to secrecy with that story but I'm pretty sure Carter knew the jig was up when she started asking him random questions like "Hey Carter, have you seen that new movie 'Donkey Punch' yet?" or "Claire and I were thinking about taking a kick-boxing class, what do you think Carter?"

I was happy to find out that the sex between us was just as awesome when we were alone and didn't have to fear that a child would walk in on us at any moment. I earned five gold stars that night in "Blow Jobs 101" and did not get kicked out of class. Or in the face.

I drastically cut my hours back at the bar, so I had more time to get everything ready for the store opening. Basically, right now, I worked when I could. If I had a few hours of free time, I gave them a call to see if they could use me. Even though it wasn't my dream job and I never planned on being there forever, it was still bittersweet not spending every night there. The Fosters had been good to me, giving me a job, no questions asked, when I showed up five years ago as a college drop-out and pregnant.

I cried like a baby when I called up there last night and T.J. told me they didn't need me. That bar was my home away from home and held so many memories. My water broke in the storage room when I was grabbing a bottle of vodka. Gavin took his first steps over by the door when my dad brought him by for lunch one afternoon. But most importantly, it was where I found Carter again.

The bar was right down the street from the store, and I knew I'd still spend a lot of time in there; it was just strange not to be there every day. I'd be lying if I said a big part of my sadness wasn't also due to the absence of P.O.R.N in my life. However, T.J. came through with flying colors while I stocked the front cooler of my store with chocolate last night. I heard the door chime behind me and figured it was Carter stopping by with Gavin. As soon as I turned around I was hit right in the face with three ping-pong balls. T.J. screamed something about how I'd never had that many balls smack me in the face while I was sober and then turned and ran out the door.

I spent the rest of the evening drafting up a couple of new rules for P.O.R.N, one of which included a penalty shot if multiple balls were handled without prior approval. A cup would be placed on a table, a ball would be thrown and if it made it into the cup, you were in the clear. However, if the ball failed to land in said cup, the thrower of the ball had to take a direct shot to the face. I called this the "Cupping of the Balls" rule.

Drew stopped by to help lift a few heavy boxes for me and found a copy of the rules by the register. Three hours later he came back with shirts for everyone that said "I Love P.O.R.N." and made himself an honorary team captain.

Before I even had a chance to be worried about how I would pay my bills until the store started making money, Carter sat me down the night after Gavin and I first spent the night and told me he was going to take over paying for everything until I was up and running. It was the night of our first fight. I had been on my own and provided for Gavin and I all this time. There was no way I wanted to take Carter's hand-out. My stubborn ass refused to see it from his point of view, hence the big fight. He had missed out on so much, and he felt guilty about that every single day, even though it wasn't his fault. Being able to pay my phone bill and buy Gavin new shoes and pay for his doctor's appointments made Carter feel like he was finally a full part of our lives and not just some guy with the title of "Dad." As independent as I was and as much as I hated the idea of someone paying my way, I couldn't deny him this if it was what he really wanted and it would make him happy. I ended my temper tantrum, agreed to what Carter was asking and then we had hot as hell make-up "phone calls" locked in the laundry room while Gavin watched a movie in the living room.

So, with Carter's help and my decreased hours at the bar, I was able to get almost everything done a few days before the opening. The only thing left to do this far ahead of time was fold all of the brochures Jenny made for me. Carter took Gavin for the night so I could have some down time with the girls and they could help me with the folding.

Jim and Drew were going to keep Carter company since I would have their women all evening. I had to put my foot down though with Drew. I told him I would buy a tennis racket and go John McEnroe on his ass if my son came home with any new, colorful words.

Liz, Jenny and I were sitting on the floor of my living room surrounded by thousands of folded and unfolded brochures and four empty bottles of wine.

Wait, make that five. I emptied the fifth bottle into Liz's glass after she jumped up and ran to the bathroom holding her hands between her legs like a toddler because she had to pee so badly.

I got up and walked to the kitchen to grab another bottle of wine. As I passed by the bathroom, I found the door wide open.

"Liz, are you peeing with the door open?"

She looked up at me with crazy, drunk eyes while she swayed back and forth on the toilet and peed.

"Yes. Does it bother you?"

"Only if you fall off the toilet and piss on my floor," I told her as I walked away.

"Fair enough, hairy muff!" she yelled to me.

After I popped the cork on another bottle of wine and refilled everyone's glasses, Liz came back into the living room, shoved the brochures out of the way and lay down on her belly with her chin in her hands.

"Okay, skank whores. Time for a little Truth or Dare," she slurred. "Jenny, what nickname have you given your vagina?"

Jenny blushed and bit her lip, looking down in her lap. After several long minutes of Liz and I goading her, she finally mumbled something that sounded like, "Water."

"Repeat that, please. I don't have dog hearing," I told her.

"You do have a vagina that smells like a dog though," Liz laughed.

"Fuck you, anal warts."

"I call my vagina, Waterford," Jenny said, interrupting the banter between Liz and me.

We turned to her with equal looks of confusion on our faces.

"Explain," Liz said as she took a sip of wine.

Jenny shrugged. "You know, Waterford is like, good dishes and stuff. So, I only let the best eat off of my Waterford."

Liz snorted. "Why don't you just call it China then?"

Jenny thought about this for a minute.

"But, I've never been to China," she replied with a puzzled look on her face.

"Okay, next!" I announced. "Liz, same question. Name that beaver!"

Why is this room tilty?

Liz took another big gulp of her wine.

"Vajingo. As in 'maybe the vajingo ate your penis,' she said in an

Australian accent.

The radio that played from the kitchen finally stopped the sequence of commercials and switched to music.

"I love this song. It really envelopes me," Jenny said dreamily.

"Does it put a stamp on you too?" Liz laughed.

"Yeah, a tramp stamp!" I yelled.

Why am I yelling?

"I don't have a tattoo," Jenny argued.

"It's Claire's turn and I'm choosing dare," Liz stated.

"Hey, I'm the one that gets to choose," I protested.

"Shut up, whore! I dare you to send Carter a picture of your tits."

"Wait, what did you say?" Jenny asked. "I can't hear you without my glasses on," she mumbled as she poured more wine into her glass. Liz ignored her and scooted across the floor army-style, grabbed my phone that lay in the middle of us and handed it to me. I only hesitated for a second before I snatched it out of her hand and pressed the button for the camera, chugging the rest of my glass of wine for liquid courage.

I lifted my shirt and bra up to my neck, held my arm out in front of me as far as I could and quickly snapped a picture. My shirt and bra were back down and I was scrolling through the contacts in my phone before anyone said anything.

"Holy shit, dude! I just meant a cleavage picture. I didn't need you to whip out the fun bags right in front of us. I have to say though, I'm kind of proud of you right now," Liz said in awe.

"Claire has pretty boobies," Jenny muttered while she looked down the front of her shirt.

I attached the boob shot to a blank text message and typed the words, "We miss you," then hit send.

That was empowering! I felt all sorts of Joan of Arc-like now. But maybe more "The Legend of Billie Jean" movie version of her. Burning at the stake doesn't sound like fun. But I could totally rock a short hair cut and get people to chant "fair is fair" as they follow me and my outlaw friends across state lines. I turned my phone towards Liz and showed her the text.

"Oh, young grasshopper, it is clear you can be taught," Liz said as she wiped a fake tear out of her eye.

"I don't feel very lurid right now," Jenny slurred as she flopped onto her back and stared at the ceiling.

"Lucid! It's lucid, Jenny. For fuck's sake, someone get this bitch an Encyclopedia Britannica," Liz yelled from her spot on the floor.

"FAIR IS FAIR!" I yelled as I fist pumped.

I started folding some more of the flyers while Liz crawled over to Jenny and tried to lead her in a Hooked on Phonics boot camp. While Liz made her do push-ups and repeat words back to her, I got up and went to the kitchen to cut up some cheese and grab a plate of crackers.

In hindsight, wielding a cheese grater when my blood type was currently Merlot positive wasn't the best idea.

"KICK HIM IN the nut sack!"

I sat down on the couch and rolled my eyes as the UFC fight we watched started a new round.

"Okay, seriously. Enough with the nut kicking talk," I scolded.

Drew looked at me and pouted, "Oh come on, your kid isn't even awake."

I looked behind me where Gavin had fallen asleep on the couch. His little body was draped over the arm of the couch, his head and arms dangling down towards the floor, his knees pushed into the cushions. How in the hell does he fall asleep like that?

"I'm just trying to save you from the wrath of Claire. Really, it's for your own safety," I told him as I looked at his shirt that showed a couple walking in the sand with the words, "I enjoy long walks on the beach...after anal."

"I'll put my nuts on all of you," Gavin's muffled voice said from his hanging position off the end.

I looked at Drew pointedly.

"Hey, Carter," Jim said as he walked back in from the kitchen. "Why is Claire sending me a picture of her tits with the words, 'Me fish Lou,' in it?"

"What?" Drew and I both asked in unison.

Jim held his cell phone out to me as I leaned forward to see it.

"Seriously? Claire's tits are on that phone?" Drew yelled as he jumped up from the couch and tried to grab the phone before I got to it.

I panicked, flew off the recliner in the corner and onto Drew's back, wrapping my arms around his neck.

"What the fuck are you doing? Get off my back you dumbass," Drew yelled as he twisted and turned, trying to throw me off.

"Don't you even think about looking at that picture, dick licker," I threatened as I tried holding on to his neck with one arm and reached for Jim' phone with the other.

The phone suddenly beeped and Jim pulled it towards him, rolling his eyes at what he saw.

Drew stopped moving and we both just stood there. Well, Drew just stood there; I was still hanging from his back like a wet noodle.

"Okay, now Jenny is asking me if I want to eat in China tonight. What the fuck is wrong with your women?"

I dropped off of Drew's back and Jim handed me his phone. I scrolled to the text from Claire and my jaw dropped.

Yep, those were her tits. Sweet Jesus. I forwarded the text to my phone, you know, so I could ask her about it later…and stuff.

The phone rang in my hands and caller I.D. said it was Liz.

"Go ahead and answer it. You can ask her why Claire is sending me nudey pictures," Jim said with a laugh.

I hit "send" and put the phone to my ear, quickly pulling it away when I heard muffled screams through the receiver.

"Jesus Christ, who's screaming?" Drew asked with a cringe.

I shook my head and shrugged my shoulders, attempting to put the phone back to my ear.

"I swear to fucking God if you puke in this cab I will punch you in the neck! Stop being a pussy!"

"Hey!" I yelled, trying to be heard over the screams. "HELLO!"

The screams continued and the three of us moved into the kitchen so we wouldn't wake Gavin.

"You're a mother for Christ's sakes! It's just a little blood. Will you stop screaming?"

"LIZ! HELLO!" I yelled again, once we got to the kitchen.

Drew was laughing but I knew those screams. And hearing Liz mention the word "blood" freaked me out a little. Was Claire bleeding?

"Drew, call Jenny," I said quickly.

A few seconds later I heard ringing through my end of the phone call and the sound of Jenny's voice over Claire's screams and Liz's yelling. I hung up since I wasn't getting anywhere and turned to face Drew.

"Awww, I love you too, Snuggie!"

I punched Drew in the shoulder and indicated that he should get to the point by giving him the finger.

"Hey, baby, what's going on? Why is Claire screaming?" he asked, pulling the phone back and hitting the speaker button.

The screaming and arguing burst into the room and we all winced.

"Claire's got nice boobies," Jenny said.

I rolled my eyes.

"Baby, focus. What is going on? Where are you?" Drew asked her.

"I'm dying! Oh my God, I'm going to bleed to death in a cab that smells like pee and curry!"

Why the fuck is Claire bleeding in a cab?

"Claire had an assident. Axiscent. She's got a boo boo," Jenny slurred.

"Alright ladies, Butler General Hospital. No, don't pay me; just get the hell out of my cab."

DREW AND JIM stayed at my house with Gavin and I raced to the hospital.

What if Claire had a freak garbage disposal incident and lost a hand?

Or a really heavy meat cleaver fell on her leg and they needed to amputate? My house was not wheelchair accessible. Fuck! Could you buy wheelchair ramps at Walmart?

By the time I made it to the emergency room, I sorely regretted leaving Jim and Drew back at the house. I was stuck in a room with three drunken women. One of whom was sobbing hysterically about orphaning our son while the other two knocked shit over and yelled random things to people who walked by.

"Excuse me sir, do you know where we can get an x-ray of the stapler stuck in her vagina?" Liz asked an orderly that walked by as she pointed her thumb at Claire.

I gave the guy an apologetic look before focusing my attention on Claire.

"Baby, it's fine. It's just a little cut on your finger. Two stitches really aren't that big of a deal," I told her as I held her in my arms and rubbed her back.

I snapped my fingers at Jenny and Liz who were now in the corner of the room trying to get rubber gloves on their heads. They gave me innocent looks, smacked each other and kept giggling.

"Not a big deal? Not a big deal?" she said loudly. "They asked me if I had a living will. I almost DIED tonight!"

I chuckled, but quickly masked it when she shot me a dirty look.

"Claire, that's normal. They ask everyone that," I reassured her.

"I concur, do you concur?" Liz asked.

"Not helping," I growled.

"Not caring," she replied before turning back to the supply cabinet in the room.

"What if I died? My baby would be alone," she sobbed.

"Um, hello? Father, standing right here," I reminded her.

"Fine. But what if something happens to both of us? They could ship him off to my Aunt Gertie the hoarder who talks to her curtains and eats soap," she whined.

I grabbed her face in my hands and wiped away the tears, giving her a soft kiss on the lips.

"Okay, if there's a natural disaster tomorrow and neither one of us is here, I'm sure your dad wouldn't mind stepping in. Why are you so worried about this right now?"

"They asked me if in the event of an emergency, someone could administer Last Rites to me. They thought I was going to die tonight, Carter. This is serious!" she cried. "What if my dad has a heart attack tomorrow or an asteroid lands on him when he's walking to his car after work?"

No more Sci-Fi channel before bed for Claire.

"I swear to you that they ask everyone about Last Rites. But would it make you feel better if we get something in writing so you don't have to worry about this? We can make a list of people that is ten pages long if it will make you feel better."

She nodded happily and threw her arms around my neck.

"Thank you so much, baby. I love you more than a hooker loves free VD testing day at the clinic," she told me drunkenly.

I rubbed her back and shot dirty looks to Liz and Jenny when I saw that they'd taken over the dry-erase board with important hospital phone numbers that hung on the wall. Instead of "Order Meals" it now said "Order Hookers", and instead of "For a Chapel Visit, ask a nurse" it now said "For a Happy Ending, ask a nurse."

The doctor walked in then with Claire's discharge papers and a prescription for an antibiotic. He explained everything to us and turned to leave the room.

"Doctor, wait! This patient needs an enema STAT!" Liz yelled while Jenny waved a rubber tube over her head like a lasso.

I think we could safely say that some people will already be crossed off of the guardian list.

20.

Have You Seen Mike Hunt?

O*H JESUS FUCKING hell. Where's the monkey that kicked me in the head and shit in my mouth?*

"I think I'm dying," I croaked.

Carter's laughter shook the bed and forced a little bit of vomit up into my throat. I clamped my hand over my mouth and started breathing through my nose to make it stop.

"Please don't start the 'I'm dying' thing again. It's too early and I'm not awake enough to say anything comforting," Carter replied as he slowly rubbed circles on my back.

I started to ask him what the hell he was talking about when the pounding in my head turned into flashes of memories from the night before.

"Oh my God, I sent a picture of my boobs to Jim," I moaned as a fresh wave of nausea rolled through me.

"You also threw up in the emergency room parking lot, called Drew and told him you were the Donkey Punch Dick Queen and filled out a Last Will and Testament on a Burger King napkin and then asked the drive-thru worker to notarize it."

I am never drinking again. I am never drinking again.

"Why can't I be one of those people who black out when they drink? It would be really nice right now if I didn't have to remember these things," I muttered.

I felt the bed shift behind me and a few seconds later, Carter's arm came around me and held a napkin in front of my face.

"Sorry, baby, even if you did black out, I still have proof of your stupidity," he said with a laugh. I grabbed the napkin from his hand and squinted at the messy writing that was all over it as he got back under the covers behind me.

"I don't wanna be def. Death. Dead. This Burger Twin nappykin just got served as my will, BEOTCH! The fries here suck, by the way. If I die, don't feed my son your shitty fries. Don't give my son to the creepy child molester king you put in your commercials either. What the fuck is wrong with that guy? He's got a normal body and a plastic face that is always smiley. It's not right, man. It's just not right. My ears feel funny."

I wondered if someone gave me a roofie last night. This was the one time in my life I hoped I got roofied, so I could blame it on something other than me being a horrible drunk.

"Wow, okay, so I've been meaning to bring up the subject of having a will drafted by a lawyer and getting a new birth certificate for Gavin that has your name on it. I probably should have done that before I drank my weight in wine," I explained.

"Well, lucky for you, I'm fluent in Claire's Drunken Ramblings. Even though you barely knew what you were saying last night, I could tell this is important to you. It's important to me too. God forbid anything should ever happen to us, but if something does, it would make me feel better knowing Gavin is going to be okay. I mean, I know we have your dad and even though you haven't met them yet, my parents are absolutely on board with anything that has to do with Gavin, but I agree that we should also have someone younger as a back-up plan just in case. I know you're going to be insanely busy for the next month or so once the shop opens tomorrow, and we'll have no time to really sit down and discuss this, so I thought maybe we could just sort of pop in on our friends in the next few days and see how they do when they're around Gavin. You know, sort of like a secret interview."

I really wanted to throw up right now, but I had to choke it back because Carter deserved my undivided, non-spewing attention.

"I can't believe you actually took me seriously about anything last night."

Carter slid over to my side of the bed, pressing his body up against mine as he wrapped his arms around my waist.

"I take everything you say seriously. Even when you're sexting our friends and screaming into the drive-thru window that whoever is making your burger better not spit in it," Carter said, placing a kiss to my temple.

I lifted my hand up in front of my face and noticed the bandage wrapped around my middle finger for the first time.

"I guess it's fitting I almost sliced off my middle finger. It will be fun to flip everyone off when they ask me what happened," I said with a sigh. "You know what I just remembered? Liz and Jim are babysitting his little cousin for a few hours today. I was planning on going over there so she and Gavin could play while Liz and I filled out the last of our paperwork. You could come with us and we could do our first super secret spy interview."

Carter leaned up on his elbow so he could look down at me.

"Will I get to wear a secret decoder ring and make up a spy code name, like Ichybon Snagglewhip or Bonanza Challywag?"

I turned my head and looked up at him.

"Will I ever have to say those names out loud, in front of people we know?" I asked.

"Only if our cover is blown."

He laid his head back down on the pillow behind me and within seconds, I could feel his hard penis up against my ass.

"Really? Talking about Bonanza Challywag excites you?" I asked with a laugh, trying not to grimace when the action made my stomach churn.

His hand, that rested on my stomach, snuck under my tank top and slid up the front of my body until it came in contact with my bare breast.

"Anything I say, do or think about with you excites me," he said softly as his palm feathered over my nipple. I pushed my hips back and rubbed my ass up against his length while he kneaded my breast and pressed a kiss to the side of my neck. His head jerked away from me abruptly and his hand stopped its exploration of my flesh.

"You're going to throw up, aren't you?" he asked as I squeezed my eyes shut and thought about rainbows and kittens and other things that didn't make me want to puke.

It didn't work. Rainbows made me think of, "Taste the rainbow," which made me think of Skittles and the half-pound bag I ate last night before bed. Kittens made me think of fleas and litter boxes with little poops that looked like tootsie rolls covered in rocks and…

I bolted out of bed and raced to the bathroom, barely making it in time before I emptied the contents of my stomach—which coincidentally looked a bit like a rainbow.

"It's okay, my penis is not offended in the least that it just made you throw up," Carter yelled from the bedroom.

CARTER GOT GAVIN up, dressed and fed him breakfast while I took a shower and tried to feel human. As much as I hated to do it, puking actually helped. I exorcised the demons.

When I got out of the shower, I realized I didn't have any clothes…well, aside from the tank top I wore to bed and underwear. Where the hell did my clothes go?

I went through Carter's closet and found one of his shirts and threw it on then dug through his underwear drawer for a pair of boxers. Instead, buried way in the back, I found a teeny, tiny pair of red banana-hammock briefs.

The revenge gods were smiling down on me today, my friends.

I shimmied into them and made my way out to the kitchen where Carter was cleaning up breakfast and Gavin was giving him a run for his money.

"Mommy always lets me have candy right after breakfast."

I stood just outside of the doorway so I could see them but they couldn't see me. Gavin was seated at the kitchen table and Carter had his back to him, loading things in the dishwasher.

"Right, candy after breakfast. And I'm Santa Claus," Carter muttered quietly.

"You're Santa Claus?!!" Gavin asked excitedly, standing up on his chair.

Carter whipped around to face him with a panicked look on his face.

"What? No. Well, technically… Wait, no. No, no, no. I am not Santa Claus. That was just a figure of speech," he explained.

"What's a finger of peach?"

"Shit!" Carter muttered.

Gavin pointed at him.

"Awwwwww, you said *shit*," he accused, making sure to whisper the bad word.

"So did you," Carter argued. "Don't tell your mother."

"Don't tell me what?" I asked, walking through the doorway with a smile.

Carter sighed. "You heard that didn't you?"

I walked up to Gavin and scooped him off of the chair and into my arms for a hug.

"I have no idea what you're talking about," I told him as I kissed both of Gavin's cheeks.

"How did you sleep last night, little man?"

He squeezed me as hard as he could until I had to pry his arms from around my neck so I could breathe.

"I slept good. But you crawled into my bed wif me last night and told me never to talk to kings with smiley faces," he told me.

Carter laughed while I groaned.

I gave Gavin one last squeeze and then set him down on his feet.

"Run into your room and find your shoes, okay? We're going to see Aunt Liz and Uncle Jim in a little bit."

He let out a cheer of excitement and ran out of the room.

I walked over to Carter and leaned my body into his while he lounged against the kitchen counter.

"You look good wearing my shirt," he said as he wrapped his arms around me.

I kissed his chin and looked up at him.

"I look even better wearing your tighty underoos," I said with a laugh as I reached back and lifted up a corner of his shirt so he could see.

He shook his head and sighed.

"I can't believe you found those. My boxers made me chafe at work so I thought I'd try…"

"Don't worry," I interrupted him. "I'll make sure everyone knows you wear big boy undies now."

I laughed and wrapped my arms around his neck. He bent down and gave me a sweet kiss, sucking my top lip into his mouth and making my toes curl.

"Where are my clothes?" I asked between kisses.

"Your shirt is in the garbage. You threw it there last night when we got here and you saw the blood all over it. You said you couldn't possibly ever wear something again that reminded you of how you almost died in a horrific accident. I took your jeans from you before you did the same to them. They're in the dryer right now."

I shook my head and sighed while Carter tightened his hold on me and placed another kiss on my lips.

"Move in with me," he said suddenly.

His lips stayed against mine and I opened my eyes so I could see him. He stared at me so intently there was no way I misheard him.

"I love you," he continued quickly. "I love Gavin. I love waking up to both of you in this house with me. I don't want to miss seeing him tie his shoes for the first time or write his name. I don't want to wake up in the morning and not see you drooling on the pillow next to me."

I laughed and smacked his arm, the conversation immediately turning lighter.

"Besides, I need a woman here to be barefoot and pregnant in the kitchen making me chicken pot pies every night," he said with a smile.

"Well, then we've obviously never met if you want me to take on that role."

We stood there in the kitchen, wrapped in each other's arms with Carter's junior jockey's creeping up my ass, and I realized I had never been happier.

"Yes," I told him.

His eyebrows went up and his face lit up with a huge smile.

"Yes? Really?" he asked. "I thought for sure I'd have to resort to bribery or extortion."

I nodded my head and laughed. "Yes! We will move in with you so I can monitor the stupid shit you say and punch you in the kidney when you suggest I should be barefoot and pregnant in the kitchen again."

A FEW HOURS later, Liz and I were just finishing our paperwork at her kitchen table. Jim and Carter were sitting at the table with us carrying on their own conversation while Gavin and Jim's eight-year-old little cousin Melissa played.

Gavin was currently in the living room watching a movie, but Melissa had been running through the kitchen at warp speed, yelling as loud as she could for the past fifteen minutes. Carter and I passed each other secret looks every so often about the conversation we had in the car on the way over here. We weren't going to discipline Gavin at all the entire time at their house. We would let Liz and Jim take over and see what they did. I had first hand experience on the type of care-givers they were since they were my best friends, so this was mostly for Carter's benefit. I knew for a fact that Liz and Jim were wonderful with kids and Carter would be more than willing to assign them as Gavin's back-up guardians after today.

Surprisingly, we wouldn't need to discipline Gavin anyway. He was being very well behaved. Melissa, on the other hand, reminded me yet again while some animals in the wild eat their young. She was a terror.

After her twenty-seventh pass through the kitchen, waving her hands above her head and screaming, Liz finally had enough.

"Melissa! Stop it," she said sternly.

The little terror did indeed stop. For two seconds. Then she started back up and ran out of the room screaming like her ass was on fire. Her ass would be on fire soon if she didn't shut the hell up.

"Is that all you're going to do?" I asked.

"No," Liz replied as she looked up from the paper she was signing. "Next time she runs by I'm going to kick her."

Not conventional by any means, but I was okay with that. I was daydreaming about shoving a Roman candle in her pants and dousing it with lighter fluid.

"So, Melissa seems a little…high strung," Carter said to Jim.

Jim nodded his head in agreement. "She's a cute kid, but I can only stand her in small doses. This one time we took her to dinner with us and she was being a nightmare so Liz made her go sit out in the car while we paid the bill. We got halfway home before we realized she wasn't in the car," he laughed. "Remember that Liz? Hilarious!"

Carter looked at me in horror and I tried not to make eye contact. The whole way here all I did was brag about how good Liz and Jim were with Gavin and how they'd be naturals at parenting. Oops. I forgot about that story. In their defense, Melissa was Satan. I would have driven off without her too.

Melissa made another lap through the kitchen and true to her word, Liz stuck her foot out. The annoying third-grader went sprawling across the floor.

"NO WIRE HANGERS EVER!" Liz yelled at her.

"You're weird," Melissa stated as she stood up and went running back out of the room.

"Nice work there, Mommy Dearest," I told her.

"So, Liz, when you have kids of your own, how are you going to discipline them?" Carter asked.

I gave him a pointed look. We were supposed to be inconspicuous here. Asking blunt questions like that was sure to send up a red flag.

Liz shrugged. "Eh, I'm not big on discipline. If it's funny and no one is bleeding, you're not in trouble. That's my philosophy."

Gavin walked in then and leaned his head on my arm.

"Melissa told me no one is allowed near her no-no zone. What does that mean? I don't like her. She's loud. I told her my mommy wasn't afraid to punch a kid," he said with a sigh.

We heard Melissa yelling in the other room and some loud banging.

"What the hell is she doing in there?" Liz asked.

"The cat's being bad," Gavin said.

Liz and Jim' cat was known to be a little ball of terror, wreaking havoc on unsuspecting people when they least expected it. One time, when I was on the floor tickling Gavin, she hurtled through the air from God knows where and landed on my back with her teeth and claws inserted two inches deep into my skin. I hated that cat, but I think I hated Melissa more. Hopefully the cat was putting her in her place.

"Did the cat scratch you guys?" I asked, looking over his arms for claw marks.

"No, she won't stay in the suitcase," he explained.

All the adults at the table looked at each other in silence. At the sound of another thump from the living room, we all jumped up and ran out of the kitchen.

AFTER MAKING SURE Melissa hadn't immediately moved herself into serial killer territory by suffocating a cat, we headed home.

"That really wasn't the best representation of their parenting skills," I tried to explain as Carter pulled out of their driveway.

"Hey, Gavin," Carter said as he glanced in the rear-view mirror. "What new word did Aunt Liz teach you today?"

"Ladyboner," Gavin said as he looked out his window.

Carter gave me a pointed look.

"Aunt Liz said you got a ladyboner for Daddy. Did you buy him a present? I want one too," Gavin complained.

After stopping at my house to pick up a few things, we went back to Carter's and put Gavin down for a nap. Carter finally gave up trying to convince me that Liz and Jim were off the list when I said one word.

Drew.

If I was willing to give that giant child a try, he needed to keep an open mind with my friends. At least we agreed to wait until after the store opening tomorrow to tell Gavin that we would be moving. If we told him now, he would bug us every minute from now until we moved asking if it was time yet. I didn't need to fight the urge to lock him out of the house while I was busy with the store. One person can only take so much.

AFTER GAVIN'S NAP, Claire's dad stopped by to pick him up for a sleepover. He walked right in the front door without knocking and proceeded to make his way through every room. Once he had seen all there was to see, he told me the house was "good enough." Oddly, that was the nicest thing he had said to me since we met, and I kind of felt like we had a moment.

I leaned in to give him a hug and he stopped me with his hand to my forehead.

"You don't want to do that, son."

I stepped back and gave him a sympathetic look.

"Nam, huh? Still hard for you to get close to people?" I asked.

"No. I'm still not sure you aren't gay and if you try to play grab-ass, it's gonna get real awkward when I have to snap your fingers in two."

I was going to break that man one of these days, mark my words.

We said our good-byes to Gavin and Claire left soon after to head up to the shop and get a few last minute things made for tomorrow's opening.

I offered to meet her up there after I showered and ran a few errands.

Claire had given me a spare key to the shop, so I let myself in through the front door two hours later. It was dark outside and I left the lights to the store off as I carefully made my way to the kitchen in the back.

I heard music playing and rounded the corner of the kitchen to see Claire licking melted chocolate off of her middle finger. My dick sprang to life as I watched her swirl her finger through her mouth and sway her body to the erotic beats of the song that played.

I rounded the edge of the counter where she worked and stood behind her, placing my arms on either side of her with my hands flat on the counter. I leaned my body close to hers, bringing one hand up to move her hair away from her neck and pushed it behind her shoulder. She continued to work, flipping chocolate molds over and tapped the finished product out onto towels so nothing would break, her body swaying to the music and sliding against me every so often. When I put my mouth on the side of her neck, her motions got choppy.

"Are those chocolate penises and boobs?" I asked.

"Yes," she moaned as I let the tip of my tongue taste her skin. "Party favors…shit…mmmmm."

I smiled against her neck when she moaned and placed another open-mouth kiss there, this time letting my teeth graze her skin. I watched as goose bumps flushed her skin and listened to her take a shuddering breath. I continued to nip and gently suck on the side of her neck until she finally got fed up with concentrating on the chocolate molds. She dropped them to the counter and smacked her hands down next to mine, dumping over a bowl of melted chocolate in the process. The warm liquid splattered onto her hand and ran off the edge of the counter, pooling on the floor.

"Shit!" Claire laughed as she lifted her hands from the counter and tried to shake off some of the chocolate on them. She bowed her head to look at the puddle on the floor, and I reached up and moved her hair all the way around to the front of her other shoulder so the back of her neck was wide open. I swiped my finger through the mess of melted chocolate on the counter and then trailed it along the back of her neck, leaving a smudge of chocolate behind on her skin.

"Did you just get chocolate in my hair?" she asked distractedly.

My hand snaked around her waist and I pushed it under the hem of her shirt until I touched the smooth, warm skin of her stomach. I moved my mouth towards the back of her neck and slid my hand down into her pants. My fingers slid right inside her underwear and through the soft triangle of curls. I attached my lips to her chocolate-coated skin and gently sucked as two of my fingers slid down and glided through her.

"Oh my God," she moaned softly as I pushed and pulled my fingers through her, coating them with her wetness. "Forget it, you can put chocolate wherever you want."

She felt so good, better than anything else in the world. I could stand here touching her all night and never tire of it.

I nibbled and sucked at the back of her neck, making sure to remove all of the chocolate I'd placed there. I was happy to learn that the spot right below her hairline drove her insane. Every time my teeth grazed that area, she would moan and jerk her hips into my hand. I lifted my free hand from the counter and pushed it under her shirt, lifting the cup of her bra up and over one of her breasts as I went. I cupped the fullness of her in my palm and then took two fingers and circled them all around her nipple. I copied the same motions with my other hand, my fingers circling through the heat between her legs.

The beats of the music and the sound of her soft moans filled the room, and I was about two seconds away from exploding in my pants just by listening to her and feeling her come apart in my hands. I rocked my hips into her ass and it was my turn to moan. She was soft against my hardness, wet against my warm fingers and the skin of her neck tasted salty and sweet, like the chocolate covered pretzels she made. I was about to say something really stupid like tell her she was the yin to my yang. But in all honesty, she was. I wanted more than anything for her to be mine. Forever. That thought should have scared me. If it was any other woman, it probably would. But not Claire. Nothing about her scared me, except the thought of losing her.

Her hips started moving faster and I kissed my way over to her ear.

"I love you so much," I whispered, sliding my hand lower and pushing two fingers into her tight heat. Claire moaned loudly as I moved my fingers in and out of her and my other hand continued to tease her nipple.

My hands were suddenly empty as they were pulled out of her and off of her breast when she abruptly turned to face me. We both looked down at the front of her shirt at the mess of chocolate that was all over it from my hands and from her leaning into the spill on the counter. I laughed until she brought both of her hands of to my cheeks and wiped the chocolate on them all over my face.

"I love you more than chocolate," she said with a smile.

Her hands slid down the front of my shirt, leaving a trail of chocolate in their wake, and went to work on my pants. Before I knew it, she had them shoved down to my thighs. I reached for her hips but she batted my hands away.

"No, no, no. It's my turn to play," she said with a wicked smile on her lips.

My dick jumped against my stomach like it was getting ready to do a jig. When she licked her lips and looked down at it, I whimpered. She reached behind her back for a second, fiddling around with something. Before I could tell her that now was not the time to start cleaning up our mess, she kissed my lips and I felt something warm and wet slide around the head of my penis.

She pulled back, slid down my body and my mouth dropped open.

Oh, sweet Jesus, is that…is she going to…

She wrapped her hand around the base of me and her lips around the head and sucked me into her mouth. I didn't even know what kind of incoherent expletives flew from my mouth. I may have said the words "shamwow" and "jiggidy" somewhere in there. I leaned over her and my hands smacked onto the counter sending splatters of chocolate all over the front of my shirt as Claire began licking all around, making sure to get every last drop of melted chocolate she rubbed there with her fingers when she kissed me.

She was licking chocolate off of my dick. I felt like I was in a porno—a really, really good porno with better music and a superb story line. Not like that really creepy one with the guy who put peanut butter on his johnson and let his dog…

Her lips slid around and down my length, taking as much of me in her mouth as she could, and I forgot about the dick licking dog. Thank God. She started a slow rhythm, moving her head up and down, sucking harder every time she got to the tip, before plunging her mouth back down on me. I felt like I should pump my fists in the air or give Claire a round of applause, but that would quickly turn this into bad porno territory.

I could feel my balls tighten and I wrapped my hands around her arms and pulled her up to me. As good as it felt to be in her mouth, I needed inside of her right now. I slid my hands into the waistband of her pants and underwear and slid them down her hips far enough so she could pull one leg out.

Lifting Claire up, I sat her on the counter right at the edge, moving her to the side a little so she wasn't sitting in chocolate. I pushed her knees apart so I could get between them. Her hands fell into the puddle of chocolate on either side of her hips and I held her around her waist as she started to slip through the mess. She smacked a gooey coated hand onto my shoulder, leaving a chocolate hand-print behind and making us both laugh. She brought a chocolate coated finger from her other hand up to her mouth and spread the sugary wetness along her bottom lip.

Oh, sweet Jesus, was that porn music playing in the background? Was I starring in "Cocks and the Chocolate Factory" or "Chocolate Melts in Your Vagina, Not in your Hand"?

I swooped in and kissed her, sucking her lip into my mouth and greedily licking the chocolate off with my tongue. Once I got it all, she pushed her tongue past mine and swirled it through my mouth. She tasted like Claire and chocolate, and I had a moment where I wanted to cry like a baby because my dream for the past five years was right in front of me. I grabbed the back of both of her knees and pulled her legs up around my waist, my hands sliding down her thighs and over her ass. I sucked her tongue into my mouth and pulled her closer to the edge of the counter, my hardness resting against her wet heat.

Her arms wrapped around my shoulders and I pushed my hips forward, sinking into her slowly until my pelvis was flush against hers. My mouth never left hers as I stayed deep inside of her and swiveled my hips, grinding myself against her. She whimpered into my mouth and pushed herself harder against me, creating friction right where she needed it. Her legs tightened around my hips and I squeezed my hands onto her ass, rocking her harder and faster against me. It was killing me not move, not to slide in and out of her heat that squeezed around me, but I knew she liked what I was doing and that's all that mattered.

Our kiss never ended as I felt her start to tighten around me. Her hips moved faster and she clawed at my shoulders as I moved against her and rotated my hips, pushing her into oblivion.

I deepened the kiss and swallowed her cries as she came. Her hands latched onto my hair and I couldn't have cared less that I'd have to wash chocolate out of it tonight. I removed a hand from her ass and rested it on the counter next to her for more leverage as I pulled almost all the way out of her and slammed back inside, stars bursting behind my closed eyes at the sensations that shot up through me.

Claire's moans and muttered curses spurned me on to move faster and harder. Thank God for that because there was no way I could be gentle now. I needed to fuck her on the kitchen counter, plain and simple.

My free hand slid under one of her knees so her leg draped down over the crook of my elbow. I lifted her leg higher and pushed deeper inside of her until we both moaned.

I thrust into her hard and fast, my hips moving at lightening speed. The smell of chocolate filled the air, her hot wetness coated me as I pumped in and out of her and the sounds of our bodies slapping together shot my orgasm through me like a freight train. I only lasted a few more seconds, shouting her name as I came, my thrusts never slowing down. My orgasm ripped through me and I swore it was the best one I ever had. I pushed into her one last time and held still until the last few tingles of my release disappeared.

I dropped my forehead to hers and we stayed where we were, trying to catch our breaths. My arm slid out from under her leg and it fell limply down my side. I felt myself pulse inside of her as I wrapped my arms around her and pulled her body close.

After a few minutes of staying just like that, I finally recovered the ability to speak.

"I'm really going to like this whole chocolate business you own if this is how we get to spend our evenings."

Claire laughed and looked around. "It looks like a chocolate bomb went off in here."

There was chocolate in both of our hair, I could feel dried chocolate on my face and arms and our shirts were completely covered. I looked down and saw chocolate hand prints on Claire's thighs and hips and the half of her pants that hung off of her were sopping wet from the chocolate that still dripped off the edge of the counter. We were so busy with our post coital glow and laughing at the mess we made, that we didn't hear the connecting door to Liz's store open.

"SURPRISE!" Several voices yelled as we looked towards the door in shock.

"Oh my fucking God, are you kidding me?" Liz yelled as she cringed and tried not to drop the cake she held in her hands.

"Oh Jesus, my eyes. MY EYES!" Jim screamed as he covered his face with both hands and turned around.

"Are those chocolate boobs?" Drew asked, walking towards us and grabbing a piece off of the counter and popping it into his mouth.

My dick, completely shrunken now, was still in Claire. This was like the damn finger in the vagina day all over again. What the fuck was wrong with my life?

"Sorry I'm late! Claire, were you surprised?" Jenny asked as she pushed her way past Liz and Jim, stopping suddenly when she saw the position we were in. On the counter. With both of our asses showing, covered in chocolate.

"Heh, heh, Claire has boobs and penises stuck to her ass!" Drew laughed.

So that explains the weird bumps I felt on her ass. I was a little worried there for a minute that she might have boils or some creepy skin condition I didn't know about.

"I hope to God you bleach this counter," Liz scolded.

"And my eyes," Jim mutter with his back still to us.

Claire hadn't moved or said a word and I almost wanted to stick my finger under her nose to see if she was still breathing.

"We wanted to surprise you with a 'Good luck with the store opening' cake but it looks like you guys started celebrating without us," Jenny laughed. "Drew, why haven't we played with chocolate yet? We need to remedial that."

"Remedy, babe. Remedy," Drew corrected as he grabbed another chocolate boob from the counter a few inches from Claire's ass and ate it.

Why the fuck was everyone still standing in this kitchen?

"I brought you a sample of my new edible lotion. It's funnel cake flavor. I figured you and Carter-boy could spice it up by playing dirty carnie and innocent fair-goer," Liz said as she tossed the bottle of lotion on the counter. "Looks like I should have brought you a drop cloth instead."

"I'm guessing you and Jim already tested out the funnel cake lotion, right? Did you pretend to be the slutty clown car with millions of midgets flocking out of your vagina?" Claire said sarcastically.

"This is the Butler Broadcasting System, coming to you live from the kitchen of the snacks side of 'Seduction and Snacks,' the new business opening tomorrow, right in the heart of Butler."

A woman in a business suit suddenly walked through the door with a microphone in her hand and a man with a camera followed behind her.

The giant spotlight on top of the camera blinded us and everyone started yelling, but not before we heard the words, "Coming to you live…"

This is a dream. It has to be a fucking dream.

The perfectly coiffed woman with the bouffant hair stopped in her tracks when she saw my chocolate covered ass. Her shout of, "Holy fuck," was now being broadcast into several thousand Butler living rooms.

Thankfully, the camera man took in the scene in front of him and reacted faster than she did. He whipped around, smacking his camera into Jim's head before stumbling backwards, slipping through the spilled, melted chocolate and crashing down on the floor on his back.

"SON OF A bitch that hurt," Jim could be heard shouting off-camera as the view on the television suddenly flew to a shot of the ceiling and a loud "ooomf" came through the speakers, signifying the point in the broadcast when the camera man landed on his ass.

Liz fell off the couch, landing on her side in a fit of giggles. Jim managed to stay on the couch but bent over at the waist, holding on to his stomach as he laughed right along with her.

All Claire and I could do was stare in shock at the replay of tonight's broadcast that Liz managed to catch on her DVR. After the kitchen debacle and plenty of apologies from the staff of BBS for deciding a surprise interview would be fun, we came back to Liz and Jim's house to clean up and see if by some miracle there was a cable outage in the area.

No such luck.

"Ooooh, here comes my part!" Drew said excitedly as he jumped up from his spot on the floor and reached over to turn up the volume on the television.

Drew's face suddenly came into the shot as he bent over the downed camera man, the view of the shop's kitchen ceiling behind his head.

"Stop by Seduction and Snacks for the grand opening tomorrow and try some of Claire's boobs. They're delicious!" he said with a smile as he bit off one of the chocolate boobs he held in his hand.

The camera turned to the side where the stunned TV anchor stood with Liz and Jenny, waving frantically into the camera behind her and Jim off to the side rubbing his head and muttering, "Fuck that hurt."

"B-b-back to you in the studio, Sam," she stuttered as she stared wide eyed into the camera without blinking.

The shot went back to the studio where they immediately began talking about the weather.

"Well, the good news is the camera man managed to avoid showing Butler that you guys were taste testing the chocolate with your penis and vagina," Liz said from her spot on the floor.

"If that's the good news, what the hell is the bad news?" Claire asked.

"Well, Drew is now the face of Seduction and Snacks," Liz laughed.

We all glanced over at Drew as he picked lint off of the front of his shirt that had been the main focus of the camera shot.

I guess there were worse things Seduction and Snacks could be famous for than a tee shirt that read, "Have you seen Mike Hunt?"

21.

Itchy Feet and Fading Smiles

SURPRISINGLY THE AIRING of our dirty laundry, or should I say dirty kitchen and mouths, didn't deter anyone from stopping by the grand opening of Seduction and Snacks today. But if one more person asks me if Mr. Hunt is available, I'm going to punch them in the kidney.

Carter, Gavin, Liz, Jim and I all arrived at the shop a few hours before we opened to finish last-minute details and set everything up. Thankfully, today's opening didn't require the chocolate boobs and penises. Drew ate all the ones that weren't stuck to my ass last night. Come to think of it, he may have eaten those as well. I remembered him saying something about a "Five Second Ass Rule", not to be confused with the original "Five Second Rule" for when you drop food on the floor. I tuned him out when he told Carter, "Her ass better be so clean you can see your face in it!"

Much to our shock, there was a line of people on the sidewalk waiting for us to open.

Was this really my life right now? How did I get to this point? A few months ago I was a single mother with no social life or romantic prospects anywhere in my future, and I was stuck at a dead-end job at a bar. Now, I was opening a business, doing what I loved every single day, and found the love of my life who was the best father in the world to our son.

Oh, and my vagina was getting regular work-outs on an almost-daily basis. Couldn't forget that tidbit since it was probably the most important. I thought if my vagina had to wait any longer for some action, she would have just got up and walked out of my underwear to find another pair of legs to sit between. I would have turned into a fake woman. If you spread my legs, I'd look like Barbie with her plastic who-ha that had no hole. At least Ken wasn't missing out on sticking it to her. Poor guy just had a pair of tighty-whities with no bulge. That's probably why when I was younger I always made them dry hump. There wasn't much else they could do, really.

The store had been open for two hours and it had yet to be empty. Liz and I kept the adjoining door to our places open so people could file back and forth. I was a little leery about how the good people of Butler would take to having a sex toy shop downtown, but I was pleasantly surprised to find out how many dirty people lived here. Liz was going to resurrect the sex lives of everyone in this town one dildo at a time.

She kept the front of her store to the bare minimum, mostly lingerie, lubes, massage lotions, candles and other things that were PG rated and wouldn't freak anyone out that walked by. She kept catalogs on the counter with pictures of all the other items that were located in the back of the store. You could simply point to what you wanted and she'd go in the back and get it for you, wrapping it in a small black bag so no one would know what you got.

My dad took in Liz's side of the store with as much enthusiasm as I expected him to. He walked through the adjoining doors and stopped dead in his tracks in the middle of a rack of garters and corsets. He took a look around and proclaimed joyously, "Humph," then walked back over to my side.

Gavin was the life of the store, naturally. He walked around handing out samples with the motto, "One for you, six for me." He was so hopped up on sugar by twelve o'clock, I was going to have to scrape him off of the ceiling by the end of the day.

I stood at the cash register ringing up a customer's cookie order when I noticed Carter talking to a guy by the front window. He was holding a small boy in his arms and Carter was laughing at something the guy said. He had his back to me so I had no idea who it was but something about him was familiar. I thanked the customer, gave her a flyer and headed over to Carter.

Carter noticed me walking towards him and smiled.

"There's my girl," he said as he lifted his arm so I could ease into his side.

The guy turned at Carter's words and when we saw each other, I wasn't sure who had the more shocked expression on their face.

"Oh my God, Max?"

"Claire?" he answered, equally surprised.

Carter looked between the two of us, obviously puzzled.

"Wait, you two know each other?" he asked.

"Um, yes. But more importantly, how do *you* know him?" I asked.

This was so awkward right now I kind of wished a meteor would crash out in the street. I needed total chaos right now to distract everyone from this insane situation.

"I met Max at the library when I took Gavin that one afternoon so you could work, remember? He gave me some tips on the joys of fatherhood," Carter laughed.

Max hadn't taken his eyes off me during the exchange and I laughed nervously. I didn't see this ending well. At all.

"So, anyway, how do you two know each other?" Carter asked again.

I looked at him and tried to convey with my eyes that this was about to get really weird really fast. Carter didn't get the hint and just stared at me expectantly.

"Hello, earth to Claire," Carter said with a laugh. "What's wrong with your face?"

I sighed, figuring I might as well get this over with.

"Carter, this is Max," I said, with a raise of my eyebrows, hoping he would get it.

He just laughed and shook his head.

"Yeah. We've already established that. Are you okay?" he asked as he leaned towards me.

"Carter. This. Is. MAX," I said again, punctuating Max's name with a big, fake smile.

Carter looked at me like I was insane for all of three point two more seconds when the light bulb finally went off in his brain. Really, how many fucking Max's did he know? It wasn't like the guy's name was John or Mike and he might have just assumed it was someone else. His name was Max for fuck's sake. As soon as he met him, shouldn't a red flag have gone off in his head?

It was certainly going off now. Carter's head jerked back and forth between Max and me so quickly it almost looked like he was shaking his head no. Maybe he was. His brain might just be on overload right now and it was screaming, "Noooooooooooo! Does not compute!"

"You're Max?" he asked.

Max just nodded, finally looking away from me and at his son squirming in his arms.

"You're Max," he stated.

I laughed uncomfortably. "I think we've covered that already, hon," I said through a smile and clenched teeth.

Let the insanity commence.

Carter started chuckling.

I closed my eyes, not wanting to witness what surely was going to follow. Why had I ever though it was necessary to share every detail of this story? Why?

"Two pumps!" Carter said excitedly, followed by more laughing.

Max just stood there with a befuddled look on his face.

Then Carter raised his arm and pointed at him, still laughing, I might add.

"You're the chump!"

"Oh Jesus," I muttered.

"What?" Max asked.

Carter was smiling like a nut job.

"Nothing," I told Max. "Don't mind him."

"Where's her underwear?" Carter asked, suddenly serious.

Max's son started kicking his little legs around in an attempt to get down. He hefted him up higher in his arms and gave me a smile.

"Well, I better get going. It was good seeing you again, Claire. Good luck with the store," he said as he moved to the door and used his back to push it open.

"Could you say that TWO more times," Carter laughed.

I smacked his arm as Max lifted his hand in a wave.

Carter waved good-bye to him, shaking his hand in the air frantically like he was a little kid watching a parade.

"Come back again!" Carter shouted as Max got out the door and onto the sidewalk. "Claire likes it when people stay more than TWO seconds."

Max finally disappeared out of sight and Carter turned to face me, a lingering smile still on his face.

"What?" he asked when he saw the look on mine.

"When you're ready to start acting like an adult, let me know," I told him.

"Adults are the little ones, right?" he shouted to me as I walked away.

I shook my head as I made my way to the counter. Just then my dad walked back over from Liz's side with a black bag clutched firmly in his hand.

Oh sweet Jesus, my brain couldn't handle anymore crazy today.

We stopped in front of each other and he tried to hide the bag behind his back.

"Dad, did you just buy something from Liz's store?" I asked bewilderingly.

What in the fuck of fuckery would he need from over there? WHAT? Oh God, where's Jim? I need his eye bleach.

"Well, I've got a date tonight," he stated matter-of-factly.

"So take her some chocolates! Or a box of cookies. I'm pretty sure what's in that store isn't first-date material," I said in a panic.

There could be flavored lube in that bag right now. Or a cock ring. Or a strap on. Oh sweet mother fucking Jesus, what if's been so long since my dad has been with a woman that he bat for the other team now? Nothing against gay men. I love gay men. I had a gay friend in college that I wish I still kept in contact with. He liked to show me the awesome gaydar he possessed by pointing out every gay man within a two mile radius. What would he say if he was here right now? "Oh, Claire, that man is gayer than Richard Simmons sweatin' to the oldies on a rainbow."

When I took Gavin to the library last week there was a book called "Daddy's Roommate" in the children's section. Should I go back and get that book? Maybe I should buy a copy for future reference. There was also a book called "I Wish Daddy Didn't Drink So Much" and "It Hurts When I Poop."

What the fuck has happened to children's literature since I was little?

I knew no matter what, I would love my father. That was a fact. To quote my favorite movie, "I love my dead, gay son!"

Well, I love my dead, gay father. Er, I mean my gay father.

I need a drink.

"Never fear, Mr. Hunt is here!" Drew proclaimed as he walked through the door holding Jenny's hand. My dad raised his eyebrow at Drew's shirt that read, "Jam out with your clam out."

"Hey there, Mr. M, how's it hanging?" he asked as he walked over and shook my dad's hand.

It's hanging a little to the left of Perez Hilton Avenue.

"Oooooh, look at you already sampling the merchandise," Drew said, patting my dad on the back in a congratulatory way as he smiled at the black bag still tightly clutched in his hands.

"Claire, the store looks great!" Jenny told me as she gave me a quick hug.

"Thanks, my dad has a roommate," I blurted.

All three of them looked at me in silence.

"Mommy, can I have another cookie?" Gavin asked, running up to me and slamming into my leg.

"No, no more cookies. You already had a chocolate chip cookie. Obviously it wasn't enough for you and now you want to try a different one. I bet you want to try a peanut butter cookie which is the exact opposite. Peanut butter cookies are on a different team than chocolate chip cookies. I guess chocolate chip cookies just don't satisfy you anymore do they? One day you just woke up and decided you wanted to eat a completely different cookie from the one you've always liked since you were born. You can't just decide at your age that you want a different cookie. It doesn't work that way. You pick a cookie and you stick with it!"

Gavin looked up at me in confusion. His poor four-year-old brain was probably going to explode.

"Fine, can I have a chocolate sucker then?" he asked innocently.

I was well aware that no one was moving and they were all standing there looking at me like I was having a nervous breakdown. Maybe I was. I had a gay father; I was allowed to freak out.

"Hey, Mom, guess what? Last night Papa was kissing somebody," Gavin said with a smile.

Oh God, here it comes. Who was it? Bill from the hardware store? Tom from the corner coffee shop? Who would be my new step-father-in-law-uncle-friend?

"Gavin, that was supposed to be a secret," my dad laughed uncomfortably.

Ha, ha, what a funny story. My dad and Gavin had a secret. Isn't that cute? Isn't that fucking cute? I like how my son isn't at all fazed to see two men kissing. It shows great promise for the future of this country. However, I don't like that he isn't at all fazed that he saw his grandpa sucking face with a dude!

"Oh, ha, ha, a secret!" I laughed hysterically. "I guess the cat is out of the bag huh, Dad? Or should I say, out of the closet? Whew, is it hot in here?" I rambled, fanning my face with my hand.

Carter walked over then, leaving his station at the front door greeting customers. He must have seen my crazy eyes from across the store and knew I was seriously freaking out. Worse than that one time I ate a pot cookie in high school and then watched *The Wizard of Oz* while listening to Pink Floyd's "The Wall", when every pot smoker worth his weight in gold knows you're supposed to listen to "The Dark Side of the Moon", and I started crying because Toto was looking at me funny and when he barked it came out as, "Hey you, standing in the aisles with itchy feet and fading smiles, can you hear me?" and I could totally hear him and my feet started to itch. I cried for three hours telling everyone the cookie was evil and would kill me in my sleep.

Don't do drugs.

"Claire, you okay?" Carter asked, picking Gavin up into his arms to stand next to me.

"I'm super! I've never been better! This is the best day of my whole life!" I said with a big smile. "We should all go out back and smoke some pot."

What the hell was I spewing out of my mouth?

"George, you forgot your receipt," Liz said as she walked over from her side with a slip of paper in her hand.

"Sue is going to love that nightgown, I'm telling you. The silk is so soft and that peach color is going to look awesome with her skin tone," Liz said, coming up next to my dad and handing him the receipt.

Wait, what? Sue? There was a guy named Sue in Butler? Shouldn't I know this?

My dad actually blushed and quickly glanced at me.

"Uh, yeah. Thanks, Liz. I'm sure she'll love it."

She! Sue's a she. She's a Sue-she.

"She's a she!" I proclaimed.

Carter's arm that wasn't supporting Gavin wrapped around my waist to hold me up. I was sure he figured any minute now I was going to crack up permanently, probably even fall face-first onto the floor without putting my hands out to stop me like some of those idiots on Tosh.0.

I could hear Tosh's voice in my head, *"Okay, let's watch that one again in slow motion. Now watch as she just falls forward, never putting her arms out and then BAM! Face plant! Wow, that's gotta hurt!"*

"I probably should have told you this sooner, Claire. I'm kinda seeing Sue Zammond. You know, that woman who runs the travel agency over on Short Avenue? So, yeah. I'm seeing her," George said, shuffling his feet.

"Good for you, George," Carter told him as I gave him a quick hug in congratulations. My dad hadn't dated anyone seriously since my mom left. By the look on his face, I'd say things with Sue just might be heading in that direction and I was happy for him.

Carter, George and Drew walked over to the front counter to help out a few customers while the girls and I stood back and watched.

"I am so in love with Drew," Jenny said with a sigh. "I just can't look at him without thinking about his orgasm face."

"Jesus, Jenny! Over share," Liz complained.

"So you guys are really serious, huh?" I asked her, trying not to dry heave thinking about the words Drew and orgasm face all in one sentence.

She nodded her head and smiled.

"We are! He's taking me to Chicago next week to meet his parents. I'm so excited! I've never been to the Windy Cindy," she said happily.

Liz opened her mouth and I quickly covered it with my hand.

"Don't. Just…don't," I told her.

Drew came up behind Jenny then and wrapped his arms around her waist, leaning down to kiss her cheek.

"Excuse me, I was wondering if you had someplace I could put my boner?"

Jenny giggled and Liz gagged.

"So Liz, have you and Jim set a wedding date yet?" Drew asked, keeping his arms firmly around Jenny.

"As a matter of fact we did. So you guys all better keep your calendars wide open for the next couple of months. There will be meetings and discussions and appointments and fittings," she said as she ticked the items off on her fingers. "Oh and Claire, we want Gavin to be our ring bearer."

I looked at her like she was insane.

"Have you met my son?" I asked her.

She just laughed at me.

Poor, confused Liz. She'll find out soon enough. Like when she's standing at the back of the church on the most important day of her life and my son runs down the aisle at full speed in front of her, chucking the pillow at her grandma's head and calling Jim's uncle a dirty nut sack.

"Liz, how do you feel about facial hair for the wedding?" Drew asked seriously as he ran his fingers down his chin.

"Don't even think about having a soul patch at my wedding, Drew. No douche-tags allowed," she replied.

Liz turned her attention in my direction. "Speaking of the future, what's next for Claire and Carter?"

What's next? What isn't next is the better question. So much was changing. Jesus, so much already HAD changed.

I watched Carter walk towards me with Gavin in his arms, tickling him and making him giggle. I took a few deep breaths and calmed down. Everyone I loved was standing here in this room, in my store, happy and healthy. Carter walked to my side and draped his arm around my waist, reminding me that no matter what came my way, I wouldn't have to face it alone. I had my friends, I had my family and I had Carter.

Next week I was putting my house on the market. It freaked me out just a little. I became a mother in that house. I learned how to love another human being more than my own life in that house. But it was time to say good-bye and move on to bigger and better things. In a few months we would begin our future together and handle whatever life threw our way. I knew we would have hard times. I knew we would have a lot of adjusting to do as we learned how to live with each other, but I also knew we would do whatever it took to make it work.

I met a boy at a frat party, beat him at beer pong and let him take my virginity and give me a baby in return. Not a fair trade, but one I wouldn't change for the world.

I turned towards Carter and wrapped both of my arms around his waist and stood on my tip toes to kiss Gavin's cheek while our friends chatted behind us with my dad.

"Hey Gavin, guess what? Daddy and I have something to tell you."

Carter looked down at me with a surprised look. We agreed to wait until the time was closer to tell Gavin, but I couldn't hold it in anymore. I didn't care if he drove me insane asking if it was time yet. I was happy and excited and I wanted my little man to feel it too.

I waited for Carter to give me the go-ahead to continue. I mouthed the words "I love you" to him and tried not to cry. This man was everything I had ever dreamed of and more. And he was all mine.

He nodded his head in agreement and his lips formed an "I love you" back to me.

I reached up and smoothed Gavin's hair off of his forehead, letting my fingers trail down his cheeks and over his sweet dimples.

"We're going to sell our house and then you and I are going to live in Daddy's house with him," I explained.

Gavin stared at me for a few minutes and then shifted his focus to Carter.

"Really?" he asked.

Carter nodded his head, "Really, buddy."

Gavin looked back at me and smiled, opening his mouth to hopefully tell us how happy he was.

"HOLY SHIT!"

The End

Website: www.tarasivec.com

To stay up to date on all Tara Sivec news,
please join her mailing list:
http://eepurl.com/H4uaf

CPSIA information can be obtained
at www.ICGtesting.com
Printed in the USA
FFOW01n1343170416
23317FF

9 781682 304334